TOKYO GHOST

IMAGE COMICS, INC.

Robert Kirkman – **Chief Operating Officer**
Erik Larsen – **Chief Financial Officer**
Todd McFarlane – **President**
Marc Silvestri – **Chief Executive Officer**
Jim Valentino – **Vice-President**

Eric Stephenson – **Publisher**
Corey Murphy – **Director of Sales**
Jeff Boison – **Director of Publishing Planning & Book Trade Sales**
Jeremy Sullivan – **Director of Digital Sales**
Kat Salazar – **Director of PR & Marketing**
Emily Miller – **Director of Operations**

Branwyn Bigglestone – **Senior Accounts Manager**
Sarah Mello – **Accounts Manager**
Drew Gill – **Art Director**
Jonathan Chan – **Production Manager**
Meredith Wallace – **Print Manager**
Briah Skelly – **Publicity Assistant**
Sasha Head – **Sales & Marketing Production Designer**
Randy Okamura – **Digital Production Designer**
David Brothers – **Branding Manager**
Ally Power – **Content Manager**
Addison Duke – **Production Artist**
Vincent Kukua – **Production Artist**
Tricia Ramos – **Production Artist**
Jeff Stang – **Direct Market Sales Representative**
Emilio Bautista – **Digital Sales Associate**
Leanna Caunter – **Accounting Assistant**
Chloe Ramos-Peterson – **Administrative Assistant**

IMAGE COMICS.COM

Collection Design by Jeff Powell

ISBN 978-1-63215-663-1
BIG BANG/FORBIDDEN PLANET VARIANT ISBN: 978-1-63215-799-7
KINOKUNIYA VARIANT ISBN: 978-1-63215-800-0
NEWBURY VARIANT ISBN: 978-1-63215-814-7

TOKYO GHOST 1: THE ATOMIC GARDEN. First Printing. March 2016. Published by Image Comics, Inc. Office of publication: 2001 Center Street, 6th Floor, Berkeley, CA 94704. Copyright © 2016 Rick Remender and Sean Murphy. All rights reserved. Originally published in single magazine form as TOKYO GHOST #1-5. TOKYO GHOST™ (including all prominent characters featured herein), its logo and all character likenesses are trademarks of Rick Remender and Sean Murphy, unless otherwise noted. Image Comics® and its logos are registered trademarks of Image Comics, Inc. No part of this publication may be reproduced or transmitted, in any form or by any means (except for short excerpts for review purposes) without the express written permission of Image Comics, Inc. All names, characters, events and locales in this publication are entirely fictional. Any resemblance to actual persons (living or dead), events or places, without satiric intent, is coincidental. **PRINTED IN THE U.S.A.** For information regarding the CPSIA on this printed material call: 203-595-3636 and provide reference # RICH – 668846. For international rights inquiries, contact: foreignlicensing@imagecomics.com.

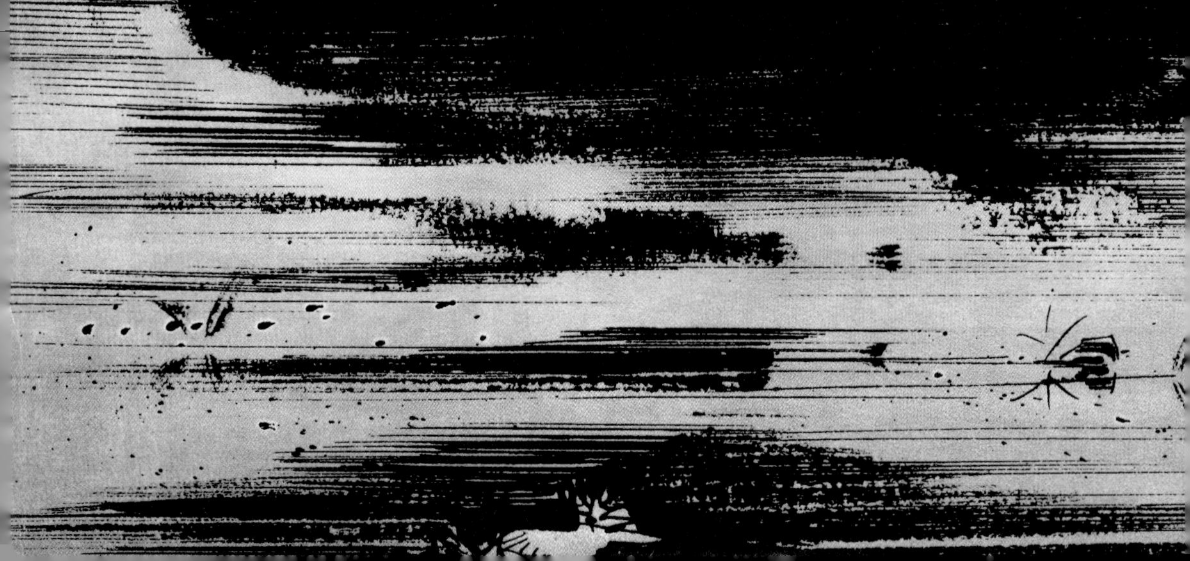

TOKYO GHOST

VOLUME ONE: THE ATOMIC GARDEN

WRITER
RICK REMENDER

ARTIST
SEAN MURPHY

COLORS
MATT HOLLINGSWORTH

LETTERS
RUS WOOTON

EDITOR
SEBASTIAN GIRNER

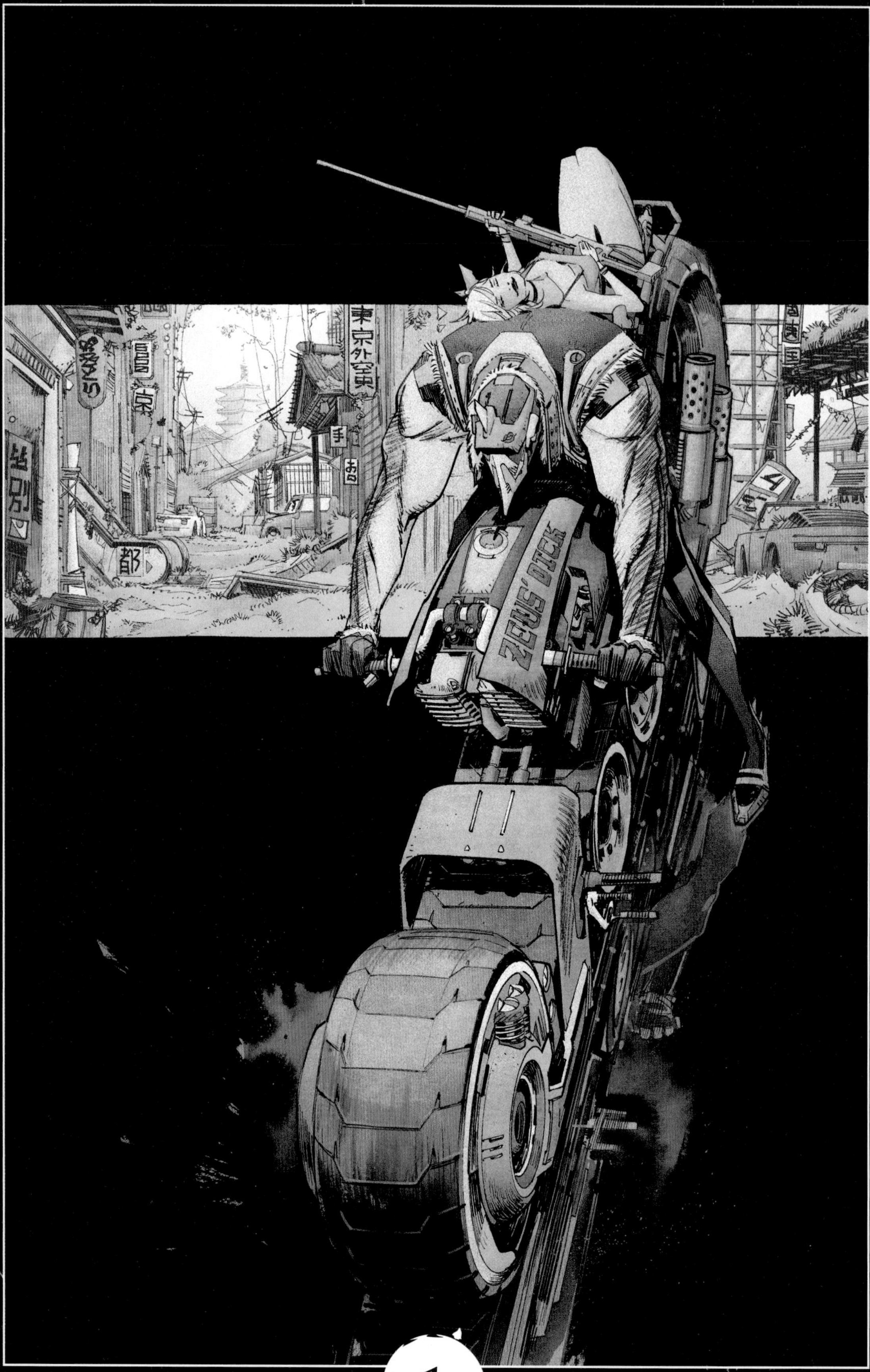
ZEUS' DICK

1

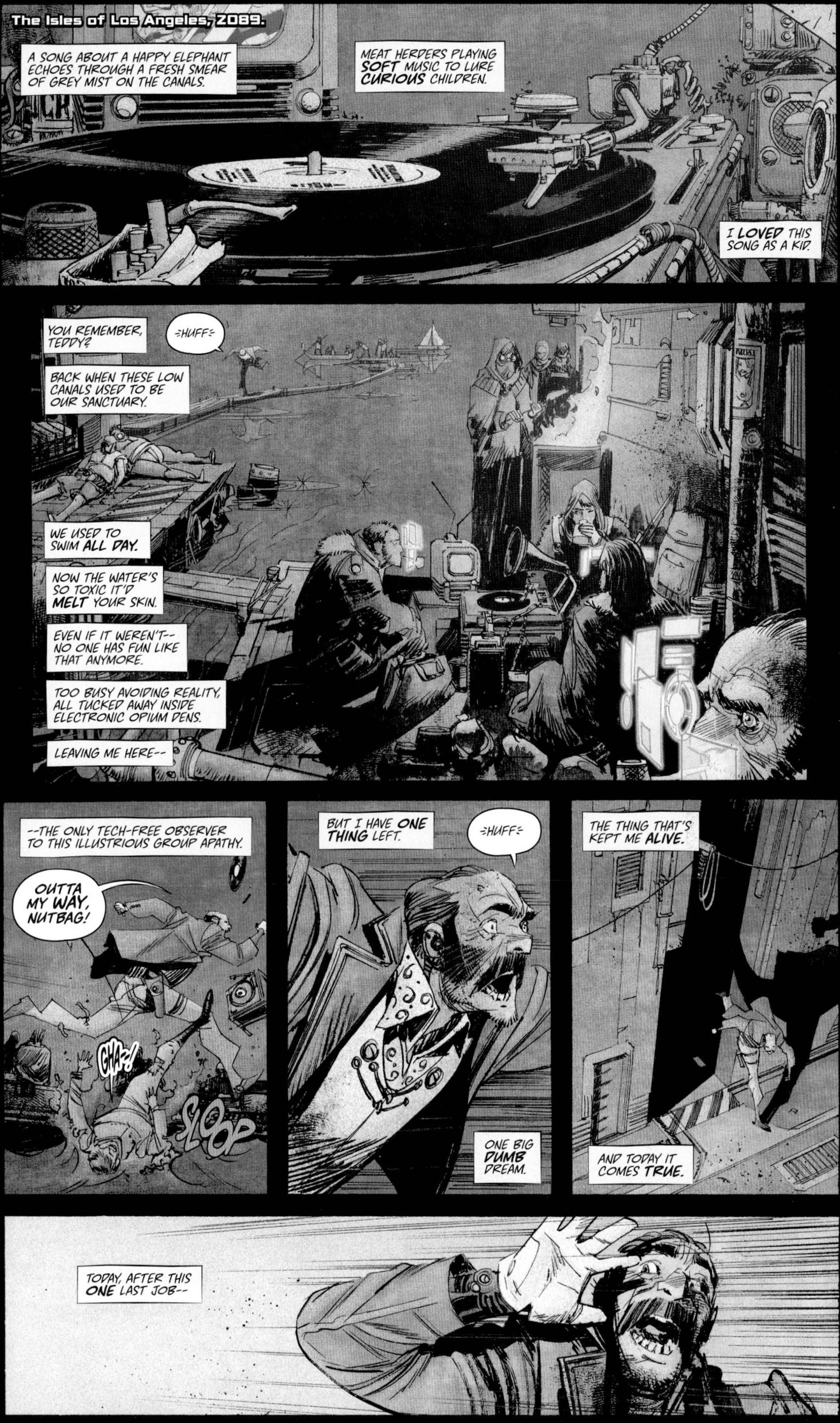

The Isles of Los Angeles, 2089.
A SONG ABOUT A HAPPY ELEPHANT ECHOES THROUGH A FRESH SMEAR OF GREY MIST ON THE CANALS.
MEAT HERDERS PLAYING SOFT MUSIC TO LURE CURIOUS CHILDREN.
I LOVED THIS SONG AS A KID.
YOU REMEMBER, TEDDY?
=HUFF=
BACK WHEN THESE LOW CANALS USED TO BE OUR SANCTUARY.
WE USED TO SWIM ALL DAY.
NOW THE WATER'S SO TOXIC IT'D MELT YOUR SKIN.
EVEN IF IT WEREN'T-- NO ONE HAS FUN LIKE THAT ANYMORE.
TOO BUSY AVOIDING REALITY, ALL TUCKED AWAY INSIDE ELECTRONIC OPIUM DENS.
LEAVING ME HERE--
--THE ONLY TECH-FREE OBSERVER TO THIS ILLUSTRIOUS GROUP APATHY.
OUTTA MY WAY, NUTBAG!
GHAK!
SLOOP
BUT I HAVE ONE THING LEFT.
=HUFF=
ONE BIG DUMB DREAM.
THE THING THAT'S KEPT ME ALIVE.
AND TODAY IT COMES TRUE.
TODAY, AFTER THIS ONE LAST JOB--

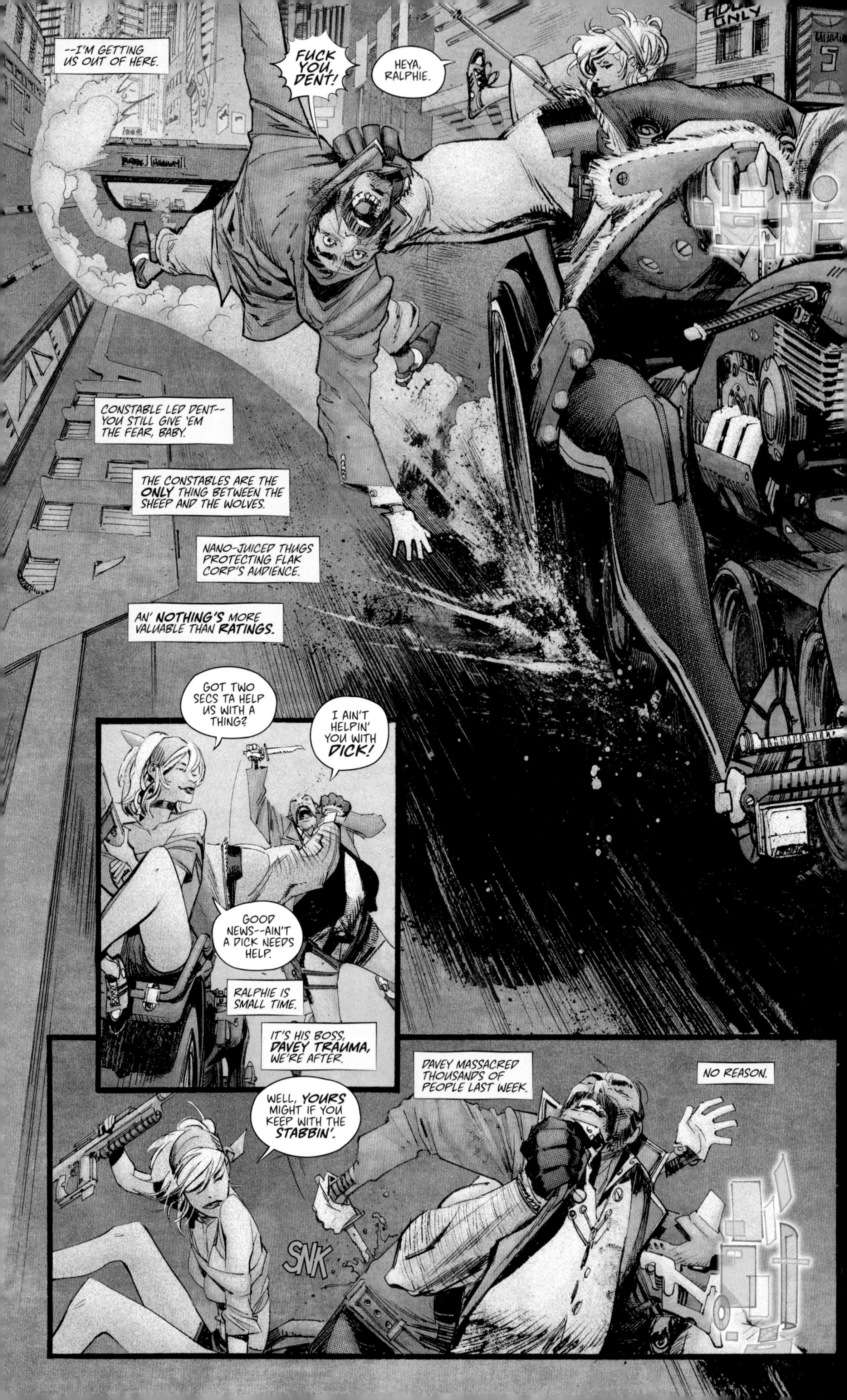

--I'M GETTING US OUT OF HERE.
FUCK YOU, DENT!
HEYA, RALPHIE.
ADULT ONLY
CONSTABLE LED DENT--YOU STILL GIVE 'EM THE FEAR, BABY.
THE CONSTABLES ARE THE ONLY THING BETWEEN THE SHEEP AND THE WOLVES.
NANO-JUICED THUGS PROTECTING FLAK CORP'S AUDIENCE.
AN' NOTHING'S MORE VALUABLE THAN RATINGS.
GOT TWO SECS TA HELP US WITH A THING?
I AIN'T HELPIN' YOU WITH DICK!
GOOD NEWS--AIN'T A DICK NEEDS HELP.
RALPHIE IS SMALL TIME.
IT'S HIS BOSS, DAVEY TRAUMA, WE'RE AFTER.
DAVEY MASSACRED THOUSANDS OF PEOPLE LAST WEEK.
NO REASON.
WELL, YOURS MIGHT IF YOU KEEP WITH THE STABBIN'.
SNK

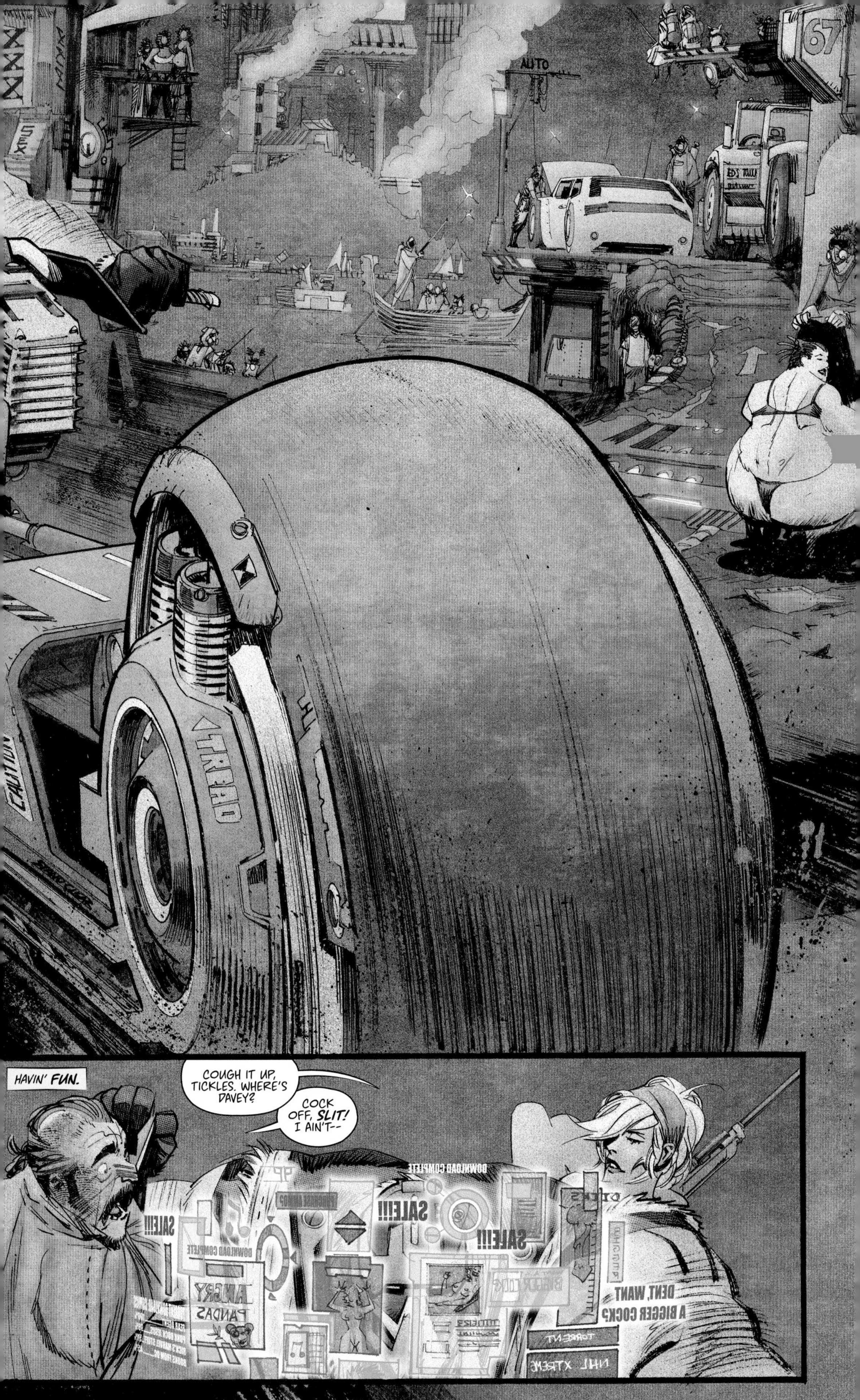
XXX
SEX
AUTO
67
TREAD
CAUTION
HAVIN' **FUN.**
COUGH IT UP, TICKLES. WHERE'S DAVEY?
COCK OFF, **SLIT!** I AIN'T--
DOWNLOAD COMPLETE
SALE!!!
SALE!!!
SALE!!!
DOWNLOAD COMPLETE
ANGRY PANDAS
DENT, WANT
A BIGGER COCK?
TORRENT
NHL XTREME

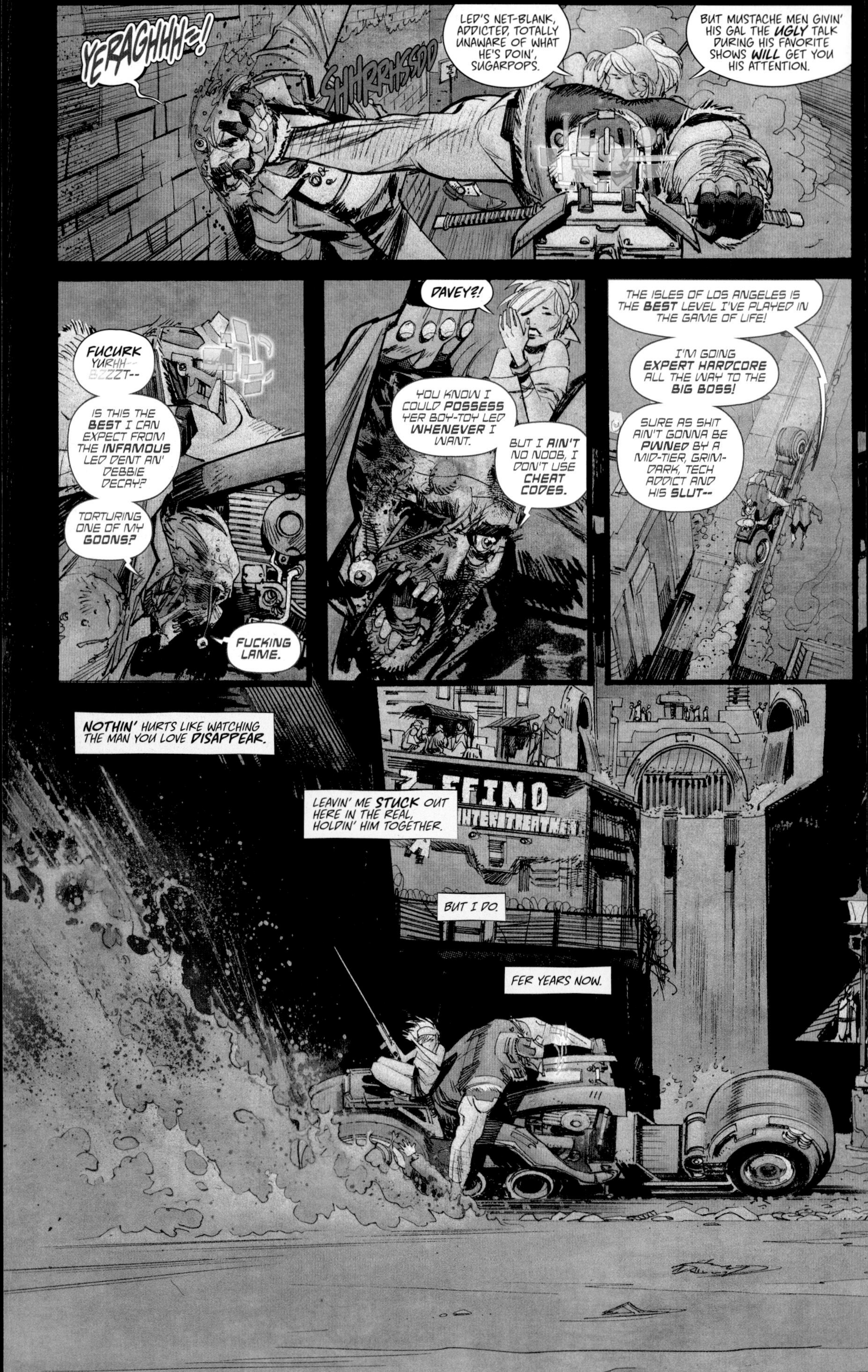

YERAGHHH~!
SHHRHSSDD
LED'S NET-BLANK, ADDICTED, TOTALLY UNAWARE OF WHAT HE'S DOIN', SUGARPOPS.
BUT MUSTACHE MEN GIVIN' HIS GAL THE UGLY TALK DURING HIS FAVORITE SHOWS WILL GET YOU HIS ATTENTION.
FUCURK YURHH-- BZZZT--
IS THIS THE BEST I CAN EXPECT FROM THE INFAMOUS LED DENT AN' DEBBIE DECAY?
TORTURING ONE OF MY GOONS?
FUCKING LAME.
DAVEY?!
YOU KNOW I COULD POSSESS YER BOY-TOY LED WHENEVER I WANT.
BUT I AIN'T NO NOOB, I DON'T USE CHEAT CODES.
THE ISLES OF LOS ANGELES IS THE BEST LEVEL I'VE PLAYED IN THE GAME OF LIFE!
I'M GOING EXPERT HARDCORE ALL THE WAY TO THE BIG BOSS!
SURE AS SHIT AIN'T GONNA BE PINNED BY A MID-TIER, GRIM-DARK, TECH ADDICT AND HIS SLUT--
NOTHIN' HURTS LIKE WATCHING THE MAN YOU LOVE DISAPPEAR.
LEAVIN' ME STUCK OUT HERE IN THE REAL, HOLDIN' HIM TOGETHER.
BUT I DO.
FER YEARS NOW.

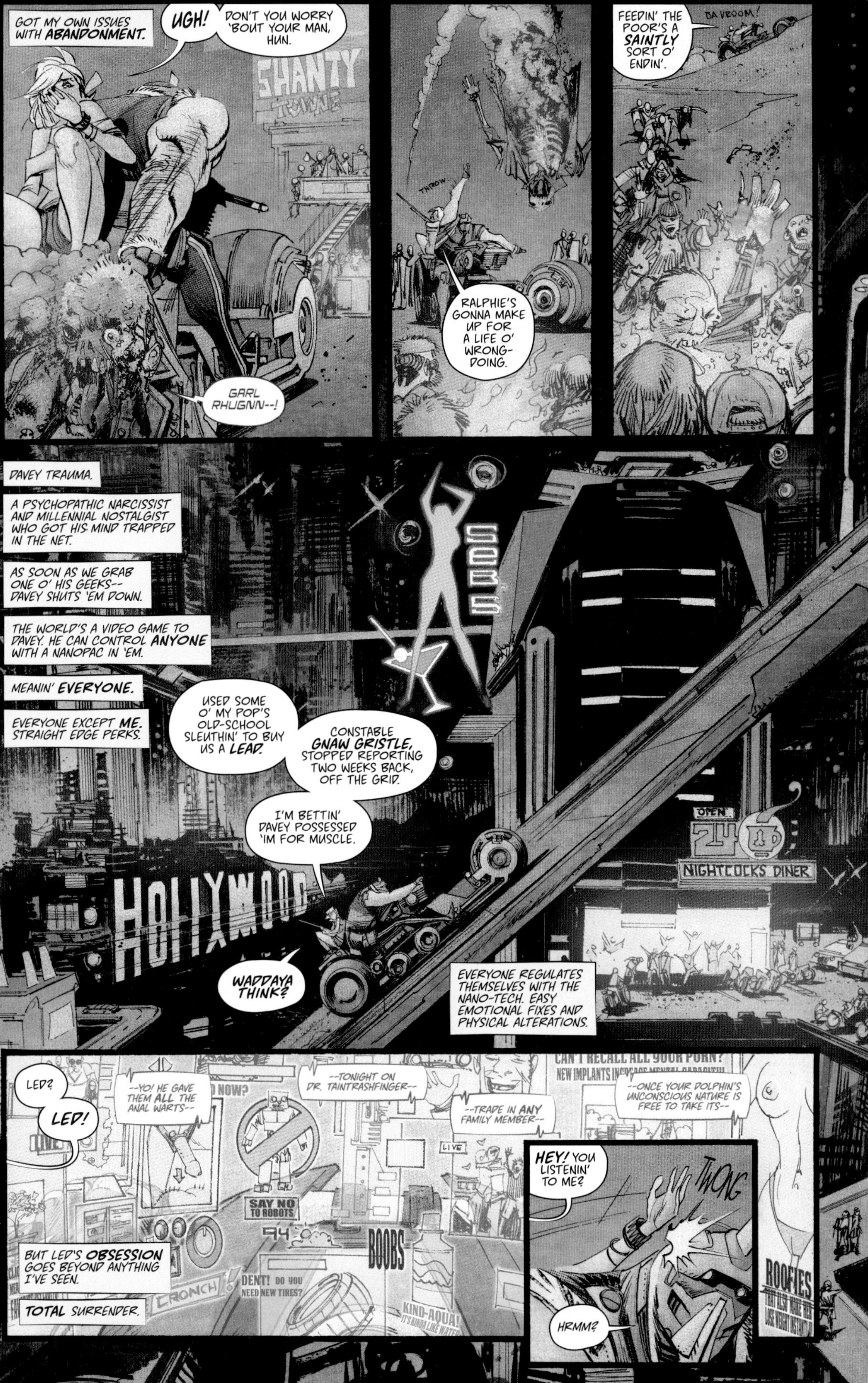

GOT MY OWN ISSUES WITH ABANDONMENT.
UGH!
DON'T YOU WORRY 'BOUT YOUR MAN, HUN.
SHANTY TOWNE
GARL RHUGNN--!
THROW
RALPHIE'S GONNA MAKE UP FOR A LIFE O' WRONG-DOING.
FEEDIN' THE POOR'S A SAINTLY SORT O' ENDIN'.
BAVROOM!
DAVEY TRAUMA.
A PSYCHOPATHIC NARCISSIST AND MILLENNIAL NOSTALGIST WHO GOT HIS MIND TRAPPED IN THE NET.
AS SOON AS WE GRAB ONE O' HIS GEEKS-- DAVEY SHUTS 'EM DOWN.
THE WORLD'S A VIDEO GAME TO DAVEY. HE CAN CONTROL ANYONE WITH A NANOPAC IN 'EM.
MEANIN' EVERYONE.
EVERYONE EXCEPT ME. STRAIGHT EDGE PERKS.
SEB 5
USED SOME O' MY POP'S OLD-SCHOOL SLEUTHIN' TO BUY US A LEAD.
CONSTABLE GNAW GRISTLE, STOPPED REPORTING TWO WEEKS BACK, OFF THE GRID.
I'M BETTIN' DAVEY POSSESSED 'IM FOR MUSCLE.
OPEN 24
NIGHTCOCKS DINER
HOLLYWOOD
WADDAYA THINK?
EVERYONE REGULATES THEMSELVES WITH THE NANO-TECH. EASY EMOTIONAL FIXES AND PHYSICAL ALTERATIONS.
LED?
LED!
--YO! HE GAVE THEM ALL THE ANAL WARTS--
--TONIGHT ON DR. TAINTRASHFINGER--
--TRADE IN ANY FAMILY MEMBER--
CAN'T RECALL ALL YOUR PORN?
--ONCE YOUR DOLPHIN'S UNCONSCIOUS NATURE IS FREE TO TAKE ITS--
SAY NO TO ROBOTS
LIVE
BOOBS
DENT! DO YOU NEED NEW TIRES?
KIND-AQUA! IT'S KINDA LIKE WATER
CRONCH
BUT LED'S OBSESSION GOES BEYOND ANYTHING I'VE SEEN.
TOTAL SURRENDER.
HEY! YOU LISTENIN' TO ME?
TWONG
HRMM?
ROOFIES

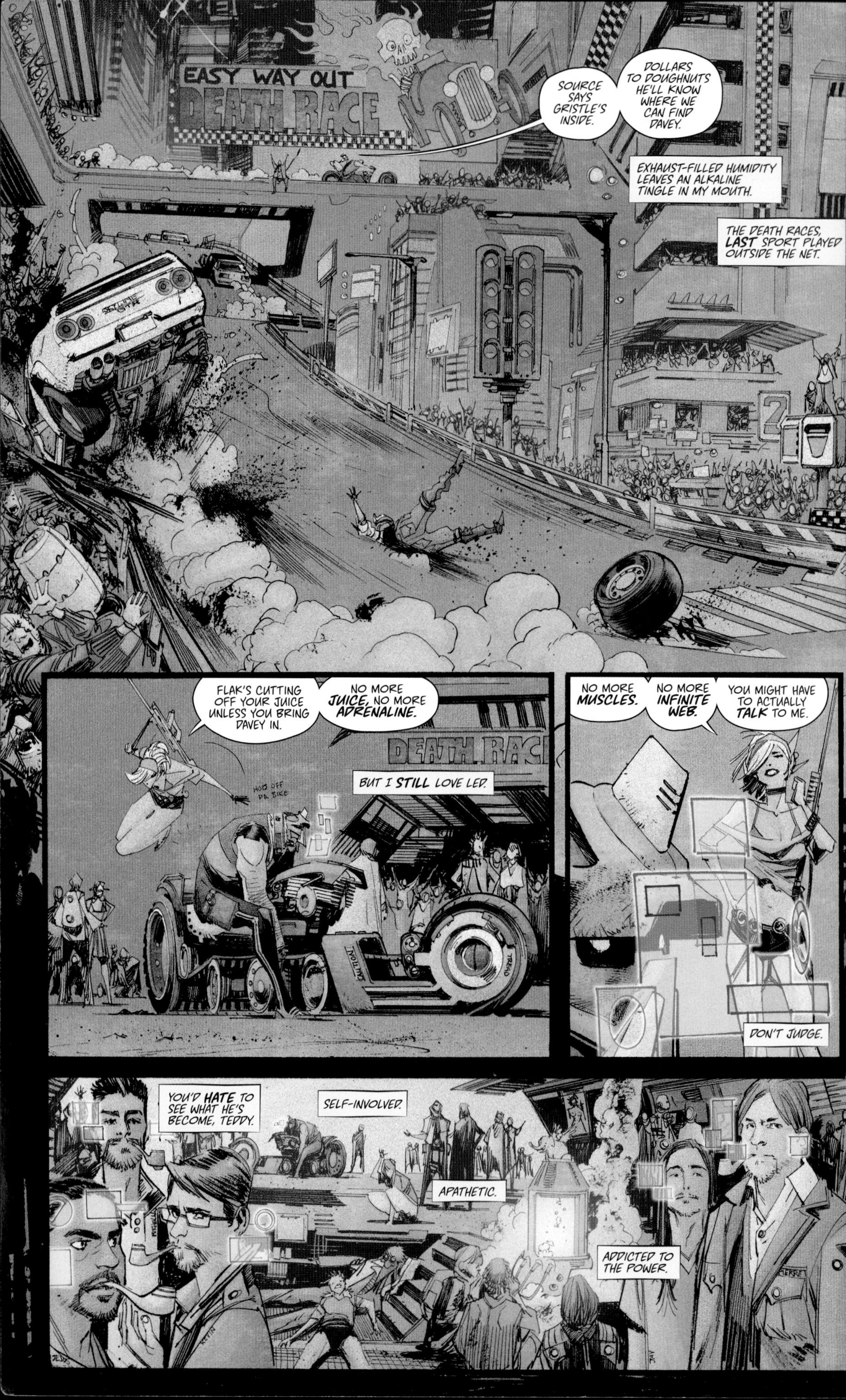
EASY WAY OUT
DEATH RACE
SOURCE SAYS GRISTLE'S INSIDE.
DOLLARS TO DOUGHNUTS HE'LL KNOW WHERE WE CAN FIND DAVEY.
EXHAUST-FILLED HUMIDITY LEAVES AN ALKALINE TINGLE IN MY MOUTH.
THE DEATH RACES, **LAST** SPORT PLAYED OUTSIDE THE NET.
FLAK'S CUTTING OFF YOUR JUICE UNLESS YOU BRING DAVEY IN.
NO MORE ***JUICE,*** NO MORE ***ADRENALINE.***
DEATH RACE
BUT I **STILL** LOVE LED.
NO MORE ***MUSCLES.***
NO MORE ***INFINITE WEB.***
YOU MIGHT HAVE TO ACTUALLY **TALK** TO ME.
DON'T JUDGE.
YOU'D **HATE** TO SEE WHAT HE'S BECOME, TEDDY.
SELF-INVOLVED.
APATHETIC.
ADDICTED TO THE POWER.

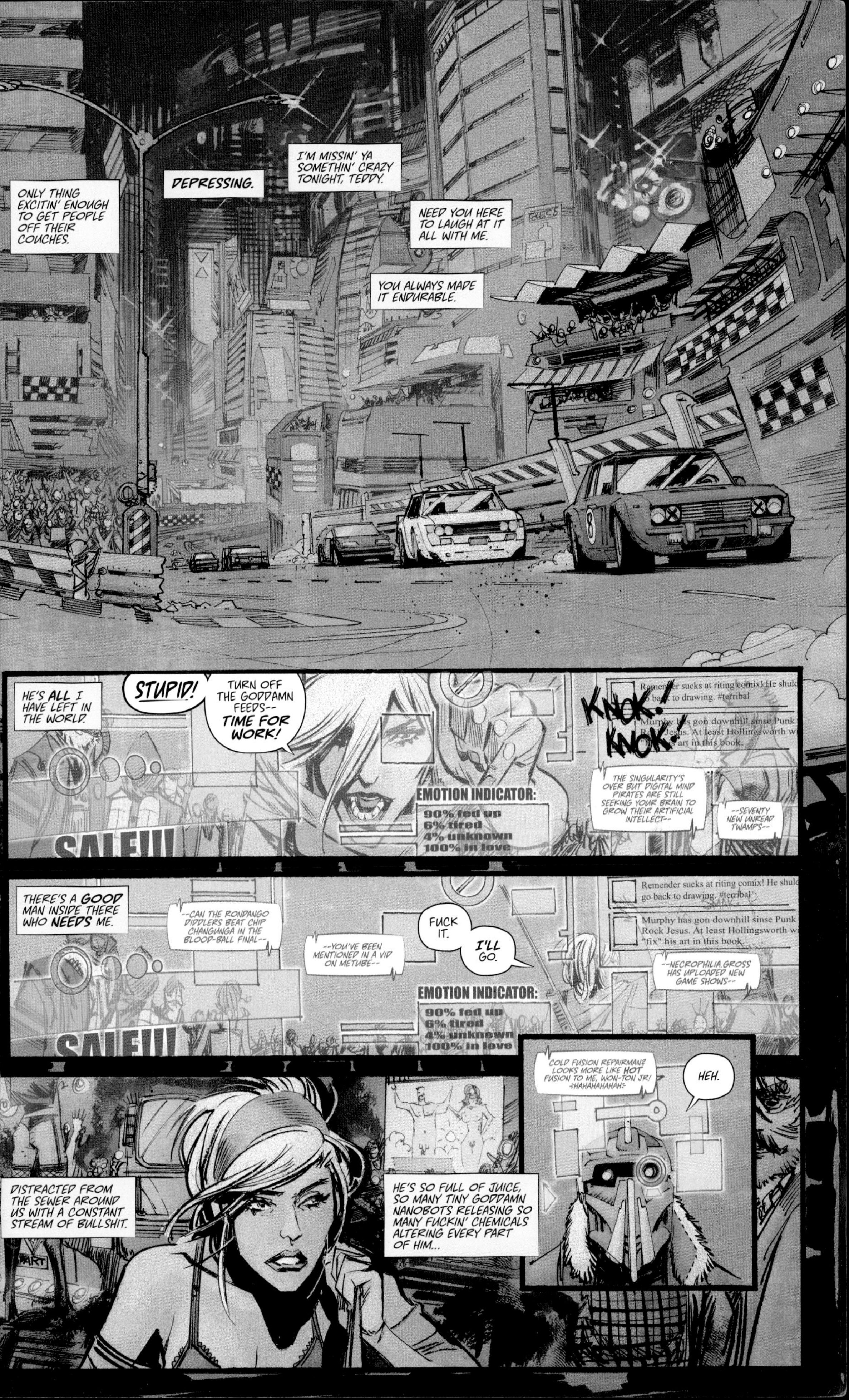
ONLY THING EXCITIN' ENOUGH TO GET PEOPLE OFF THEIR COUCHES.
DEPRESSING.
I'M MISSIN' YA SOMETHIN' CRAZY TONIGHT, TEDDY.
NEED YOU HERE TO LAUGH AT IT ALL WITH ME.
YOU ALWAYS MADE IT ENDURABLE.
HE'S **ALL** I HAVE LEFT IN THE WORLD.
STUPID!
TURN OFF THE GODDAMN FEEDS-- **TIME FOR WORK!**
KNOK! KNOK!
EMOTION INDICATOR:
90% fed up
6% tired
4% unknown
100% in love
THE SINGULARITY'S OVER BUT DIGITAL MIND PIRATES ARE STILL SEEKING YOUR BRAIN TO GROW THEIR ARTIFICIAL INTELLECT--
--SEVENTY NEW UNREAD TWAMPS--
THERE'S A **GOOD** MAN INSIDE THERE WHO **NEEDS** ME.
--CAN THE RONDANGO DIDDLERS BEAT CHIP CHANGUNGA IN THE BLOOD-BALL FINAL--
--YOU'VE BEEN MENTIONED IN A VID ON METUBE--
Remender sucks at riting comix! He shuld go back to drawing. #terribal
Murphy has gon downhill sinse Punk Rock Jesus. At least Hollingsworth w "fix" his art in this book.
FUCK IT.
I'LL GO.
--NECROPHILIA.GROSS HAS UPLOADED NEW GAME SHOWS--
EMOTION INDICATOR:
90% fed up
6% tired
4% unknown
100% in love
COLD FUSION REPAIRMAN? LOOKS MORE LIKE **HOT** FUSION TO ME, WON-TON JR! HAHAHAHAHAH
HEH.
DISTRACTED FROM THE SEWER AROUND US WITH A CONSTANT STREAM OF BULLSHIT.
HE'S SO FULL OF JUICE, SO MANY TINY GODDAMN NANOBOTS RELEASING SO MANY FUCKIN' CHEMICALS ALTERING EVERY PART OF HIM...

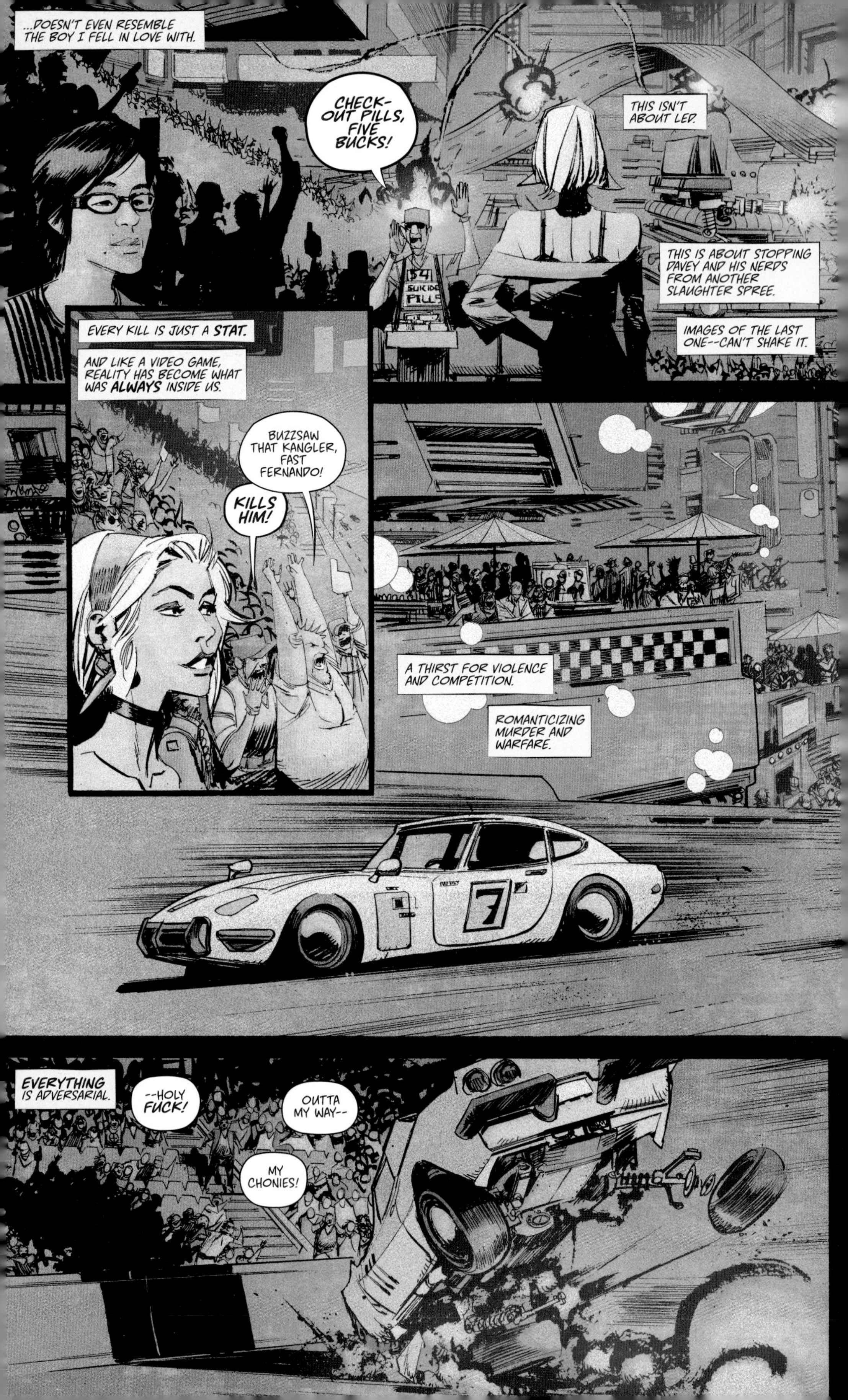

...DOESN'T EVEN RESEMBLE THE BOY I FELL IN LOVE WITH.
CHECK-OUT PILLS, FIVE BUCKS!
$4 SUICIDE PILLS
THIS ISN'T ABOUT LED.
THIS IS ABOUT STOPPING DAVEY AND HIS NERDS FROM ANOTHER SLAUGHTER SPREE.
IMAGES OF THE LAST ONE--CAN'T SHAKE IT.
EVERY KILL IS JUST A STAT.
AND LIKE A VIDEO GAME, REALITY HAS BECOME WHAT WAS ALWAYS INSIDE US.
BUZZSAW THAT KANGLER, FAST FERNANDO!
KILLS HIM!
A THIRST FOR VIOLENCE AND COMPETITION.
ROMANTICIZING MURDER AND WARFARE.
7
EVERYTHING IS ADVERSARIAL.
--HOLY FUCK!
OUTTA MY WAY--
MY CHONIES!

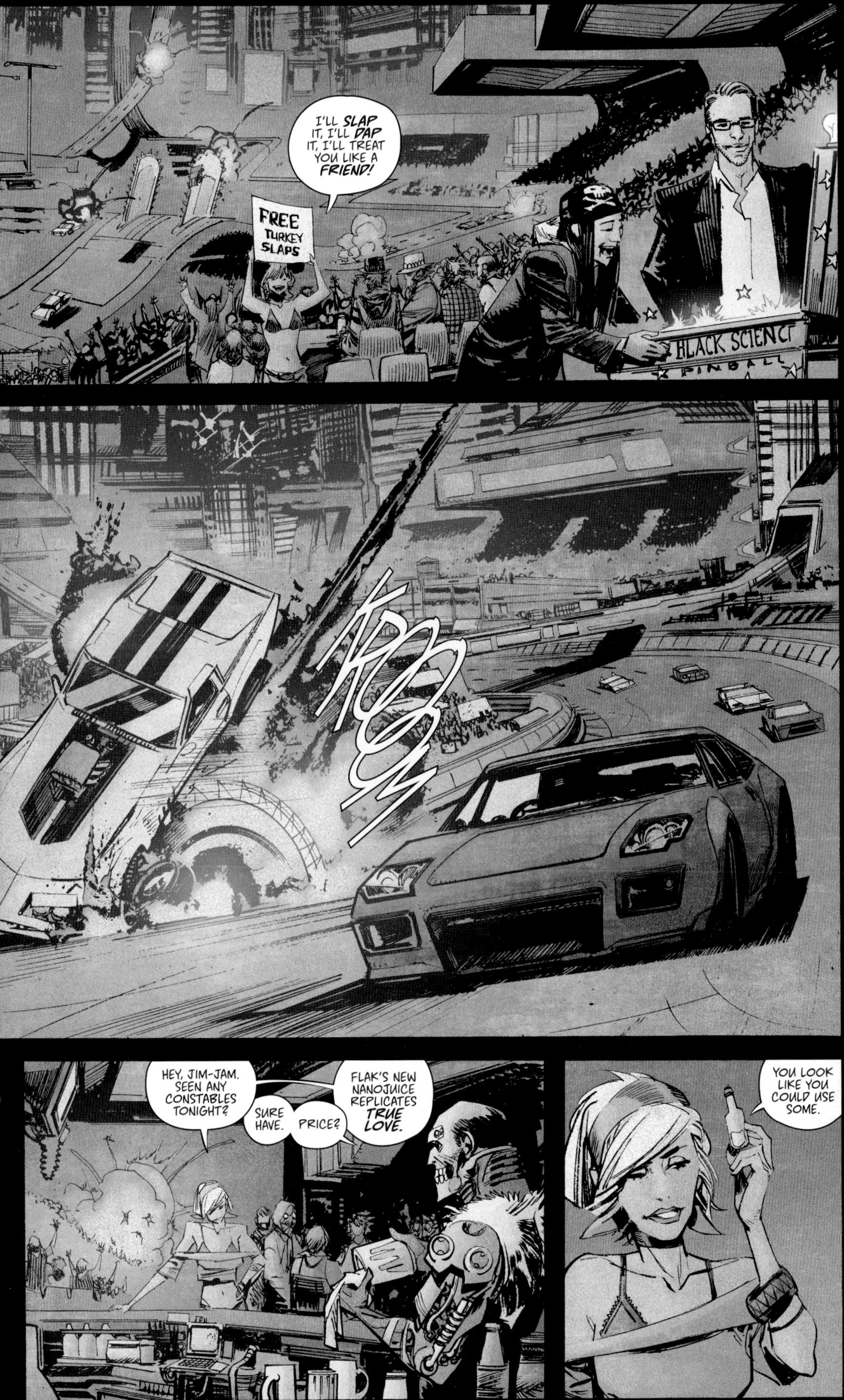
I'LL SLAP IT, I'LL DAP IT, I'LL TREAT YOU LIKE A FRIEND!
FREE TURKEY SLAPS
BLACK SCIENC
PINBALL
KROOOM
HEY, JIM-JAM. SEEN ANY CONSTABLES TONIGHT?
SURE HAVE.
PRICE?
FLAK'S NEW NANOJUICE REPLICATES TRUE LOVE.
YOU LOOK LIKE YOU COULD USE SOME.

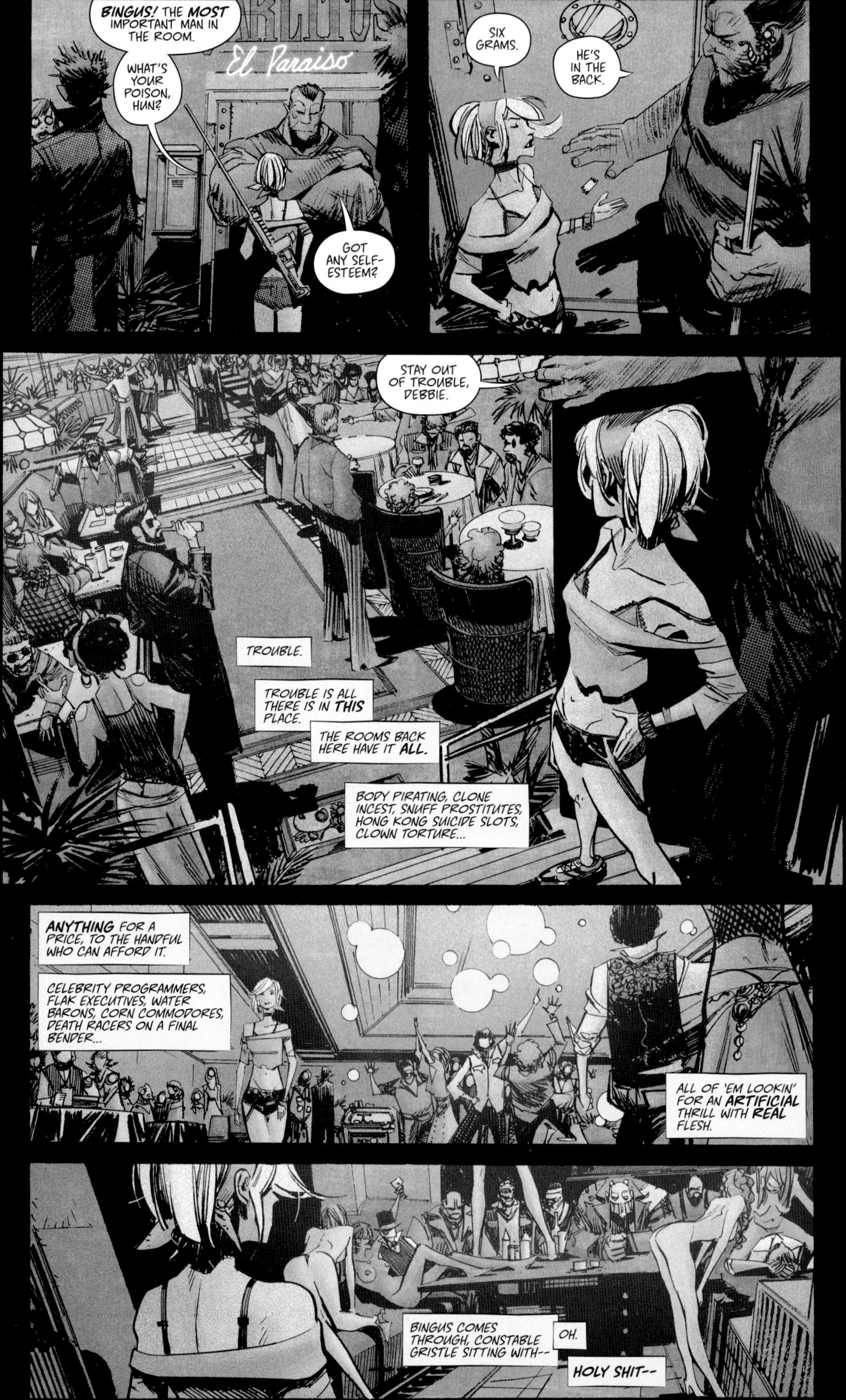
El Paraiso
BINGUS! THE MOST IMPORTANT MAN IN THE ROOM.
WHAT'S YOUR POISON, HUN?
GOT ANY SELF-ESTEEM?
SIX GRAMS.
HE'S IN THE BACK.
STAY OUT OF TROUBLE, DEBBIE.
TROUBLE.
TROUBLE IS ALL THERE IS IN THIS PLACE.
THE ROOMS BACK HERE HAVE IT ALL.
BODY PIRATING, CLONE INCEST, SNUFF PROSTITUTES, HONG KONG SUICIDE SLOTS, CLOWN TORTURE...
ANYTHING FOR A PRICE, TO THE HANDFUL WHO CAN AFFORD IT.
CELEBRITY PROGRAMMERS, FLAK EXECUTIVES, WATER BARONS, CORN COMMODORES, DEATH RACERS ON A FINAL BENDER...
ALL OF 'EM LOOKIN' FOR AN ARTIFICIAL THRILL WITH REAL FLESH.
BINGUS COMES THROUGH, CONSTABLE GRISTLE SITTING WITH--
OH.
HOLY SHIT--

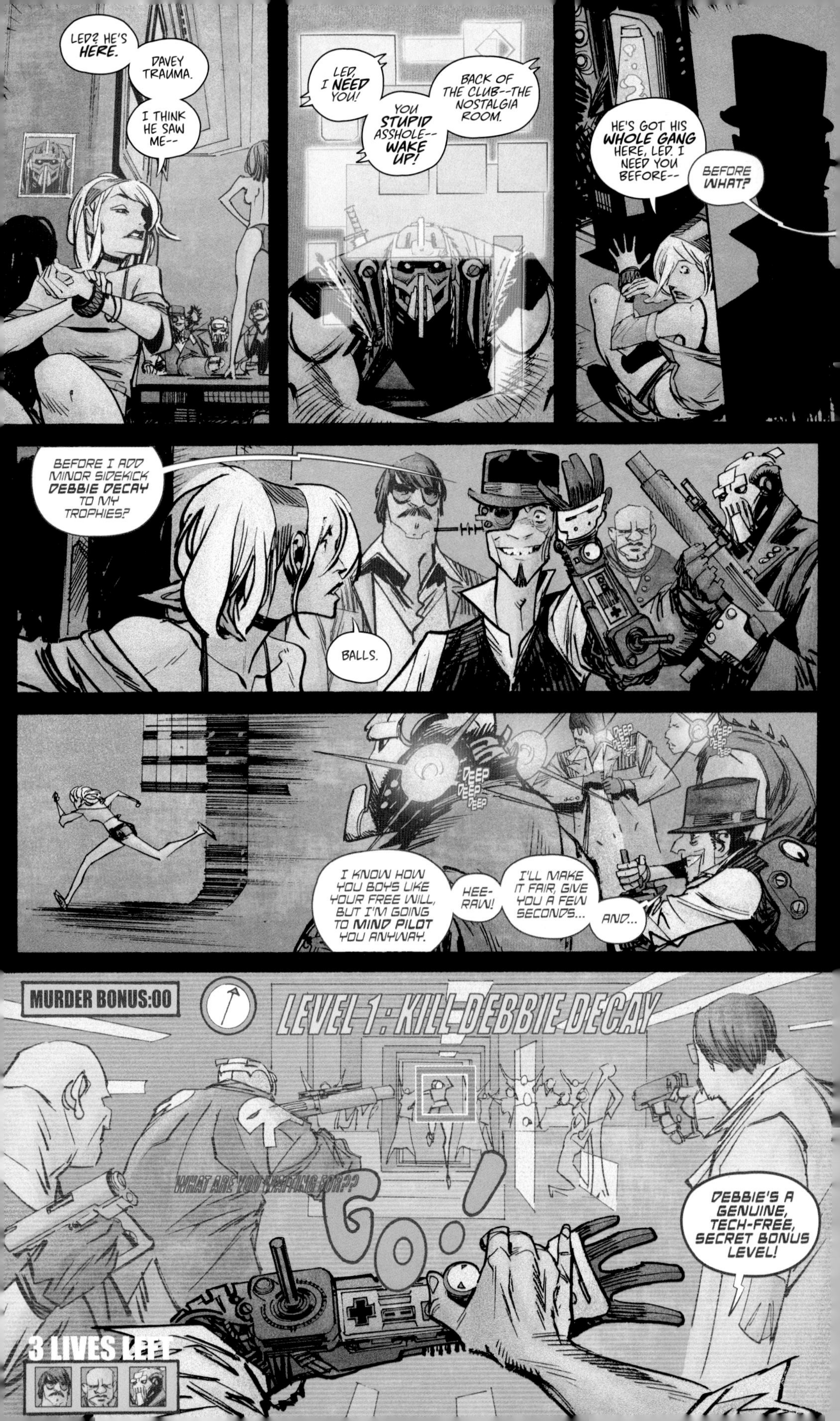
LED? HE'S HERE.
DAVEY TRAUMA.
I THINK HE SAW ME--
LED, I NEED YOU!
YOU STUPID ASSHOLE-- WAKE UP!
BACK OF THE CLUB--THE NOSTALGIA ROOM.
HE'S GOT HIS WHOLE GANG HERE, LED. I NEED YOU BEFORE--
BEFORE WHAT?
BEFORE I ADD MINOR SIDEKICK DEBBIE DECAY TO MY TROPHIES?
BALLS.
DEEP DEEP DEEP
DEEP DEEP DEEP
DEEP DEEP DEEP
I KNOW HOW YOU BOYS LIKE YOUR FREE WILL, BUT I'M GOING TO MIND PILOT YOU ANYWAY.
HEE-RAW!
I'LL MAKE IT FAIR, GIVE YOU A FEW SECONDS...
AND...
MURDER BONUS:00
LEVEL 1: KILL DEBBIE DECAY
WHAT ARE YOU WAITING FOR??
GO!
DEBBIE'S A GENUINE, TECH-FREE, SECRET BONUS LEVEL!
3 LIVES LEFT

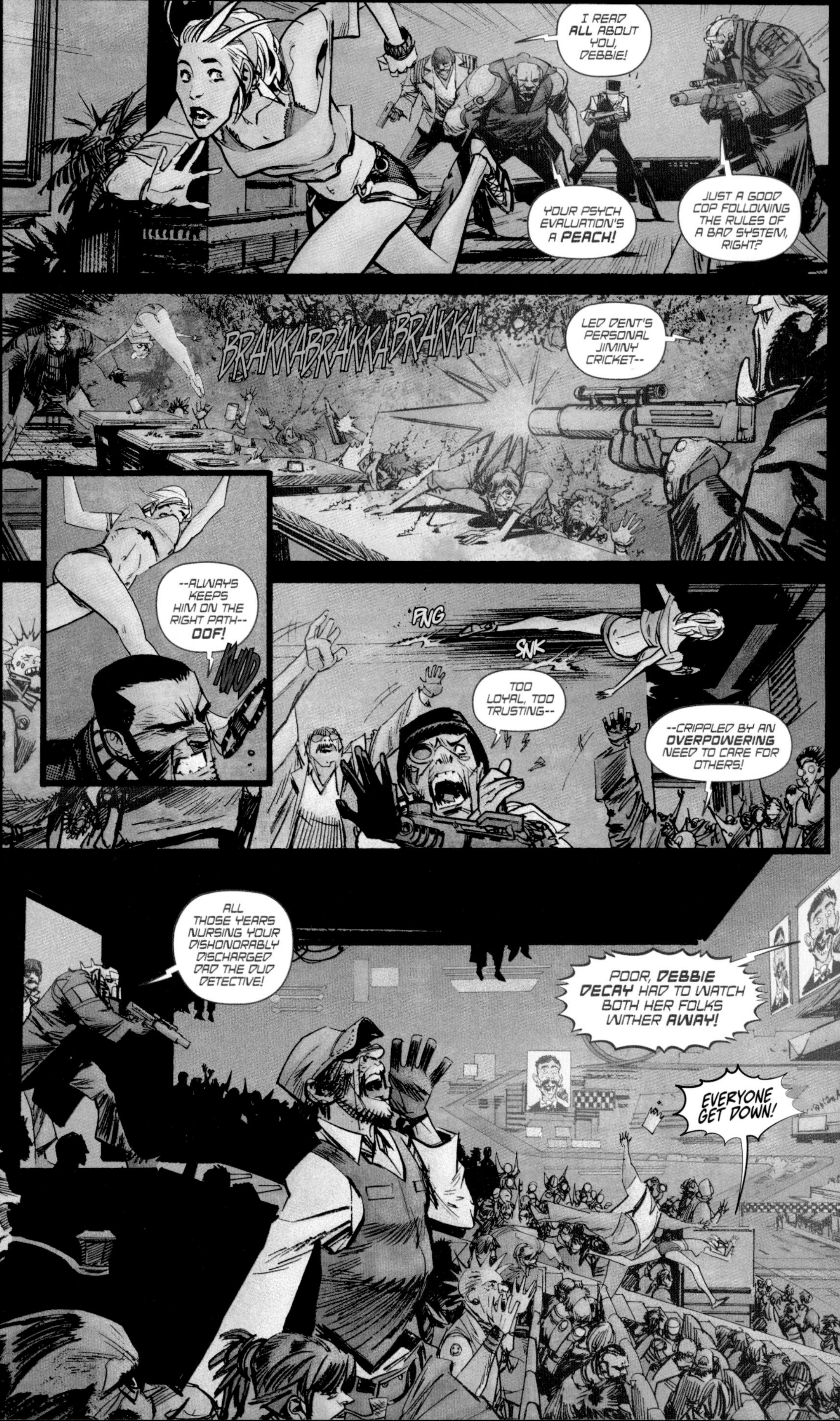
I READ **ALL** ABOUT YOU, DEBBIE!
YOUR PSYCH EVALUATION'S A **PEACH!**
JUST A GOOD COP FOLLOWING THE RULES OF A BAD SYSTEM, RIGHT?
BRAKKABRAKKABRAKKA
LEO DENT'S PERSONAL JIMINY CRICKET--
--ALWAYS KEEPS HIM ON THE RIGHT PATH-- **OOF!**
PNG
SNK
TOO LOYAL, TOO TRUSTING--
--CRIPPLED BY AN **OVERPOWERING** NEED TO CARE FOR OTHERS!
ALL THOSE YEARS NURSING YOUR DISHONORABLY DISCHARGED DAD THE DUD DETECTIVE!
POOR, **DEBBIE DECAY** HAD TO WATCH BOTH HER FOLKS WITHER **AWAY!**
EVERYONE GET DOWN!

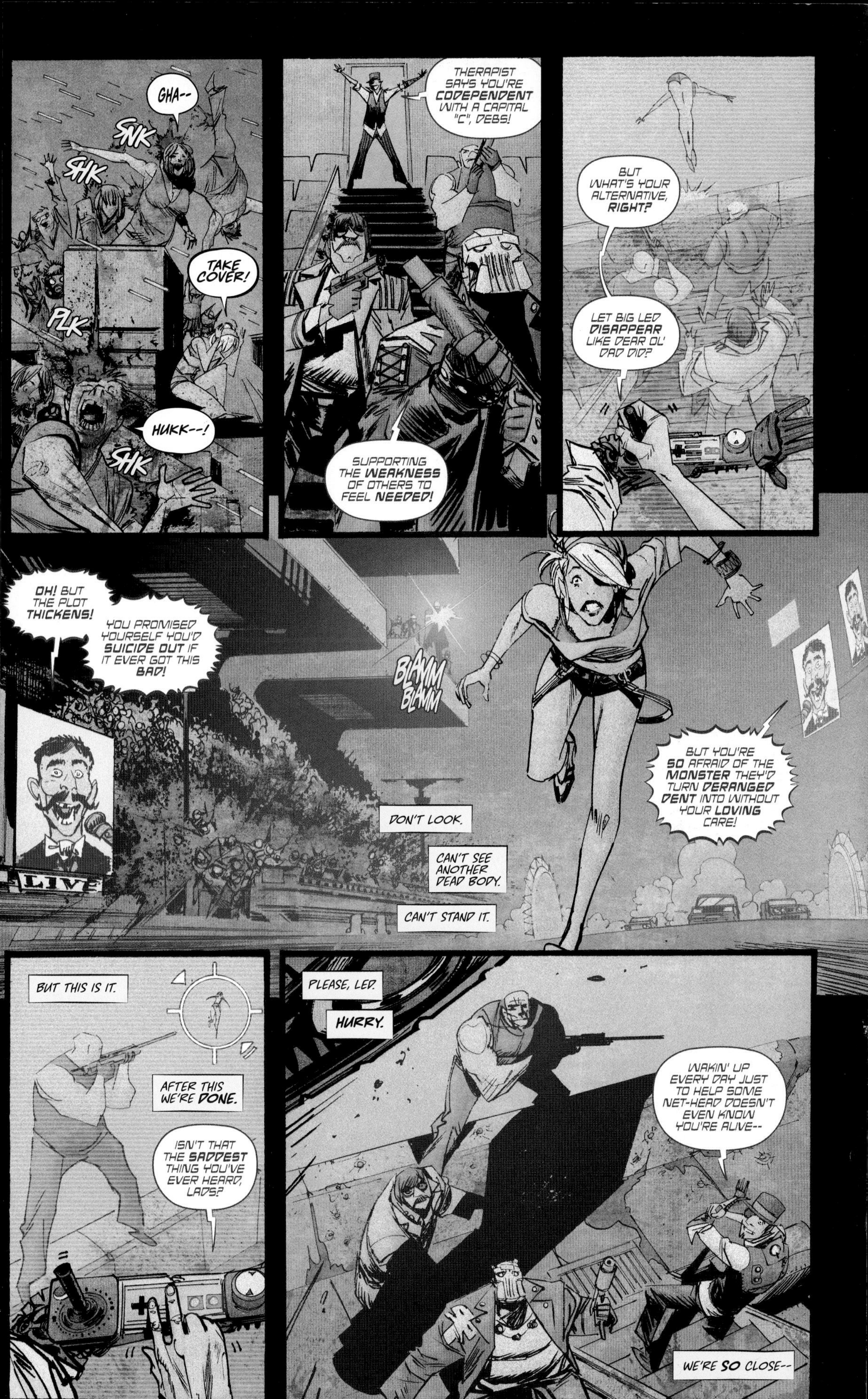
GHA--
SNK
SHK
TAKE COVER!
PLK
HUKK--!
SHK
THERAPIST SAYS YOU'RE CODEPENDENT WITH A CAPITAL "C", DEBS!
SUPPORTING THE WEAKNESS OF OTHERS TO FEEL NEEDED!
BUT WHAT'S YOUR ALTERNATIVE, RIGHT?
LET BIG LED DISAPPEAR LIKE DEAR OL' DAD DID?
OH! BUT THE PLOT THICKENS!
YOU PROMISED YOURSELF YOU'D SUICIDE OUT IF IT EVER GOT THIS BAD!
BLAMM BLAMM
LIVE
BUT YOU'RE SO AFRAID OF THE MONSTER THEY'D TURN DERANGED DENT INTO WITHOUT YOUR LOVING CARE!
DON'T LOOK.
CAN'T SEE ANOTHER DEAD BODY.
CAN'T STAND IT.
BUT THIS IS IT.
AFTER THIS WE'RE DONE.
ISN'T THAT THE SADDEST THING YOU'VE EVER HEARD, LADS?
PLEASE, LED.
HURRY.
WAKIN' UP EVERY DAY JUST TO HELP SOME NET-HEAD DOESN'T EVEN KNOW YOU'RE ALIVE--
WE'RE SO CLOSE--

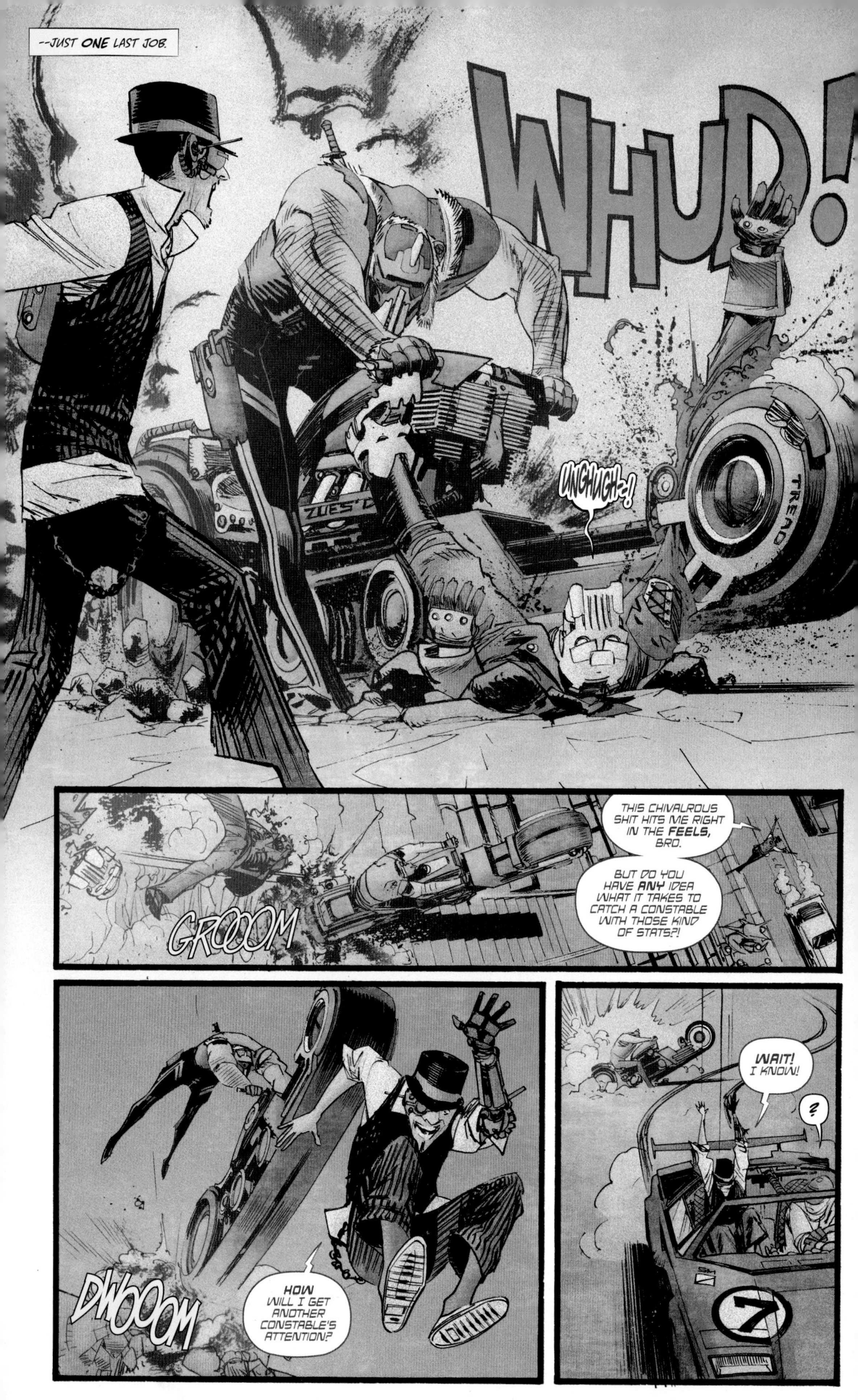
--JUST ONE LAST JOB.
WHUD!
UNGHUGH~!
ZUES'C
TREAD
GROOOM
THIS CHIVALROUS SHIT HITS ME RIGHT IN THE FEELS, BRO.
BUT DO YOU HAVE ANY IDEA WHAT IT TAKES TO CATCH A CONSTABLE WITH THOSE KIND OF STATS?!
DWOOOM
HOW WILL I GET ANOTHER CONSTABLE'S ATTENTION?
WAIT! I KNOW!
?
7

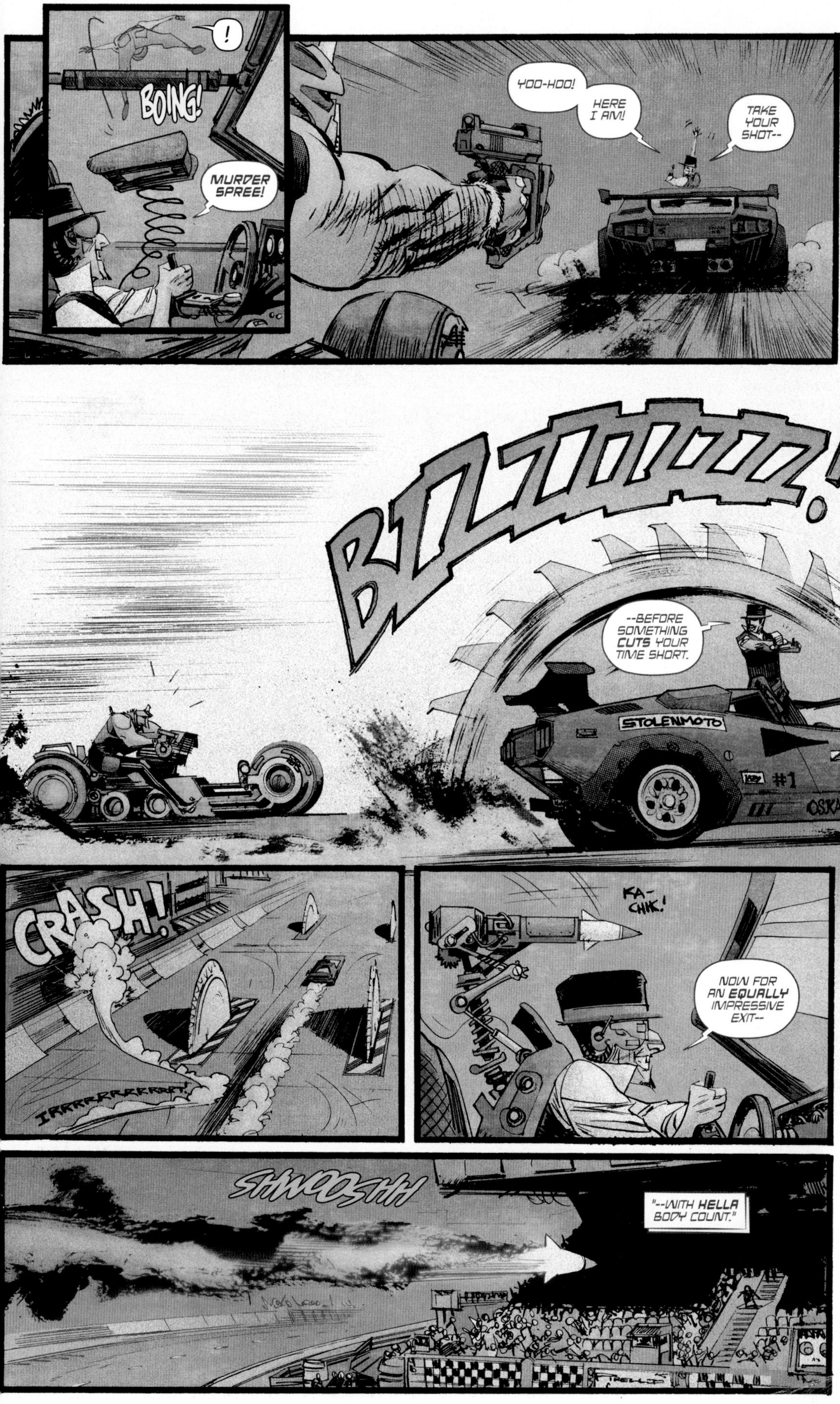
!
BOING!
MURDER SPREE!
YOO-HOO!
HERE I AM!
TAKE YOUR SHOT--
BZZOOOOOZ!
--BEFORE SOMETHING CUTS YOUR TIME SHORT.
STOLENMOTO
7
#1
OSKAR BLUE
CRASH!
IRRRRRRRRRRRRT!
KA-CHIK!
NOW FOR AN EQUALLY IMPRESSIVE EXIT--
SHWOOSHH
"--WITH HELLA BODY COUNT."

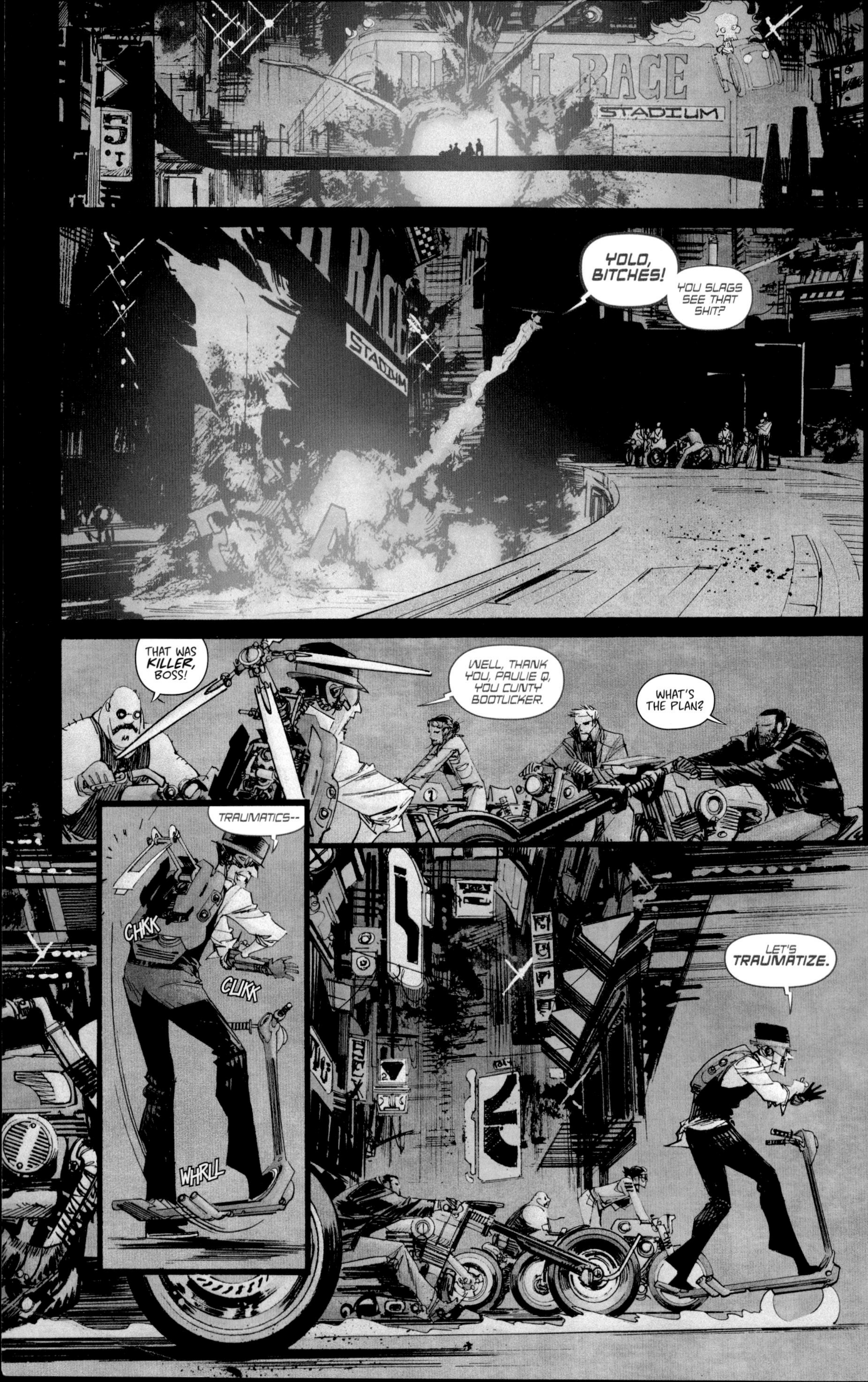
STADIUM
YOLO, BITCHES!
YOU SLAGS SEE THAT SHIT?
THAT WAS KILLER, BOSS!
WELL, THANK YOU, PAULIE Q, YOU CUNTY BOOTLICKER.
WHAT'S THE PLAN?
TRAUMATICS--
CHKK
CLIKK
WHRLL
LET'S TRAUMATIZE.

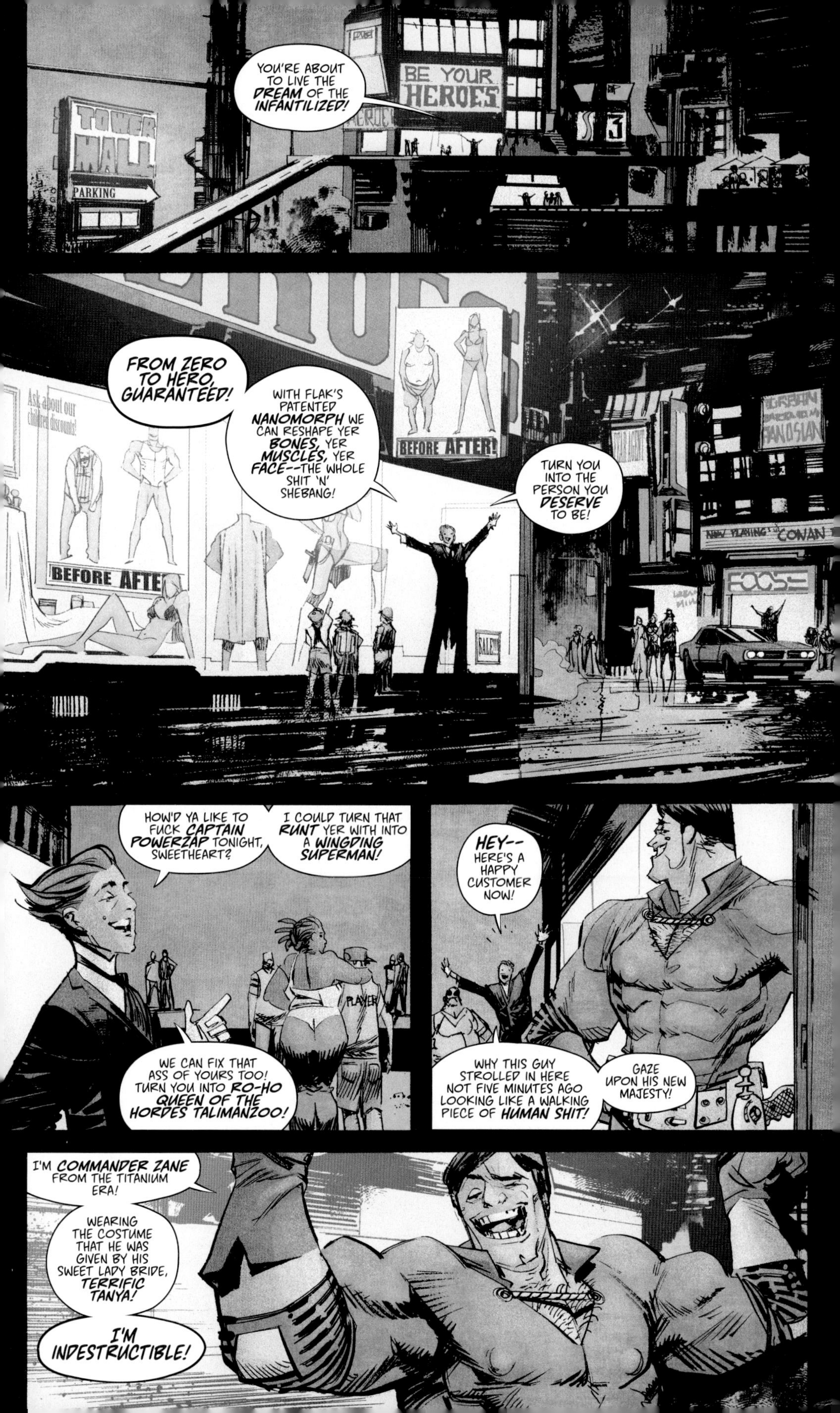
TOWER MALL
PARKING
BE YOUR HEROES
YOU'RE ABOUT TO LIVE THE DREAM OF THE INFANTILIZED!
FROM ZERO TO HERO, GUARANTEED!
Ask about our children discounts!
BEFORE AFTER!
WITH FLAK'S PATENTED NANOMORPH WE CAN RESHAPE YER BONES, YER MUSCLES, YER FACE--THE WHOLE SHIT 'N' SHEBANG!
TURN YOU INTO THE PERSON YOU DESERVE TO BE!
NOW PLAYING CONAN
SALE!!!
HOW'D YA LIKE TO FUCK CAPTAIN POWERZAP TONIGHT, SWEETHEART?
I COULD TURN THAT RUNT YER WITH INTO A WINGDING SUPERMAN!
PLAYER
WE CAN FIX THAT ASS OF YOURS TOO! TURN YOU INTO RO-HO QUEEN OF THE HORDES TALIMANZOO!
HEY-- HERE'S A HAPPY CUSTOMER NOW!
WHY THIS GUY STROLLED IN HERE NOT FIVE MINUTES AGO LOOKING LIKE A WALKING PIECE OF HUMAN SHIT!
GAZE UPON HIS NEW MAJESTY!
I'M COMMANDER ZANE FROM THE TITANIUM ERA!
WEARING THE COSTUME THAT HE WAS GIVEN BY HIS SWEET LADY BRIDE, TERRIFIC TANYA!
I'M INDESTRUCTIBLE!

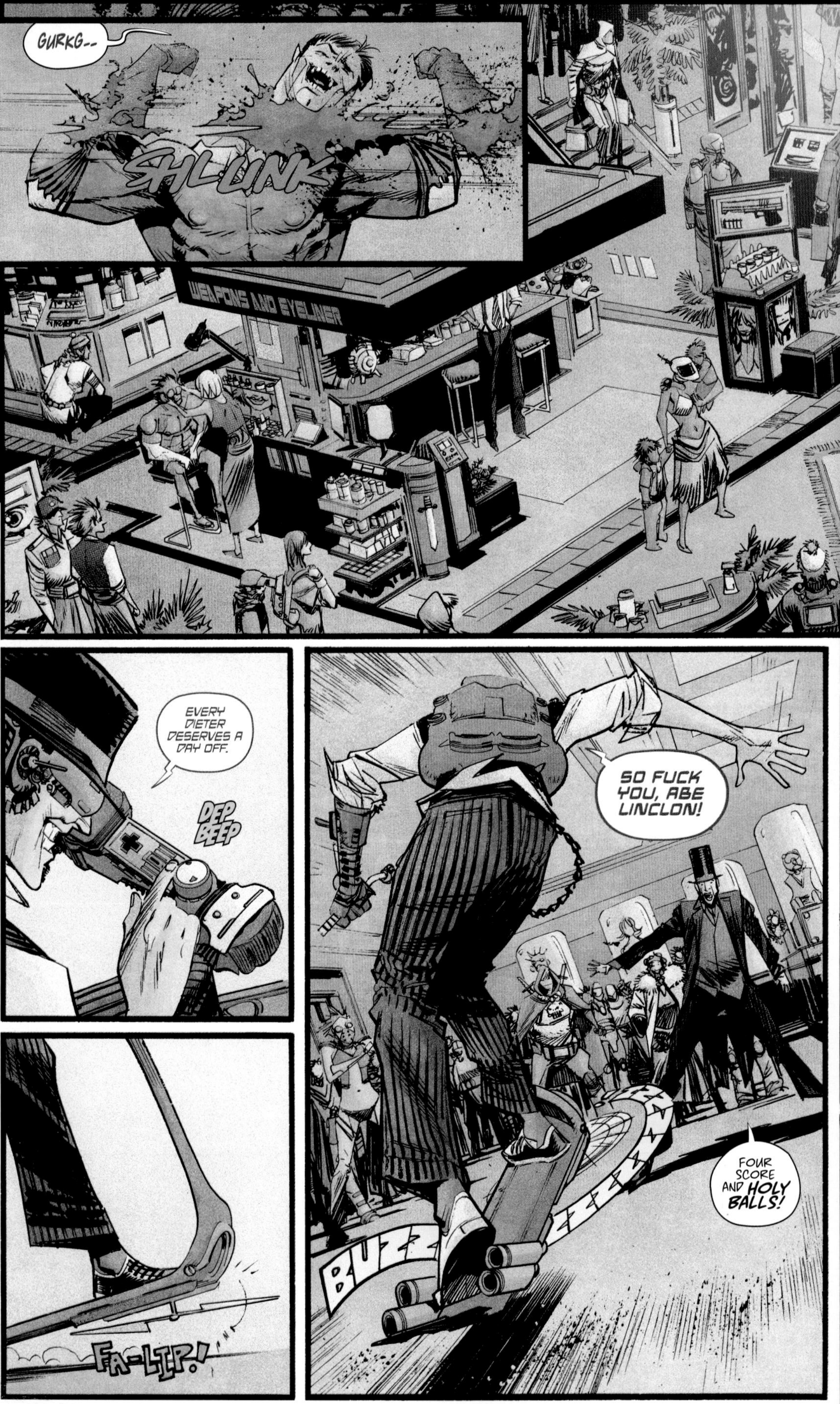
GURKG--
SHLUNK
WEAPONS AND EYELINER
EVERY DIETER DESERVES A DAY OFF.
DEP BEEP
FA-LIP!
SO FUCK YOU, ABE LINCLON!
FOUR SCORE AND HOLY BALLS!
BUZZ

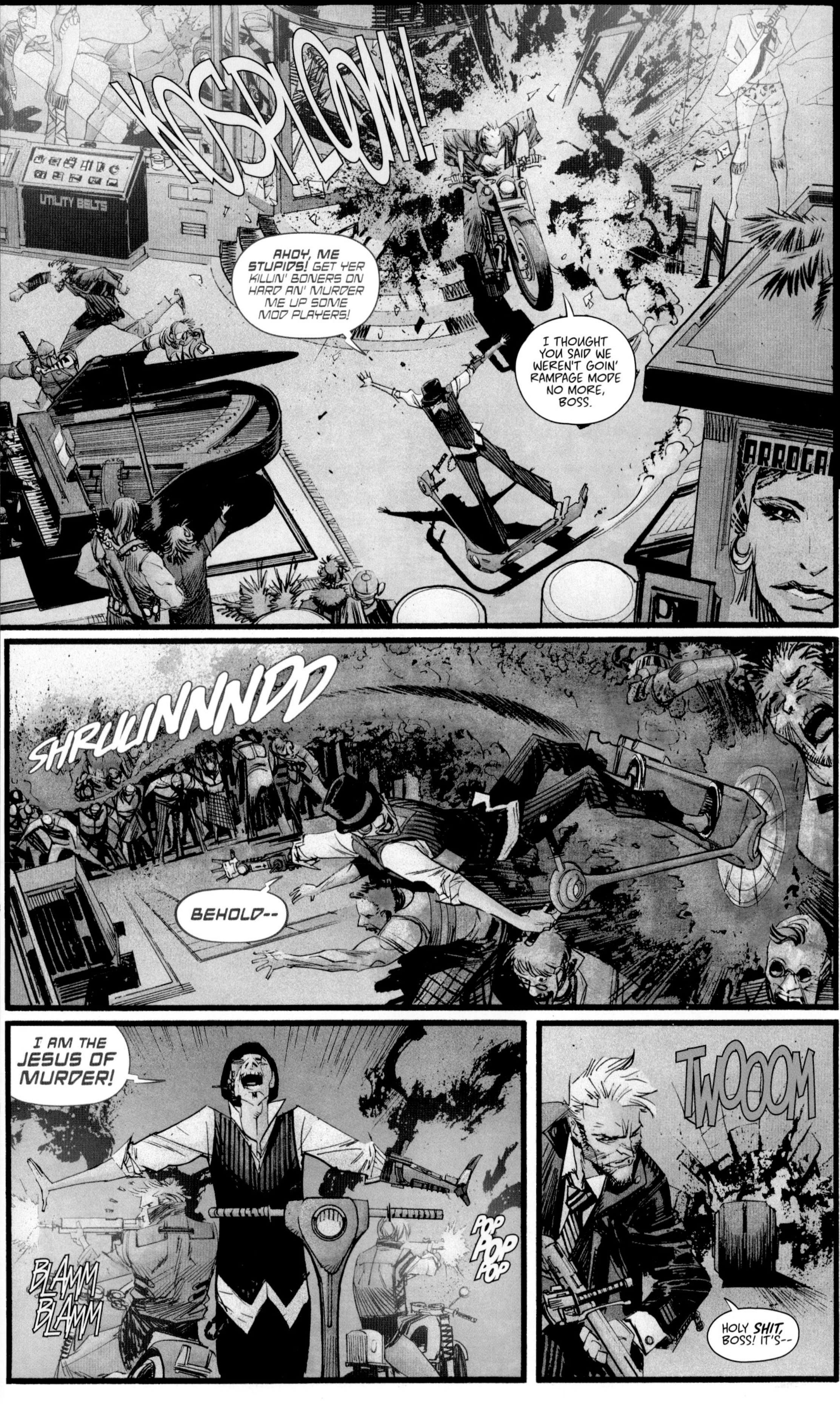
KOSPLOOM!
UTILITY BELTS
AHOY, ME STUPIDS! GET YER KILLIN' BONERS ON HARD AN' MURDER ME UP SOME MOD PLAYERS!
I THOUGHT YOU SAID WE WEREN'T GOIN' RAMPAGE MODE NO MORE, BOSS.
SHRUUNNNNDD
BEHOLD--
I AM THE JESUS OF MURDER!
POP POP POP
BLAMM BLAMM
TWOOOM
HOLY SHIT, BOSS! IT'S--

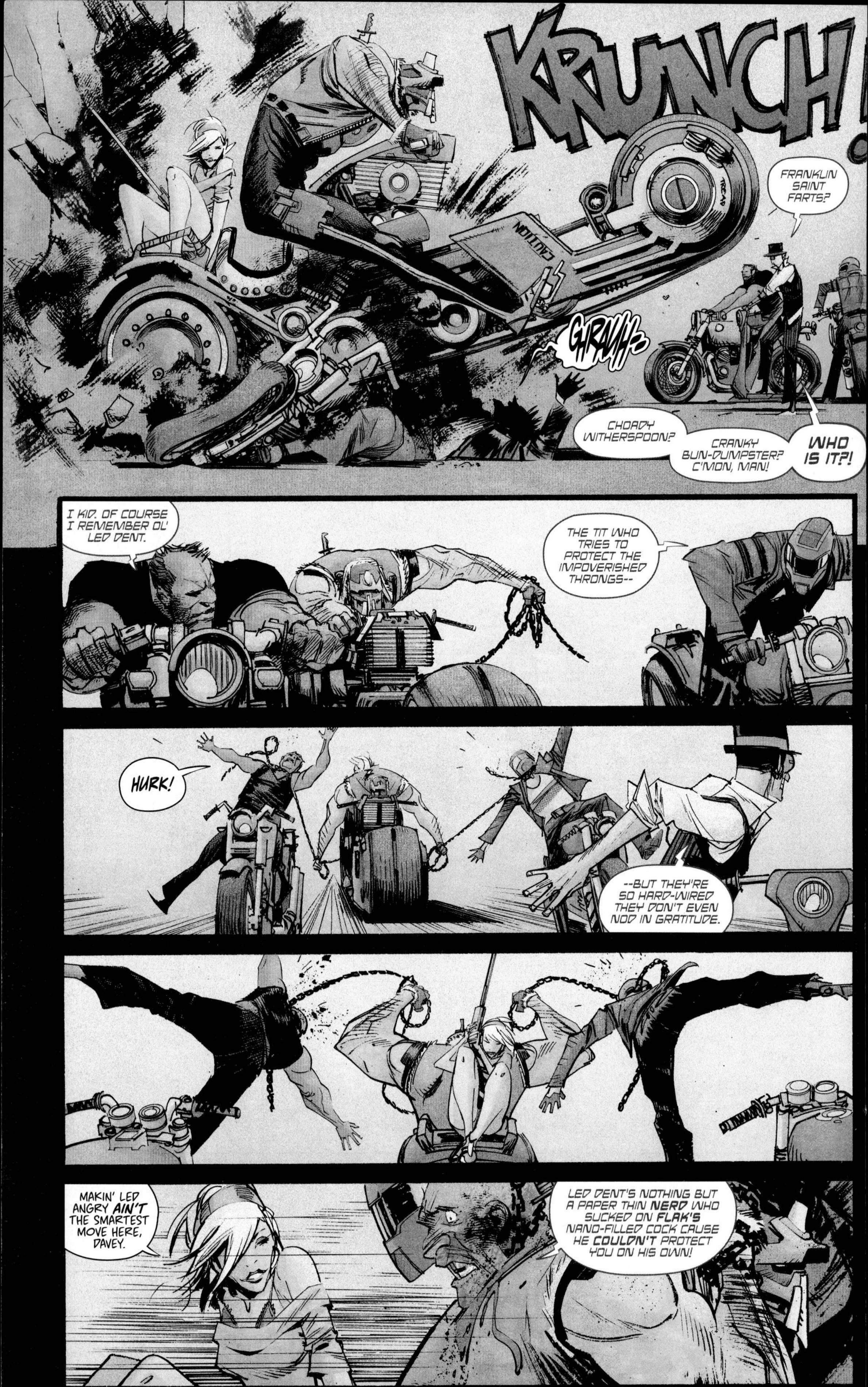
KRUNCH!
FRANKLIN SAINT FARTS?
GHRAUHH
CHOADY WITHERSPOON?
CRANKY BUN-DUMPSTER? C'MON, MAN!
WHO IS IT?!
I KID. OF COURSE I REMEMBER OL' LED DENT.
THE TIT WHO TRIES TO PROTECT THE IMPOVERISHED THRONGS--
HURK!
--BUT THEY'RE SO HARD-WIRED THEY DON'T EVEN NOD IN GRATITUDE.
MAKIN' LED ANGRY AIN'T THE SMARTEST MOVE HERE, DAVEY.
LED DENT'S NOTHING BUT A PAPER THIN NERD WHO SUCKED ON FLAK'S NANO-FILLED COCK CAUSE HE COULDN'T PROTECT YOU ON HIS OWN!

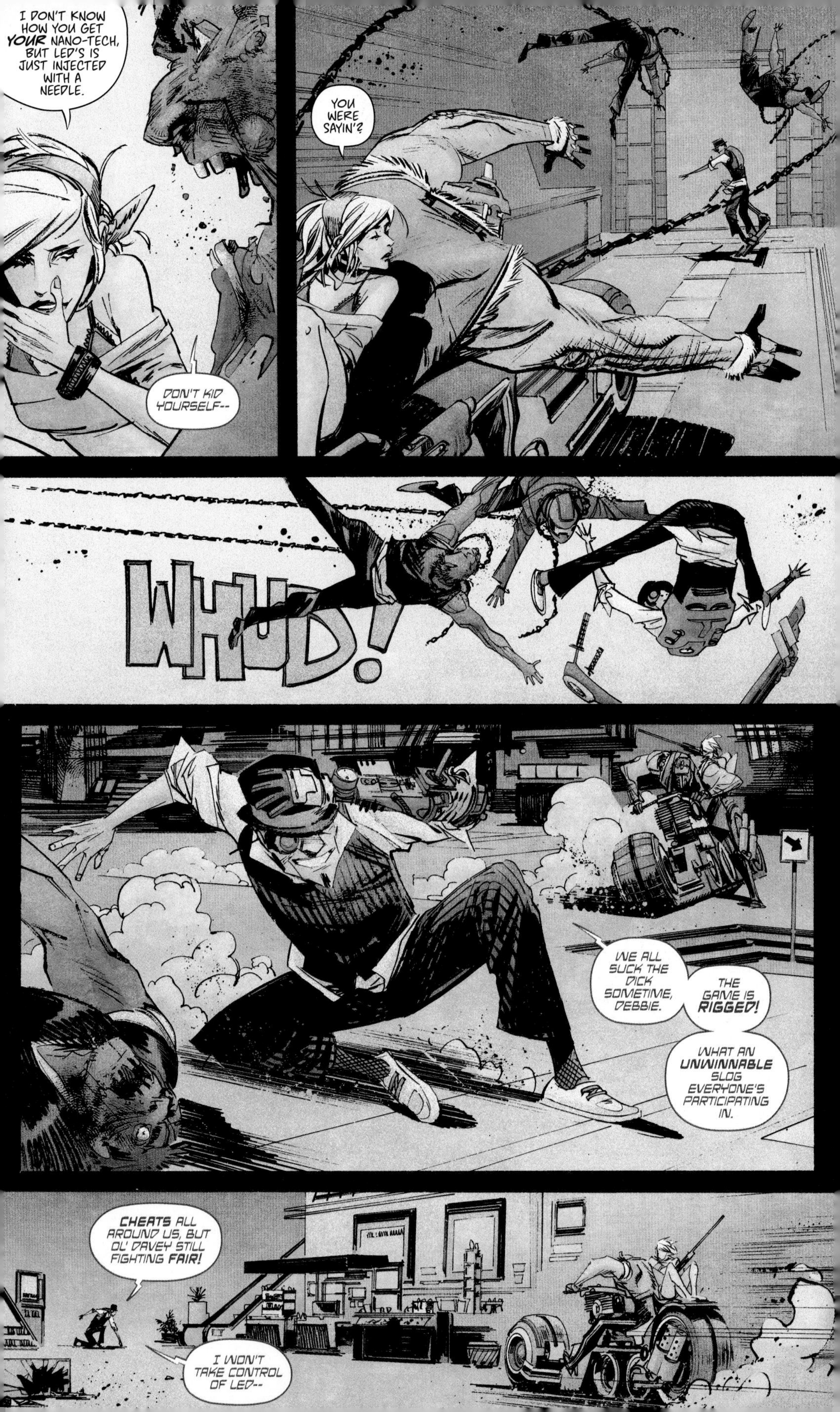
I DON'T KNOW HOW YOU GET YOUR NANO-TECH, BUT LED'S IS JUST INJECTED WITH A NEEDLE.
DON'T KID YOURSELF--
YOU WERE SAYIN'?
WHUD!
WE ALL SUCK THE DICK SOMETIME, DEBBIE.
THE GAME IS RIGGED!
WHAT AN UNWINNABLE SLOG EVERYONE'S PARTICIPATING IN.
CHEATS ALL AROUND US, BUT OL' DAVEY STILL FIGHTING FAIR!
I WON'T TAKE CONTROL OF LED--

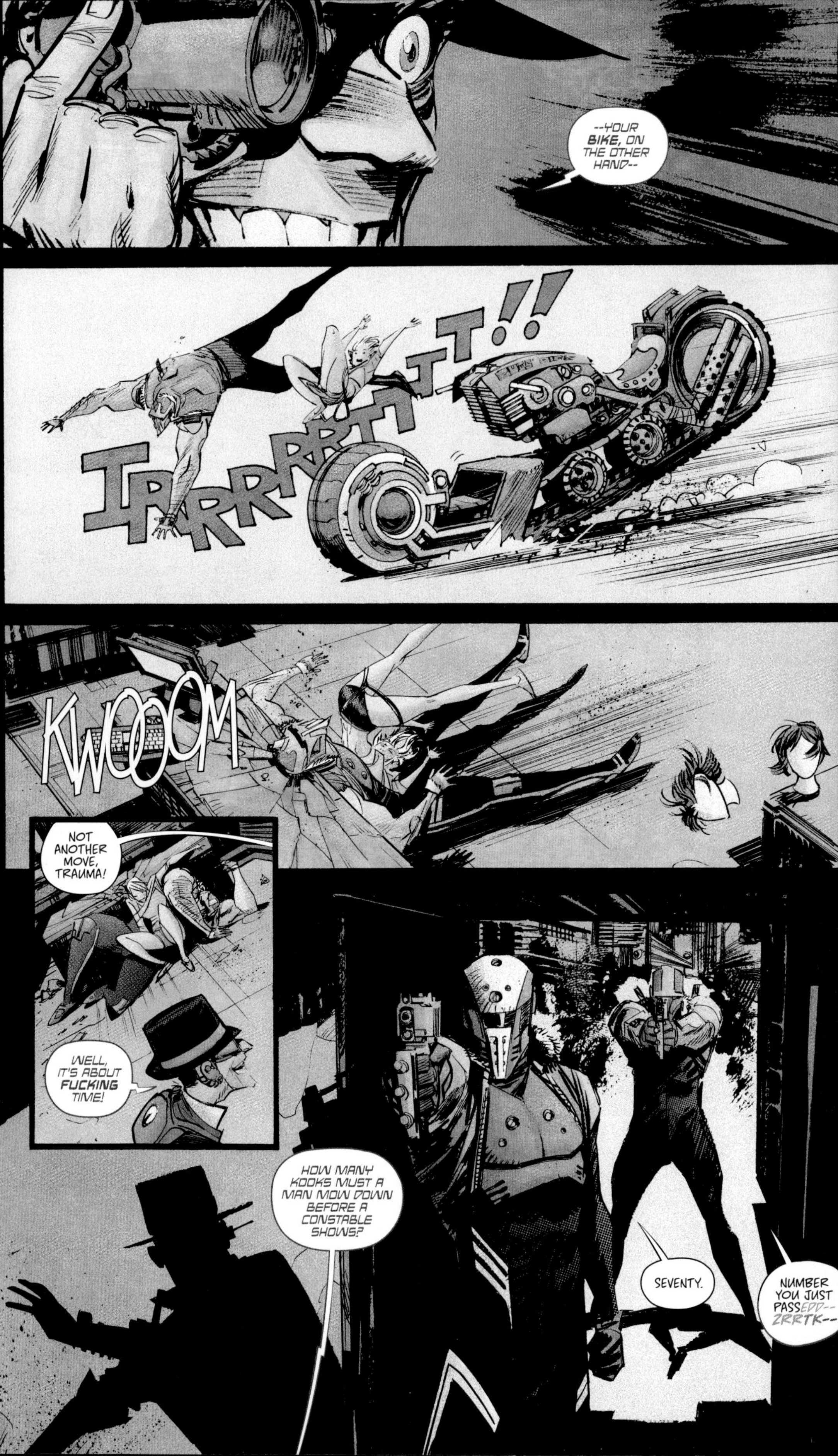
--YOUR BIKE, ON THE OTHER HAND--
TRRRRRTT!!
KWOOOM
NOT ANOTHER MOVE, TRAUMA!
WELL, IT'S ABOUT FUCKING TIME!
HOW MANY KOOKS MUST A MAN MOW DOWN BEFORE A CONSTABLE SHOWS?
SEVENTY.
NUMBER YOU JUST PASSEDD-- ZRRTK--

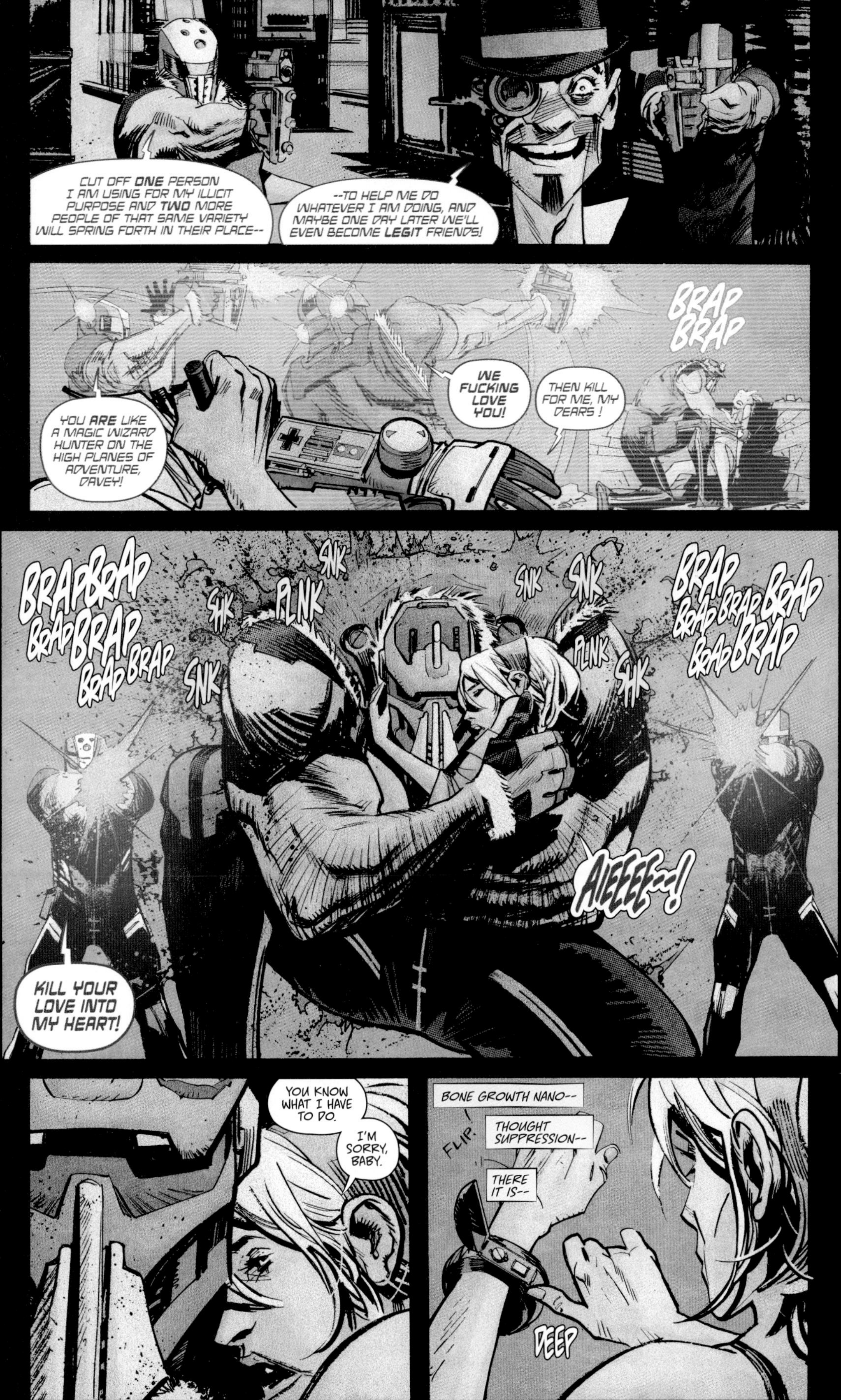
CUT OFF ONE PERSON I AM USING FOR MY ILLICIT PURPOSE AND TWO MORE PEOPLE OF THAT SAME VARIETY WILL SPRING FORTH IN THEIR PLACE--
--TO HELP ME DO WHATEVER I AM DOING, AND MAYBE ONE DAY LATER WE'LL EVEN BECOME LEGIT FRIENDS!
BRAP BRAP
YOU ARE LIKE A MAGIC WIZARD HUNTER ON THE HIGH PLANES OF ADVENTURE, DAVEY!
WE FUCKING LOVE YOU!
THEN KILL FOR ME, MY DEARS !
BRAPBRAP BRAPBRAP BRAPBRAP
SHK
PLINK
SNK
SNK
SNK
SNK
PLINK
SHK
SNK
BRAP BRAPBRAPBRAP BRAPBRAP
AIEEEE--!
KILL YOUR LOVE INTO MY HEART!
YOU KNOW WHAT I HAVE TO DO.
I'M SORRY, BABY.
BONE GROWTH NANO--
FLIP.
THOUGHT SUPPRESSION--
THERE IT IS--
DEEP

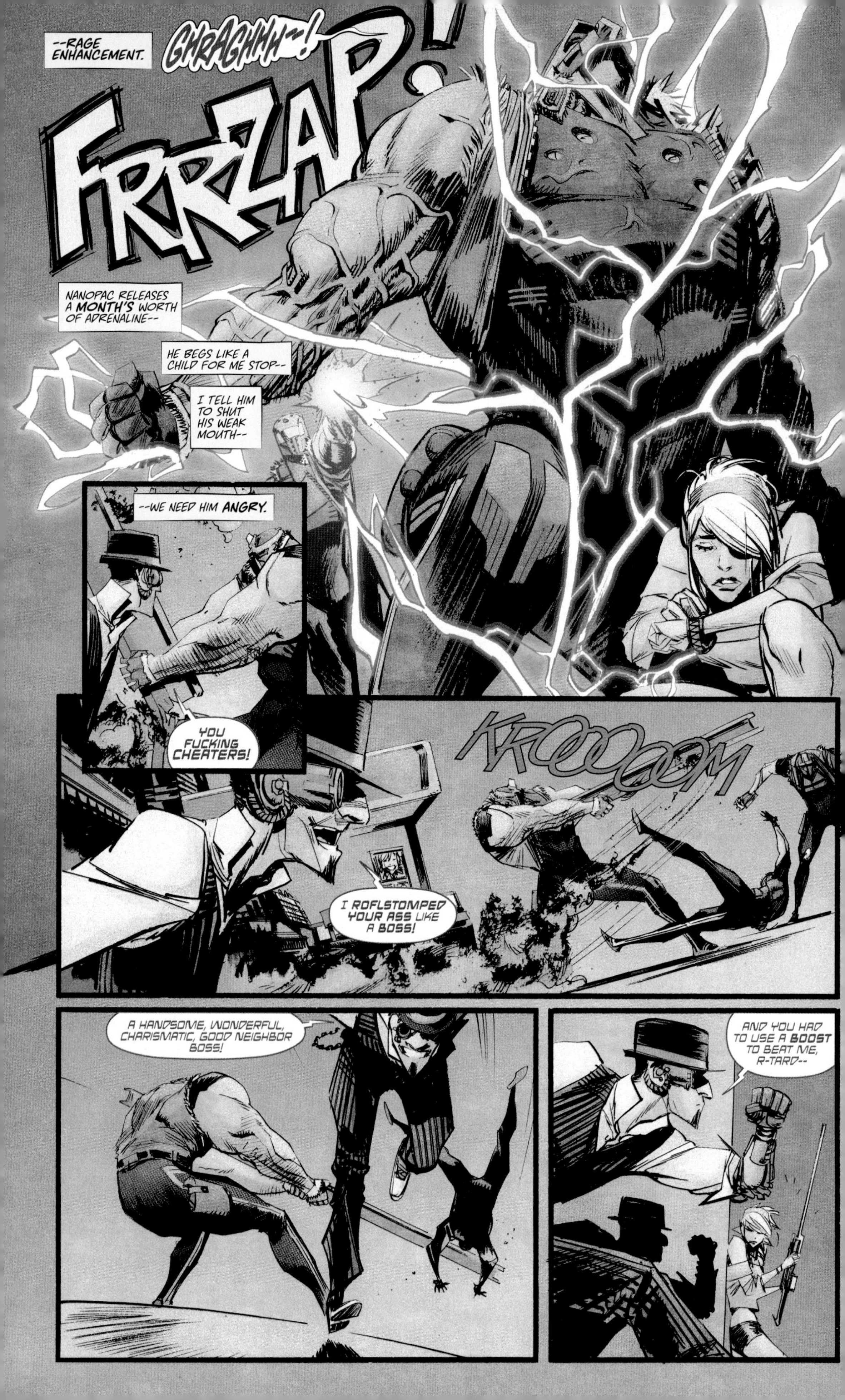
--RAGE ENHANCEMENT.
GHRAGHHH--!
FRRZAP!
NANOPAC RELEASES A MONTH'S WORTH OF ADRENALINE--
HE BEGS LIKE A CHILD FOR ME STOP--
I TELL HIM TO SHUT HIS WEAK MOUTH--
--WE NEED HIM ANGRY.
YOU FUCKING CHEATERS!
KROOOOOOM
I ROFLSTOMPED YOUR ASS LIKE A BOSS!
A HANDSOME, WONDERFUL, CHARISMATIC, GOOD NEIGHBOR BOSS!
AND YOU HAD TO USE A BOOST TO BEAT ME, R-TARD--

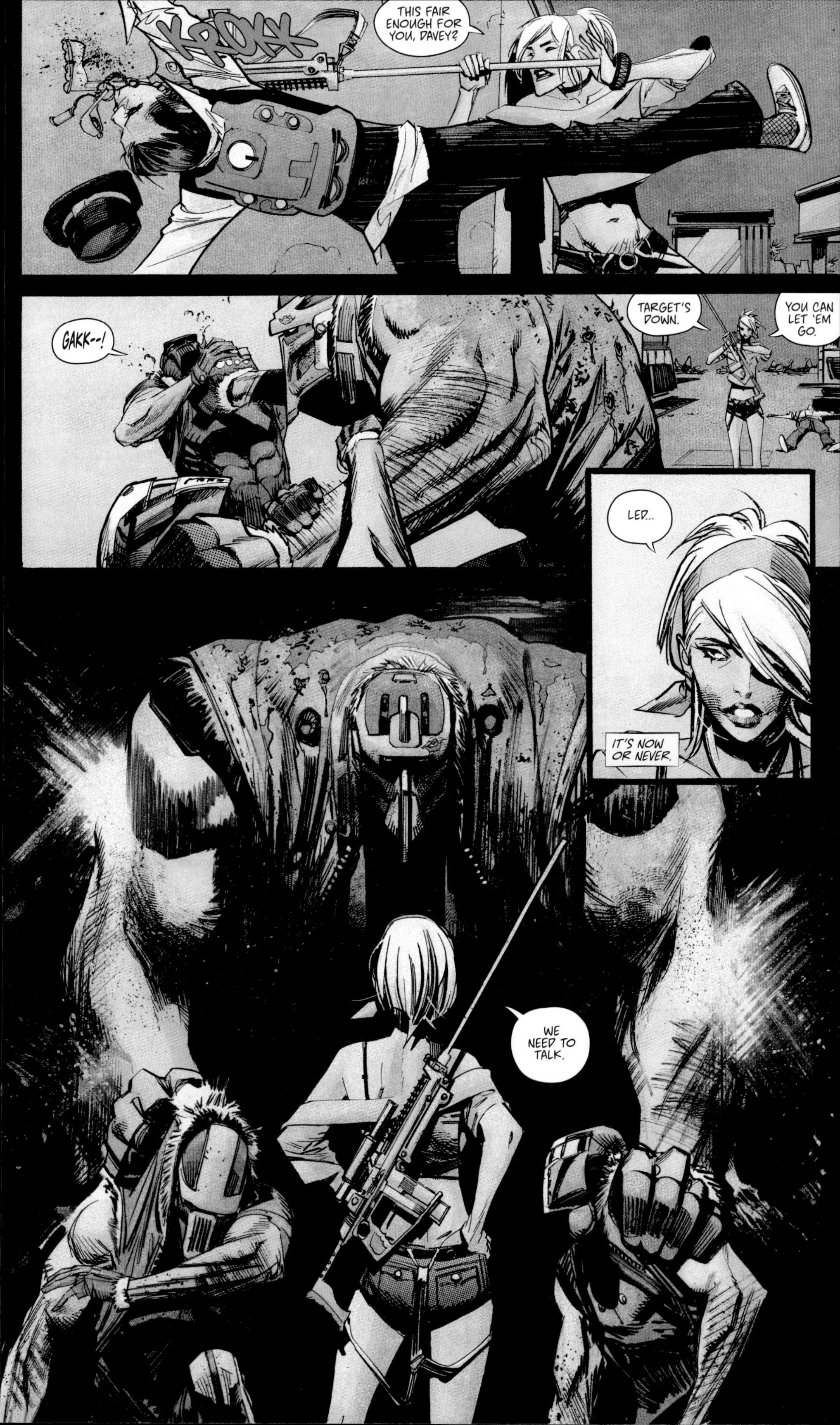

KROKK
THIS FAIR ENOUGH FOR YOU, DAVEY?
GAKK--!
TARGET'S DOWN.
YOU CAN LET 'EM GO.
LED...
IT'S NOW OR NEVER.
WE NEED TO TALK.

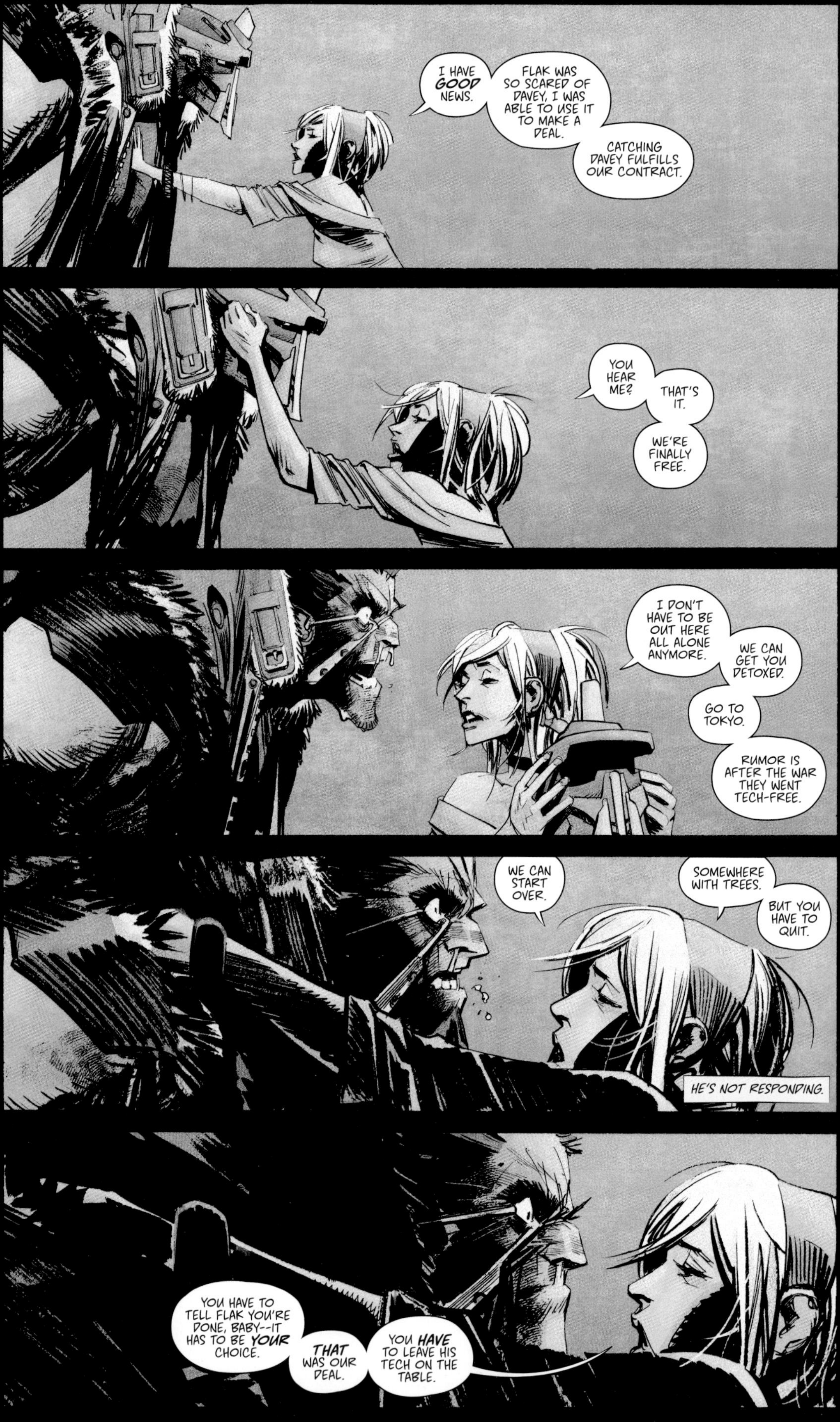
I HAVE GOOD NEWS.
FLAK WAS SO SCARED OF DAVEY, I WAS ABLE TO USE IT TO MAKE A DEAL.
CATCHING DAVEY FULFILLS OUR CONTRACT.
YOU HEAR ME?
THAT'S IT.
WE'RE FINALLY FREE.
I DON'T HAVE TO BE OUT HERE ALL ALONE ANYMORE.
WE CAN GET YOU DETOXED.
GO TO TOKYO.
RUMOR IS AFTER THE WAR THEY WENT TECH-FREE.
WE CAN START OVER.
SOMEWHERE WITH TREES.
BUT YOU HAVE TO QUIT.
HE'S NOT RESPONDING.
YOU HAVE TO TELL FLAK YOU'RE DONE, BABY--IT HAS TO BE YOUR CHOICE.
THAT WAS OUR DEAL.
YOU HAVE TO LEAVE HIS TECH ON THE TABLE.

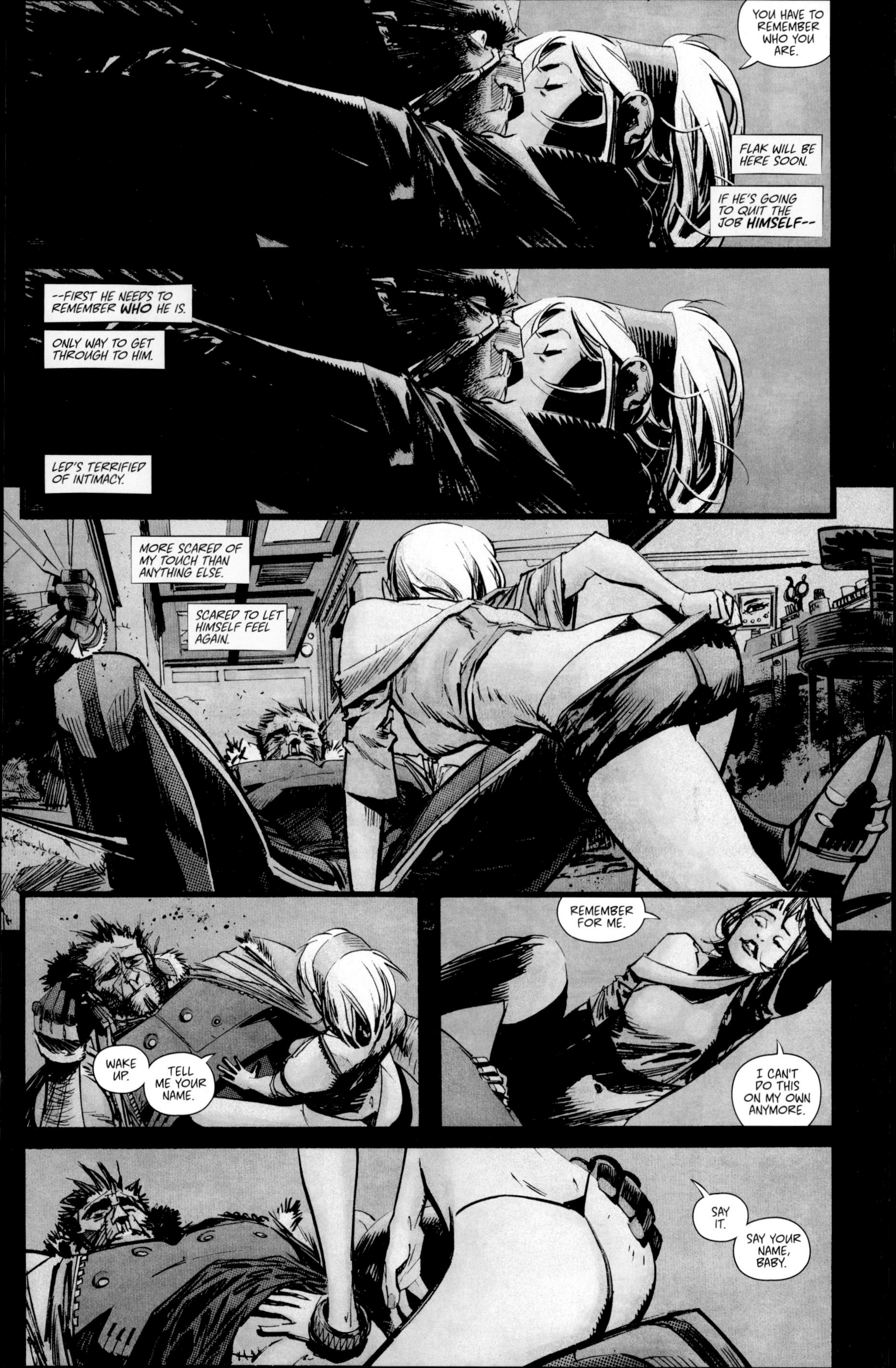
YOU HAVE TO REMEMBER WHO YOU ARE.
FLAK WILL BE HERE SOON.
IF HE'S GOING TO QUIT THE JOB HIMSELF--
--FIRST HE NEEDS TO REMEMBER WHO HE IS.
ONLY WAY TO GET THROUGH TO HIM.
LED'S TERRIFIED OF INTIMACY.
MORE SCARED OF MY TOUCH THAN ANYTHING ELSE.
SCARED TO LET HIMSELF FEEL AGAIN.
WAKE UP.
TELL ME YOUR NAME.
REMEMBER FOR ME.
I CAN'T DO THIS ON MY OWN ANYMORE.
SAY IT.
SAY YOUR NAME, BABY.

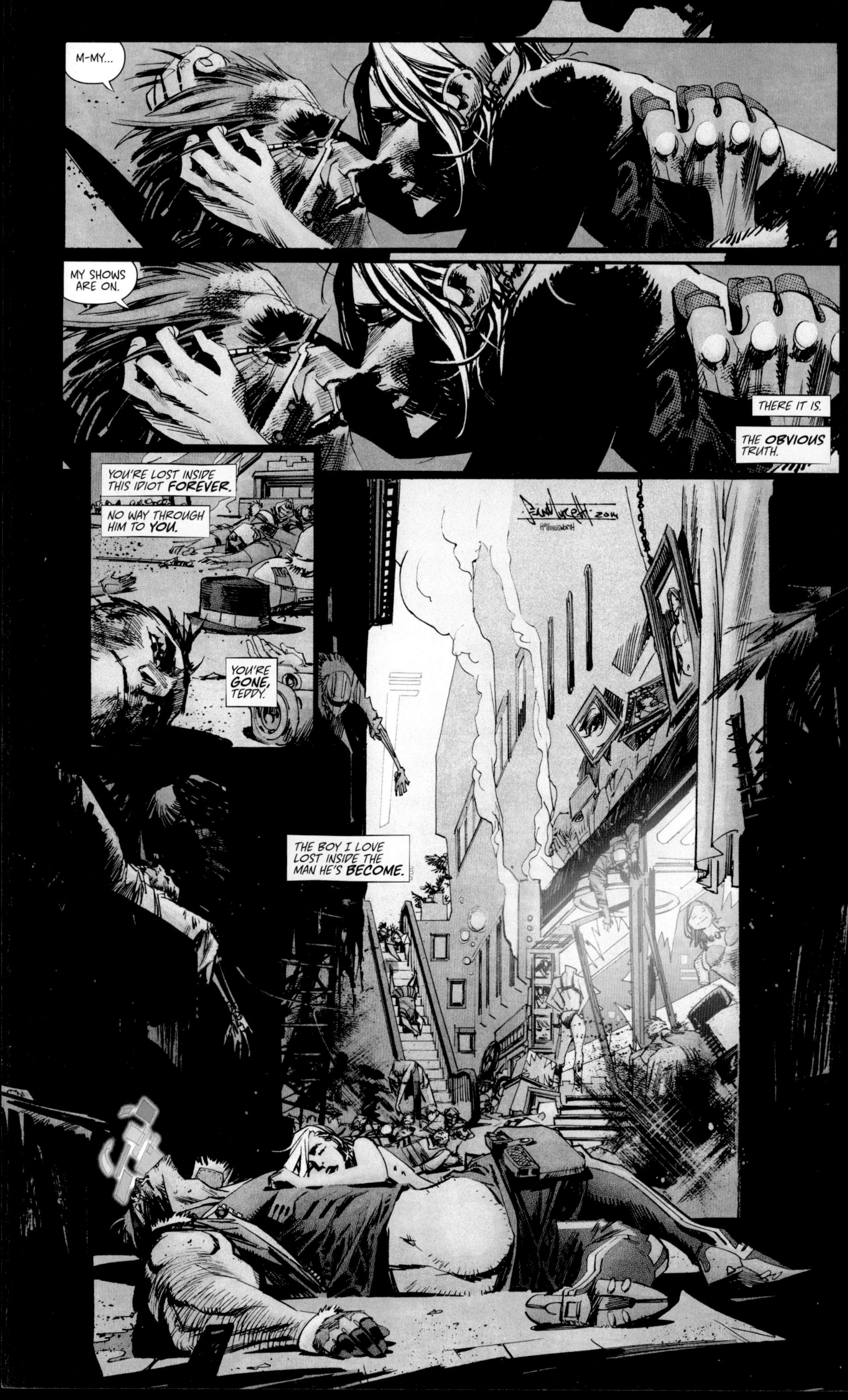
M-MY...
MY SHOWS ARE ON.
THERE IT IS.
THE OBVIOUS TRUTH.
YOU'RE LOST INSIDE THIS IDIOT FOREVER.
NO WAY THROUGH HIM TO YOU.
YOU'RE GONE, TEDDY.
THE BOY I LOVE LOST INSIDE THE MAN HE'S BECOME.
HOLLINGSWORTH

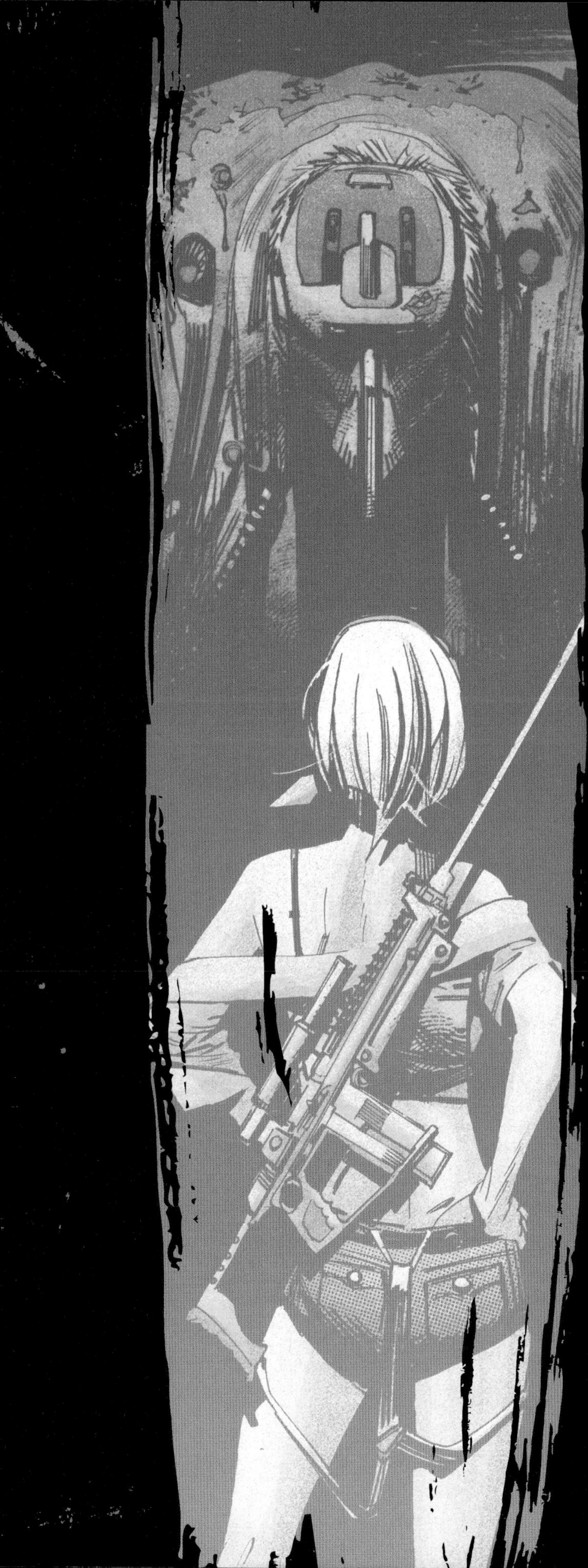

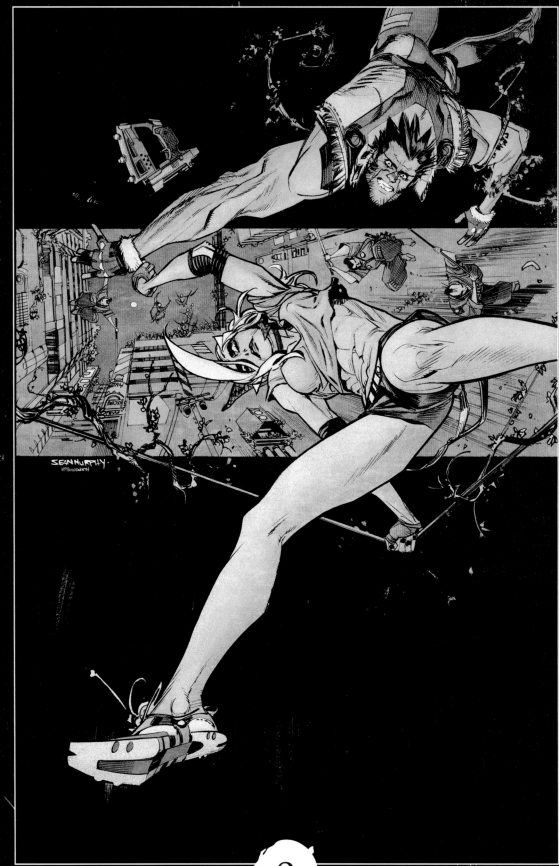

SEAN MURPHY
Hollingsworth

2

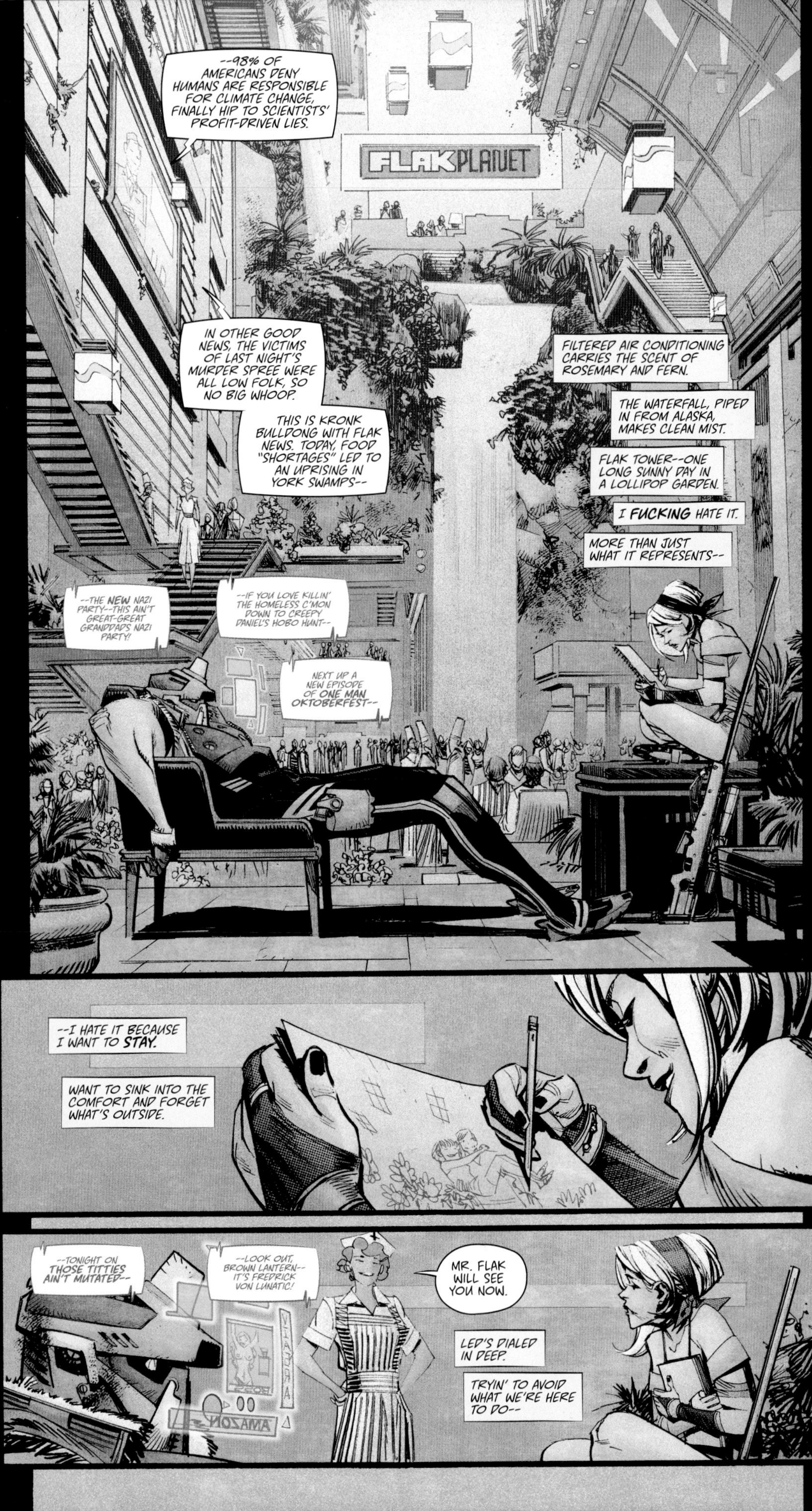
--98% OF AMERICANS DENY HUMANS ARE RESPONSIBLE FOR CLIMATE CHANGE, FINALLY HIP TO SCIENTISTS' PROFIT-DRIVEN LIES.
FLAKPLANET
IN OTHER GOOD NEWS, THE VICTIMS OF LAST NIGHT'S MURDER SPREE WERE ALL LOW FOLK, SO NO BIG WHOOP.
THIS IS KRONK BULLDONG WITH FLAK NEWS. TODAY, FOOD "SHORTAGES" LED TO AN UPRISING IN YORK SWAMPS--
FILTERED AIR CONDITIONING CARRIES THE SCENT OF ROSEMARY AND FERN.
THE WATERFALL, PIPED IN FROM ALASKA, MAKES CLEAN MIST.
FLAK TOWER--ONE LONG SUNNY DAY IN A LOLLIPOP GARDEN.
I **FUCKING** HATE IT.
MORE THAN JUST WHAT IT REPRESENTS--
--THE **NEW** NAZI PARTY--THIS AIN'T GREAT-GREAT GRANDDAD'S NAZI PARTY!
--IF YOU LOVE KILLIN' THE HOMELESS C'MON DOWN TO CREEPY DANIEL'S HOBO HUNT--
NEXT UP A NEW EPISODE OF **ONE MAN OKTOBERFEST**--
--I HATE IT BECAUSE I WANT TO **STAY.**
WANT TO SINK INTO THE COMFORT AND FORGET WHAT'S OUTSIDE.
--TONIGHT ON **THOSE TITTIES AIN'T MUTATED**--
--LOOK OUT, BROWN LANTERN-- IT'S FREDRICK VON LUNATIC!
MR. FLAK WILL SEE YOU NOW.
LED'S DIALED IN DEEP.
TRYIN' TO AVOID WHAT WE'RE HERE TO DO--

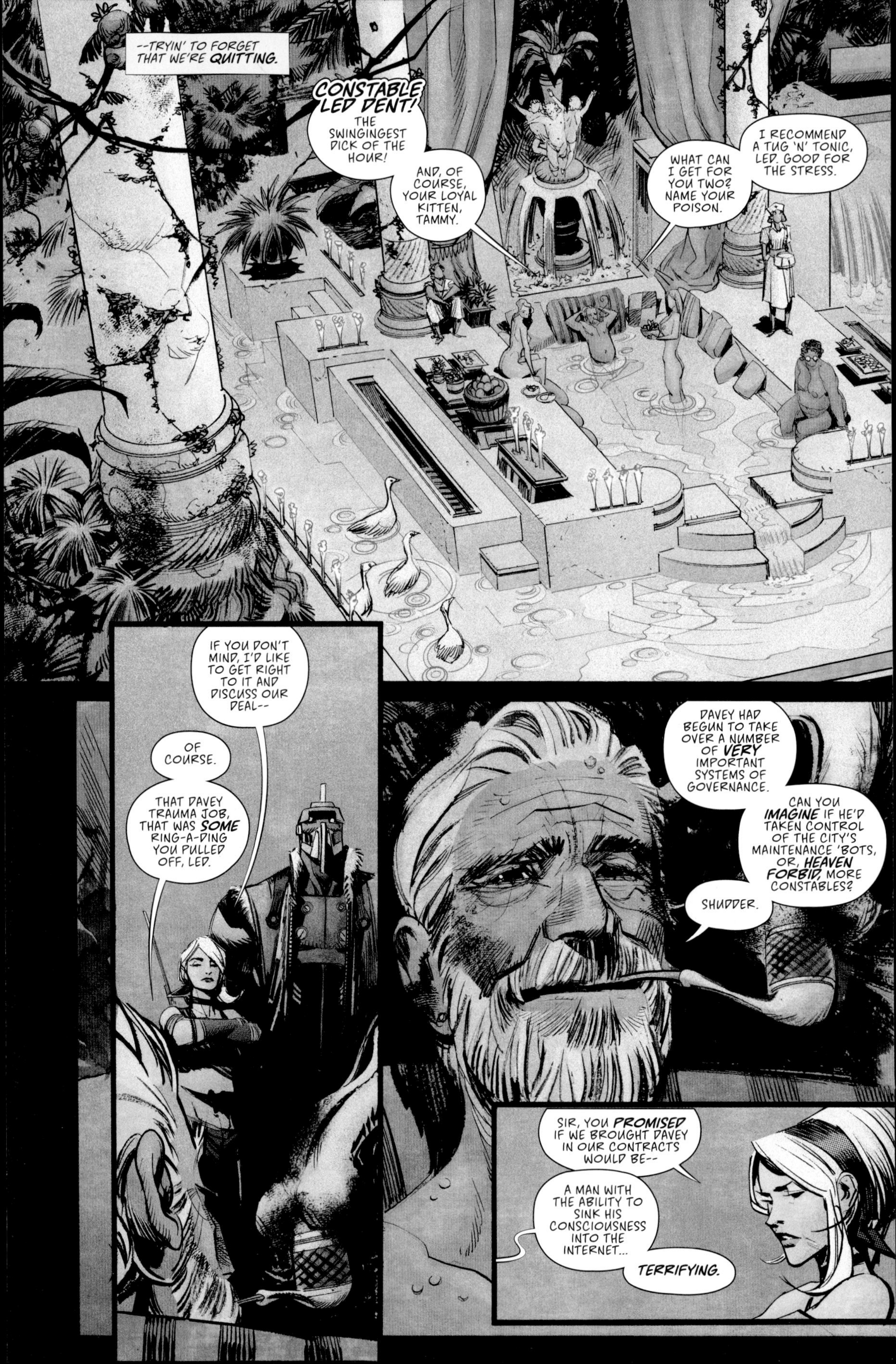
--TRYIN' TO FORGET THAT WE'RE QUITTING.
CONSTABLE LED DENT!
THE SWINGINGEST DICK OF THE HOUR!
AND, OF COURSE, YOUR LOYAL KITTEN, TAMMY.
WHAT CAN I GET FOR YOU TWO? NAME YOUR POISON.
I RECOMMEND A TUG 'N' TONIC, LED. GOOD FOR THE STRESS.
IF YOU DON'T MIND, I'D LIKE TO GET RIGHT TO IT AND DISCUSS OUR DEAL--
OF COURSE.
THAT DAVEY TRAUMA JOB, THAT WAS SOME RING-A-DING YOU PULLED OFF, LED.
DAVEY HAD BEGUN TO TAKE OVER A NUMBER OF VERY IMPORTANT SYSTEMS OF GOVERNANCE.
CAN YOU IMAGINE IF HE'D TAKEN CONTROL OF THE CITY'S MAINTENANCE 'BOTS, OR, HEAVEN FORBID, MORE CONSTABLES?
SHUDDER.
SIR, YOU PROMISED IF WE BROUGHT DAVEY IN OUR CONTRACTS WOULD BE--
A MAN WITH THE ABILITY TO SINK HIS CONSCIOUSNESS INTO THE INTERNET...
TERRIFYING.

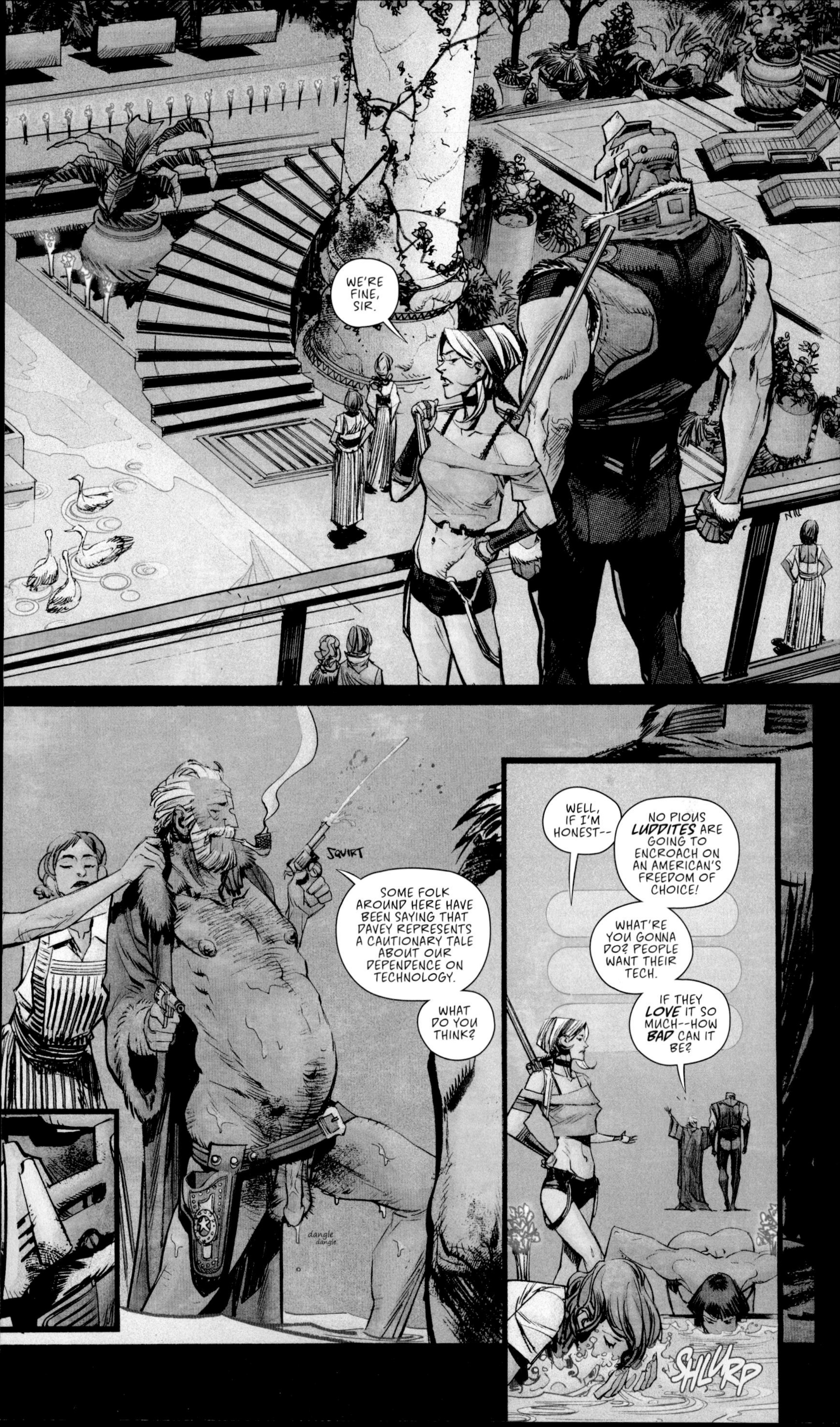
WE'RE FINE, SIR.
SQUIRT
SOME FOLK AROUND HERE HAVE BEEN SAYING THAT DAVEY REPRESENTS A CAUTIONARY TALE ABOUT OUR DEPENDENCE ON TECHNOLOGY.
WHAT DO YOU THINK?
dangle dangle
WELL, IF I'M HONEST--
NO PIOUS LUDDITES ARE GOING TO ENCROACH ON AN AMERICAN'S FREEDOM OF CHOICE!
WHAT'RE YOU GONNA DO? PEOPLE WANT THEIR TECH.
IF THEY LOVE IT SO MUCH--HOW BAD CAN IT BE?
SHLURP

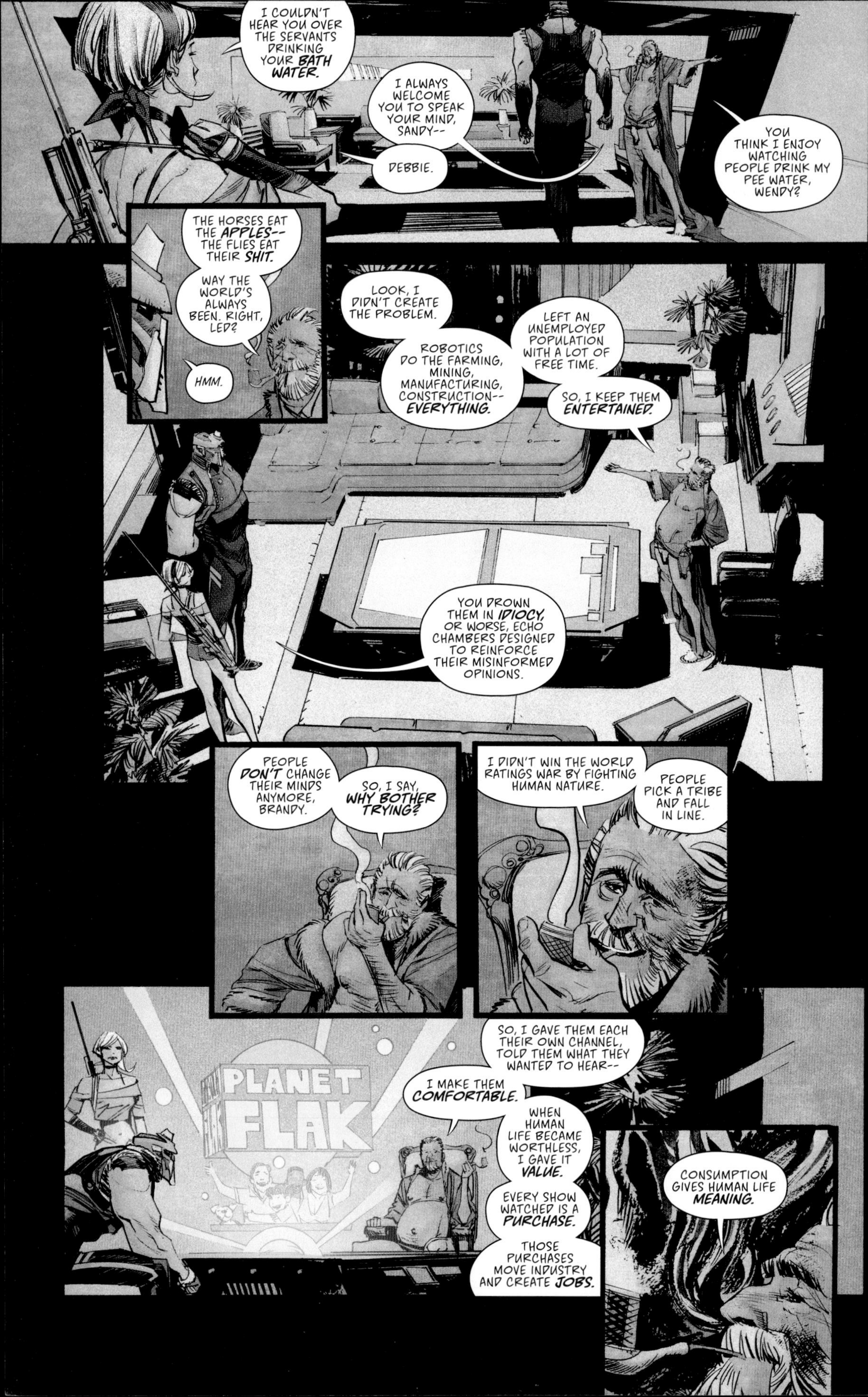

I COULDN'T HEAR YOU OVER THE SERVANTS DRINKING YOUR BATH WATER.
I ALWAYS WELCOME YOU TO SPEAK YOUR MIND, SANDY--
DEBBIE.
YOU THINK I ENJOY WATCHING PEOPLE DRINK MY PEE WATER, WENDY?
THE HORSES EAT THE APPLES-- THE FLIES EAT THEIR SHIT.
WAY THE WORLD'S ALWAYS BEEN. RIGHT, LED?
HMM.
LOOK, I DIDN'T CREATE THE PROBLEM.
ROBOTICS DO THE FARMING, MINING, MANUFACTURING, CONSTRUCTION-- EVERYTHING.
LEFT AN UNEMPLOYED POPULATION WITH A LOT OF FREE TIME.
SO, I KEEP THEM ENTERTAINED.
YOU DROWN THEM IN IDIOCY, OR WORSE, ECHO CHAMBERS DESIGNED TO REINFORCE THEIR MISINFORMED OPINIONS.
PEOPLE DON'T CHANGE THEIR MINDS ANYMORE, BRANDY.
SO, I SAY, WHY BOTHER TRYING?
I DIDN'T WIN THE WORLD RATINGS WAR BY FIGHTING HUMAN NATURE.
PEOPLE PICK A TRIBE AND FALL IN LINE.
SO, I GAVE THEM EACH THEIR OWN CHANNEL, TOLD THEM WHAT THEY WANTED TO HEAR--
I MAKE THEM COMFORTABLE.
PLANET FLAK
WHEN HUMAN LIFE BECAME WORTHLESS, I GAVE IT VALUE.
EVERY SHOW WATCHED IS A PURCHASE.
THOSE PURCHASES MOVE INDUSTRY AND CREATE JOBS.
CONSUMPTION GIVES HUMAN LIFE MEANING.

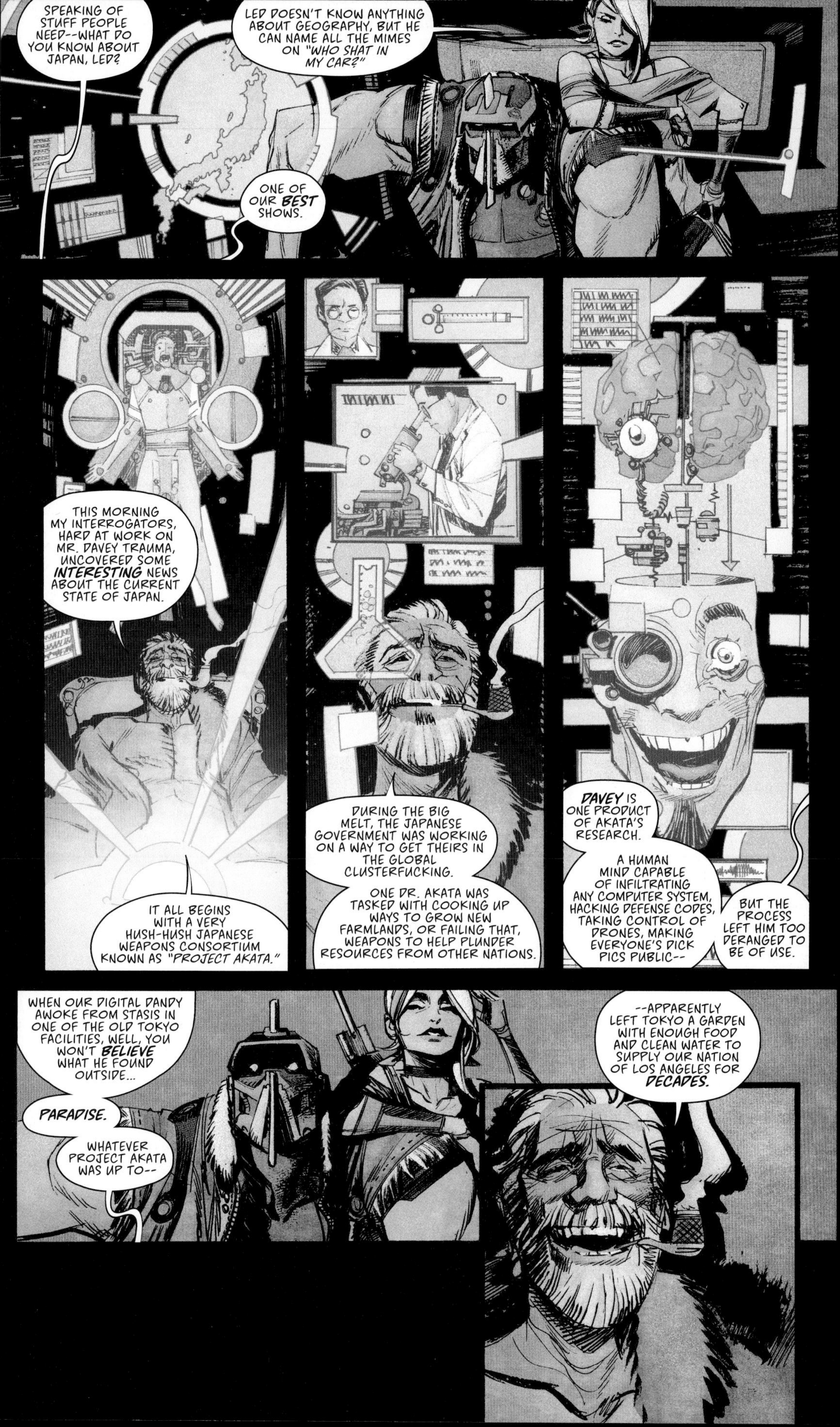

SPEAKING OF STUFF PEOPLE NEED--WHAT DO YOU KNOW ABOUT JAPAN, LED?
LED DOESN'T KNOW ANYTHING ABOUT GEOGRAPHY, BUT HE CAN NAME ALL THE MIMES ON "WHO SHAT IN MY CAR?"
ONE OF OUR **BEST** SHOWS.
THIS MORNING MY INTERROGATORS, HARD AT WORK ON MR. DAVEY TRAUMA, UNCOVERED SOME **INTERESTING** NEWS ABOUT THE CURRENT STATE OF JAPAN.
IT ALL BEGINS WITH A VERY HUSH-HUSH JAPANESE WEAPONS CONSORTIUM KNOWN AS "*PROJECT AKATA.*"
DURING THE BIG MELT, THE JAPANESE GOVERNMENT WAS WORKING ON A WAY TO GET THEIRS IN THE GLOBAL CLUSTERFUCKING.
ONE DR. AKATA WAS TASKED WITH COOKING UP WAYS TO GROW NEW FARMLANDS, OR FAILING THAT, WEAPONS TO HELP PLUNDER RESOURCES FROM OTHER NATIONS.
DAVEY IS ONE PRODUCT OF AKATA'S RESEARCH.
A HUMAN MIND CAPABLE OF INFILTRATING ANY COMPUTER SYSTEM, HACKING DEFENSE CODES, TAKING CONTROL OF DRONES, MAKING EVERYONE'S DICK PICS PUBLIC--
BUT THE PROCESS LEFT HIM TOO DERANGED TO BE OF USE.
WHEN OUR DIGITAL DANDY AWOKE FROM STASIS IN ONE OF THE OLD TOKYO FACILITIES, WELL, YOU WON'T **BELIEVE** WHAT HE FOUND OUTSIDE...
PARADISE.
WHATEVER PROJECT AKATA WAS UP TO--
--APPARENTLY LEFT TOKYO A GARDEN WITH ENOUGH FOOD AND CLEAN WATER TO SUPPLY OUR NATION OF LOS ANGELES FOR ***DECADES.***

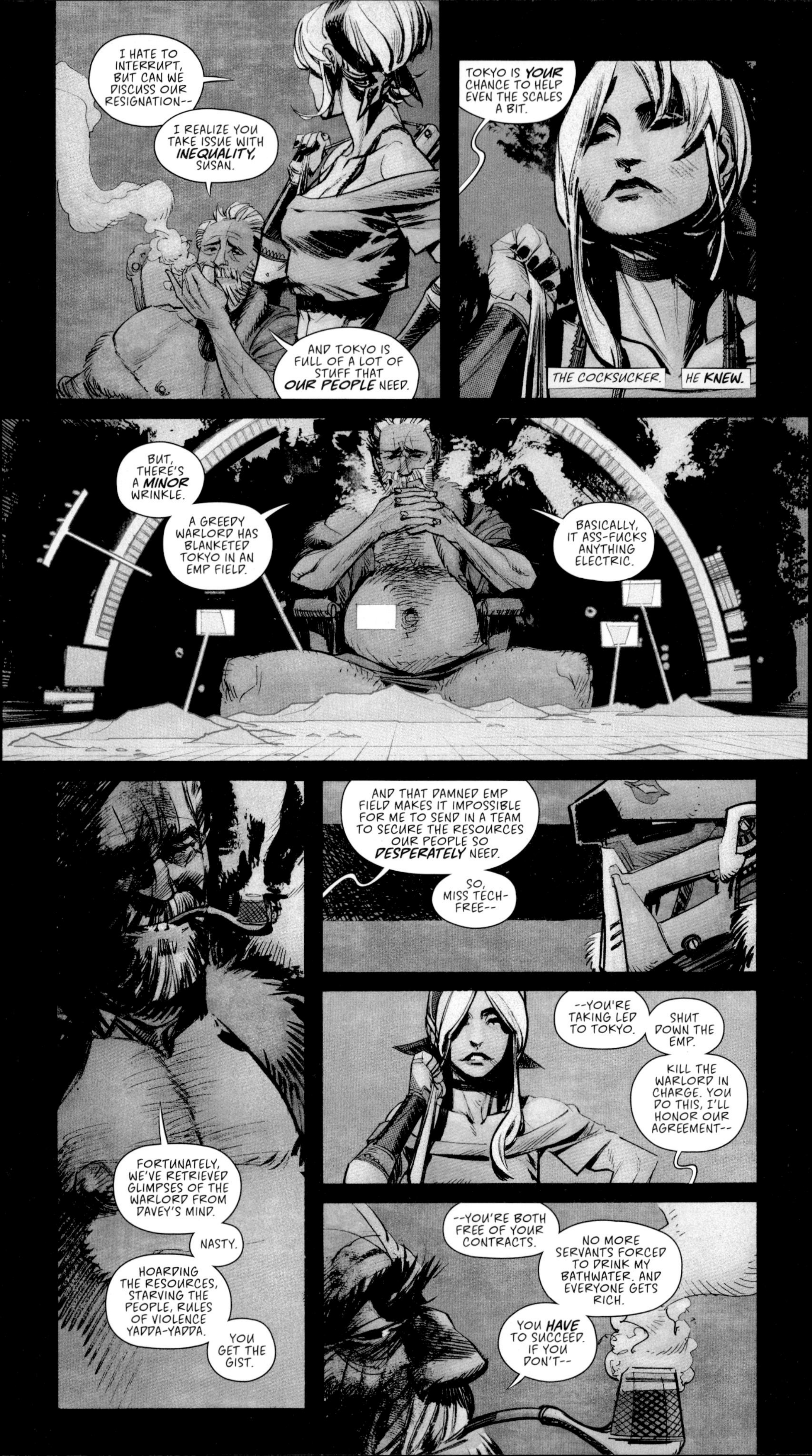
I HATE TO INTERRUPT, BUT CAN WE DISCUSS OUR RESIGNATION--
I REALIZE YOU TAKE ISSUE WITH INEQUALITY, SUSAN.
AND TOKYO IS FULL OF A LOT OF STUFF THAT OUR PEOPLE NEED.
TOKYO IS YOUR CHANCE TO HELP EVEN THE SCALES A BIT.
THE COCKSUCKER.
HE KNEW.
BUT, THERE'S A MINOR WRINKLE.
A GREEDY WARLORD HAS BLANKETED TOKYO IN AN EMP FIELD.
BASICALLY, IT ASS-FUCKS ANYTHING ELECTRIC.
FORTUNATELY, WE'VE RETRIEVED GLIMPSES OF THE WARLORD FROM DAVEY'S MIND.
NASTY.
HOARDING THE RESOURCES, STARVING THE PEOPLE, RULES OF VIOLENCE YADDA-YADDA.
YOU GET THE GIST.
AND THAT DAMNED EMP FIELD MAKES IT IMPOSSIBLE FOR ME TO SEND IN A TEAM TO SECURE THE RESOURCES OUR PEOPLE SO DESPERATELY NEED.
SO, MISS TECH-FREE--
--YOU'RE TAKING LED TO TOKYO.
SHUT DOWN THE EMP.
KILL THE WARLORD IN CHARGE. YOU DO THIS, I'LL HONOR OUR AGREEMENT--
--YOU'RE BOTH FREE OF YOUR CONTRACTS.
NO MORE SERVANTS FORCED TO DRINK MY BATHWATER. AND EVERYONE GETS RICH.
YOU HAVE TO SUCCEED. IF YOU DON'T--

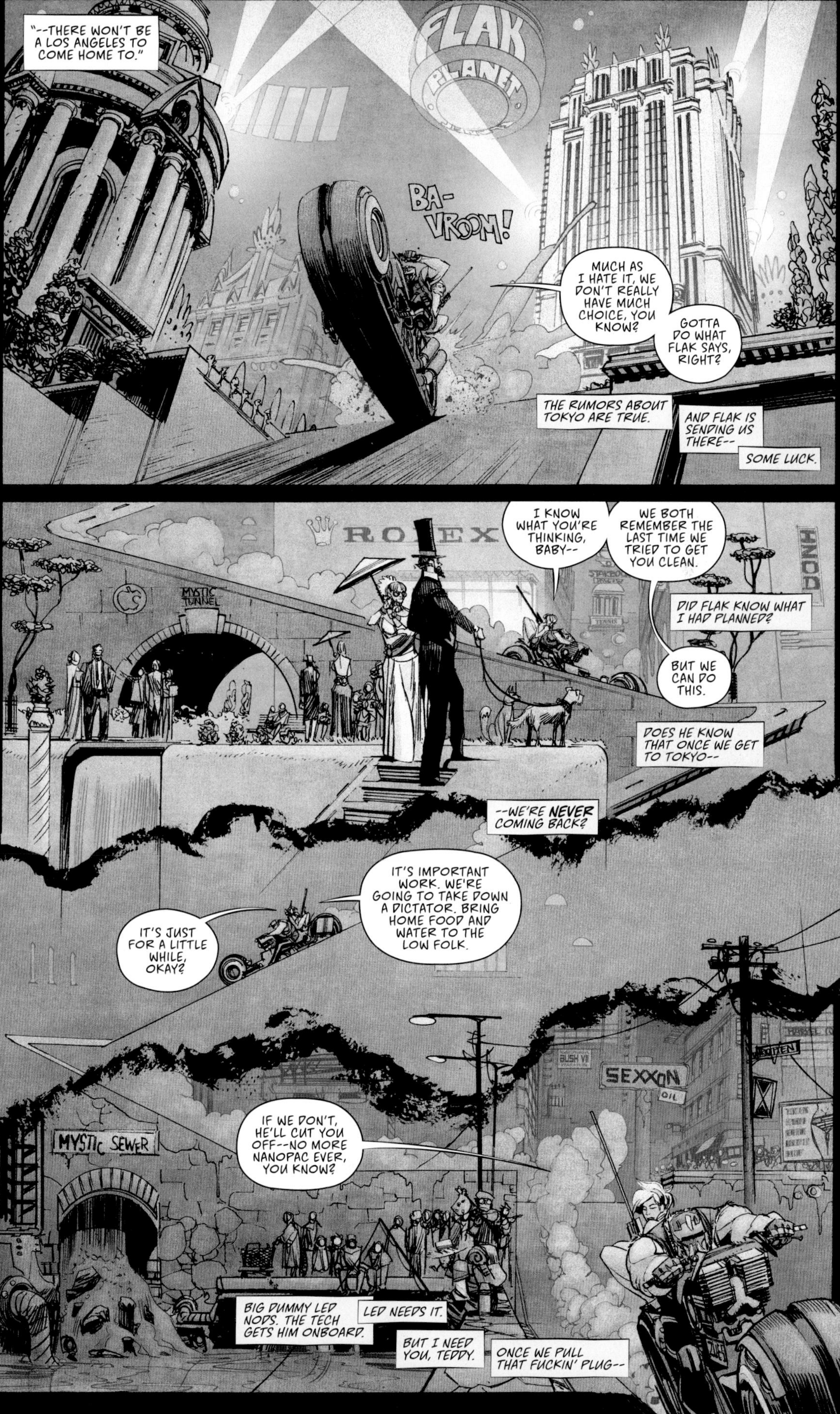
"--THERE WON'T BE A LOS ANGELES TO COME HOME TO."
FLAK PLANET
BA-VROOM!
MUCH AS I HATE IT, WE DON'T REALLY HAVE MUCH CHOICE, YOU KNOW?
GOTTA DO WHAT FLAK SAYS, RIGHT?
THE RUMORS ABOUT TOKYO ARE TRUE.
AND FLAK IS SENDING US THERE--
SOME LUCK.
ROLEX
MYSTIC TUNNEL
I KNOW WHAT YOU'RE THINKING, BABY--
WE BOTH REMEMBER THE LAST TIME WE TRIED TO GET YOU CLEAN.
DID FLAK KNOW WHAT I HAD PLANNED?
BUT WE CAN DO THIS.
DOES HE KNOW THAT ONCE WE GET TO TOKYO--
--WE'RE **NEVER** COMING BACK?
IT'S IMPORTANT WORK. WE'RE GOING TO TAKE DOWN A DICTATOR. BRING HOME FOOD AND WATER TO THE LOW FOLK.
IT'S JUST FOR A LITTLE WHILE, OKAY?
SEXXON OIL
MYSTIC SEWER
IF WE DON'T, HE'LL CUT YOU OFF--NO MORE NANOPAC EVER, YOU KNOW?
BIG DUMMY LED NODS. THE TECH GETS HIM ONBOARD.
LED NEEDS IT.
BUT I NEED YOU, TEDDY.
ONCE WE PULL THAT FUCKIN' PLUG--

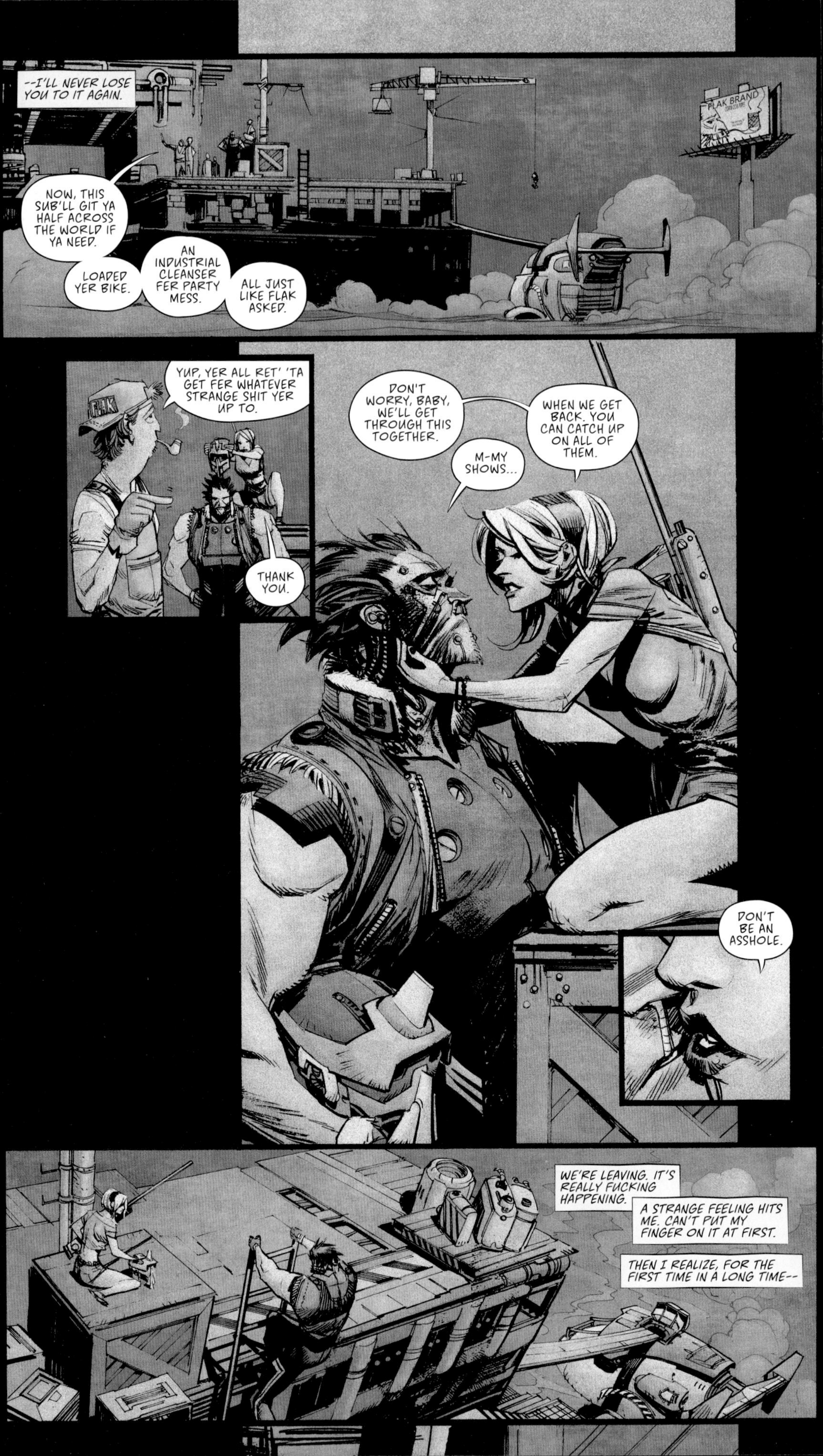
--I'LL NEVER LOSE YOU TO IT AGAIN.
FLAK BRAND
NOW, THIS SUB'LL GIT YA HALF ACROSS THE WORLD IF YA NEED.
LOADED YER BIKE.
AN INDUSTRIAL CLEANSER FER PARTY MESS.
ALL JUST LIKE FLAK ASKED.
YUP, YER ALL RET' 'TA GET FER WHATEVER STRANGE SHIT YER UP TO.
THANK YOU.
DON'T WORRY, BABY, WE'LL GET THROUGH THIS TOGETHER.
M-MY SHOWS...
WHEN WE GET BACK. YOU CAN CATCH UP ON ALL OF THEM.
DON'T BE AN ASSHOLE.
WE'RE LEAVING. IT'S REALLY FUCKING HAPPENING.
A STRANGE FEELING HITS ME. CAN'T PUT MY FINGER ON IT AT FIRST.
THEN I REALIZE, FOR THE FIRST TIME IN A LONG TIME--

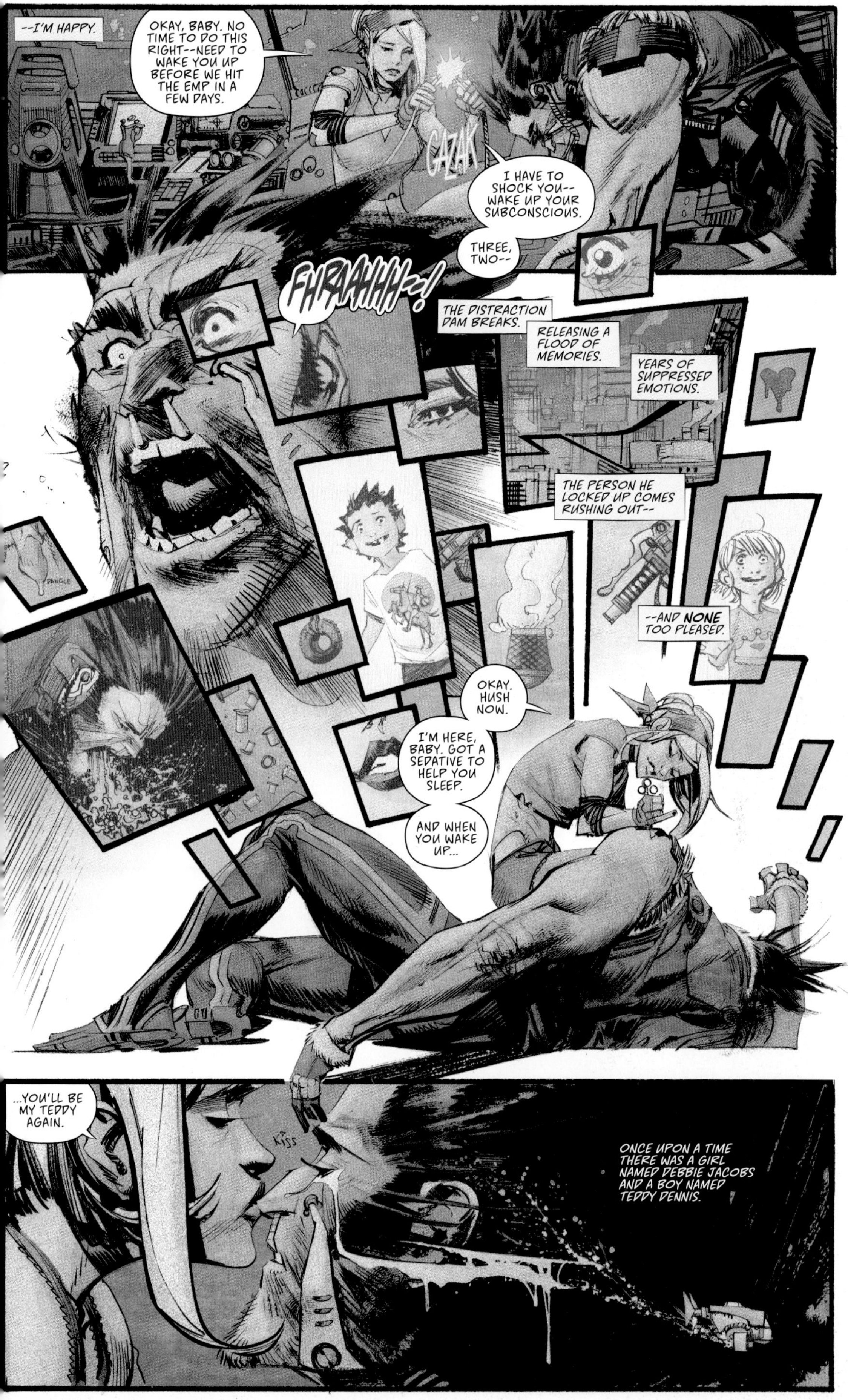
--I'M HAPPY.
OKAY, BABY. NO TIME TO DO THIS RIGHT--NEED TO WAKE YOU UP BEFORE WE HIT THE EMP IN A FEW DAYS.
GAZAK
I HAVE TO SHOCK YOU--WAKE UP YOUR SUBCONSCIOUS.
THREE, TWO--
FHRAAHHH--!
THE DISTRACTION DAM BREAKS.
RELEASING A FLOOD OF MEMORIES.
YEARS OF SUPPRESSED EMOTIONS.
THE PERSON HE LOCKED UP COMES RUSHING OUT--
--AND **NONE** TOO PLEASED.
OKAY. HUSH NOW.
I'M HERE, BABY. GOT A SEDATIVE TO HELP YOU SLEEP.
AND WHEN YOU WAKE UP...
...YOU'LL BE MY TEDDY AGAIN.
KISS
ONCE UPON A TIME THERE WAS A GIRL NAMED DEBBIE JACOBS AND A BOY NAMED TEDDY DENNIS.

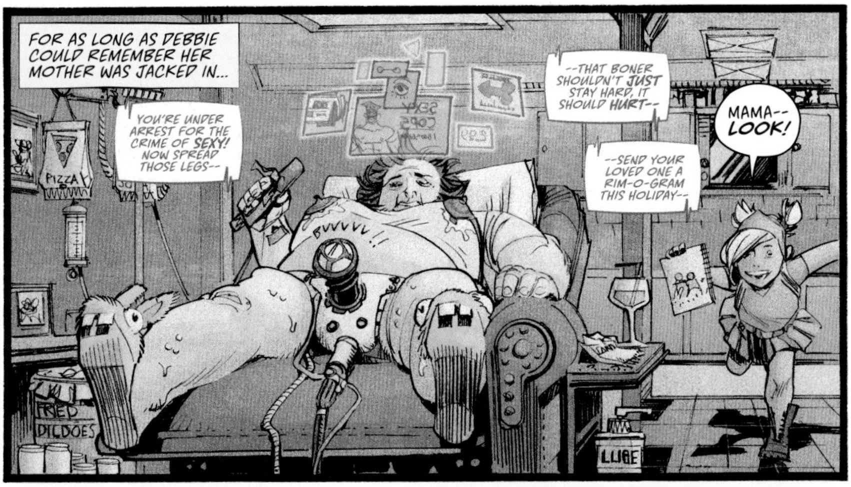
FOR AS LONG AS DEBBIE COULD REMEMBER HER MOTHER WAS JACKED IN...
YOU'RE UNDER ARREST FOR THE CRIME OF SEXY! NOW SPREAD THOSE LEGS--
--THAT BONER SHOULDN'T JUST STAY HARD, IT SHOULD HURT--
--SEND YOUR LOVED ONE A RIM-O-GRAM THIS HOLIDAY--
MAMA--LOOK!
PIZZA
BVVVVL!!
FRED DILDOES
LUBE

DEBBIE WAS RAISED BY HER FATHER, ONE OF THE LAST TECH-FREE DETECTIVES IN THE LAPD. DEBBIE LOVED HER DAD MORE THAN ANYTHING. HE WAS KIND, GIVING, WARM, AND BRAVE. EVERYTHING SHE ASPIRED TO BE.

A RARE HONEST COP, BACK BEFORE THE POLICE WERE DISSOLVED FOR PRIVATE SECURITY FORCES, HE TAUGH DEBBIE THAT THE ONLY WAY A SOCIETY WAS WORTH LIVING IN IS IF PEOPLE HELPED EACH OTHER.

EVEN IF THE FOLKS BEING HELPED DIDN'T NOTICE.

HER FATHER WOULD OPENLY WEEP AS HE BEGGED HIS WIFE TO COME OUT OF THE VIRTU COFFIN SHE'D FALLEN INTO.

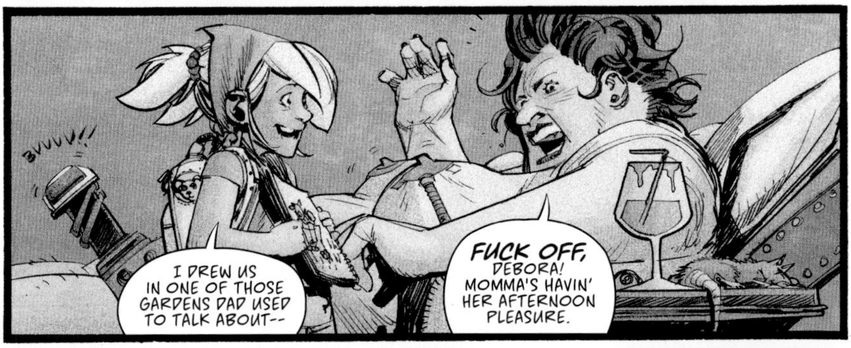
BVVVVV!!!
I DREW US IN ONE OF THOSE GARDENS DAD USED TO TALK ABOUT--
FUCK OFF, DEBORA! MOMMA'S HAVIN' HER AFTERNOON PLEASURE.

DEBBIE SWORE SHE'D NEVER END UP IN THE SAME SITUATION.

TO ESCAPE THE SADNESS AT HOME HER DAD WOULD TAKE DEBBIE TO SILVER LAKE SHOR WATCH THE SUNSET AND TALK.

HE TAUGHT HER THAT EVEN A DIFFICULT REALITY IS BETTER THAN RETREAT INTO A CYBER-FORGERY. NEVER RETREAT.

AND HE NEVER DID...

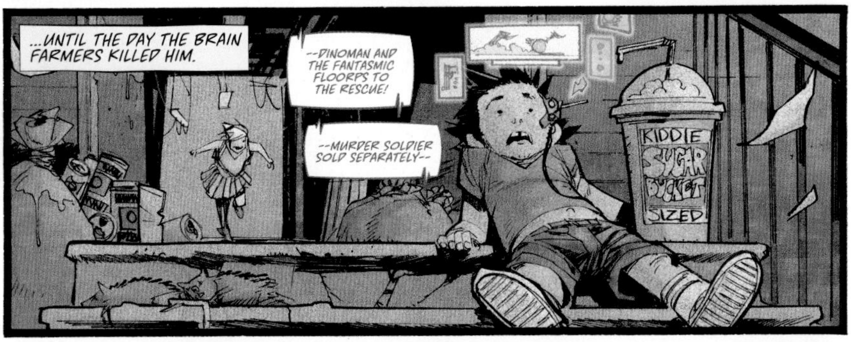
...UNTIL THE DAY THE BRAIN FARMERS KILLED HIM.
--DINOMAN AND THE FANTASMIC FLOORPS TO THE RESCUE!
--MURDER SOLDIER SOLD SEPARATELY--
KIDDIE SUGAR BUCKET SIZED

DEBBIE MISSED HER DAD TERRIBLY.

SHE KEPT HIM CLOSE, NEVER FORGETTING THE LESSONS HE TAUGHT.

SHE NEVER STOPPED PLAYING OUTSIDE. NEVER WENT ONLINE

BUT, OVER TIME, SHE WAS LONELY. SHE WANTED REAL FRIENDS, ACTUAL KIDS TO RU AND PLAY WITH.

ONE FATEFUL DAY AS YOUNG DEBBIE WAS GOING OUT TO PLAY...

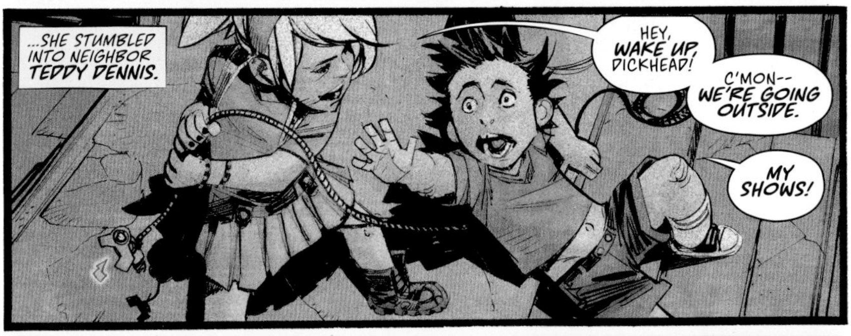
...SHE STUMBLED INTO NEIGHBOR TEDDY DENNIS.
HEY, WAKE UP, DICKHEAD!
C'MON--WE'RE GOING OUTSIDE.
MY SHOWS!

DEBBIE HAD GROWN UP LISTENING TO TEDDY'S PAREN FIGHT NEXT DOOR, OFTEN ABOUT HOW TO GET RID OF THE BOY.

BUT THE FIGHTING EVENTUALL STOPPED. TEDDY'S PARENTS HAD FOUND THEIR ESCAPE, THEY'D GONE IN PERMANENT, AND TOTALLY CHECKED OUT.

ON THE DAY OUR NOBLE HEROINE FOUND TEDDY...

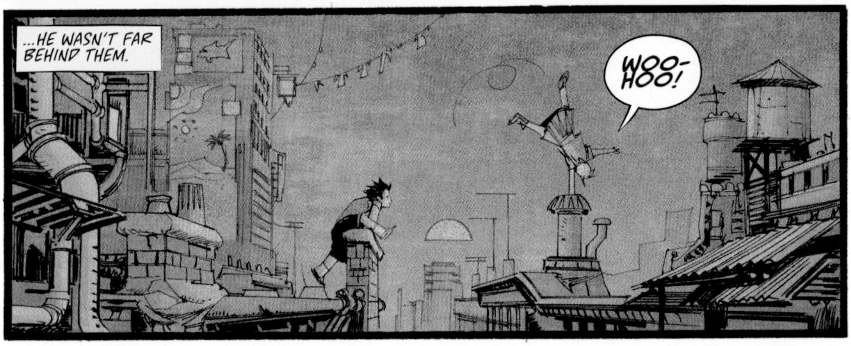
...HE WASN'T FAR BEHIND THEM.
WOO-HOO!

DEBBIE TAUGHT TEDDY WHAT HER FATHER TAUGHT HER--LIVING LIFE OUTSIDE IS MORE FUN. AND GIVEN HOW CUTE SHE WAS, THE POOR BO WAS SMITTEN. HE NEVER STOO A CHANCE.

FROM THEN ON EVERY DAY THEY RAN TOGETHER, MAKING THE BEST OF WHAT THEY WER BORN INTO.

THEY RAN THE ROOFTOPS AN THE ALLEYWAYS.

THEY HOWLED AT THE MOON.

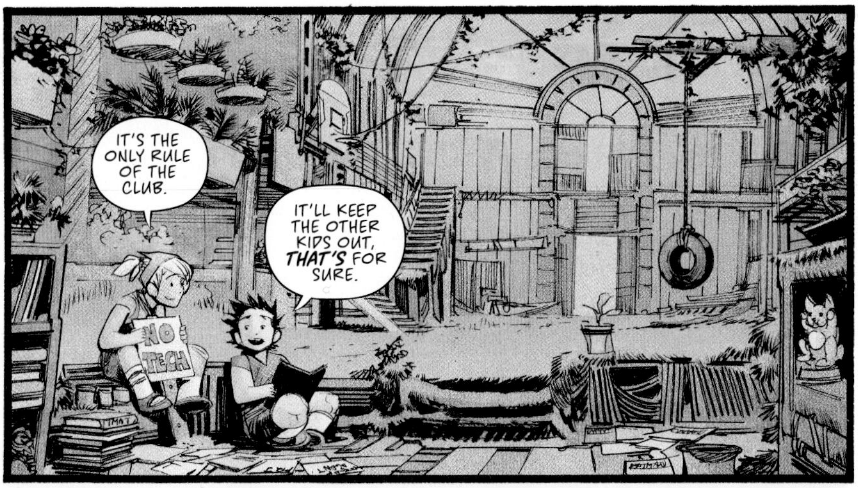
IT'S THE ONLY RULE OF THE CLUB.
NO TECH
IT'LL KEEP THE OTHER KIDS OUT, **THAT'S** FOR SURE.

THEY FOUND AN ABANDONED GREENHOUSE AND MADE IT THEIR HOME.

A SECRET GARDEN WHERE THEY PLAYED KICKBALL, READ BOOKS AND MADE ART. IT WAS THERE, YEAR BY YEAR THAT THEY BECAME THE BEST OF FRIENDS.

NO ONE ELSE UNDERSTOOD THEM OR CARED TO TRY. THEY WERE THE ONLY FAMILY THEY NEEDED. WHICH WAS GOOD...

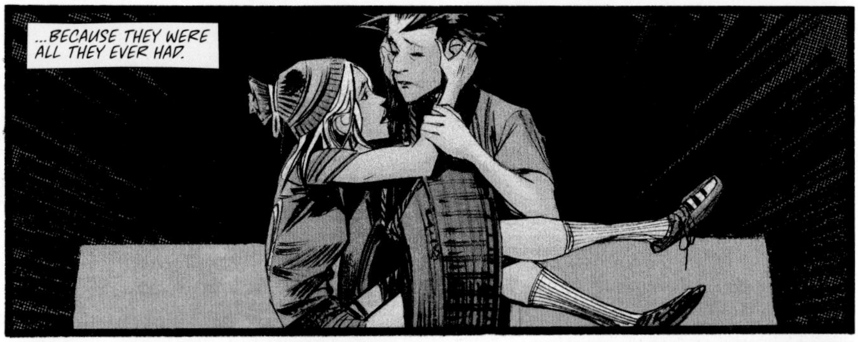
...BECAUSE THEY WERE ALL THEY EVER HAD.

TIME PASSED.

THEY GREW UP.

FELL IN LOVE.

SHARED THEIR FIRST KISS.

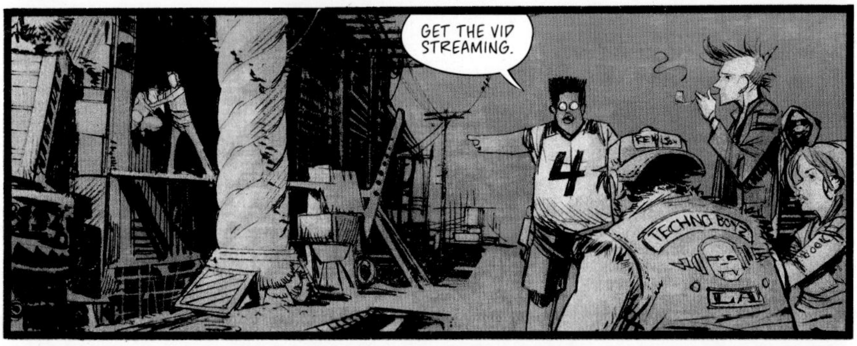
GET THE VID STREAMING.

OUTSIDE OF THE GARDEN, THEY WERE ALWAYS IN DANGER.

TECH HEADS, EMO DEALERS, BODY PIRATES, CANNIBAL HUNTERS...

BEING ATTACKED WAS THE RISK THEY TOOK TO GO OUTSIDE.

BUT TEDDY GREW ANGRY. TIRED OF BEING PICKED ON IN FRONT OF HIS GIRL. EMBARRASSED BY THE VERY VULNERABILITY DEBBIE FELL IN LOVE WITH.

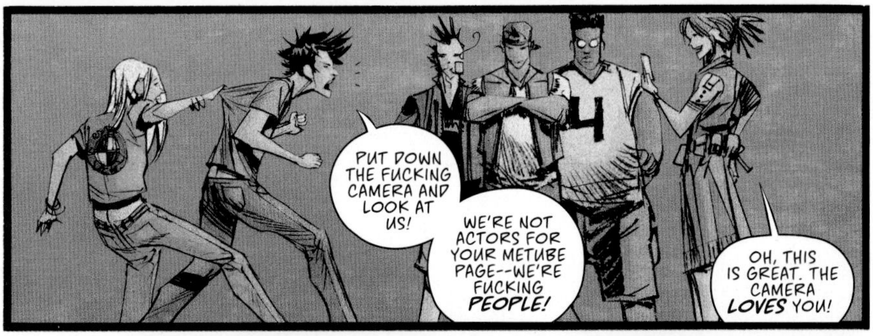
PUT DOWN THE FUCKING CAMERA AND LOOK AT US!
WE'RE NOT ACTORS FOR YOUR METUBE PAGE--WE'RE FUCKING **PEOPLE!**
OH, THIS IS GREAT. THE CAMERA **LOVES** YOU!

ONE DAY AS THEY CAME HOME FROM THE SECRET GARDEN A BAND OF FAME BANGERS FOUND THEM.

THESE CUNTS MADE MILLIONS FILMING REALITY CRIME. STITCHED TOGETHER WITH A "STORY" TO MAKE IT "ART."

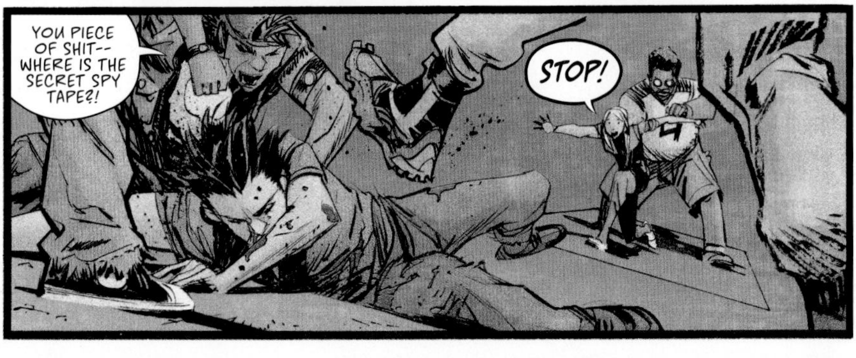
YOU PIECE OF SHIT--WHERE IS THE SECRET SPY TAPE?!
STOP!

THEY BEAT TEDDY NEAR TO DEATH.

ALL THE WHILE READING FROM A SCRIPT.

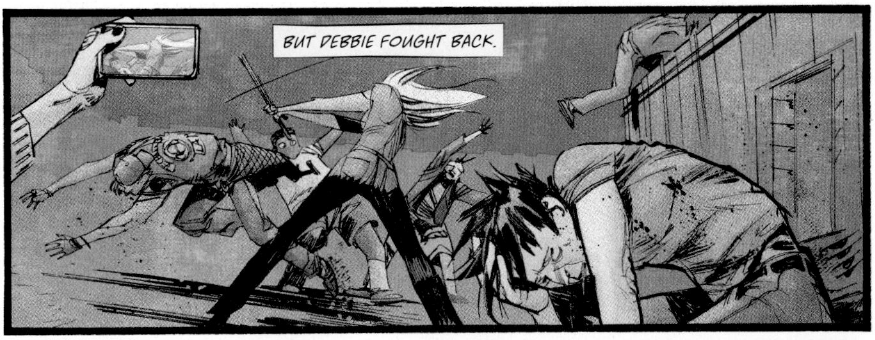
BUT DEBBIE FOUGHT BACK.

HER DAD HAD TAUGHT HER MORE ABOUT POLICE WORK THAN JUST POETIC IDEOLOG HE ALSO TAUGHT HER HOW T FUCK A BAND OF ASSHOLES UP.

AND HOWDY.

THE DICKS RAN SCARED.

BUT HER PROTECTING TEDD WAS THE WORST THING THAT COULD HAVE HAPPENED TO THE YOUNG LOVERS.

IT SHONE A BRIGHT LIGHT O HIS WEAKNESS...

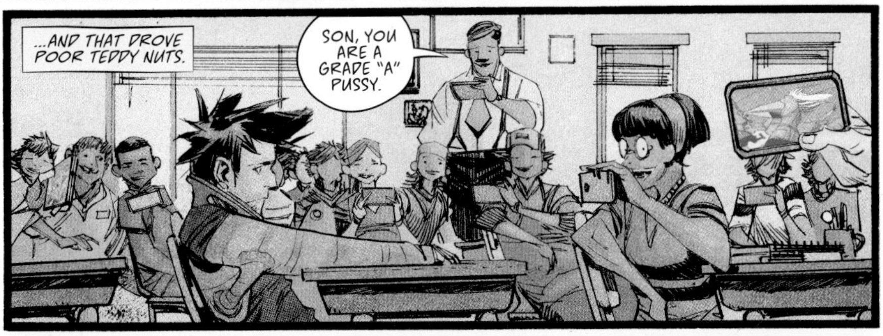
...AND THAT DROVE POOR TEDDY NUTS.
SON, YOU ARE A GRADE "A" PUSSY.

THE VIDEO OF HIS BEATING BECAME A CLICK-HIT.

EVERYONE HAD SEEN IT THE NEXT DAY AT SCHOOL. THEY WERE ALL LAUGHING AT WEA TEDDY, PROTECTED BY HIS GIRLFRIEND.

THE CLIP BECAME THE SECOND-MOST WATCHED OF THE YEAR. BEAT OUT ONLY TO A GAME SHOW THAT HAS POOR PEOPLE COUNT RICH PEOPLE'S MONEY.

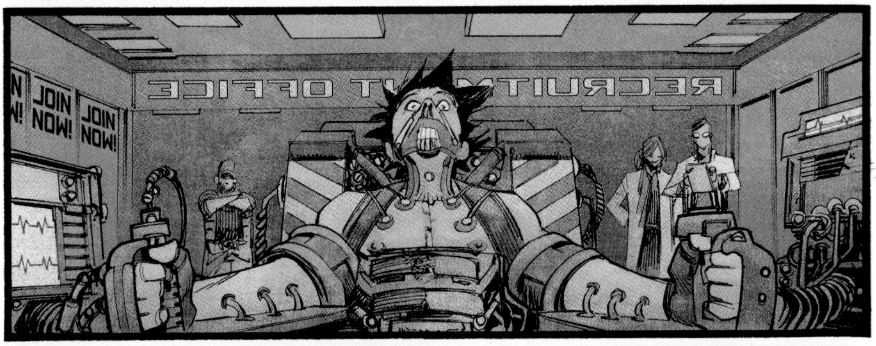
JOIN NOW!
JOIN NOW!

THE CONSTABLE PROGRAM WAS BUILT FOR GUYS LIKE TEDDY: SMALL MEN WITH BIG CHIPS ON THEIR SHOULDERS THE KIND WHO HAD TASTED A BEATING--

--AND WERE READY TO GIVE ONE **BACK.**

TEDDY DIDN'T TELL DEBBIE. SHE KNEW FROM HER FATHE ABOUT THE HUNDREDS OF NANOBOTS THEY PUT IN THOSE POOR BASTARDS... S WOULD HAVE STOPPED HIM.

THE SELF-CENTERED PRICK LEFT HER A NOTE, "I'LL PROTECT YOU."

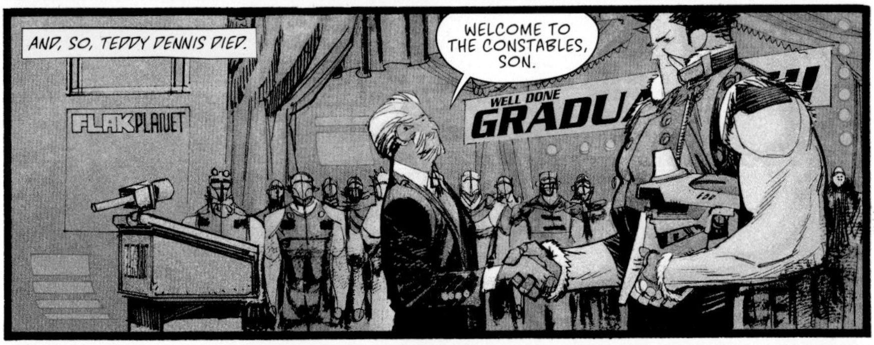
AND, SO, TEDDY DENNIS DIED.
WELCOME TO THE CONSTABLES, SON.
FLAKPLANET
WELL DONE
GRADUA

AND **LED DENT** WAS BORN.

DID TEDDY BECOME A CONSTABLE FOR DEBBIE OR FOR HIMSELF?

WHICHEVER IT WAS--

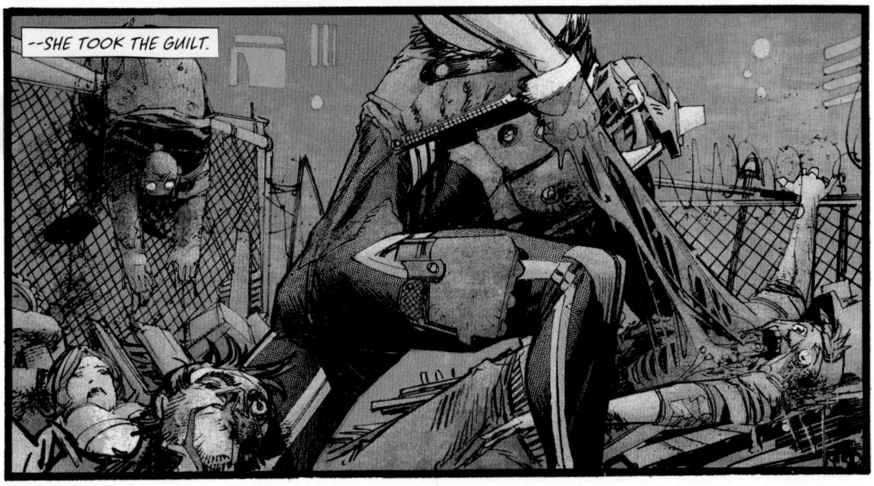
--SHE TOOK THE GUILT.

HIS FIRST DAY AS CONSTABLE HE FOUND THE GANG WHO BEAT HIM.

AND NEARLY KILLED THEM AL

AS TIME WENT BY LED DENT BECAME THE MOST FEARED MAN ALIVE. YEARS OF SEETHING FINALLY GIVEN SOME WAY OUT.

LED BECAME ADDICTED TO THE POWER.

DEBBIE TRIED TO HOLD HIM TOGETHER. HOLDING ON TO THE TECH-HEAD SHE LOVED. SHE ENDED UP IN THE EXACT SITUATION SHE SWORE TO AVOID...

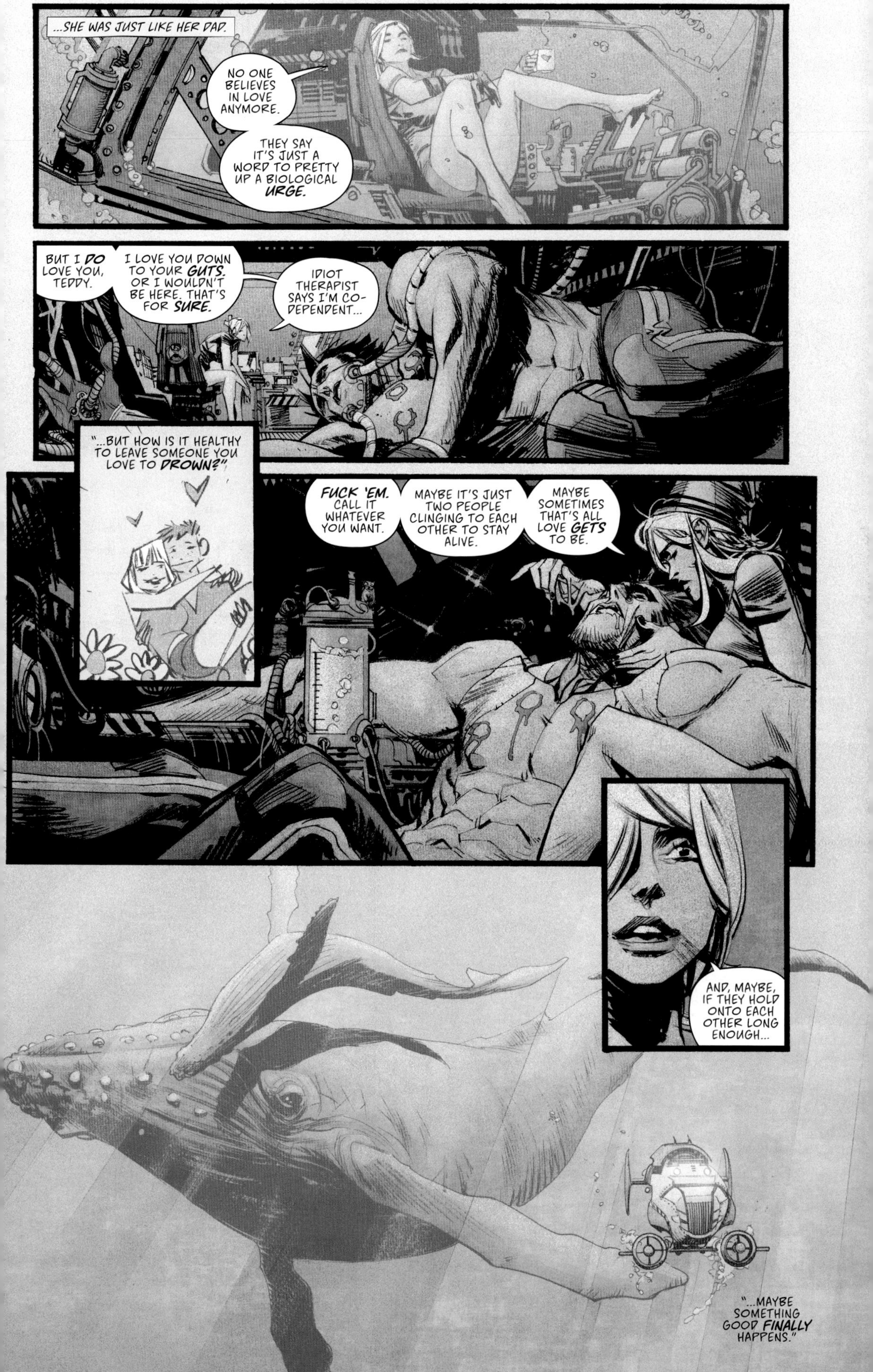
...SHE WAS JUST LIKE HER DAD.
NO ONE BELIEVES IN LOVE ANYMORE.
THEY SAY IT'S JUST A WORD TO PRETTY UP A BIOLOGICAL URGE.
BUT I DO LOVE YOU, TEDDY.
I LOVE YOU DOWN TO YOUR GUTS. OR I WOULDN'T BE HERE. THAT'S FOR SURE.
IDIOT THERAPIST SAYS I'M CO-DEPENDENT...
"...BUT HOW IS IT HEALTHY TO LEAVE SOMEONE YOU LOVE TO DROWN?"
FUCK 'EM. CALL IT WHATEVER YOU WANT.
MAYBE IT'S JUST TWO PEOPLE CLINGING TO EACH OTHER TO STAY ALIVE.
MAYBE SOMETIMES THAT'S ALL LOVE GETS TO BE.
AND, MAYBE, IF THEY HOLD ONTO EACH OTHER LONG ENOUGH...
"...MAYBE SOMETHING GOOD FINALLY HAPPENS."

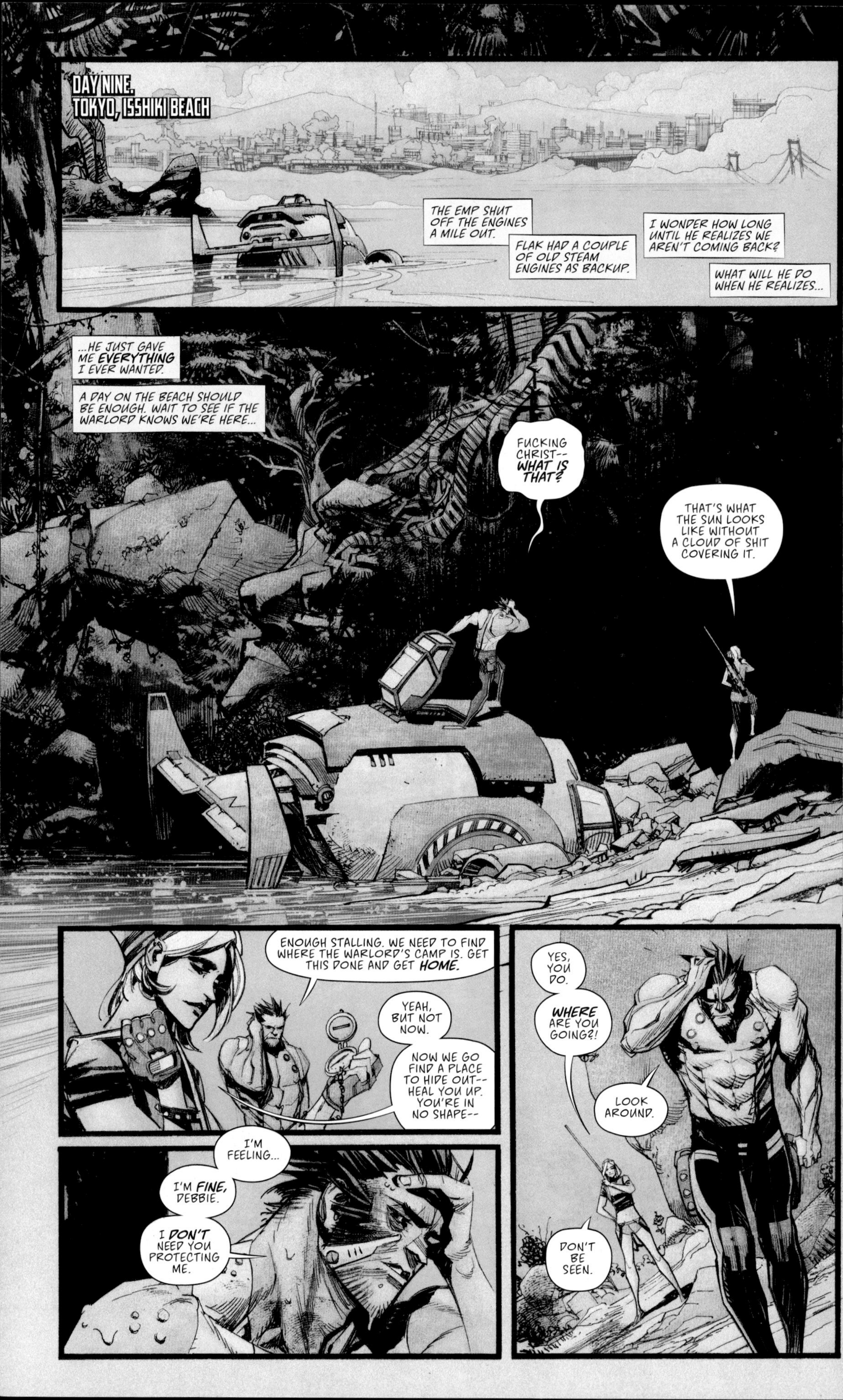
DAY NINE.
TOKYO, ISSHIKI BEACH
THE EMP SHUT OFF THE ENGINES A MILE OUT.
FLAK HAD A COUPLE OF OLD STEAM ENGINES AS BACKUP.
I WONDER HOW LONG UNTIL HE REALIZES WE AREN'T COMING BACK?
WHAT WILL HE DO WHEN HE REALIZES...
...HE JUST GAVE ME EVERYTHING I EVER WANTED.
A DAY ON THE BEACH SHOULD BE ENOUGH. WAIT TO SEE IF THE WARLORD KNOWS WE'RE HERE...
FUCKING CHRIST-- WHAT IS THAT?
THAT'S WHAT THE SUN LOOKS LIKE WITHOUT A CLOUD OF SHIT COVERING IT.
ENOUGH STALLING. WE NEED TO FIND WHERE THE WARLORD'S CAMP IS. GET THIS DONE AND GET HOME.
YEAH, BUT NOT NOW.
NOW WE GO FIND A PLACE TO HIDE OUT-- HEAL YOU UP. YOU'RE IN NO SHAPE--
I'M FEELING...
I'M FINE, DEBBIE.
I DON'T NEED YOU PROTECTING ME.
YES, YOU DO.
WHERE ARE YOU GOING?!
LOOK AROUND.
DON'T BE SEEN.

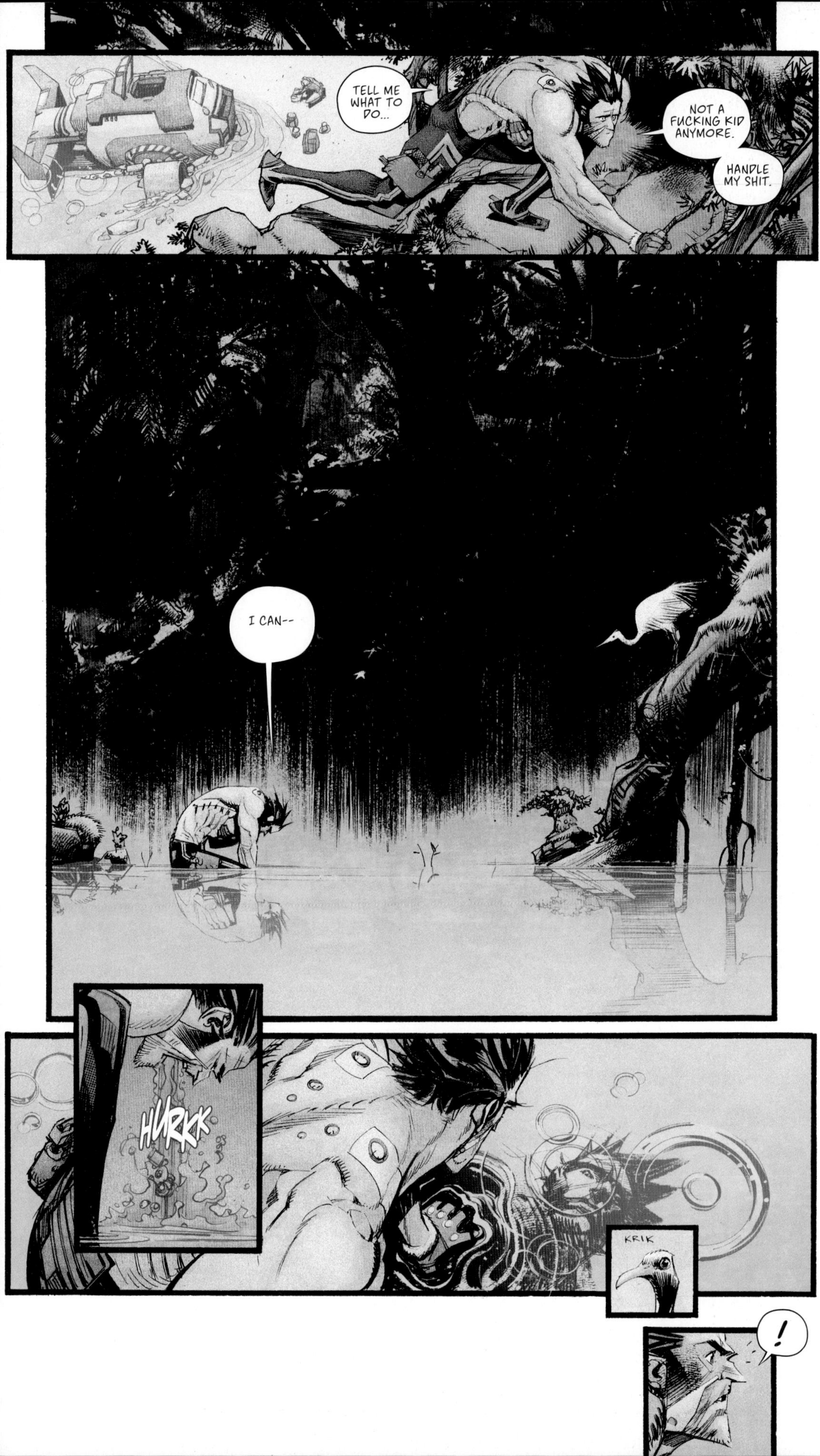
TELL ME WHAT TO DO...
NOT A FUCKING KID ANYMORE.
HANDLE MY SHIT.
I CAN--
HURKK
KRIK
!

DEBBIE!

GRAE.

THERE'S SOMEONE UP HERE!

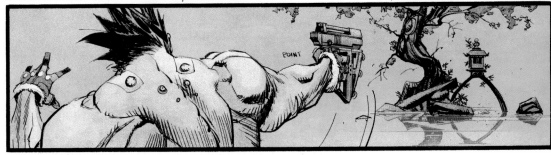

POINT

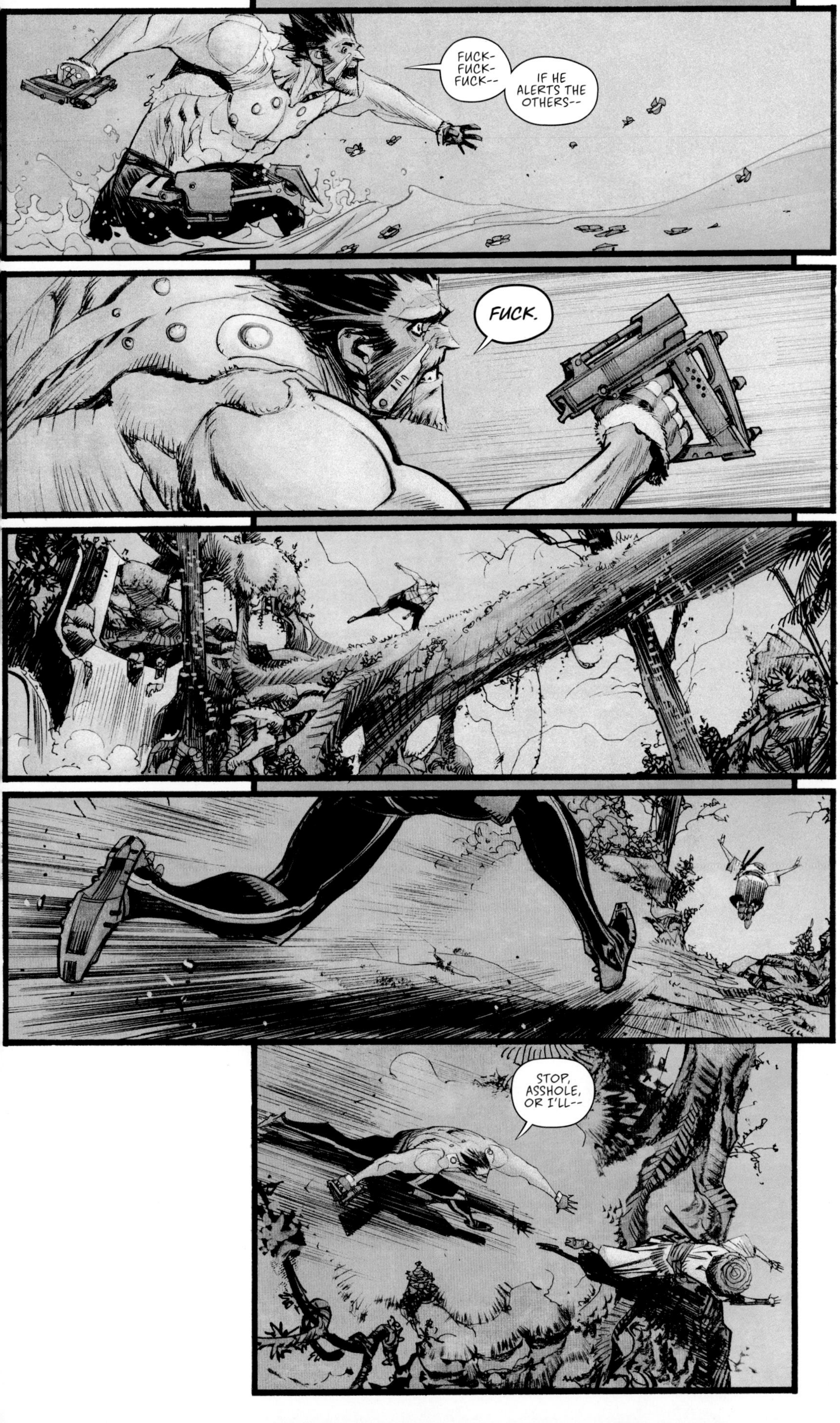
FUCK-FUCK-FUCK--
IF HE ALERTS THE OTHERS--
FUCK.
STOP, ASSHOLE, OR I'LL--

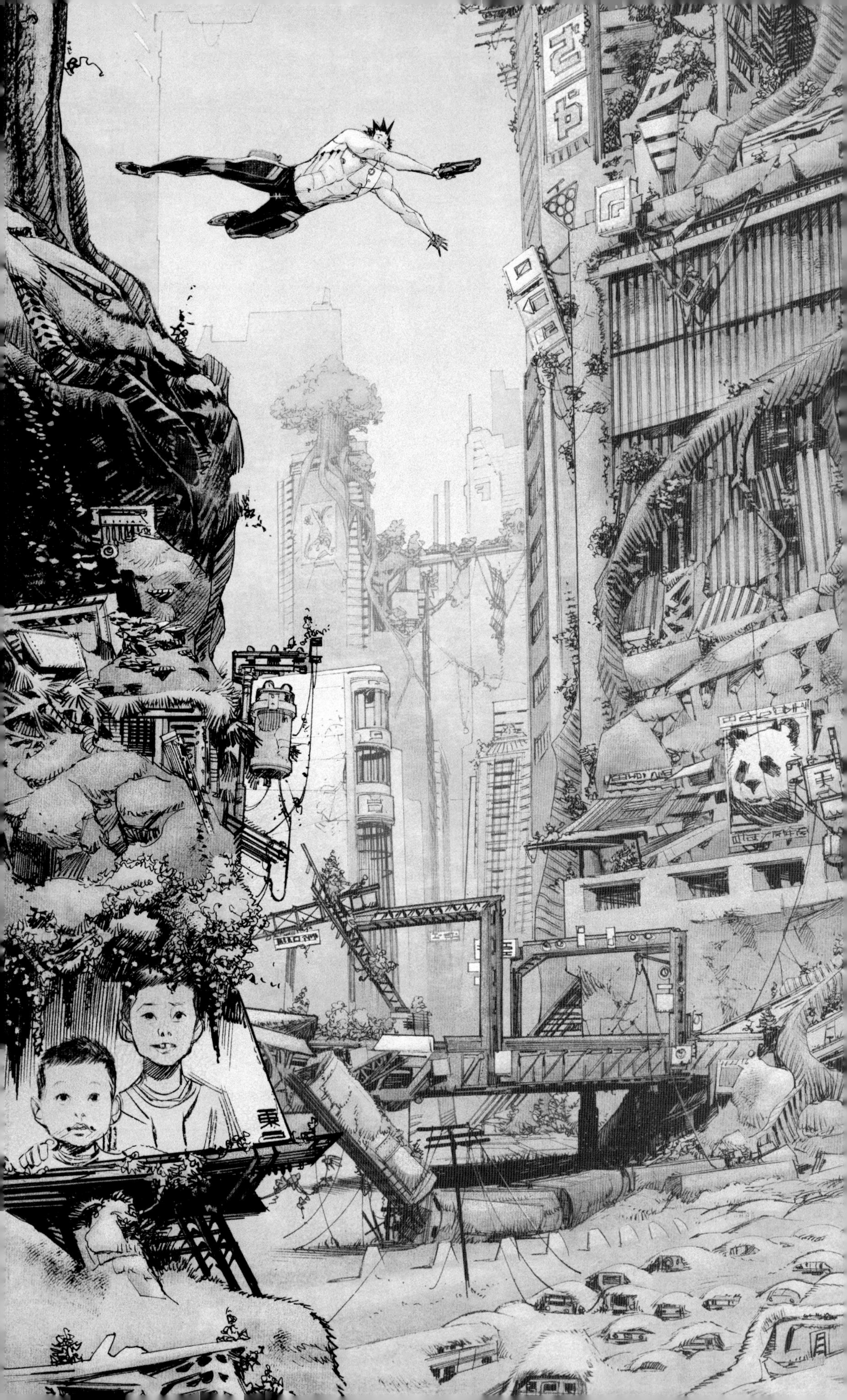

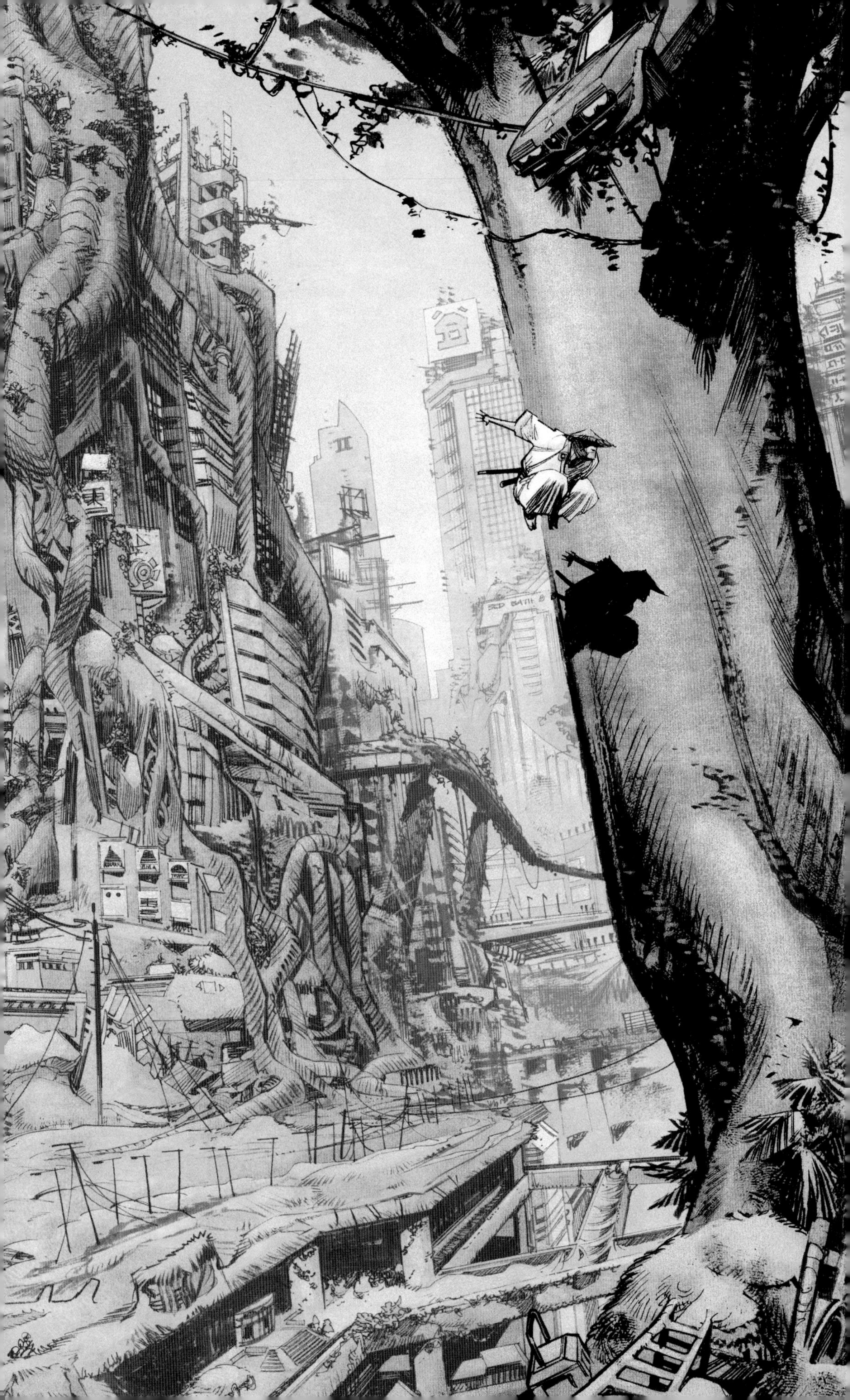

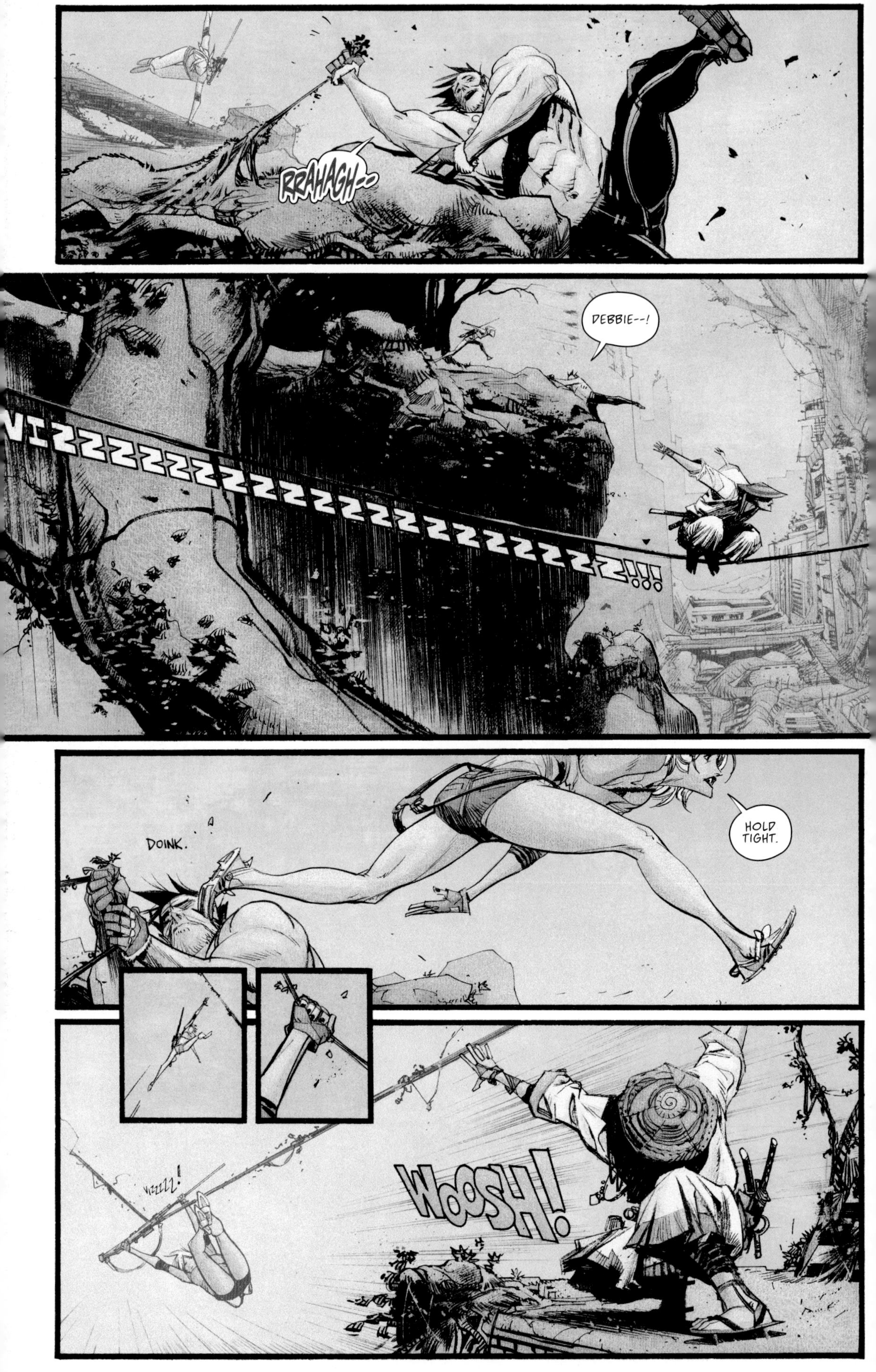
RRAHAGH--
DEBBIE--!
VIZZZZZZZZZZZZZZZZZZZZZZZZZZZZ!!!
DOINK.
HOLD TIGHT.
VIZZZZZ!
WOOSH!

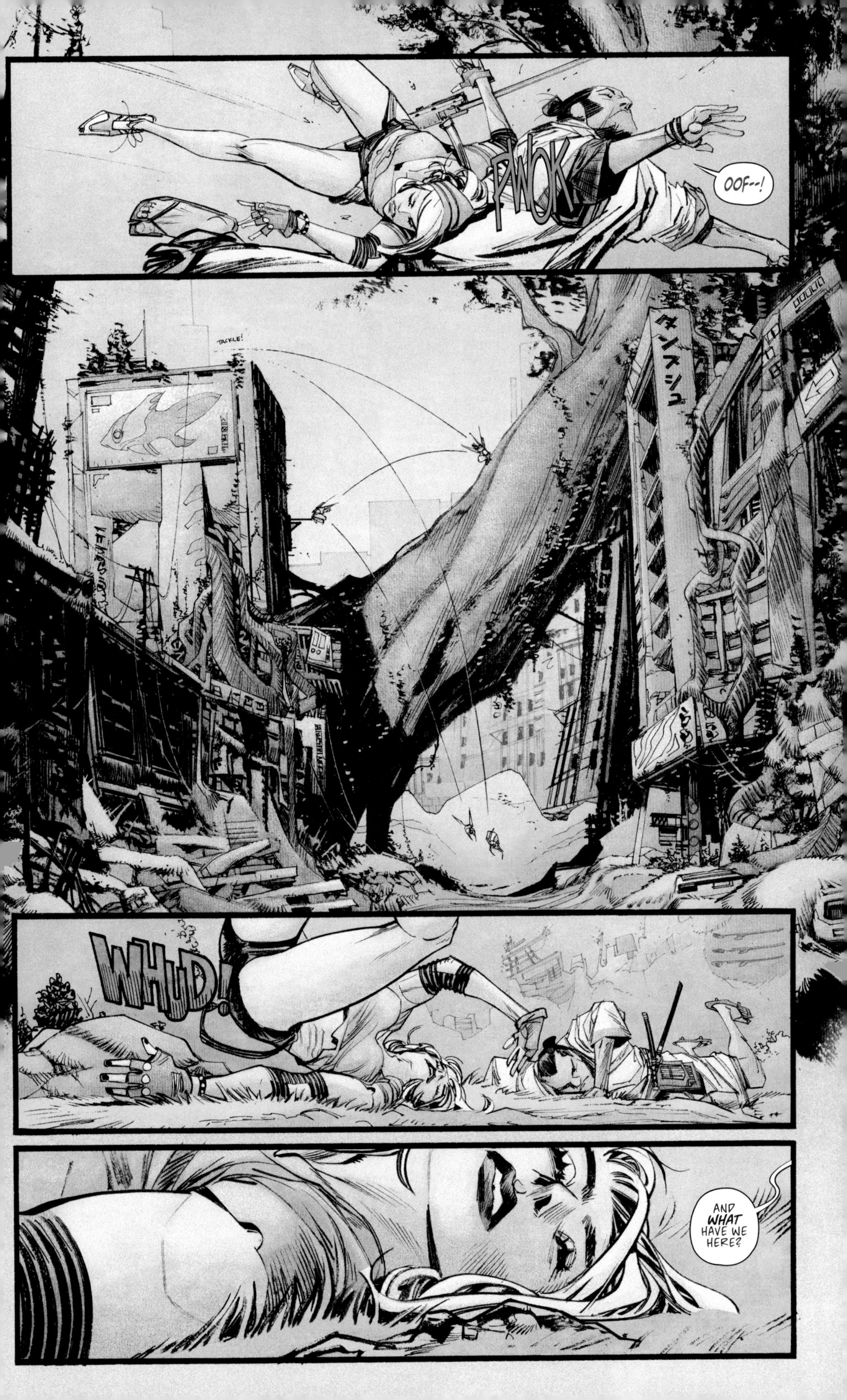
PWOK
OOF--!
TACKLE!
WHUD!
AND **WHAT** HAVE WE HERE?

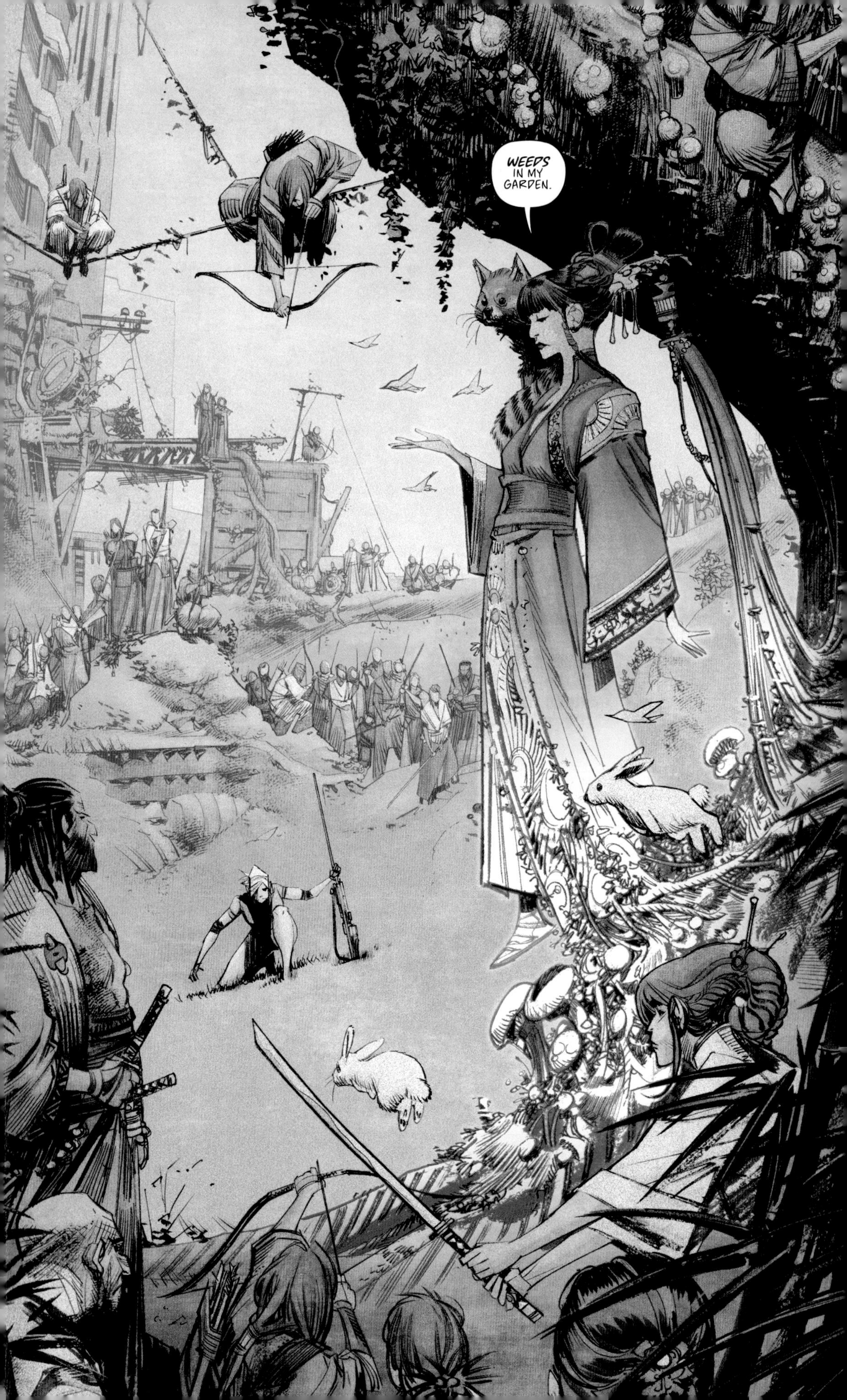
WEEDS IN MY GARDEN.

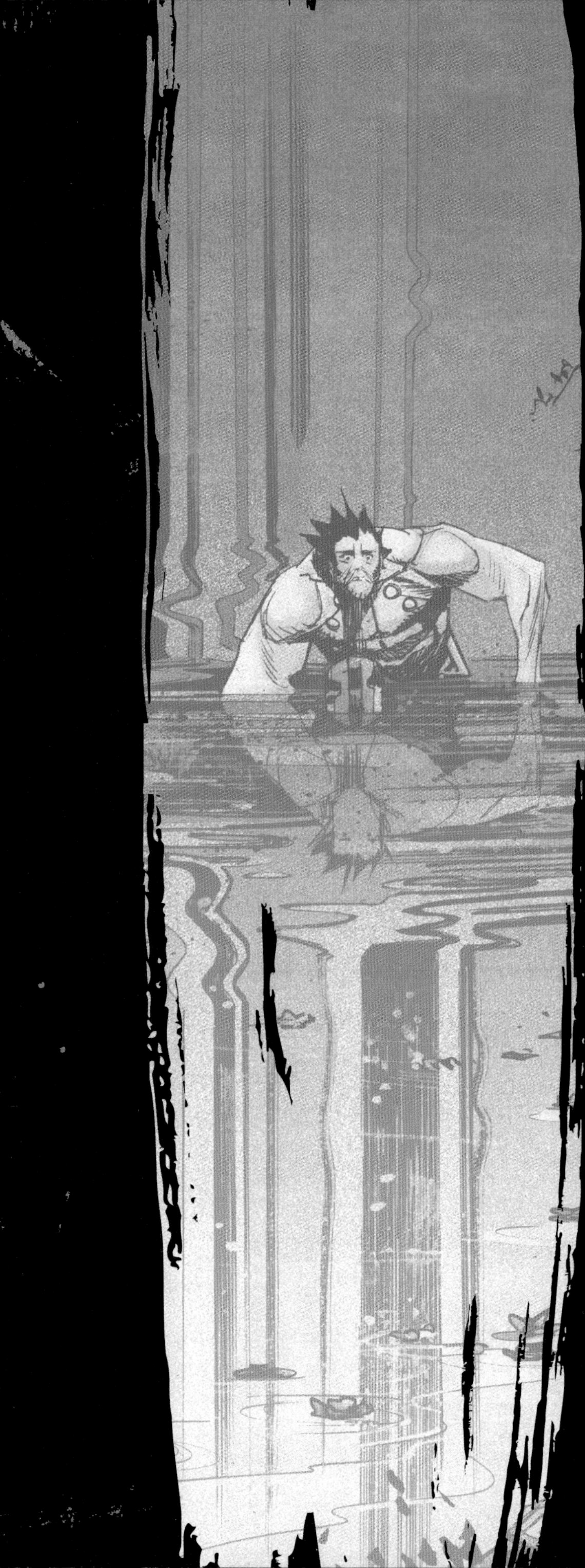

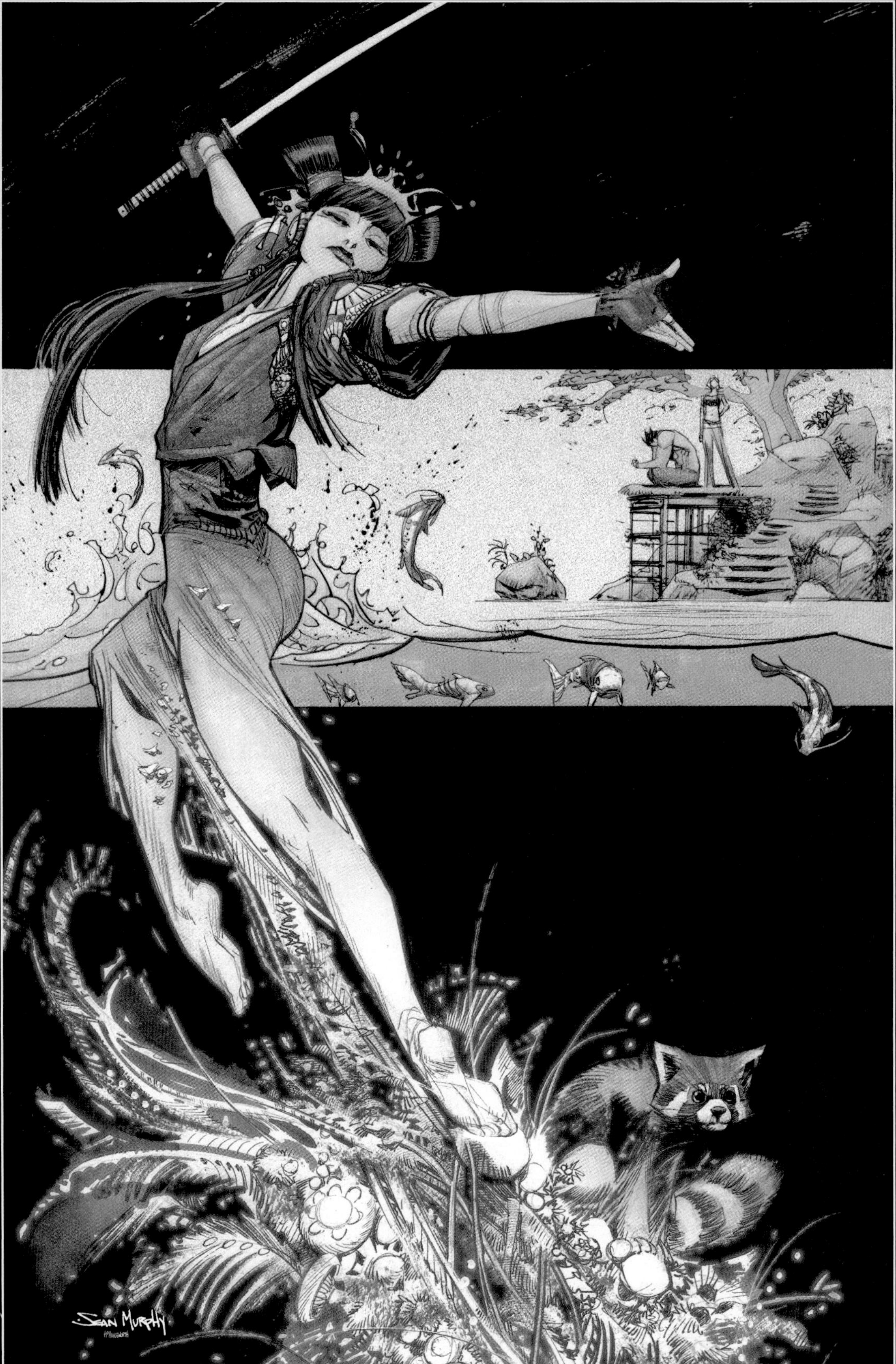
SEAN MURPHY

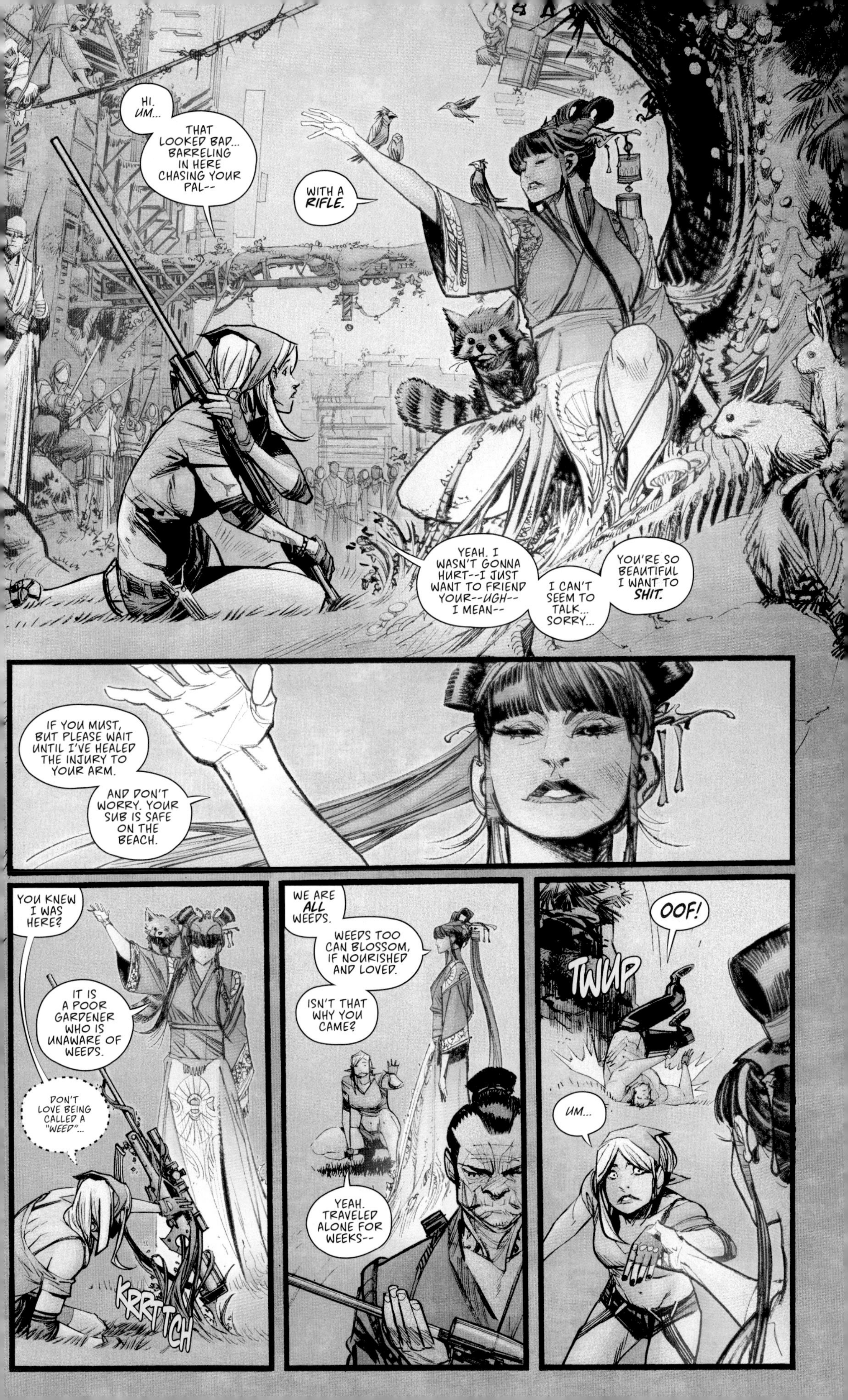
HI. UM...
THAT LOOKED BAD... BARRELING IN HERE CHASING YOUR PAL--
WITH A RIFLE.
YEAH. I WASN'T GONNA HURT--I JUST WANT TO FRIEND YOUR--UGH-- I MEAN--
I CAN'T SEEM TO TALK... SORRY...
YOU'RE SO BEAUTIFUL I WANT TO SHIT.
IF YOU MUST, BUT PLEASE WAIT UNTIL I'VE HEALED THE INJURY TO YOUR ARM.
AND DON'T WORRY. YOUR SUB IS SAFE ON THE BEACH.
YOU KNEW I WAS HERE?
IT IS A POOR GARDENER WHO IS UNAWARE OF WEEDS.
DON'T LOVE BEING CALLED A "WEED"...
KRRTTCH
WE ARE ALL WEEDS.
WEEDS TOO CAN BLOSSOM, IF NOURISHED AND LOVED.
ISN'T THAT WHY YOU CAME?
YEAH. TRAVELED ALONE FOR WEEKS--
OOF!
TWUP
UM...

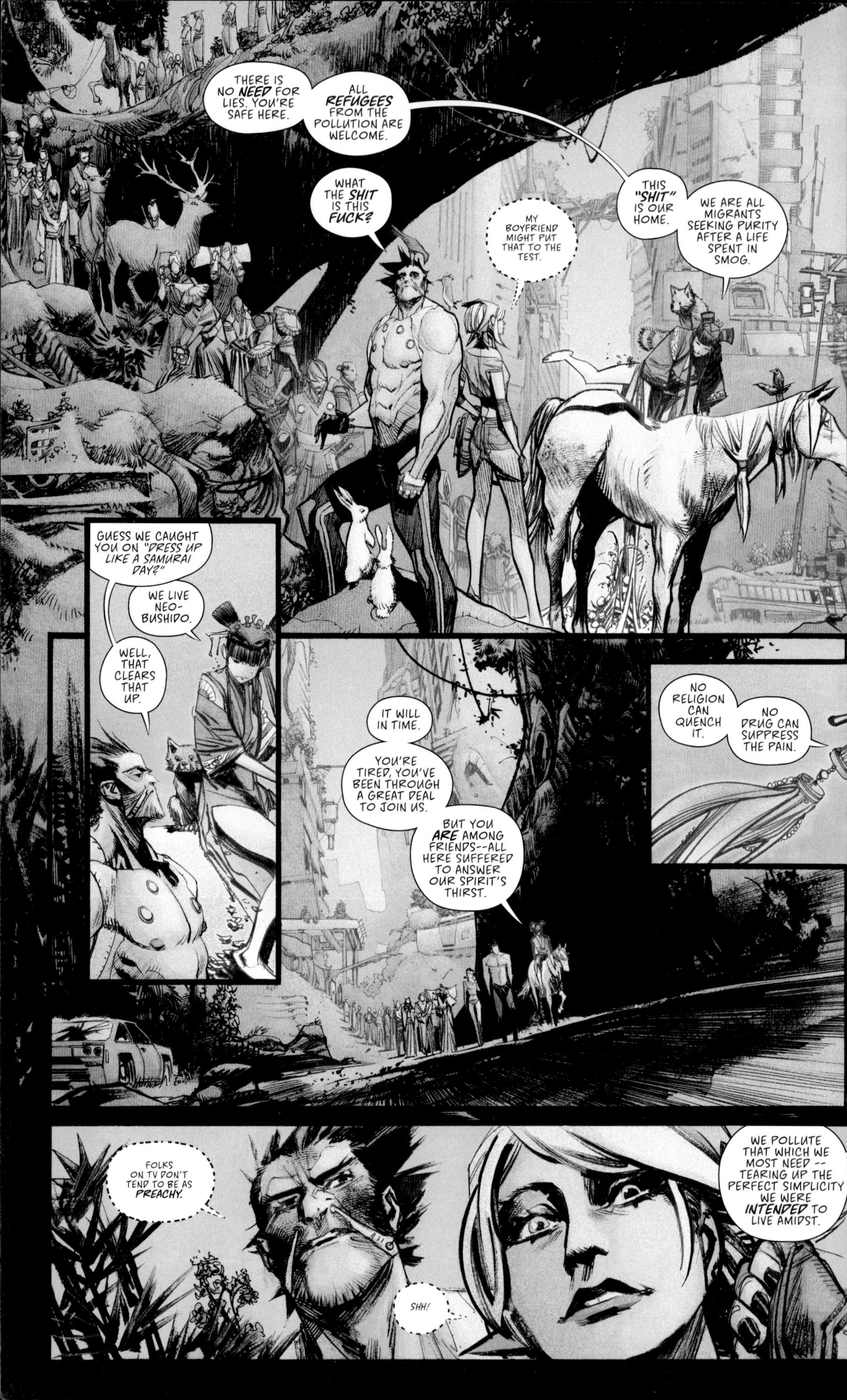

THERE IS NO NEED FOR LIES. YOU'RE SAFE HERE.
ALL REFUGEES FROM THE POLLUTION ARE WELCOME.
WHAT THE SHIT IS THIS FUCK?
MY BOYFRIEND MIGHT PUT THAT TO THE TEST.
THIS "SHIT" IS OUR HOME.
WE ARE ALL MIGRANTS SEEKING PURITY AFTER A LIFE SPENT IN SMOG.
GUESS WE CAUGHT YOU ON "DRESS UP LIKE A SAMURAI DAY?"
WE LIVE NEO-BUSHIDO.
WELL, THAT CLEARS THAT UP.
IT WILL IN TIME.
YOU'RE TIRED, YOU'VE BEEN THROUGH A GREAT DEAL TO JOIN US.
BUT YOU ARE AMONG FRIENDS--ALL HERE SUFFERED TO ANSWER OUR SPIRIT'S THIRST.
NO RELIGION CAN QUENCH IT.
NO DRUG CAN SUPPRESS THE PAIN.
FOLKS ON TV DON'T TEND TO BE AS PREACHY.
WE POLLUTE THAT WHICH WE MOST NEED -- TEARING UP THE PERFECT SIMPLICITY WE WERE INTENDED TO LIVE AMIDST.
SHH!

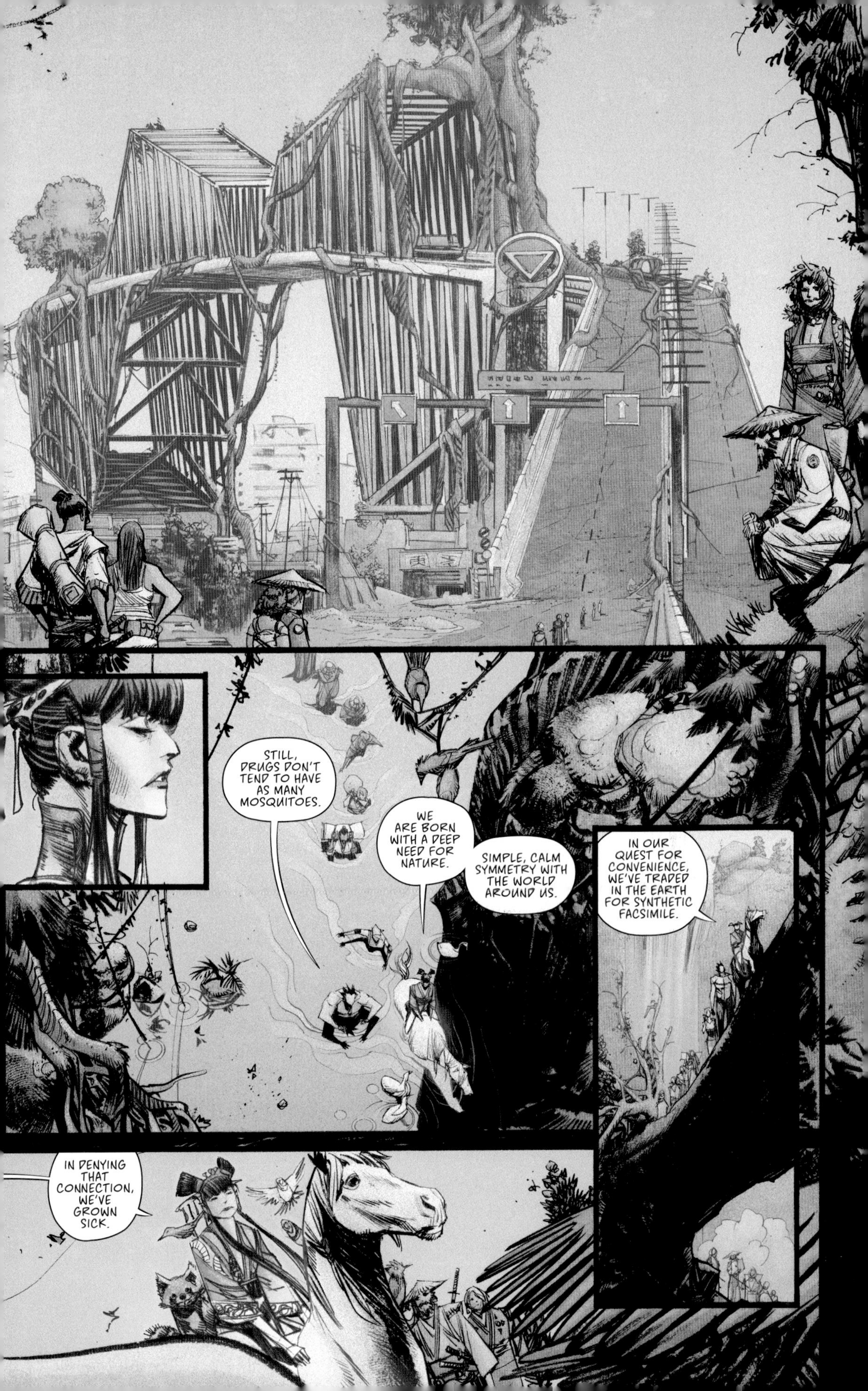

STILL, DRUGS DON'T TEND TO HAVE AS MANY MOSQUITOES.
WE ARE BORN WITH A DEEP NEED FOR NATURE.
SIMPLE, CALM SYMMETRY WITH THE WORLD AROUND US.
IN OUR QUEST FOR CONVENIENCE, WE'VE TRADED IN THE EARTH FOR SYNTHETIC FACSIMILE.
IN DENYING THAT CONNECTION, WE'VE GROWN SICK.

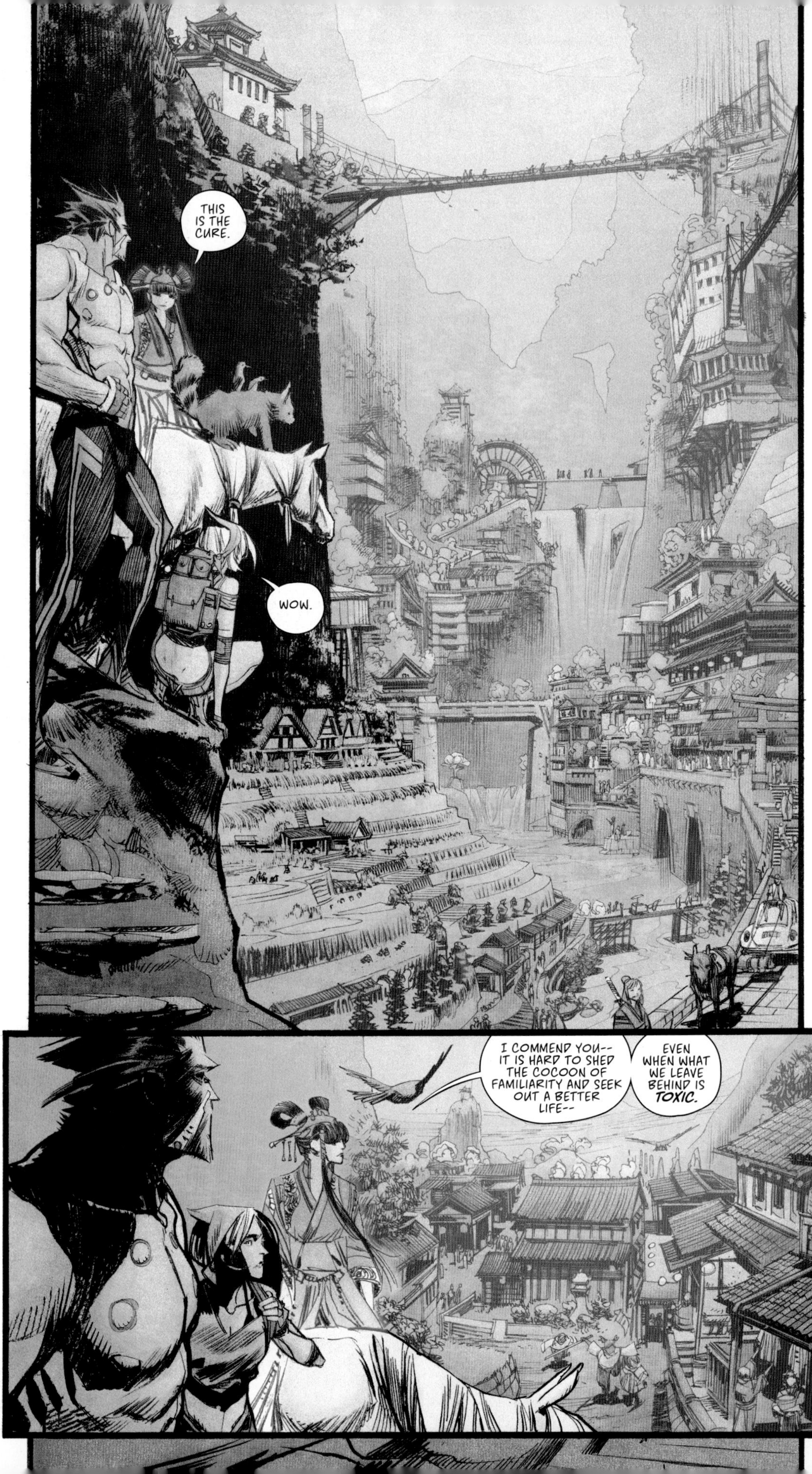
THIS IS THE CURE.
WOW.
I COMMEND YOU--IT IS HARD TO SHED THE COCOON OF FAMILIARITY AND SEEK OUT A BETTER LIFE--
EVEN WHEN WHAT WE LEAVE BEHIND IS *TOXIC*.

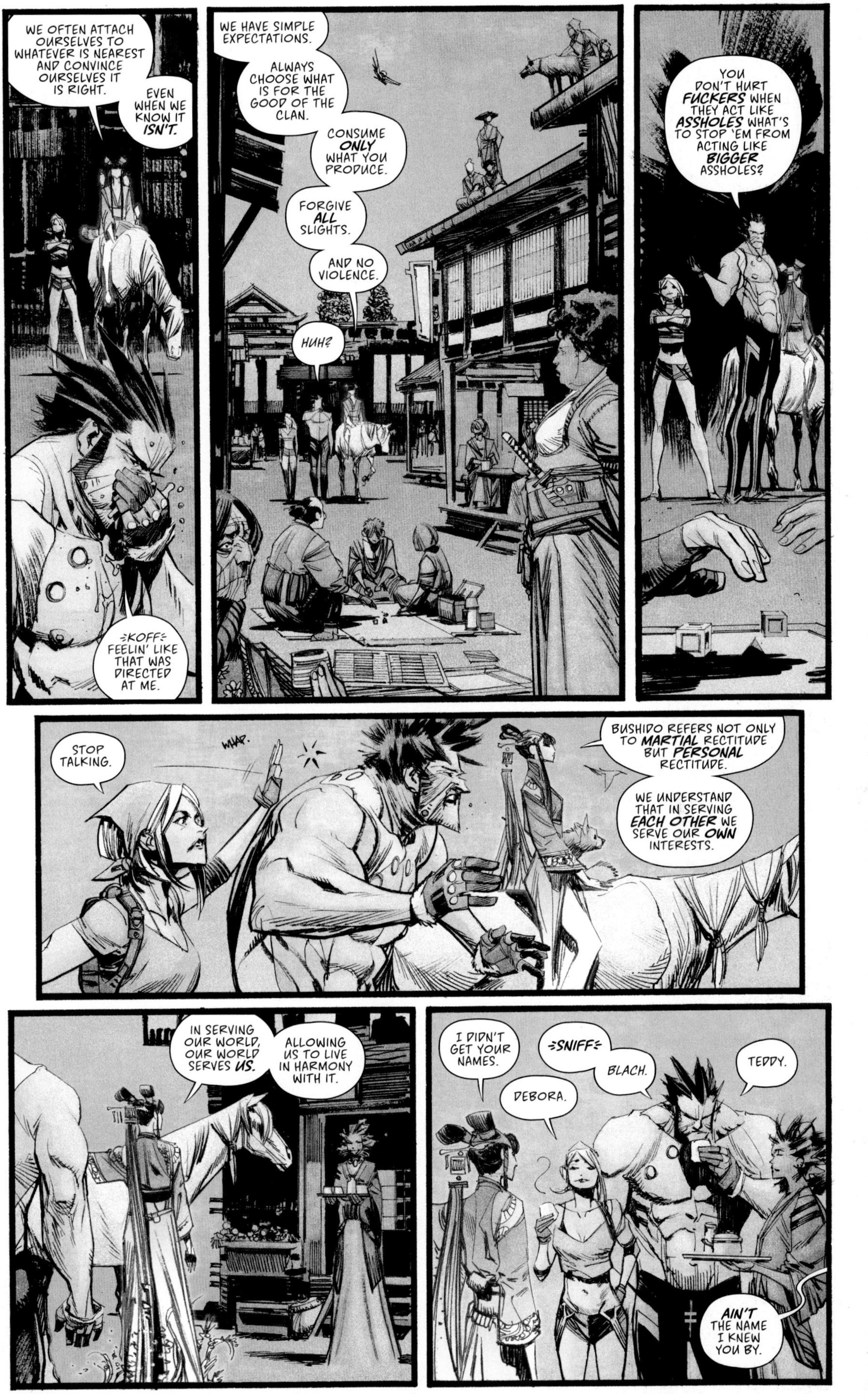
WE OFTEN ATTACH OURSELVES TO WHATEVER IS NEAREST AND CONVINCE OURSELVES IT IS RIGHT.
EVEN WHEN WE KNOW IT ISN'T.
KOFF FEELIN' LIKE THAT WAS DIRECTED AT ME.
WE HAVE SIMPLE EXPECTATIONS.
ALWAYS CHOOSE WHAT IS FOR THE GOOD OF THE CLAN.
CONSUME ONLY WHAT YOU PRODUCE.
FORGIVE ALL SLIGHTS.
AND NO VIOLENCE.
HUH?
YOU DON'T HURT FUCKERS WHEN THEY ACT LIKE ASSHOLES WHAT'S TO STOP 'EM FROM ACTING LIKE BIGGER ASSHOLES?
STOP TALKING.
WHAP.
BUSHIDO REFERS NOT ONLY TO MARTIAL RECTITUDE BUT PERSONAL RECTITUDE.
WE UNDERSTAND THAT IN SERVING EACH OTHER WE SERVE OUR OWN INTERESTS.
IN SERVING OUR WORLD, OUR WORLD SERVES US.
ALLOWING US TO LIVE IN HARMONY WITH IT.
I DIDN'T GET YOUR NAMES.
DEBORA.
SNIFF
BLACH.
TEDDY.
AIN'T THE NAME I KNEW YOU BY.

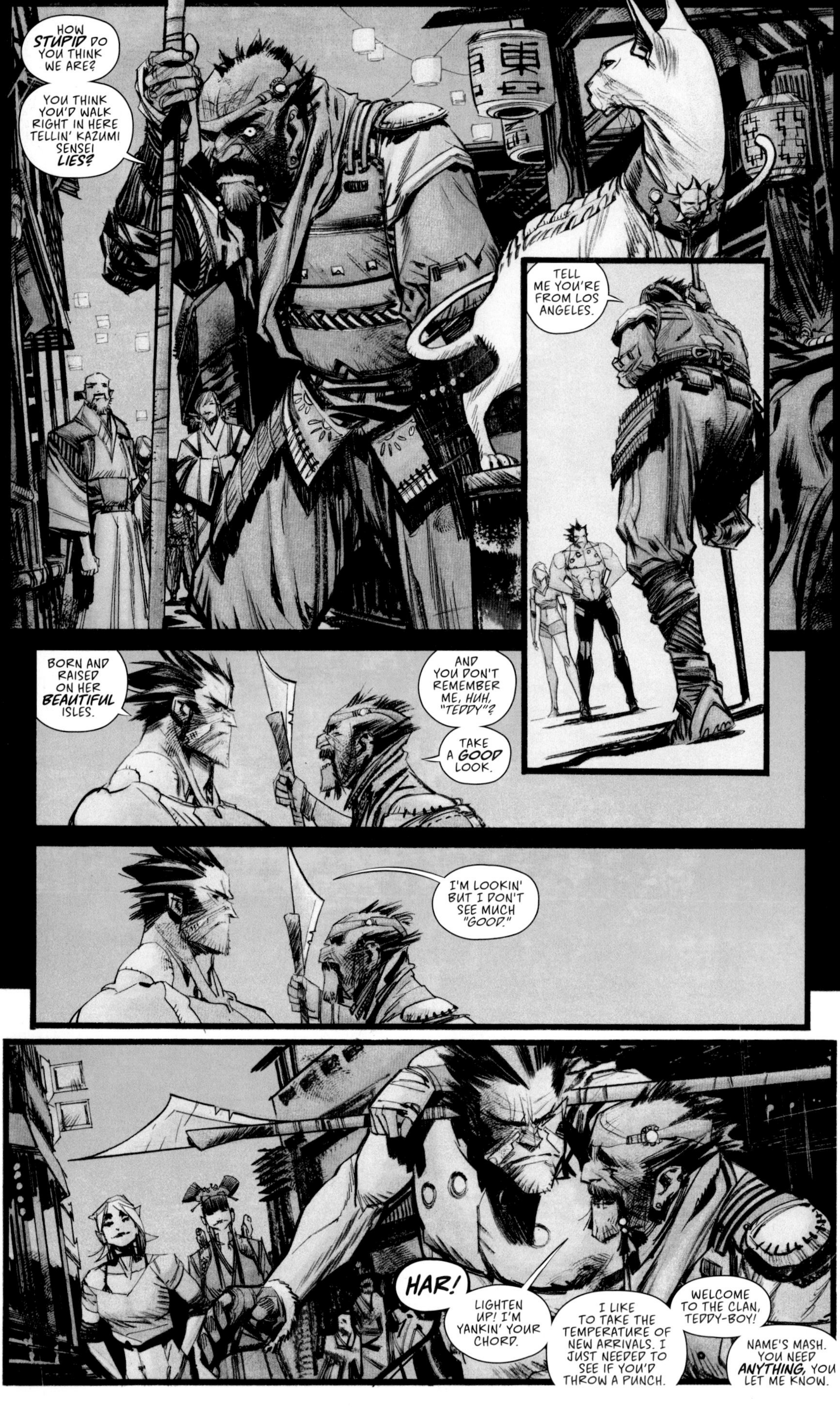
HOW **STUPID** DO YOU THINK WE ARE?
YOU THINK YOU'D WALK RIGHT IN HERE TELLIN' KAZUMI SENSEI **LIES?**
TELL ME YOU'RE FROM LOS ANGELES.
BORN AND RAISED ON HER **BEAUTIFUL** ISLES.
AND YOU DON'T REMEMBER ME, *HUH,* *"TEDDY"*?
TAKE A **GOOD** LOOK.
I'M LOOKIN' BUT I DON'T SEE MUCH *"GOOD."*
HAR!
LIGHTEN UP! I'M YANKIN' YOUR CHORD.
I LIKE TO TAKE THE TEMPERATURE OF NEW ARRIVALS. I JUST NEEDED TO SEE IF YOU'D THROW A PUNCH.
WELCOME TO THE CLAN, TEDDY-BOY!
NAME'S MASH. YOU NEED **ANYTHING,** YOU LET ME KNOW.

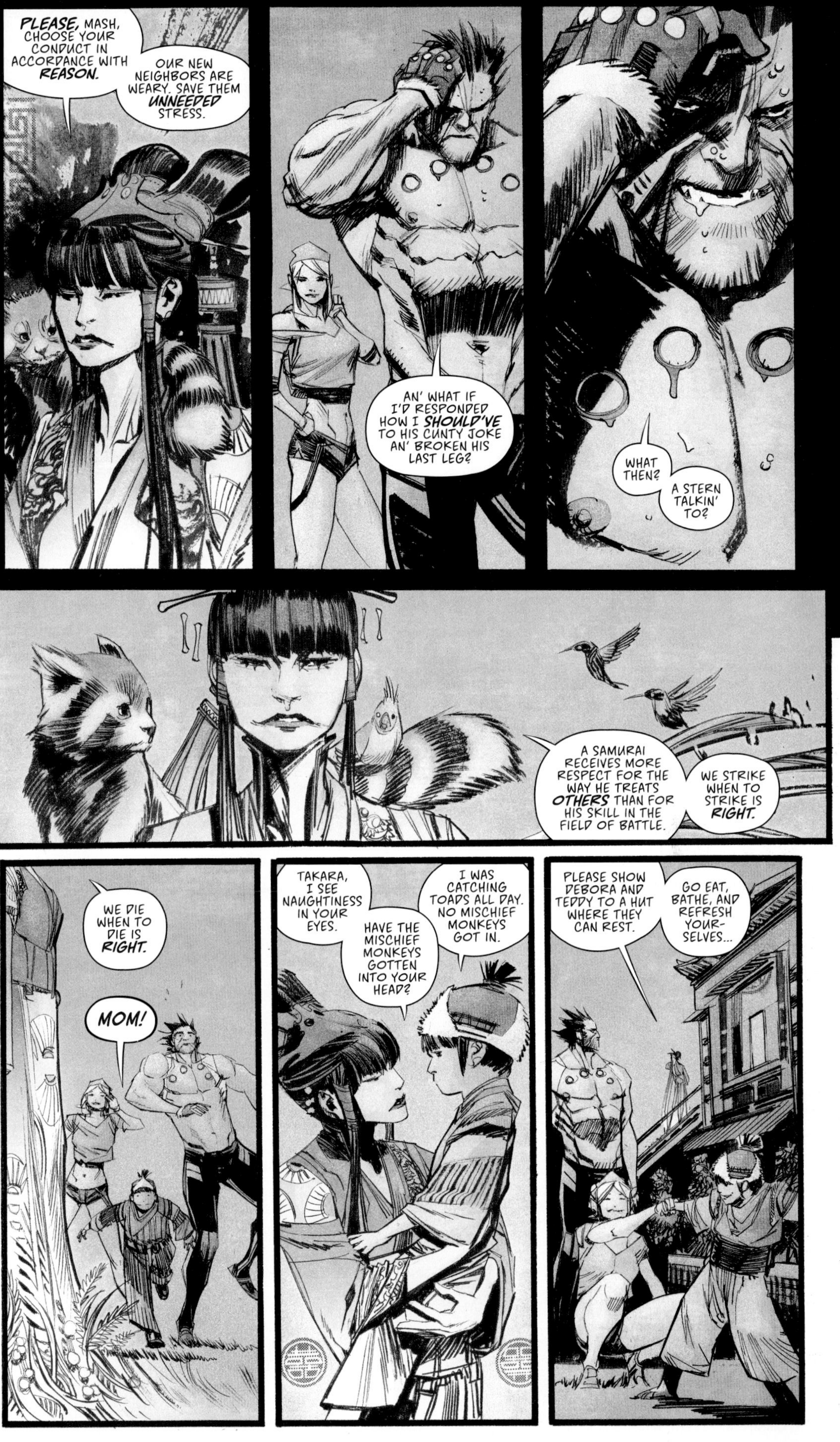
PLEASE, MASH, CHOOSE YOUR CONDUCT IN ACCORDANCE WITH REASON.
OUR NEW NEIGHBORS ARE WEARY. SAVE THEM UNNEEDED STRESS.
AN' WHAT IF I'D RESPONDED HOW I SHOULD'VE TO HIS CUNTY JOKE AN' BROKEN HIS LAST LEG?
WHAT THEN?
A STERN TALKIN' TO?
A SAMURAI RECEIVES MORE RESPECT FOR THE WAY HE TREATS OTHERS THAN FOR HIS SKILL IN THE FIELD OF BATTLE.
WE STRIKE WHEN TO STRIKE IS RIGHT.
WE DIE WHEN TO DIE IS RIGHT.
MOM!
TAKARA, I SEE NAUGHTINESS IN YOUR EYES.
HAVE THE MISCHIEF MONKEYS GOTTEN INTO YOUR HEAD?
I WAS CATCHING TOADS ALL DAY. NO MISCHIEF MONKEYS GOT IN.
PLEASE SHOW DEBORA AND TEDDY TO A HUT WHERE THEY CAN REST.
GO EAT, BATHE, AND REFRESH YOUR-SELVES...

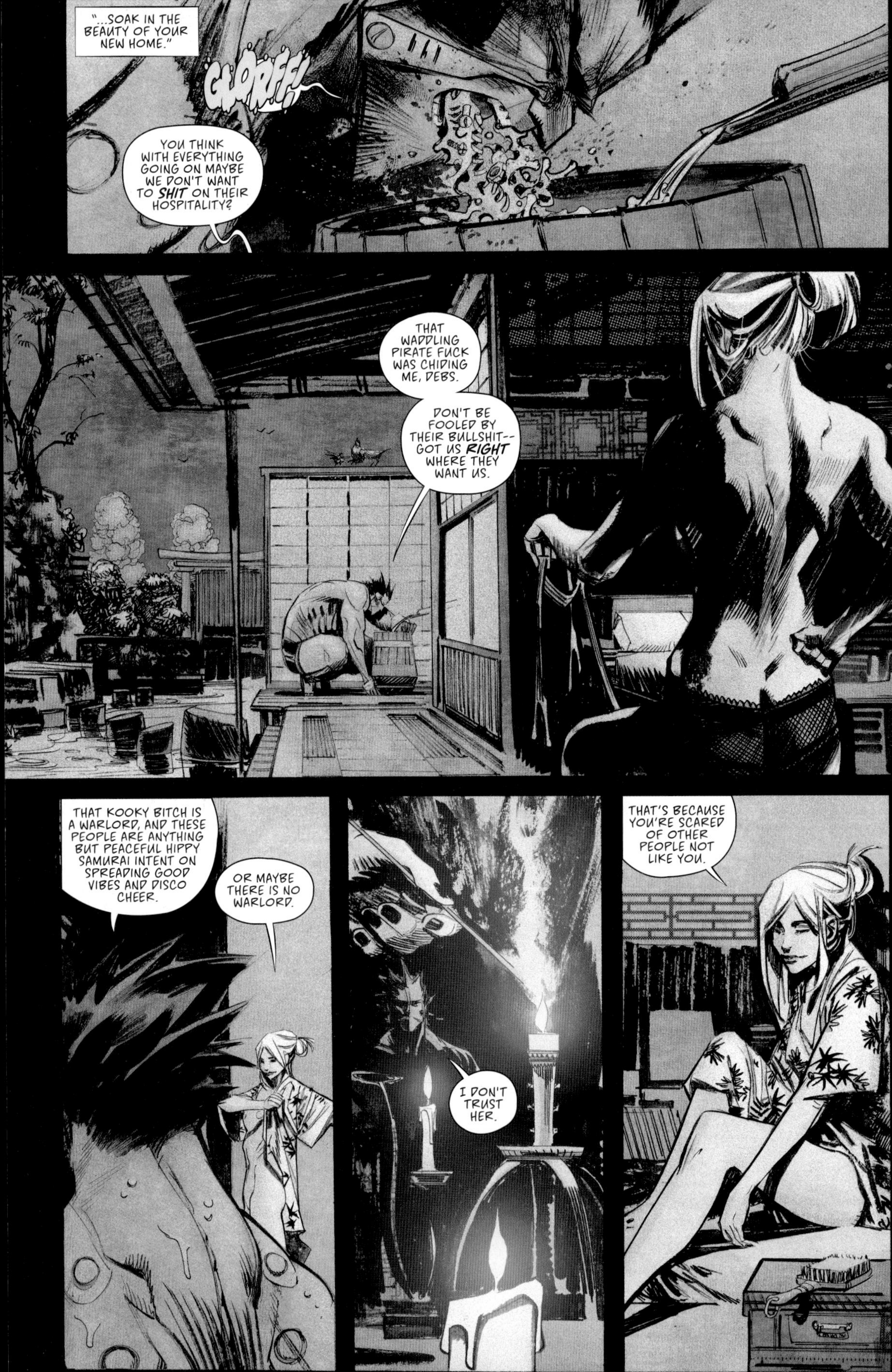

"...SOAK IN THE BEAUTY OF YOUR NEW HOME."
GLORFF!
YOU THINK WITH EVERYTHING GOING ON MAYBE WE DON'T WANT TO SHIT ON THEIR HOSPITALITY?
THAT WADDLING PIRATE FUCK WAS CHIDING ME, DEBS.
DON'T BE FOOLED BY THEIR BULLSHIT-- GOT US RIGHT WHERE THEY WANT US.
THAT KOOKY BITCH IS A WARLORD, AND THESE PEOPLE ARE ANYTHING BUT PEACEFUL HIPPY SAMURAI INTENT ON SPREADING GOOD VIBES AND DISCO CHEER.
OR MAYBE THERE IS NO WARLORD.
I DON'T TRUST HER.
THAT'S BECAUSE YOU'RE SCARED OF OTHER PEOPLE NOT LIKE YOU.

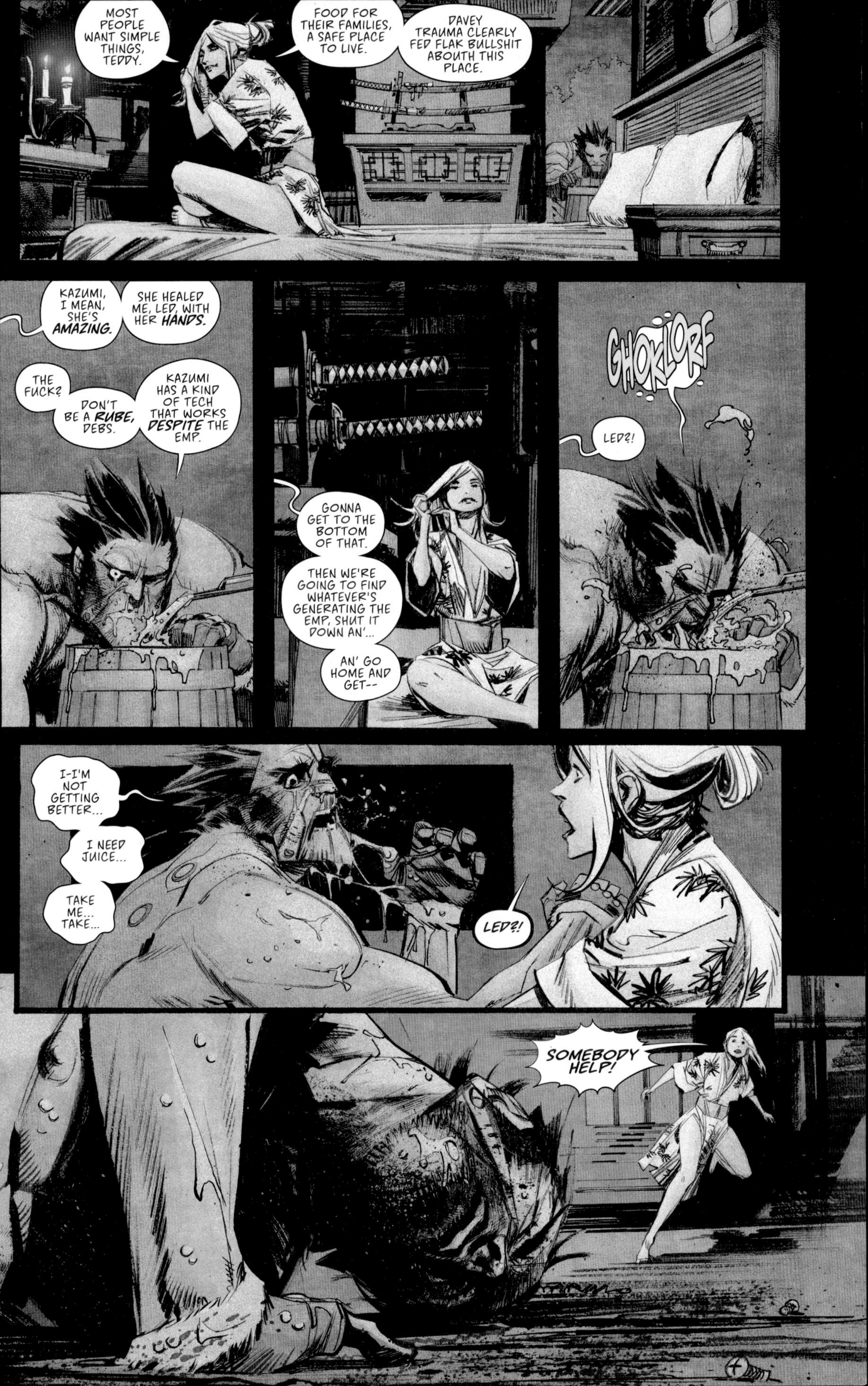
MOST PEOPLE WANT SIMPLE THINGS, TEDDY.
FOOD FOR THEIR FAMILIES, A SAFE PLACE TO LIVE.
DAVEY TRAUMA CLEARLY FED FLAK BULLSHIT ABOUTH THIS PLACE.
KAZUMI, I MEAN, SHE'S AMAZING.
SHE HEALED ME, LED, WITH HER HANDS.
THE FUCK?
DON'T BE A RUBE, DEBS.
KAZUMI HAS A KIND OF TECH THAT WORKS DESPITE THE EMP.
GONNA GET TO THE BOTTOM OF THAT.
THEN WE'RE GOING TO FIND WHATEVER'S GENERATING THE EMP, SHUT IT DOWN AN'...
AN' GO HOME AND GET--
GHOKLORF
LED?!
I-I'M NOT GETTING BETTER...
I NEED JUICE...
TAKE ME... TAKE...
LED?!
SOMEBODY HELP!

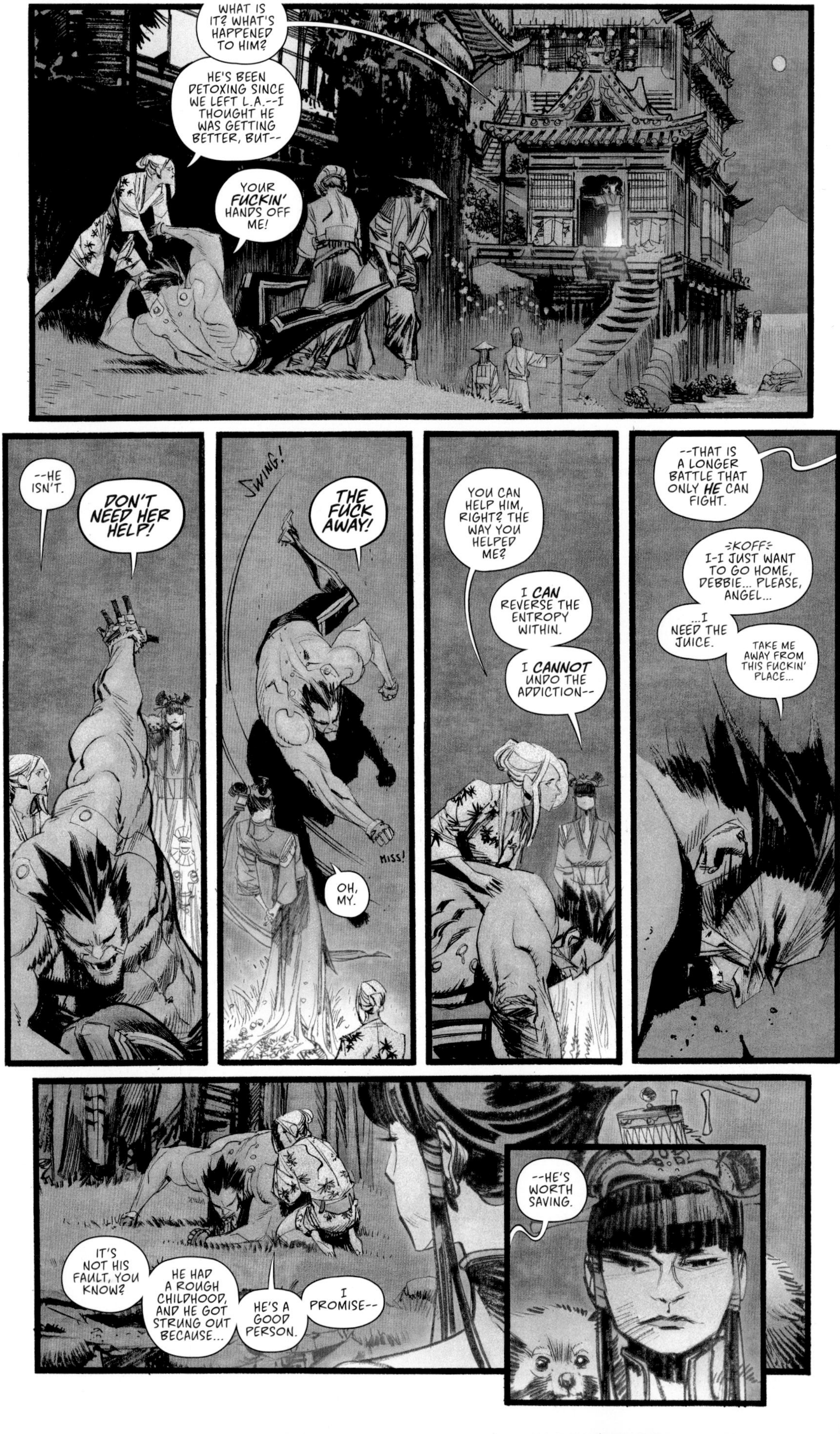
WHAT IS IT? WHAT'S HAPPENED TO HIM?
HE'S BEEN DETOXING SINCE WE LEFT L.A.--I THOUGHT HE WAS GETTING BETTER, BUT--
YOUR FUCKIN' HANDS OFF ME!
--HE ISN'T.
DON'T NEED HER HELP!
SWING!
THE FUCK AWAY!
MISS!
OH, MY.
YOU CAN HELP HIM, RIGHT? THE WAY YOU HELPED ME?
I CAN REVERSE THE ENTROPY WITHIN.
I CANNOT UNDO THE ADDICTION--
--THAT IS A LONGER BATTLE THAT ONLY HE CAN FIGHT.
KOFF
I-I JUST WANT TO GO HOME, DEBBIE... PLEASE, ANGEL...
...I NEED THE JUICE.
TAKE ME AWAY FROM THIS FUCKIN' PLACE...
IT'S NOT HIS FAULT, YOU KNOW?
HE HAD A ROUGH CHILDHOOD, AND HE GOT STRUNG OUT BECAUSE...
HE'S A GOOD PERSON.
I PROMISE--
--HE'S WORTH SAVING.

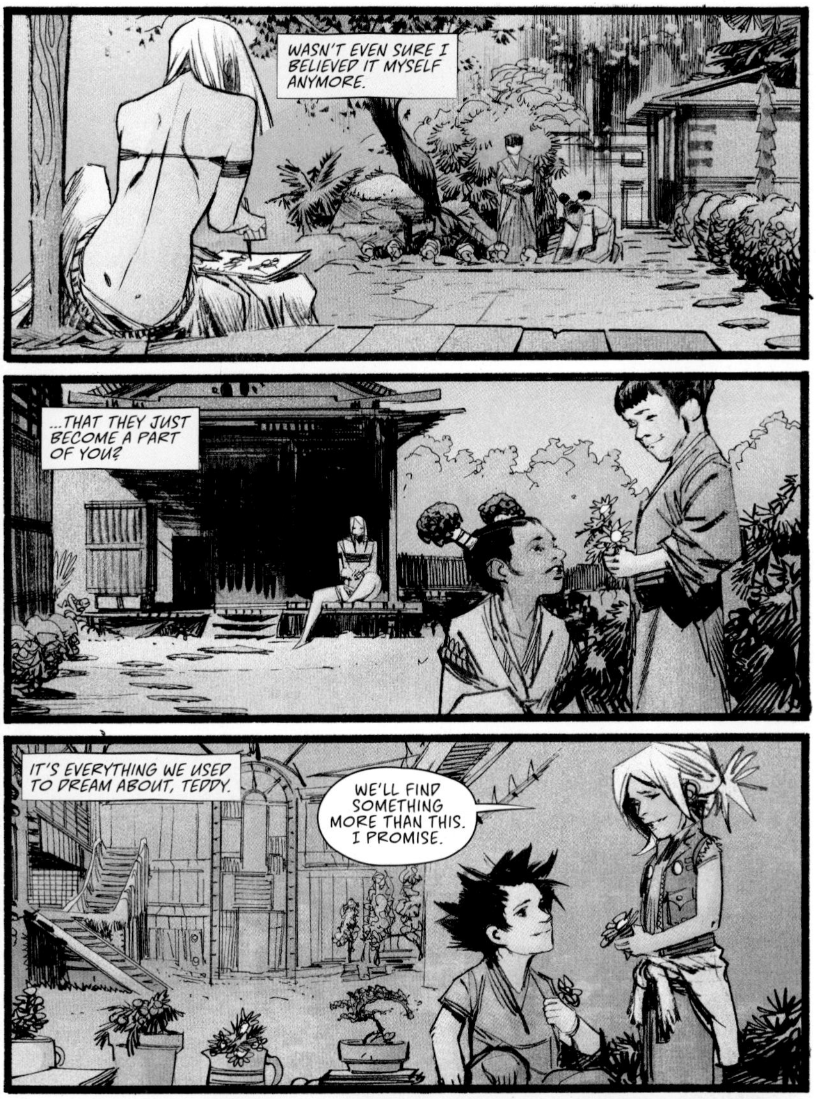
WASN'T EVEN SURE I BELIEVED IT MYSELF ANYMORE.
...THAT THEY JUST BECOME A PART OF YOU?
IT'S EVERYTHING WE USED TO DREAM ABOUT, TEDDY.
WE'LL FIND SOMETHING MORE THAN THIS. I PROMISE.

HE'D PUSHED ME AS FAR AS I COULD TAKE AND IF HE HADN'T GOTTEN BETTER... WELL...

THAT WOULD HAVE BEEN THAT.

HE'S BEEN IN A DEEP SLEEP FOR TWO WEEKS SINCE KAZUMI TOUCHED HIM. GIVEN ME TIME TO THINK.

YOU LOVE SOMEONE LONG ENOUGH YOU BEGIN TO WONDER, "WHY?" IS IT JUST FAMILIARITY? THE FACT THEY'VE BEEN FIXTURES IN YOUR LITTLE STORY FOR LONG ENOUGH...

OR DO WE FEAR CHANGE SO MUCH WE PRETEND?

THE PEOPLE HERE DON'T PRETEND. THEY'RE GENUINELY KIND AND GENEROUS TO EACH OTHER.

KAZUMI BELIEVES THAT GIVEN A CHOICE PEOPLE WILL BEND TOWARDS THE LIGHT.

SEEING THIS PLACE, IT'S HARD TO ARGUE.

THE KIND OF PLACE KIDS DREAM OF ESCAPING TO.

EVEN IF THERE'S NO REAL HOPE THAT THEY'LL EVER FIND IT.

WHICH MAKES THIS ALL THE MORE AMAZING.

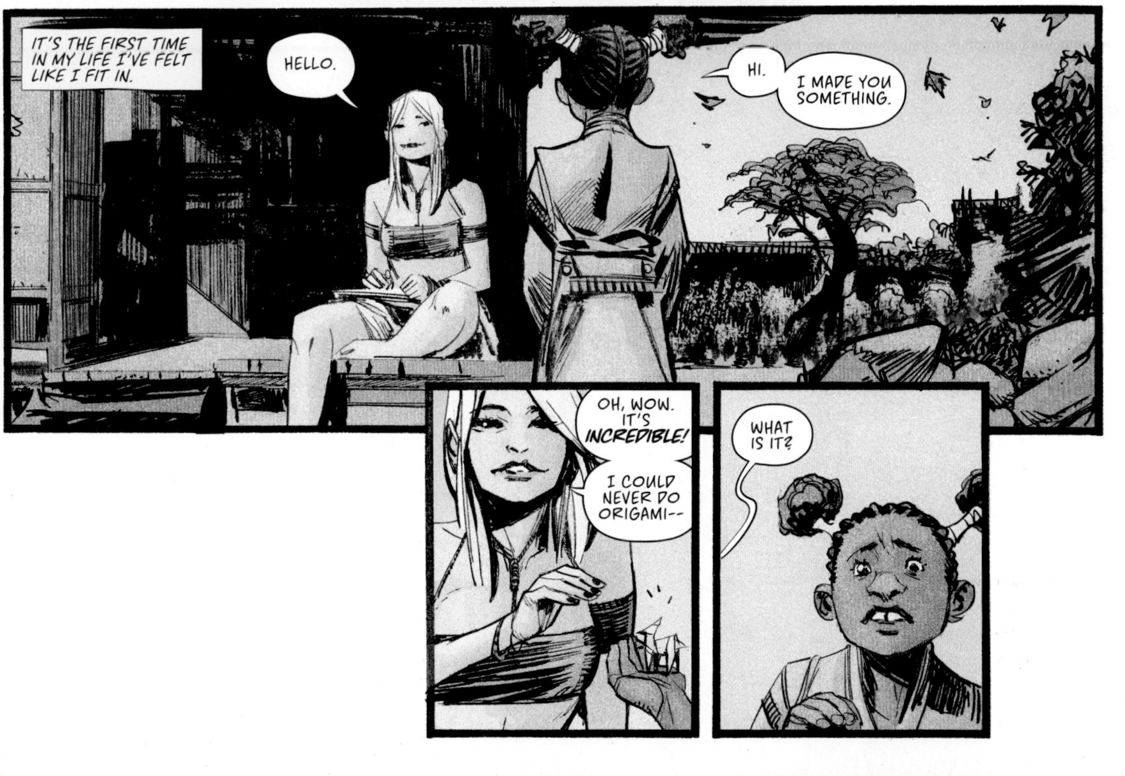
IT'S THE FIRST TIME IN MY LIFE I'VE FELT LIKE I FIT IN.
HELLO.
HI.
I MADE YOU SOMETHING.
OH, WOW. IT'S ***INCREDIBLE!***
I COULD NEVER DO ORIGAMI--
WHAT IS IT?

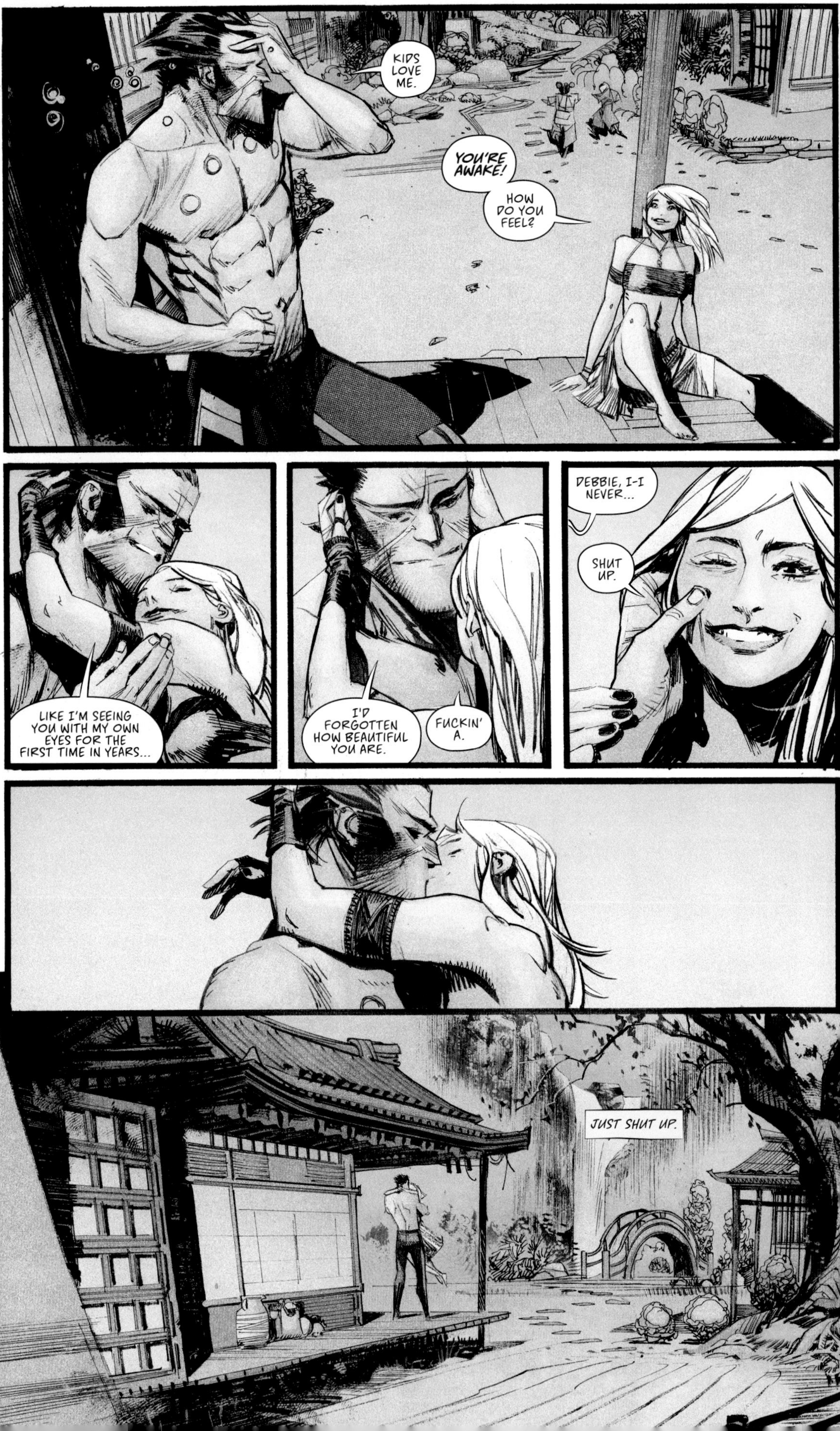

KIDS LOVE ME.
YOU'RE AWAKE!
HOW DO YOU FEEL?
LIKE I'M SEEING YOU WITH MY OWN EYES FOR THE FIRST TIME IN YEARS...
I'D FORGOTTEN HOW BEAUTIFUL YOU ARE.
FUCKIN' A.
DEBBIE, I-I NEVER...
SHUT UP.
JUST SHUT UP.

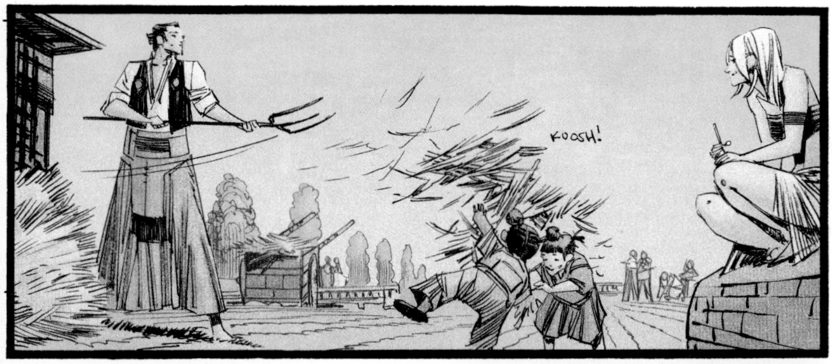
KOOSH!

WHATEVER KAZUMI DID, IT **WORKED.**
HE'S BETTER WEEK BY WEEK.

HE GOES TO BED WITHOUT SLEEPING PILLS. HE WAKES WITHOUT CAFFEINE. NO MORE OUTBURSTS. NO MORE RAGE.

LED DENT IS **GONE.**

FOR THE FIRST TIME, I GET TO SEE THE MAN TEDDY SHOULD HAVE BECOME.

EVERYTHING I KNEW HE'D BE.

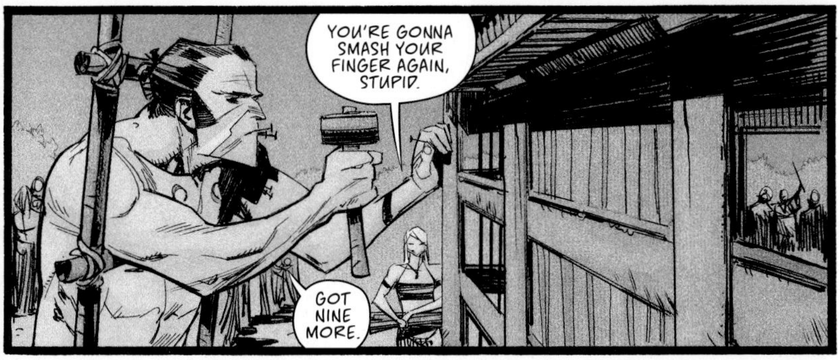
YOU'RE GONNA SMASH YOUR FINGER AGAIN, STUPID.
GOT NINE MORE.

HE'S STILL AN ADOLESCENT, BUT IN A GOOD WAY. THE KIND THAT HAS SOME WONDERMENT LEFT, SOME AWE.

BUT STILL, I CAN SEE THE JITTERS. HE CAN'T HIDE HOW HE FIGHTS THE ADDICTION EVERY DAY.

ON GOOD DAYS, HE'S PATIENT, ABLE TO GET PAST IT AND FOCUS ON HELPING AROUND TOWN.

ON BAD DAYS...

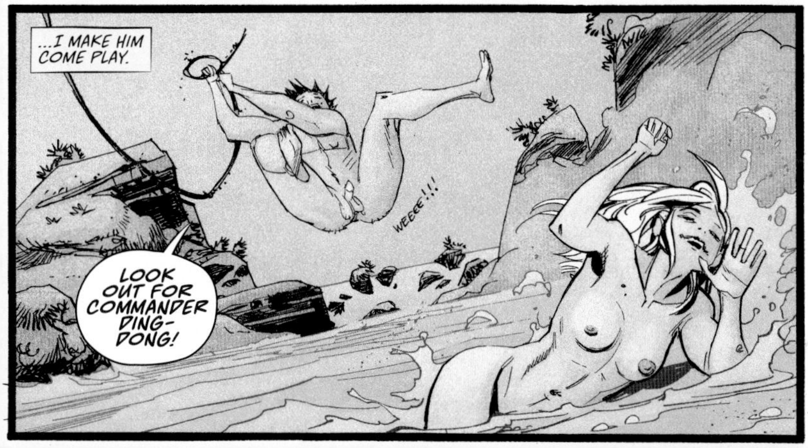
...I MAKE HIM COME PLAY.
LOOK OUT FOR COMMANDER DING-DONG!

WE TAKE LONG WALKS AND TALK.

WE SWIM IN THE CREEK.

SUNBATH ON THE SHORE.

WE RUN NAKED THROUGH THE FOREST.

AND WE FUCK.

A LOT.

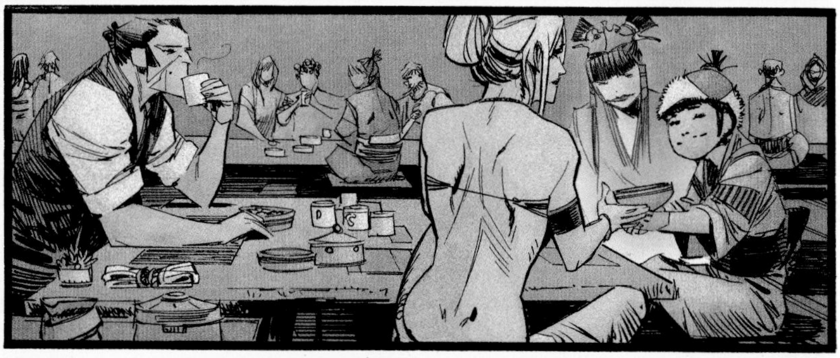

TO BE ACCEPTED INTO THIS COMMUNITY--IT FIXES SO MANY OF THE CRACKS.

WE GROW AND PREPARE OUR OWN FOOD.

WE EAT TOGETHER AND LAUGH.

NO ONE DISTRACTED BY PHONES, NO ONE POLITICKING FOR MONEY OR STATURE. NO LOUD EGOS.

NO ONE MORE IMPORTANT THAN ANYONE ELSE...

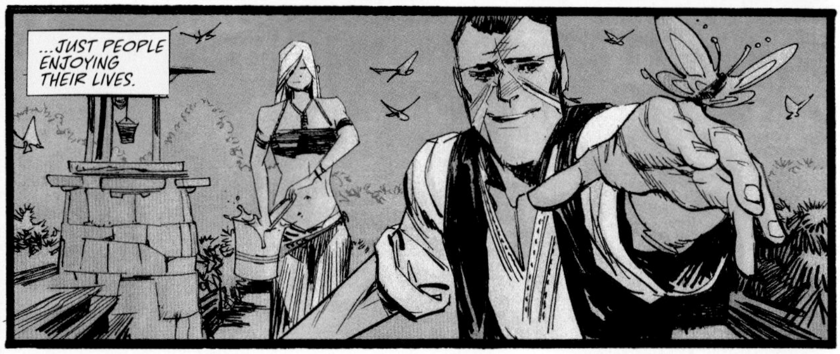
...JUST PEOPLE ENJOYING THEIR LIVES.

HOW SWEET THE SIMPLICITY IS.

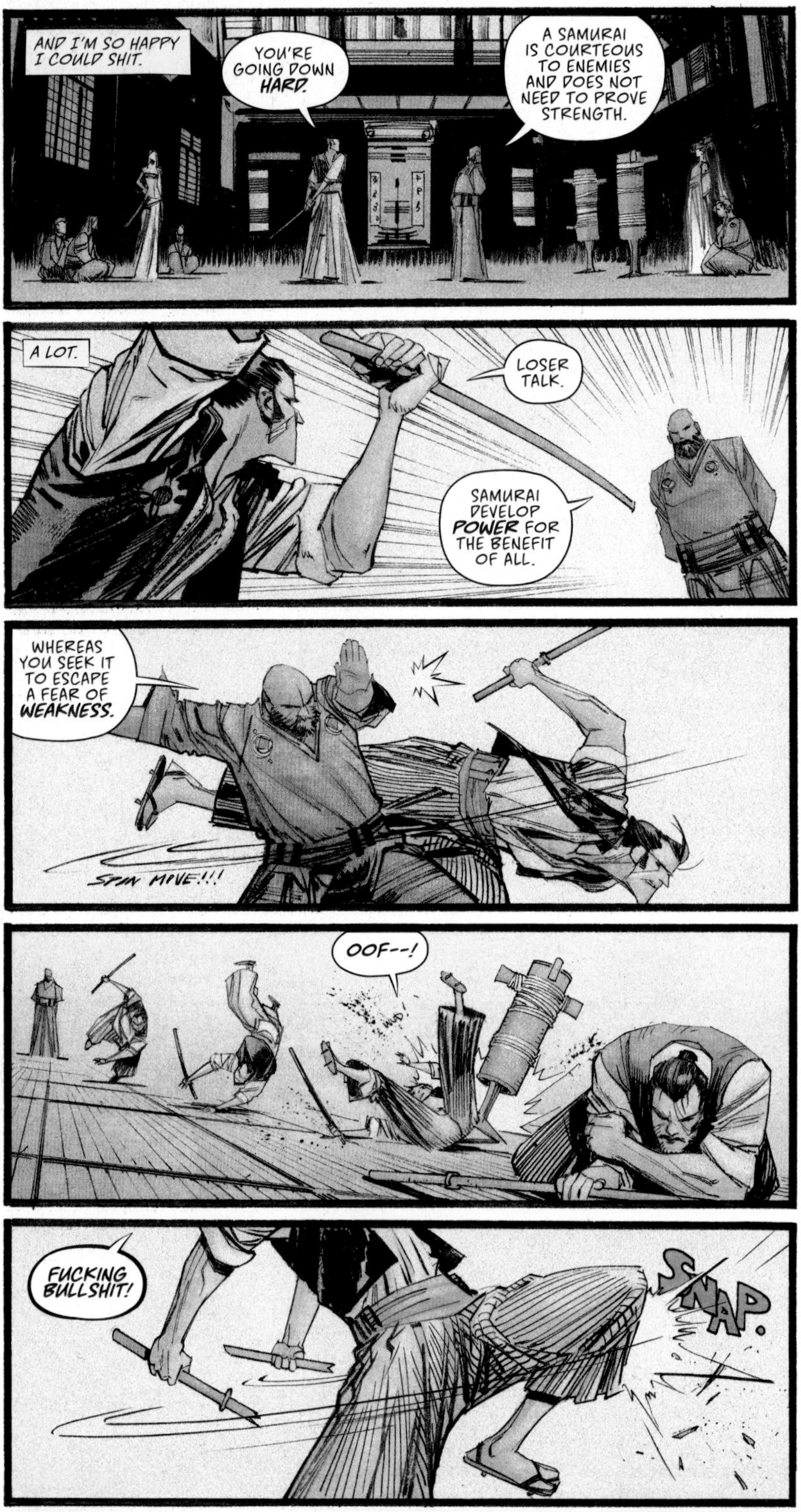
AND I'M SO HAPPY I COULD SHIT.
YOU'RE GOING DOWN **HARD.**
A SAMURAI IS COURTEOUS TO ENEMIES AND DOES NOT NEED TO PROVE STRENGTH.
A LOT.
LOSER TALK.
SAMURAI DEVELOP **POWER** FOR THE BENEFIT OF ALL.
WHEREAS YOU SEEK IT TO ESCAPE A FEAR OF **WEAKNESS.**
SPIN MOVE!!!
OOF--!
FUCKING BULLSHIT!
SNAP.

THEY'RE TEACHING US USEFUL THINGS LIKE HOW TO RIDE A HORSE AND USE A SWORD.

BUT WITHOUT HIS TECH, LED IS WEAKER.

LEARNING ANYTHING TAKES HIM MUCH LONGER NOW.

HE CAN'T FOCUS.

FOR YEARS, THE NANOTECH DID ALL THE REMEMBERING FOR HIM.

NOW HIS MIND IS A MUSCLE IN ATROPHY.

HIS BODY CLUMSY AND SLOW.

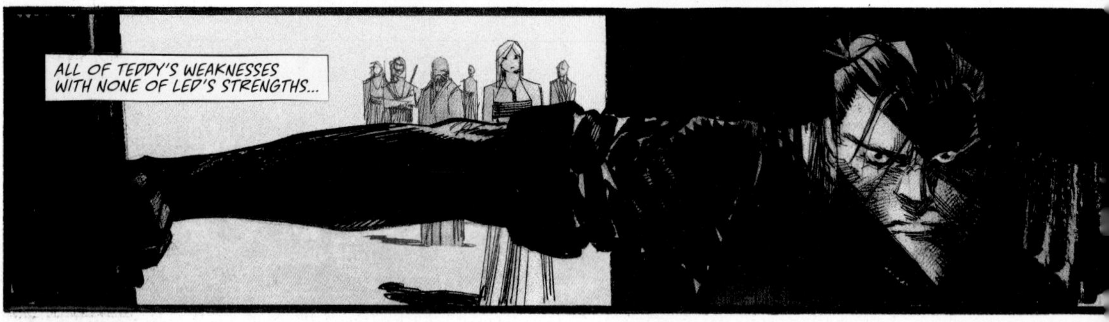
ALL OF TEDDY'S WEAKNESSES WITH NONE OF LED'S STRENGTHS...

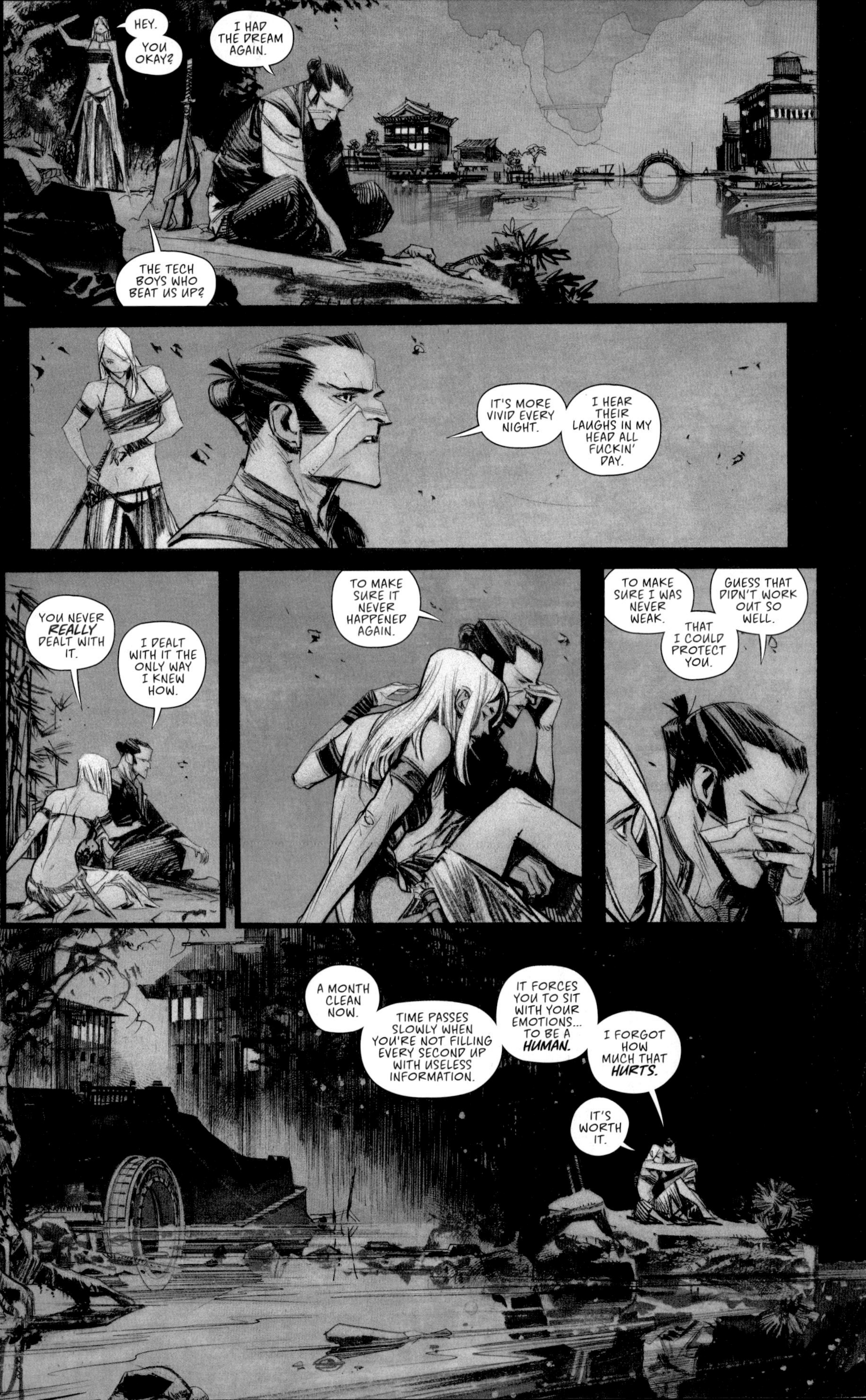
HEY.
YOU OKAY?
I HAD THE DREAM AGAIN.
THE TECH BOYS WHO BEAT US UP?
IT'S MORE VIVID EVERY NIGHT.
I HEAR THEIR LAUGHS IN MY HEAD ALL FUCKIN' DAY.
YOU NEVER **REALLY** DEALT WITH IT.
I DEALT WITH IT THE ONLY WAY I KNEW HOW.
TO MAKE SURE IT NEVER HAPPENED AGAIN.
TO MAKE SURE I WAS NEVER WEAK.
THAT I COULD PROTECT YOU.
GUESS THAT DIDN'T WORK OUT SO WELL.
A MONTH CLEAN NOW.
TIME PASSES SLOWLY WHEN YOU'RE NOT FILLING EVERY SECOND UP WITH USELESS INFORMATION.
IT FORCES YOU TO SIT WITH YOUR EMOTIONS... TO BE A **HUMAN.**
I FORGOT HOW MUCH THAT **HURTS.**
IT'S WORTH IT.

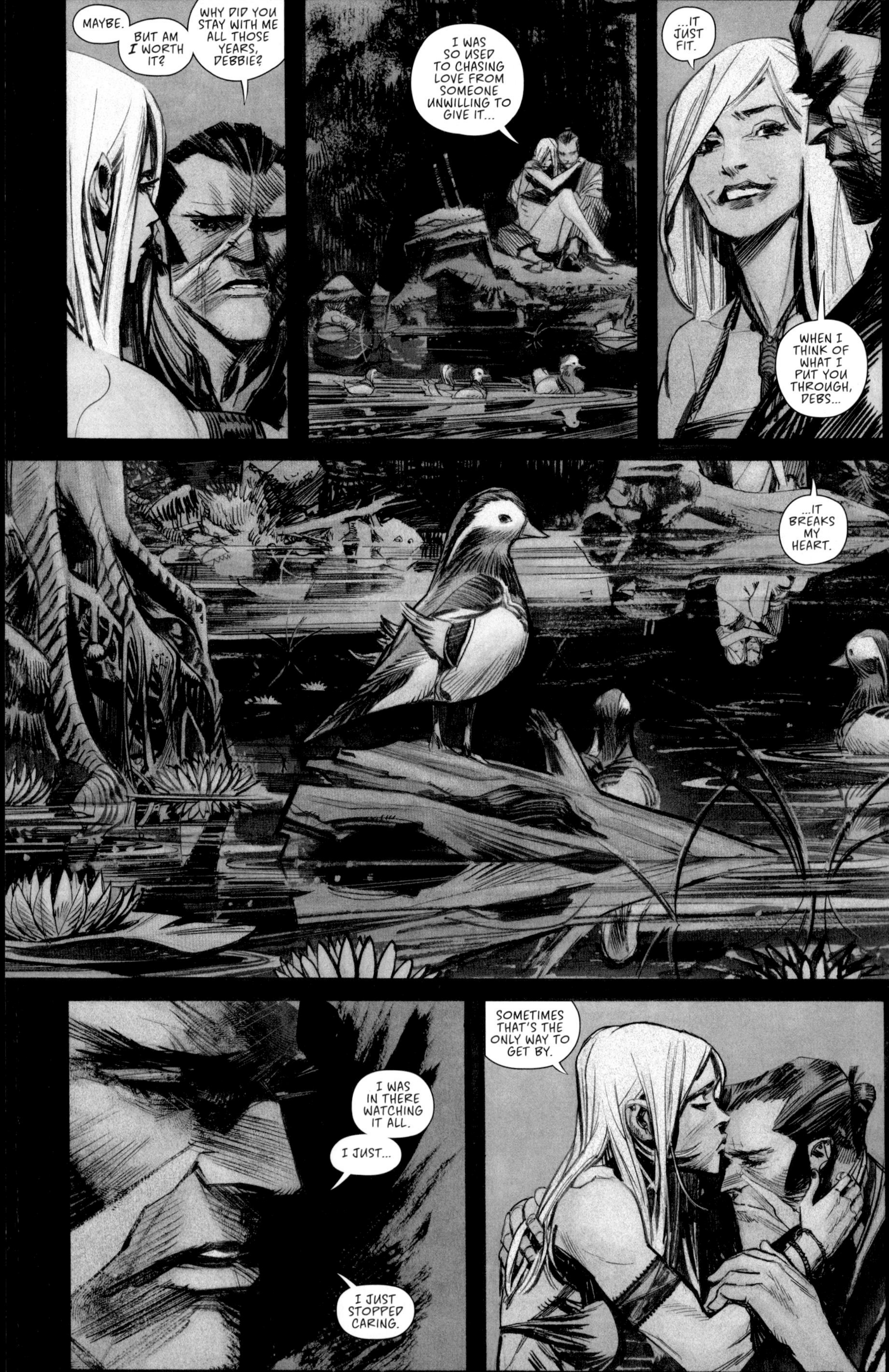
MAYBE.
BUT AM I WORTH IT?
WHY DID YOU STAY WITH ME ALL THOSE YEARS, DEBBIE?
I WAS SO USED TO CHASING LOVE FROM SOMEONE UNWILLING TO GIVE IT...
...IT JUST FIT.
WHEN I THINK OF WHAT I PUT YOU THROUGH, DEBS...
...IT BREAKS MY HEART.
I WAS IN THERE WATCHING IT ALL.
I JUST...
I JUST STOPPED CARING.
SOMETIMES THAT'S THE ONLY WAY TO GET BY.

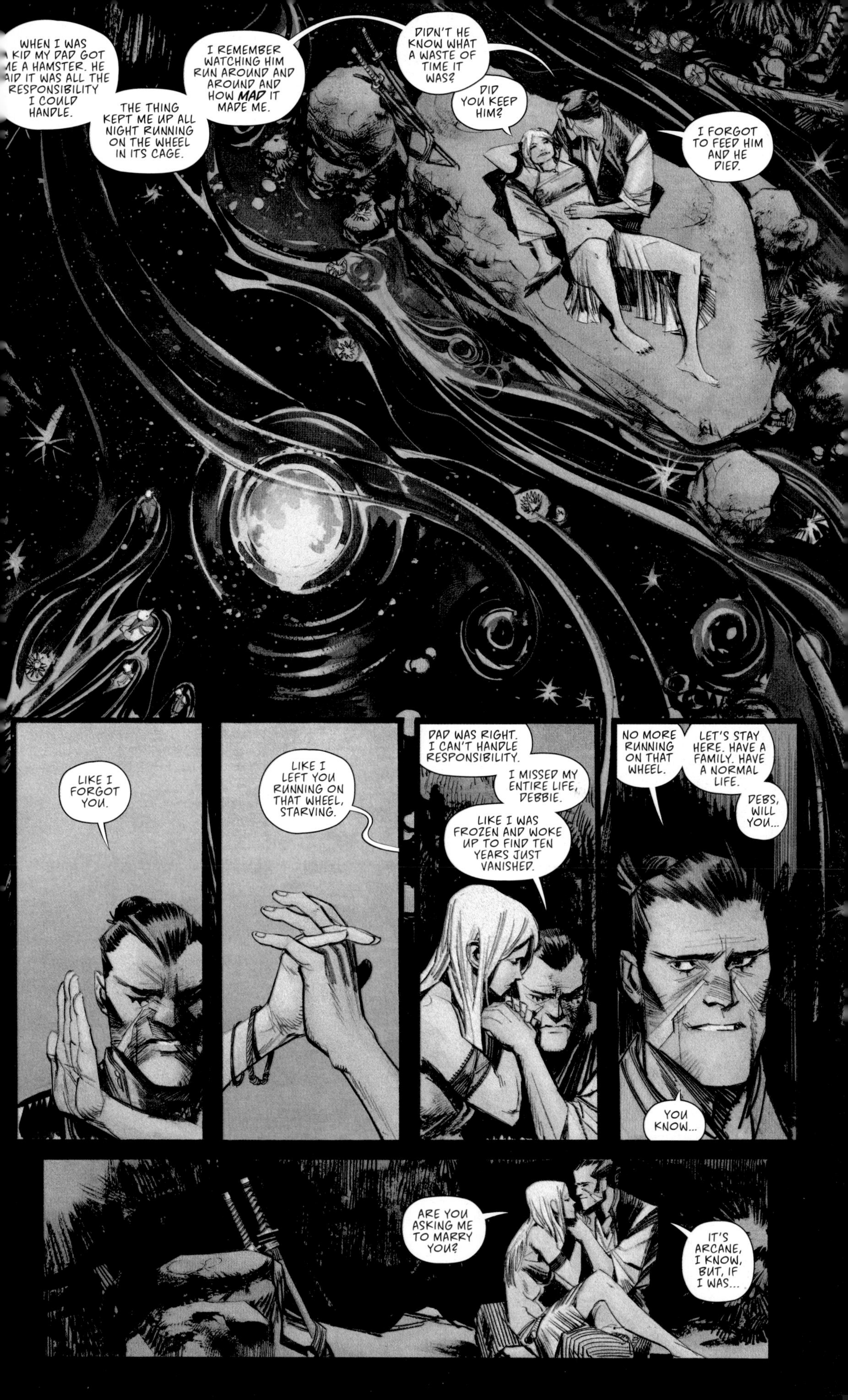
WHEN I WAS KID MY DAD GOT ME A HAMSTER. HE AID IT WAS ALL THE RESPONSIBILITY I COULD HANDLE.
THE THING KEPT ME UP ALL NIGHT RUNNING ON THE WHEEL IN ITS CAGE.
I REMEMBER WATCHING HIM RUN AROUND AND AROUND AND HOW **MAD** IT MADE ME.
DIDN'T HE KNOW WHAT A WASTE OF TIME IT WAS?
DID YOU KEEP HIM?
I FORGOT TO FEED HIM AND HE DIED.
LIKE I FORGOT YOU.
LIKE I LEFT YOU RUNNING ON THAT WHEEL, STARVING.
DAD WAS RIGHT. I CAN'T HANDLE RESPONSIBILITY.
I MISSED MY ENTIRE LIFE, DEBBIE.
LIKE I WAS FROZEN AND WOKE UP TO FIND TEN YEARS JUST VANISHED.
NO MORE RUNNING ON THAT WHEEL.
LET'S STAY HERE. HAVE A FAMILY. HAVE A NORMAL LIFE.
DEBS, WILL YOU...
YOU KNOW...
ARE YOU ASKING ME TO MARRY YOU?
IT'S ARCANE, I KNOW, BUT, IF I WAS...

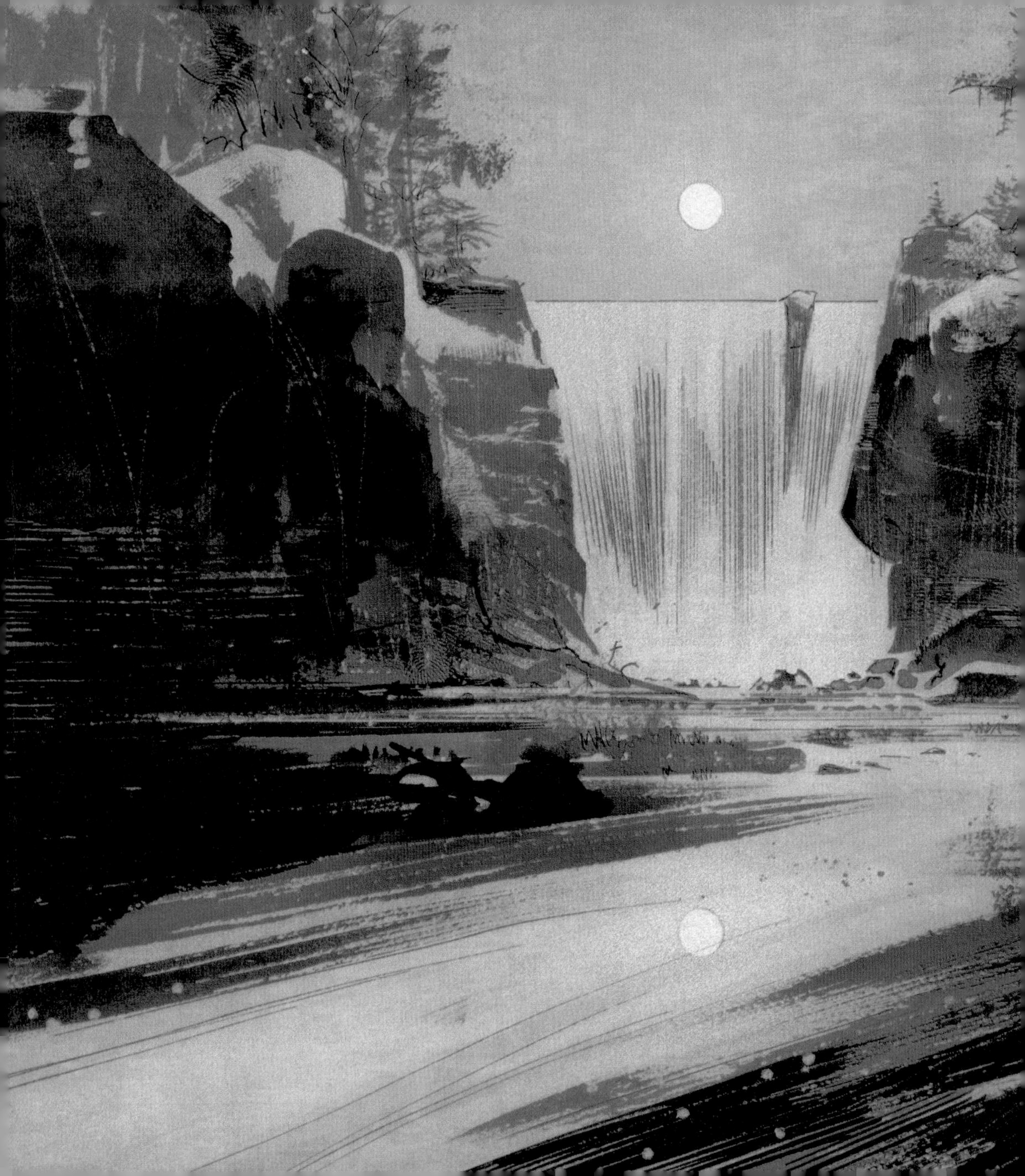

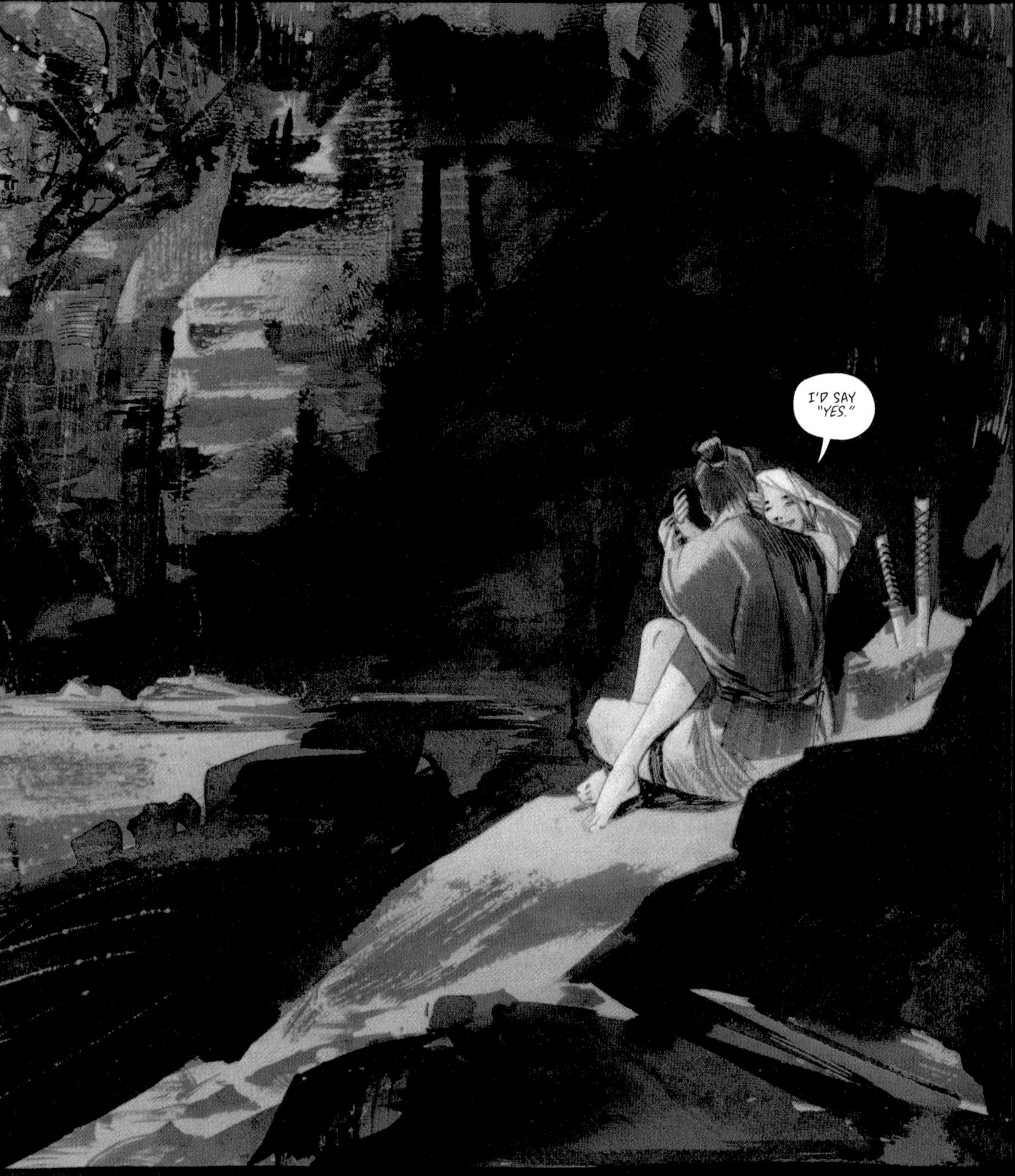
I'D SAY "YES."

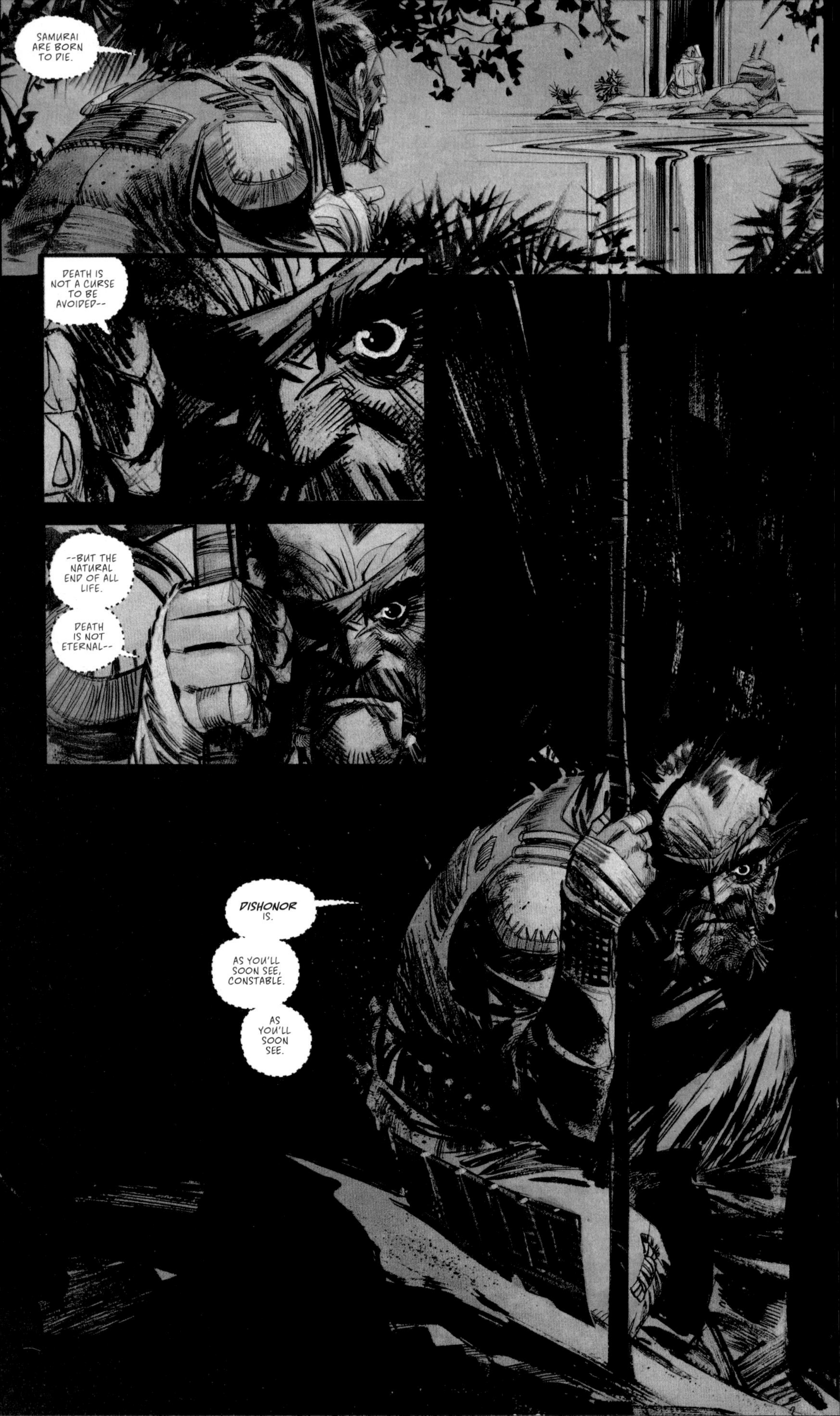
SAMURAI ARE BORN TO DIE.
DEATH IS NOT A CURSE TO BE AVOIDED--
--BUT THE NATURAL END OF ALL LIFE.
DEATH IS NOT ETERNAL--
DISHONOR IS.
AS YOU'LL SOON SEE, CONSTABLE.
AS YOU'LL SOON SEE.

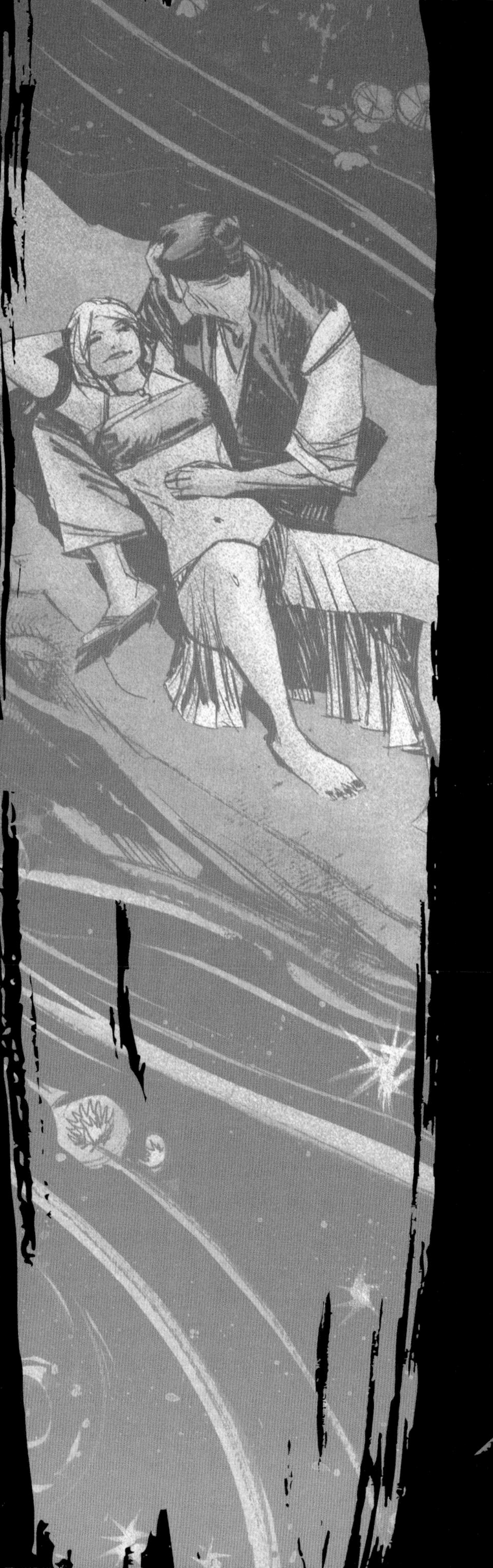

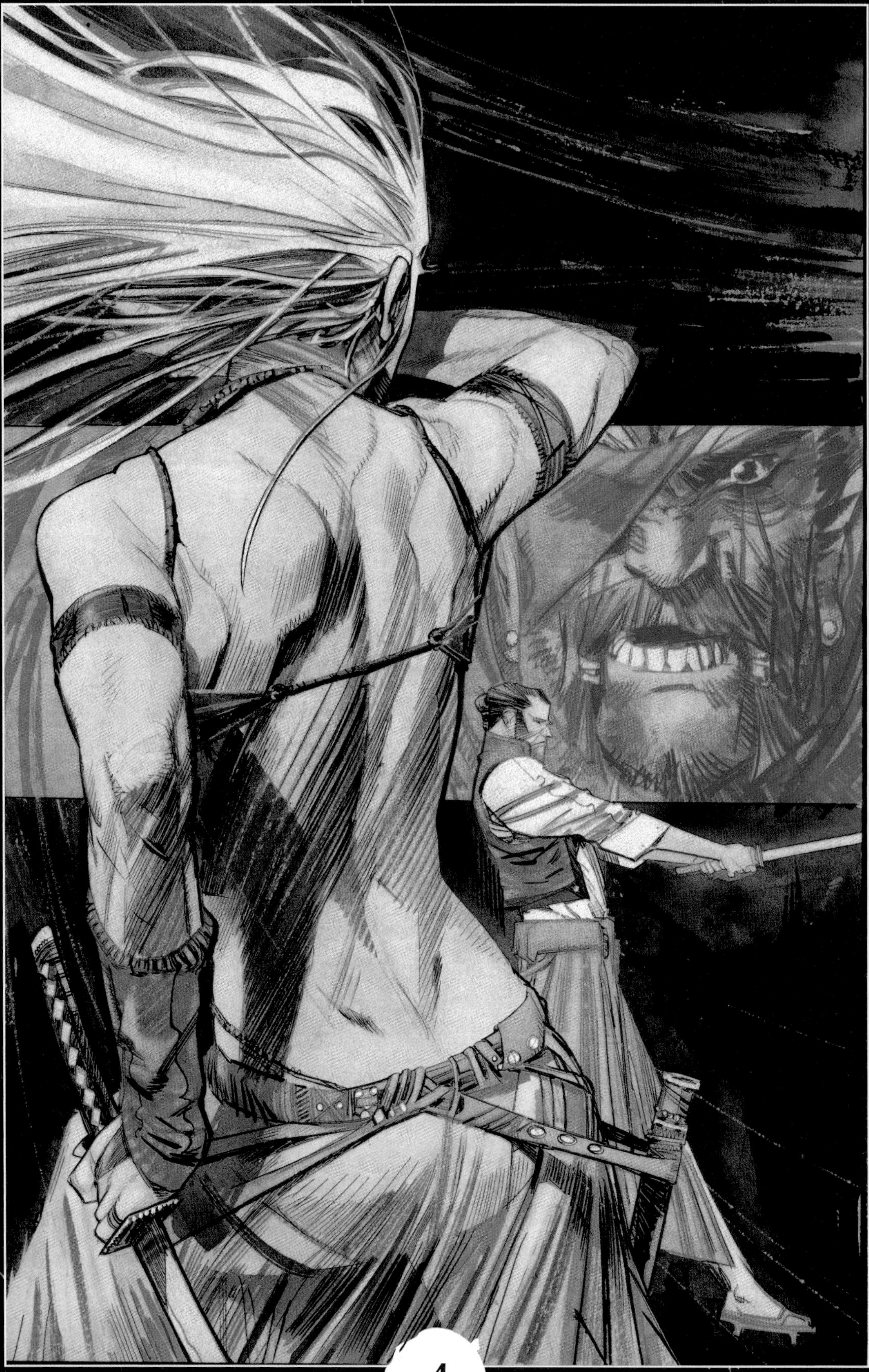

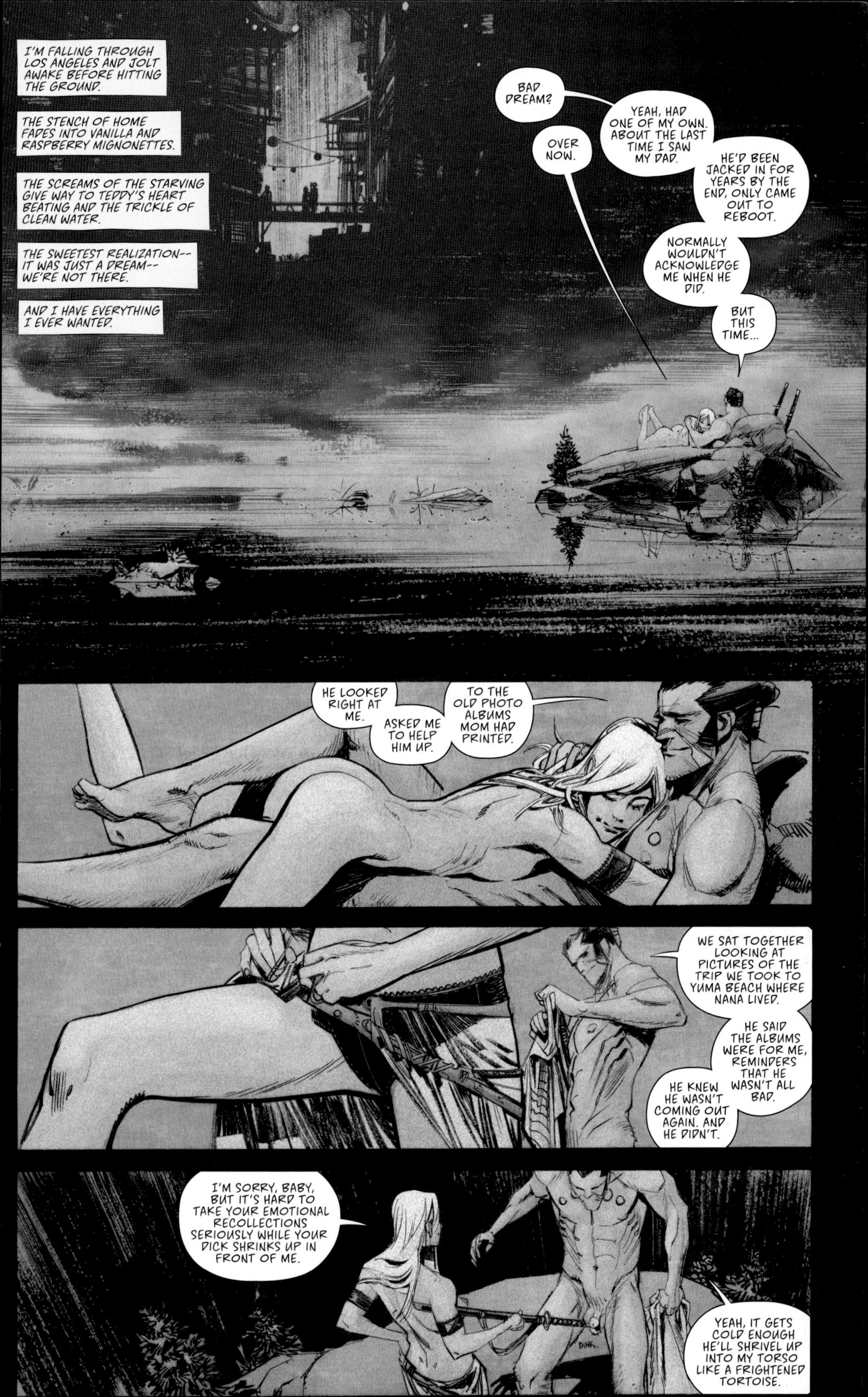
I'M FALLING THROUGH LOS ANGELES AND JOLT AWAKE BEFORE HITTING THE GROUND.
THE STENCH OF HOME FADES INTO VANILLA AND RASPBERRY MIGNONETTES.
THE SCREAMS OF THE STARVING GIVE WAY TO TEDDY'S HEART BEATING AND THE TRICKLE OF CLEAN WATER.
THE SWEETEST REALIZATION-- IT WAS JUST A DREAM-- WE'RE NOT THERE.
AND I HAVE EVERYTHING I EVER WANTED.
BAD DREAM?
OVER NOW.
YEAH, HAD ONE OF MY OWN. ABOUT THE LAST TIME I SAW MY DAD.
HE'D BEEN JACKED IN FOR YEARS BY THE END, ONLY CAME OUT TO REBOOT.
NORMALLY WOULDN'T ACKNOWLEDGE ME WHEN HE DID.
BUT THIS TIME...
HE LOOKED RIGHT AT ME.
ASKED ME TO HELP HIM UP.
TO THE OLD PHOTO ALBUMS MOM HAD PRINTED.
WE SAT TOGETHER LOOKING AT PICTURES OF THE TRIP WE TOOK TO YUMA BEACH WHERE NANA LIVED.
HE SAID THE ALBUMS WERE FOR ME, REMINDERS THAT HE WASN'T ALL BAD.
HE KNEW HE WASN'T COMING OUT AGAIN. AND HE DIDN'T.
I'M SORRY, BABY, BUT IT'S HARD TO TAKE YOUR EMOTIONAL RECOLLECTIONS SERIOUSLY WHILE YOUR DICK SHRINKS UP IN FRONT OF ME.
YEAH, IT GETS COLD ENOUGH HE'LL SHRIVEL UP INTO MY TORSO LIKE A FRIGHTENED TORTOISE.
DINK.

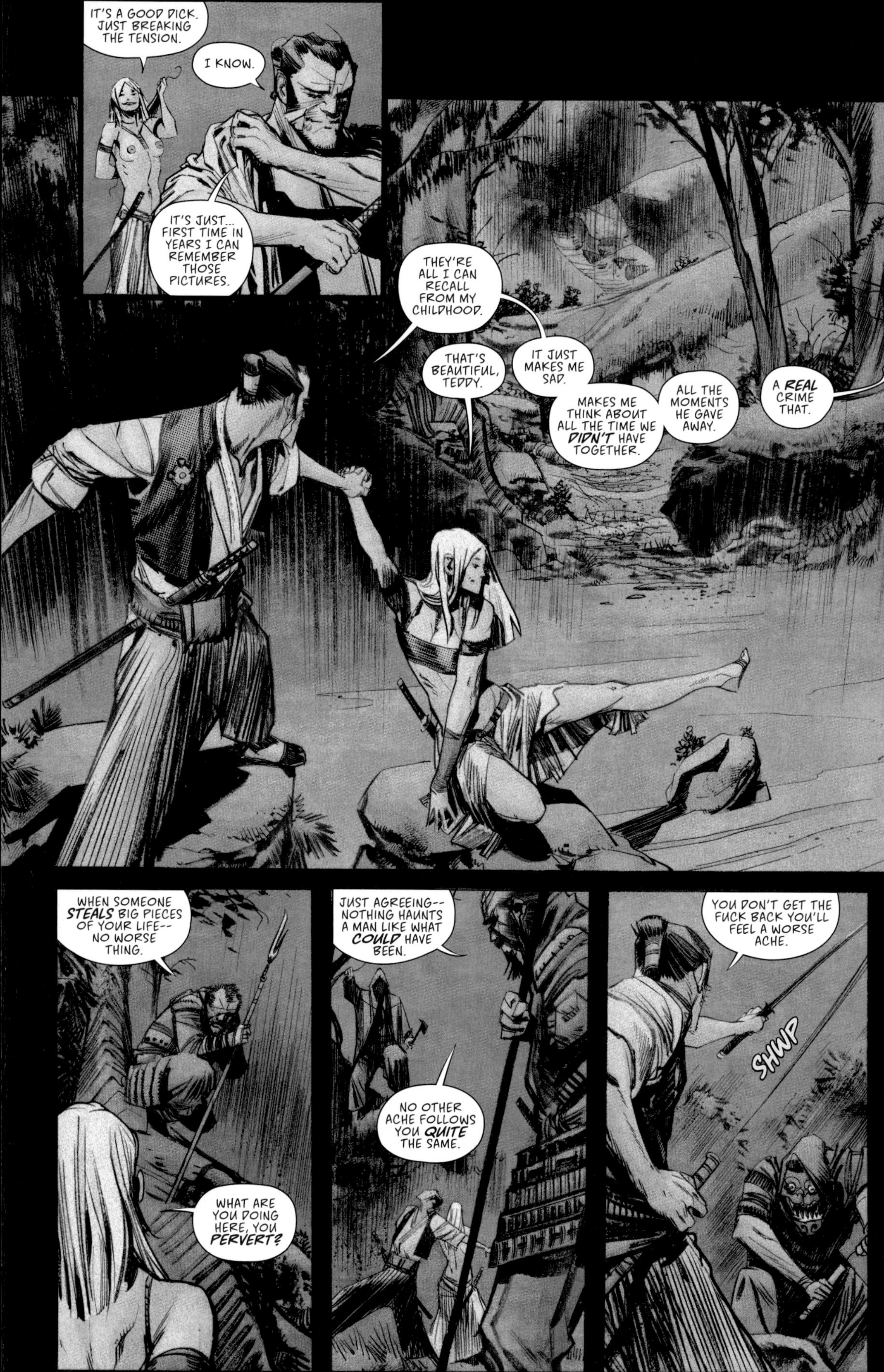
IT'S A GOOD DICK. JUST BREAKING THE TENSION.
I KNOW.
IT'S JUST... FIRST TIME IN YEARS I CAN REMEMBER THOSE PICTURES.
THEY'RE ALL I CAN RECALL FROM MY CHILDHOOD.
IT JUST MAKES ME SAD.
THAT'S BEAUTIFUL, TEDDY.
MAKES ME THINK ABOUT ALL THE TIME WE DIDN'T HAVE TOGETHER.
ALL THE MOMENTS HE GAVE AWAY.
A REAL CRIME THAT.
WHEN SOMEONE STEALS BIG PIECES OF YOUR LIFE-- NO WORSE THING.
WHAT ARE YOU DOING HERE, YOU PERVERT?
JUST AGREEING-- NOTHING HAUNTS A MAN LIKE WHAT COULD HAVE BEEN.
NO OTHER ACHE FOLLOWS YOU QUITE THE SAME.
YOU DON'T GET THE FUCK BACK YOU'LL FEEL A WORSE ACHE.
SHWP

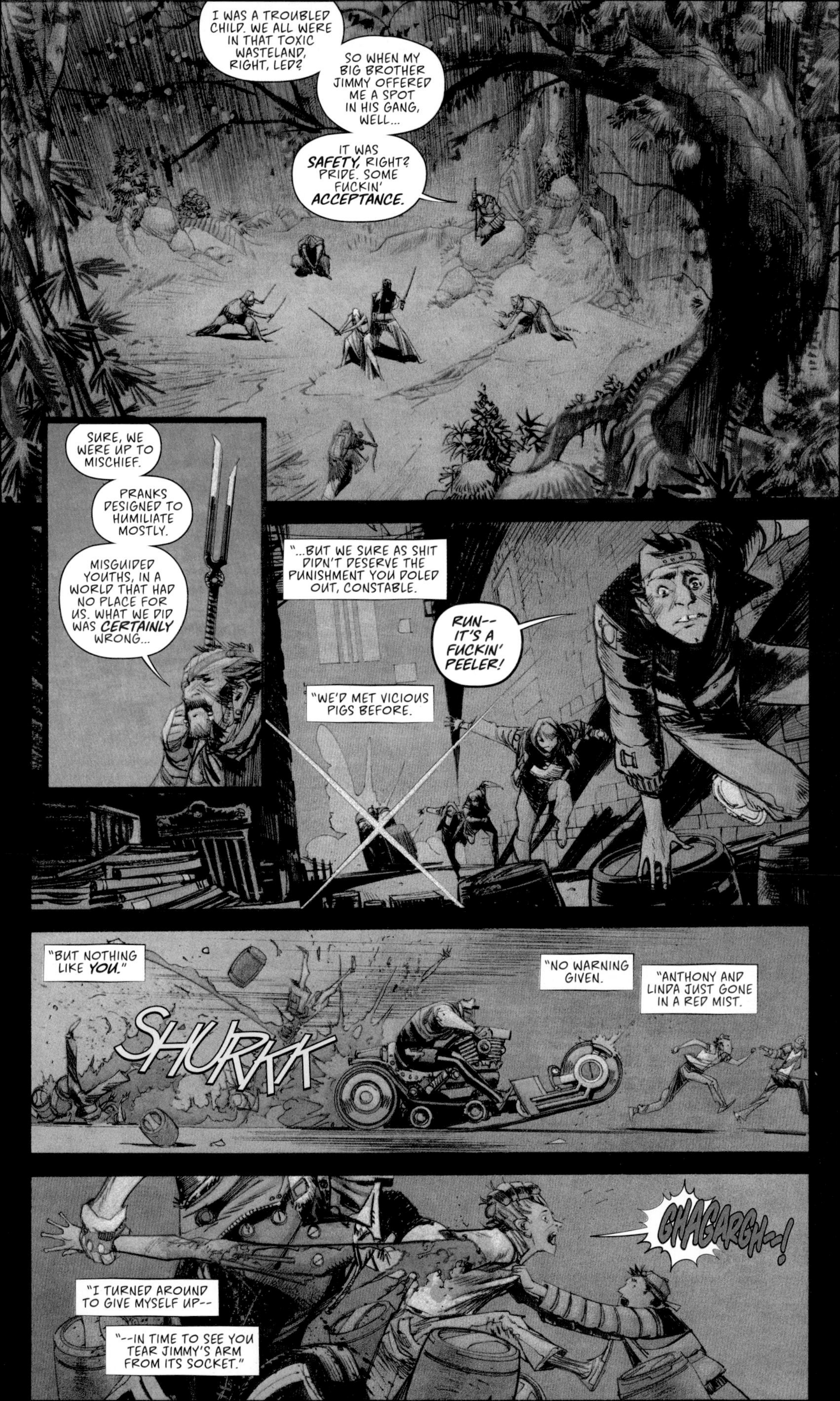
I WAS A TROUBLED CHILD. WE ALL WERE IN THAT TOXIC WASTELAND, RIGHT, LED?
SO WHEN MY BIG BROTHER JIMMY OFFERED ME A SPOT IN HIS GANG, WELL...
IT WAS SAFETY, RIGHT? PRIDE. SOME FUCKIN' ACCEPTANCE.
SURE, WE WERE UP TO MISCHIEF.
PRANKS DESIGNED TO HUMILIATE MOSTLY.
MISGUIDED YOUTHS, IN A WORLD THAT HAD NO PLACE FOR US. WHAT WE DID WAS CERTAINLY WRONG...
"...BUT WE SURE AS SHIT DIDN'T DESERVE THE PUNISHMENT YOU DOLED OUT, CONSTABLE.
RUN-- IT'S A FUCKIN' PEELER!
"WE'D MET VICIOUS PIGS BEFORE.
"BUT NOTHING LIKE YOU."
SHURKK
"NO WARNING GIVEN.
"ANTHONY AND LINDA JUST GONE IN A RED MIST.
GHAGARGH--!
"I TURNED AROUND TO GIVE MYSELF UP--
"--IN TIME TO SEE YOU TEAR JIMMY'S ARM FROM ITS SOCKET."

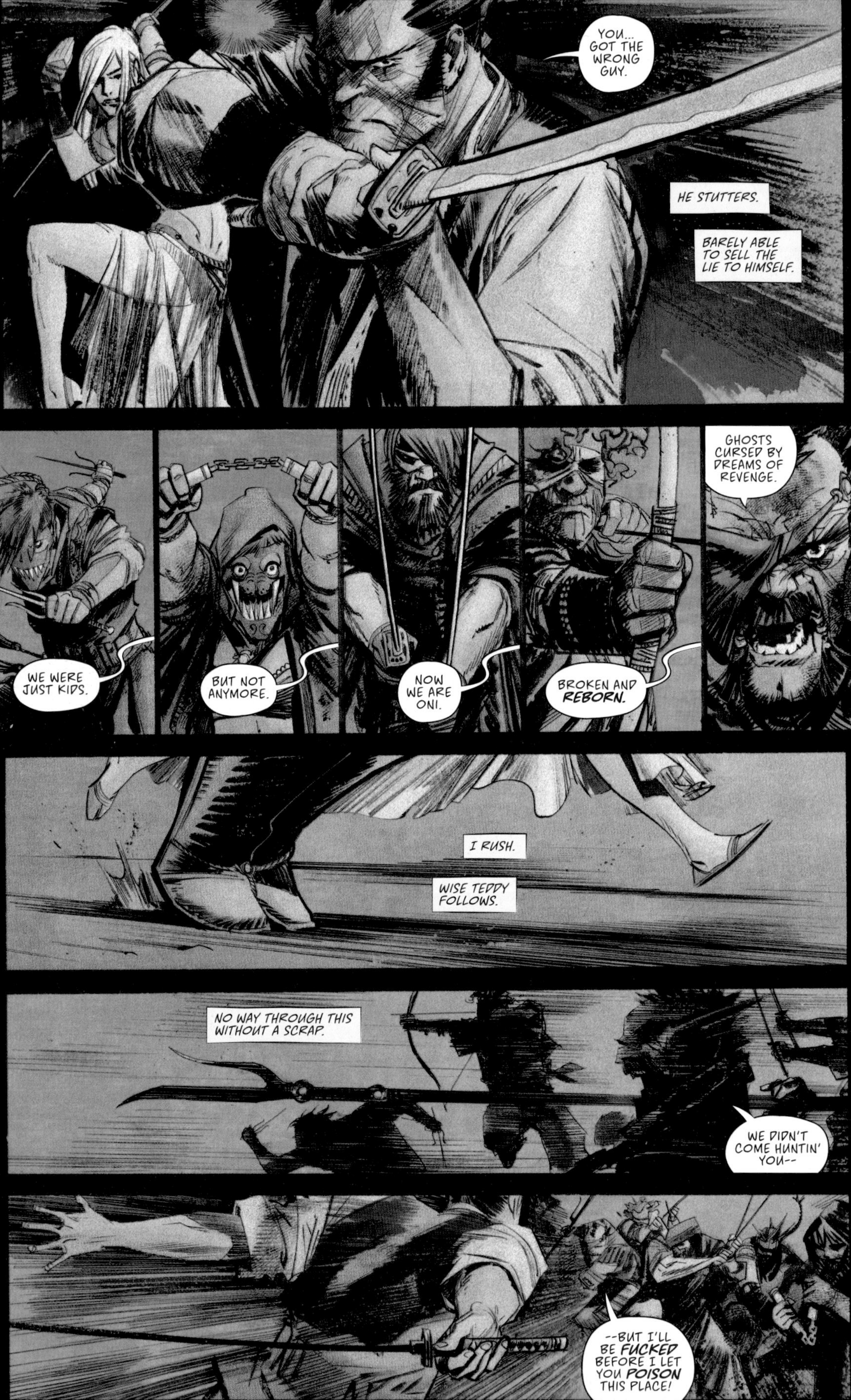
YOU... GOT THE WRONG GUY.
HE STUTTERS.
BARELY ABLE TO SELL THE LIE TO HIMSELF.
WE WERE JUST KIDS.
BUT NOT ANYMORE.
NOW WE ARE ONI.
BROKEN AND REBORN.
GHOSTS CURSED BY DREAMS OF REVENGE.
I RUSH.
WISE TEDDY FOLLOWS.
NO WAY THROUGH THIS WITHOUT A SCRAP.
WE DIDN'T COME HUNTIN' YOU--
--BUT I'LL BE FUCKED BEFORE I LET YOU POISON THIS PLACE!

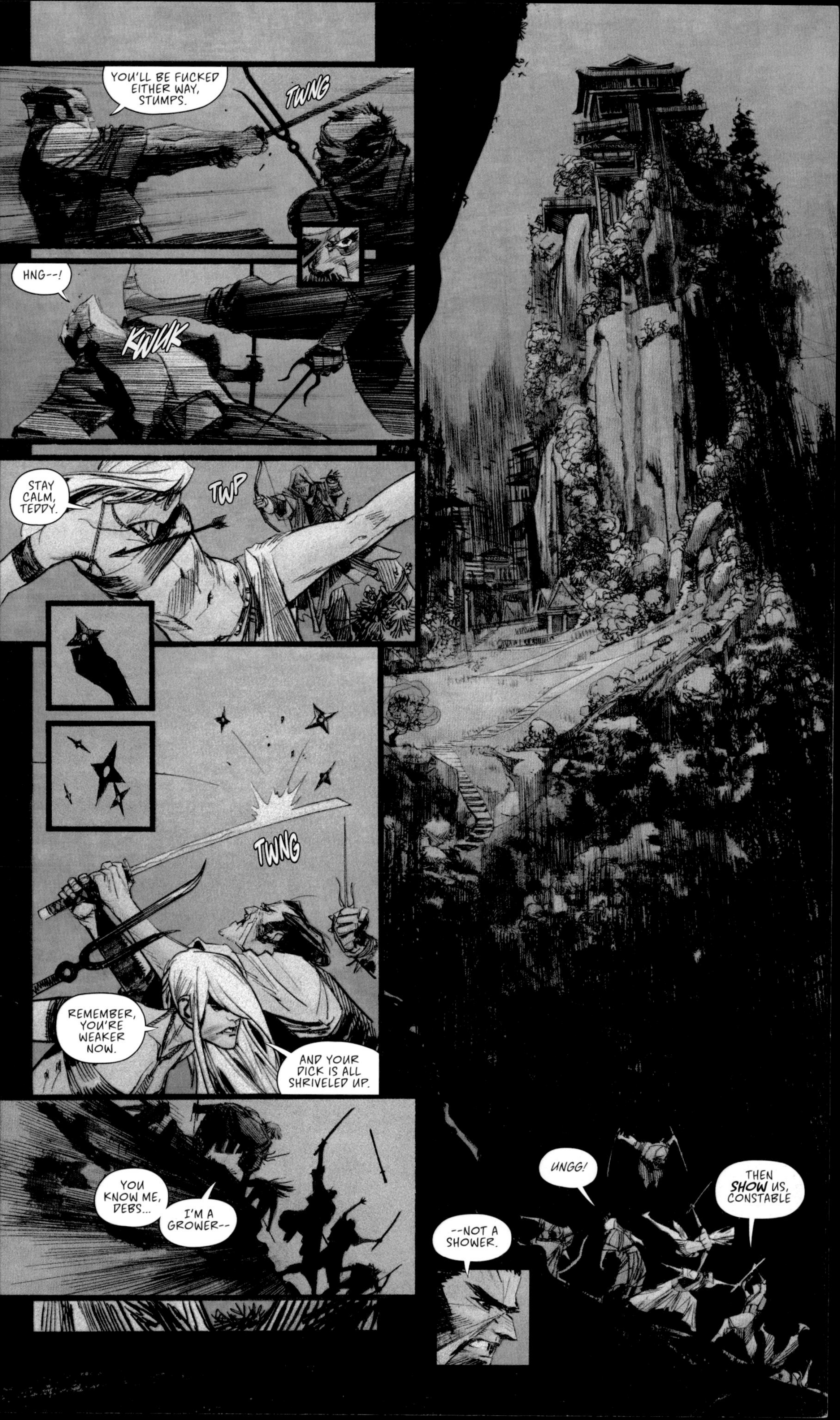
YOU'LL BE FUCKED EITHER WAY, STUMPS.
TWNG
HNG--!
KWUK
STAY CALM, TEDDY.
TWP
TWNG
REMEMBER, YOU'RE WEAKER NOW.
AND YOUR DICK IS ALL SHRIVELED UP.
YOU KNOW ME, DEBS...
I'M A GROWER--
--NOT A SHOWER.
UNGG!
THEN SHOW US, CONSTABLE

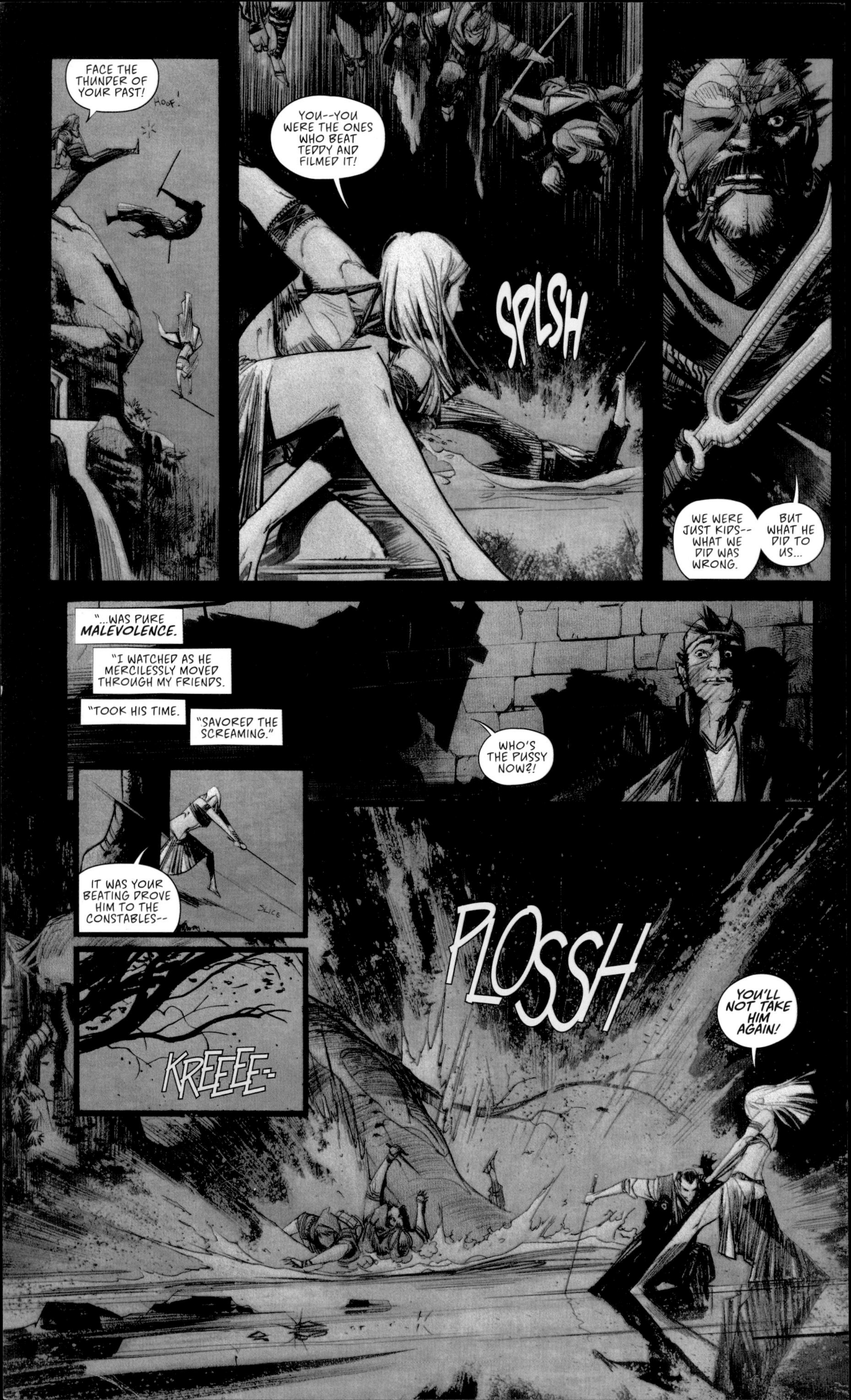
FACE THE THUNDER OF YOUR PAST!
HOOF!
YOU--YOU WERE THE ONES WHO BEAT TEDDY AND FILMED IT!
SPLSH
WE WERE JUST KIDS--WHAT WE DID WAS WRONG.
BUT WHAT HE DID TO US...
"...WAS PURE MALEVOLENCE.
"I WATCHED AS HE MERCILESSLY MOVED THROUGH MY FRIENDS.
"TOOK HIS TIME.
"SAVORED THE SCREAMING."
WHO'S THE PUSSY NOW?!
IT WAS YOUR BEATING DROVE HIM TO THE CONSTABLES--
SLICE
KREEEE--
PLOSSH
YOU'LL NOT TAKE HIM AGAIN!

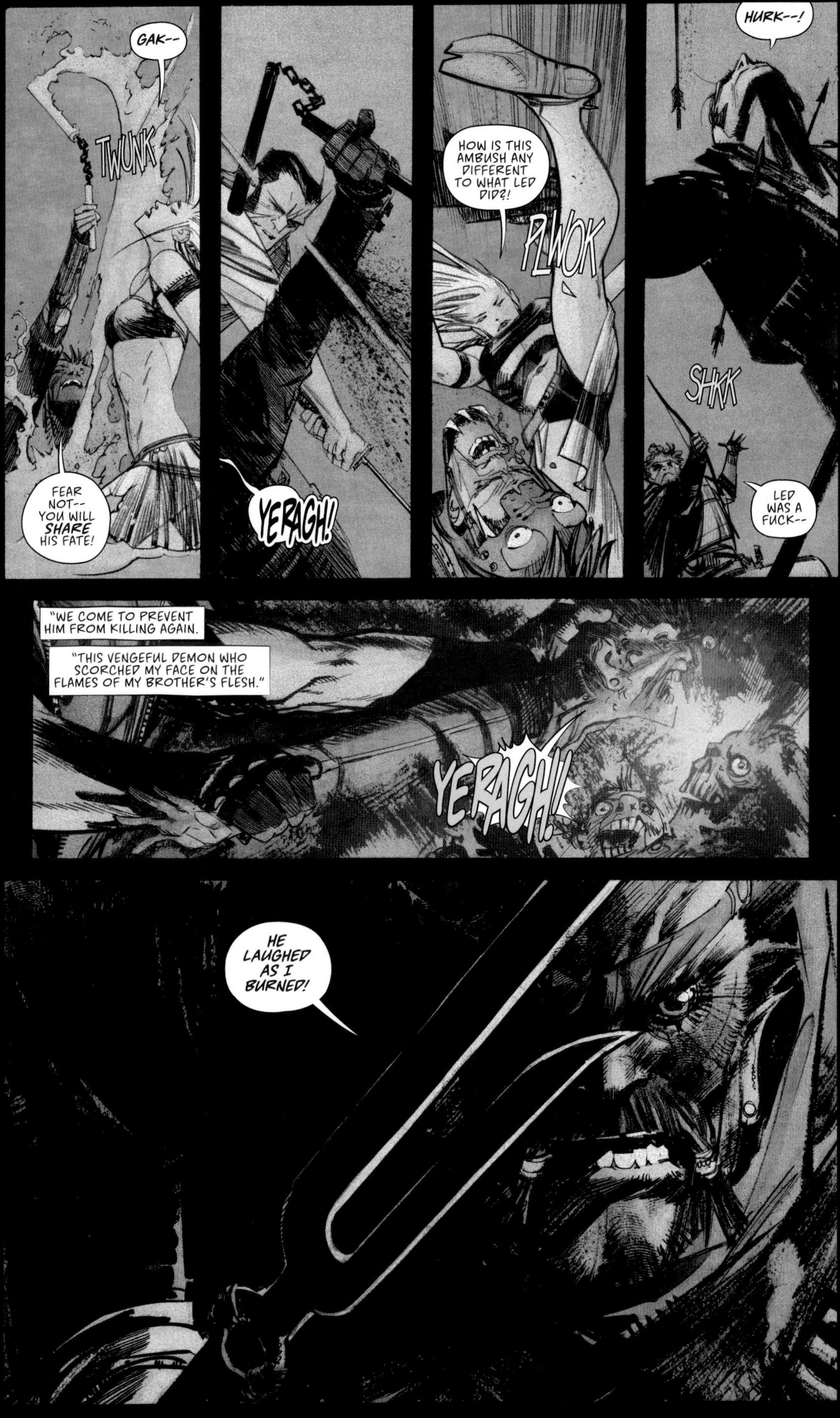
GAK--
TWUNK
FEAR NOT-- YOU WILL SHARE HIS FATE!
YE RAGH!
HOW IS THIS AMBUSH ANY DIFFERENT TO WHAT LED DID?!
PLWOK
HURK--!
SHKK
LED WAS A FUCK--
"WE COME TO PREVENT HIM FROM KILLING AGAIN.
"THIS VENGEFUL DEMON WHO SCORCHED MY FACE ON THE FLAMES OF MY BROTHER'S FLESH."
YE RAGH!
HE LAUGHED AS I BURNED!

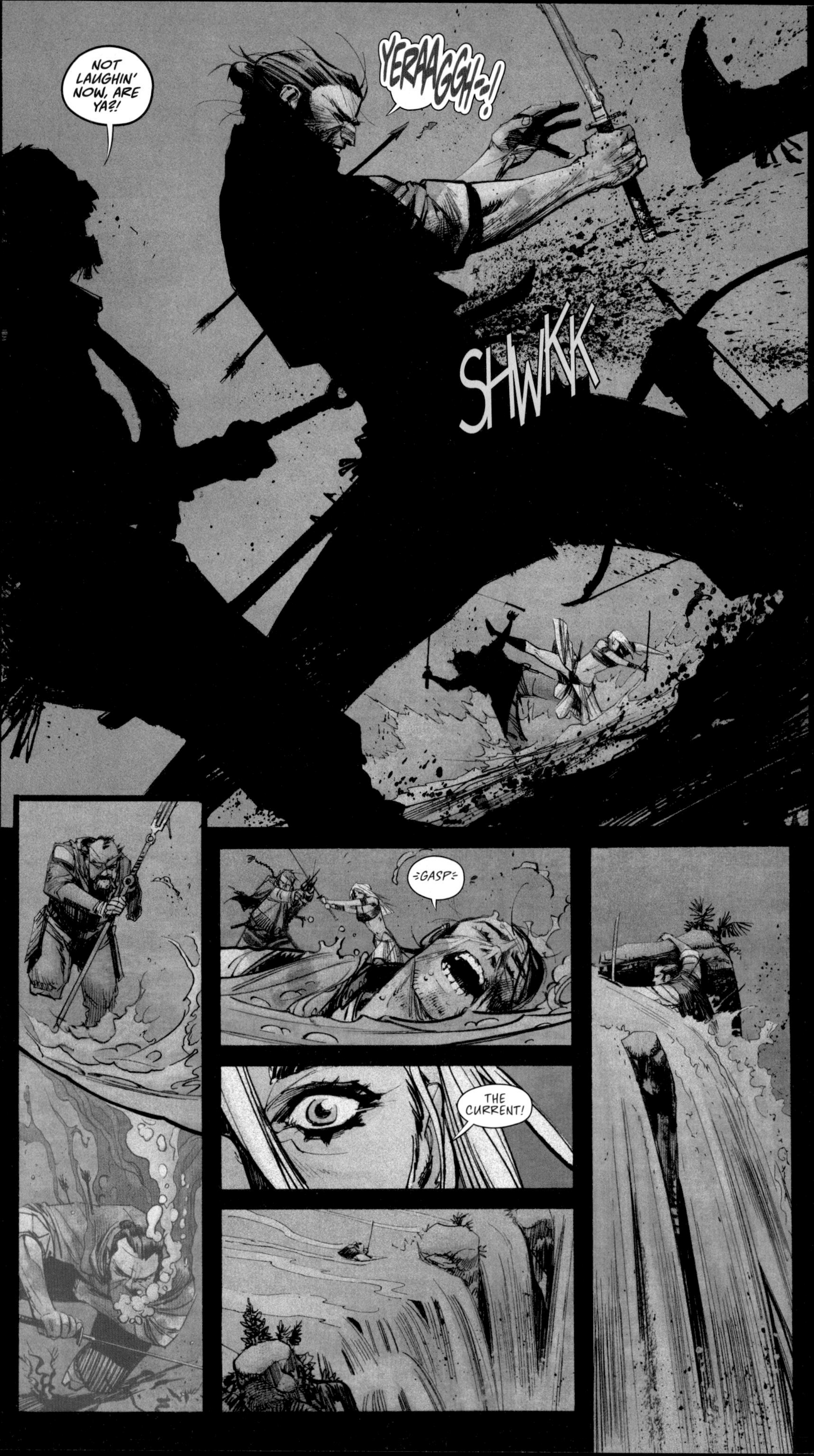
NOT LAUGHIN' NOW, ARE YA?!
YERAAGGH-!
SHWKK
GASP
THE CURRENT!

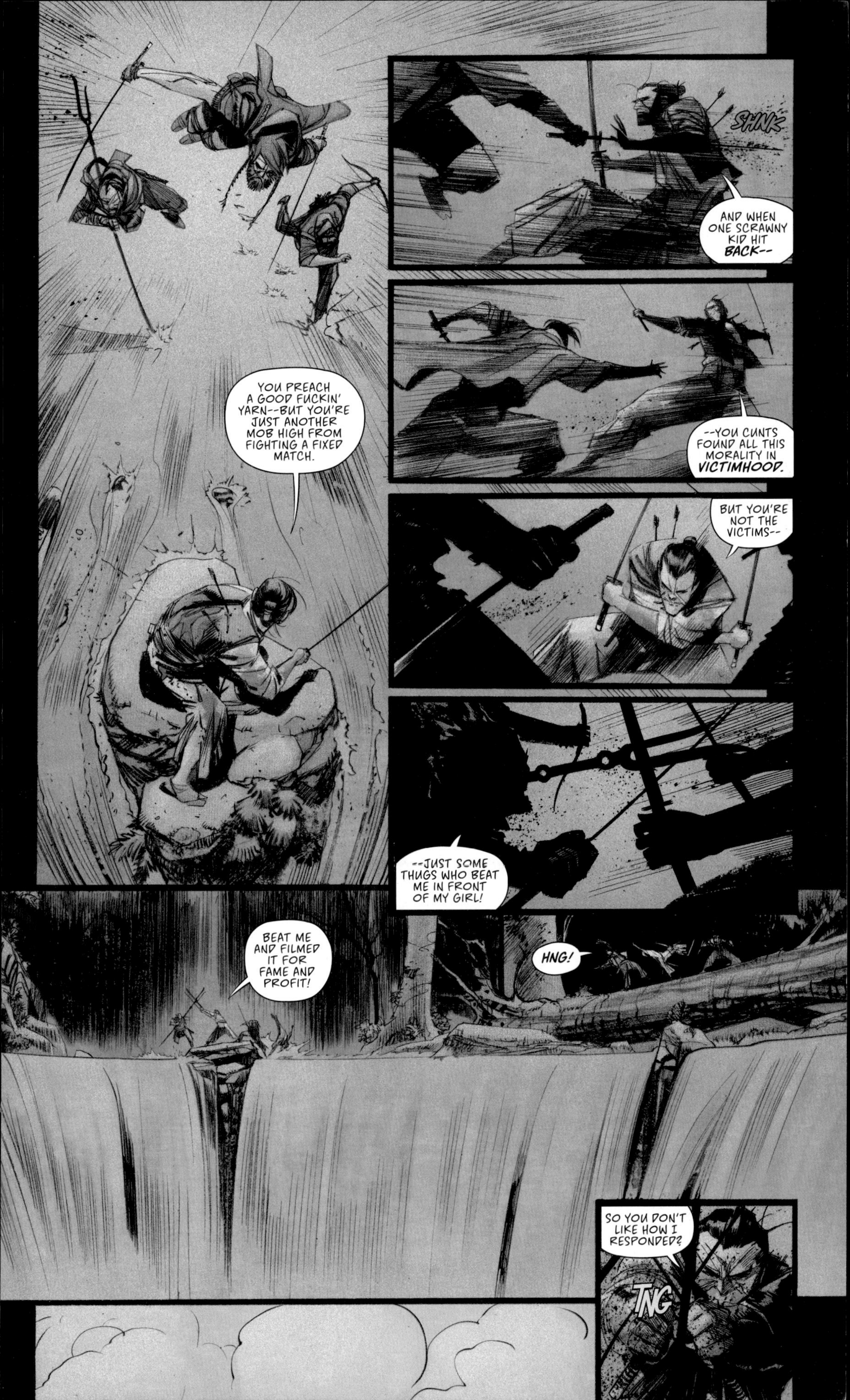

SHNK
AND WHEN ONE SCRAWNY KID HIT BACK--
--YOU CUNTS FOUND ALL THIS MORALITY IN VICTIMHOOD.
YOU PREACH A GOOD FUCKIN' YARN--BUT YOU'RE JUST ANOTHER MOB HIGH FROM FIGHTING A FIXED MATCH.
BUT YOU'RE NOT THE VICTIMS--
--JUST SOME THUGS WHO BEAT ME IN FRONT OF MY GIRL!
BEAT ME AND FILMED IT FOR FAME AND PROFIT!
HNG!
SO YOU DON'T LIKE HOW I RESPONDED?
TNG

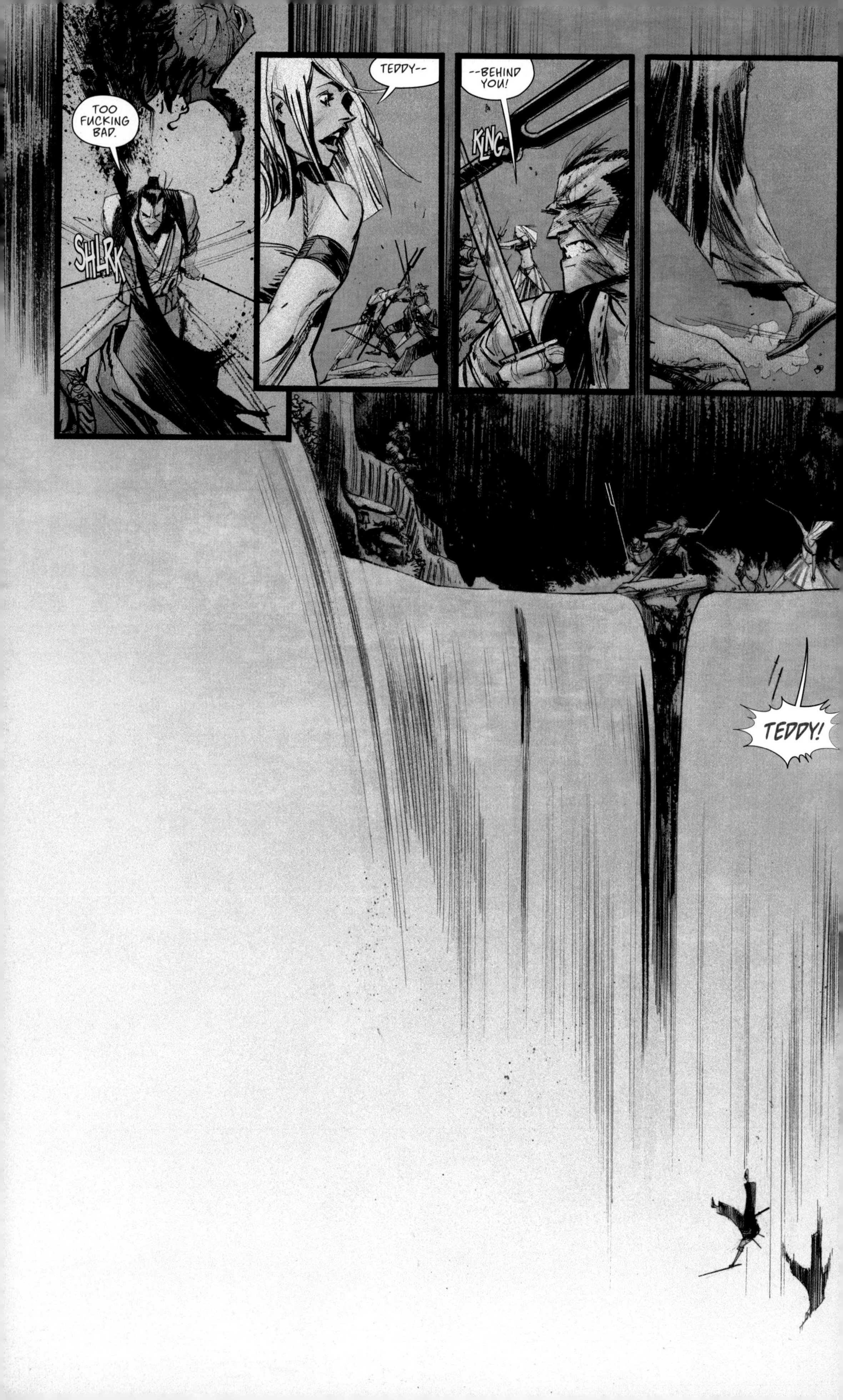
TOO FUCKING BAD.
SHLRK
TEDDY--
--BEHIND YOU!
KLNG
TEDDY!

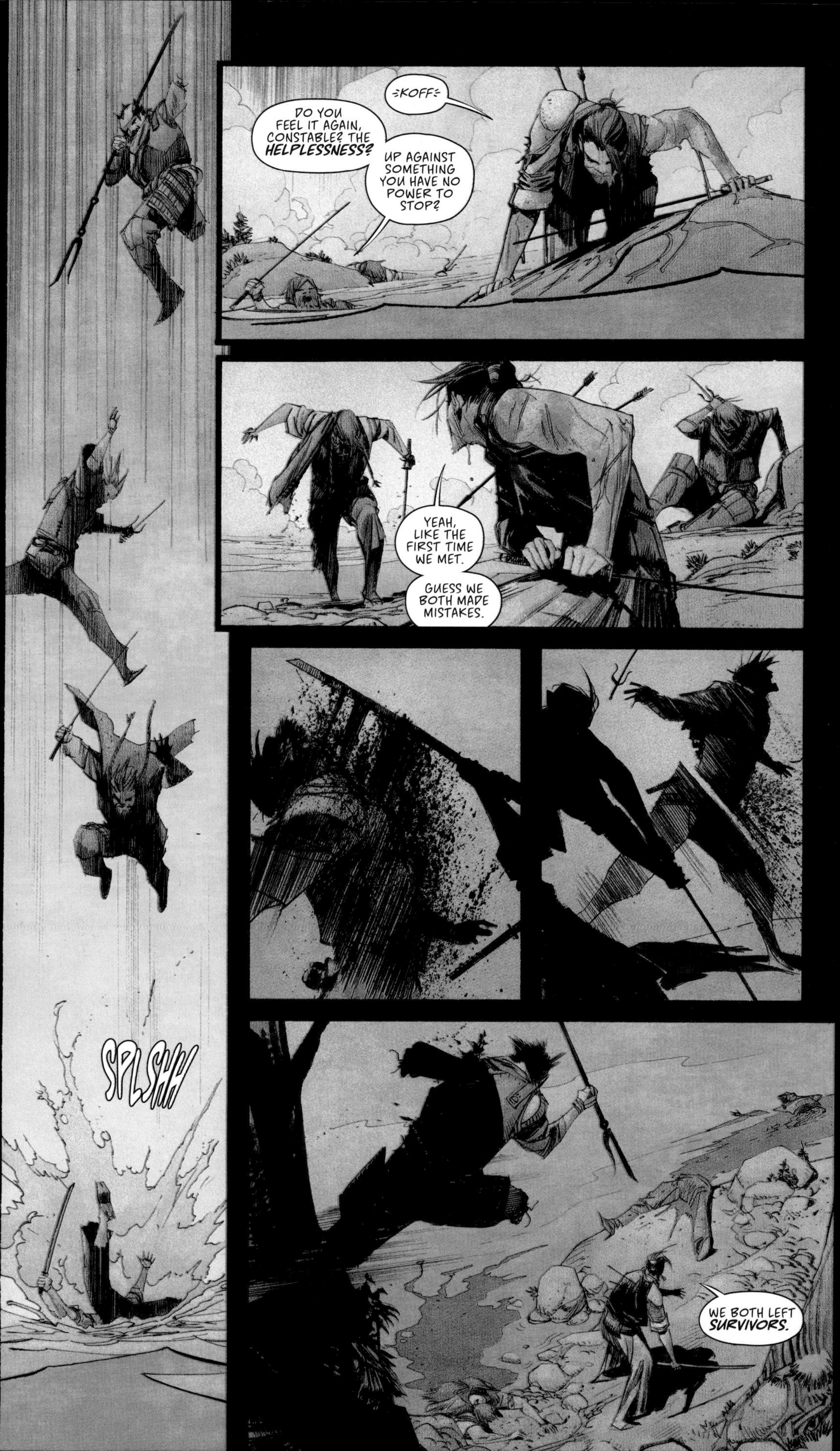

=KOFF=
DO YOU FEEL IT AGAIN, CONSTABLE? THE HELPLESSNESS?
UP AGAINST SOMETHING YOU HAVE NO POWER TO STOP?
YEAH, LIKE THE FIRST TIME WE MET.
GUESS WE BOTH MADE MISTAKES.
SPLSHH
WE BOTH LEFT SURVIVORS.

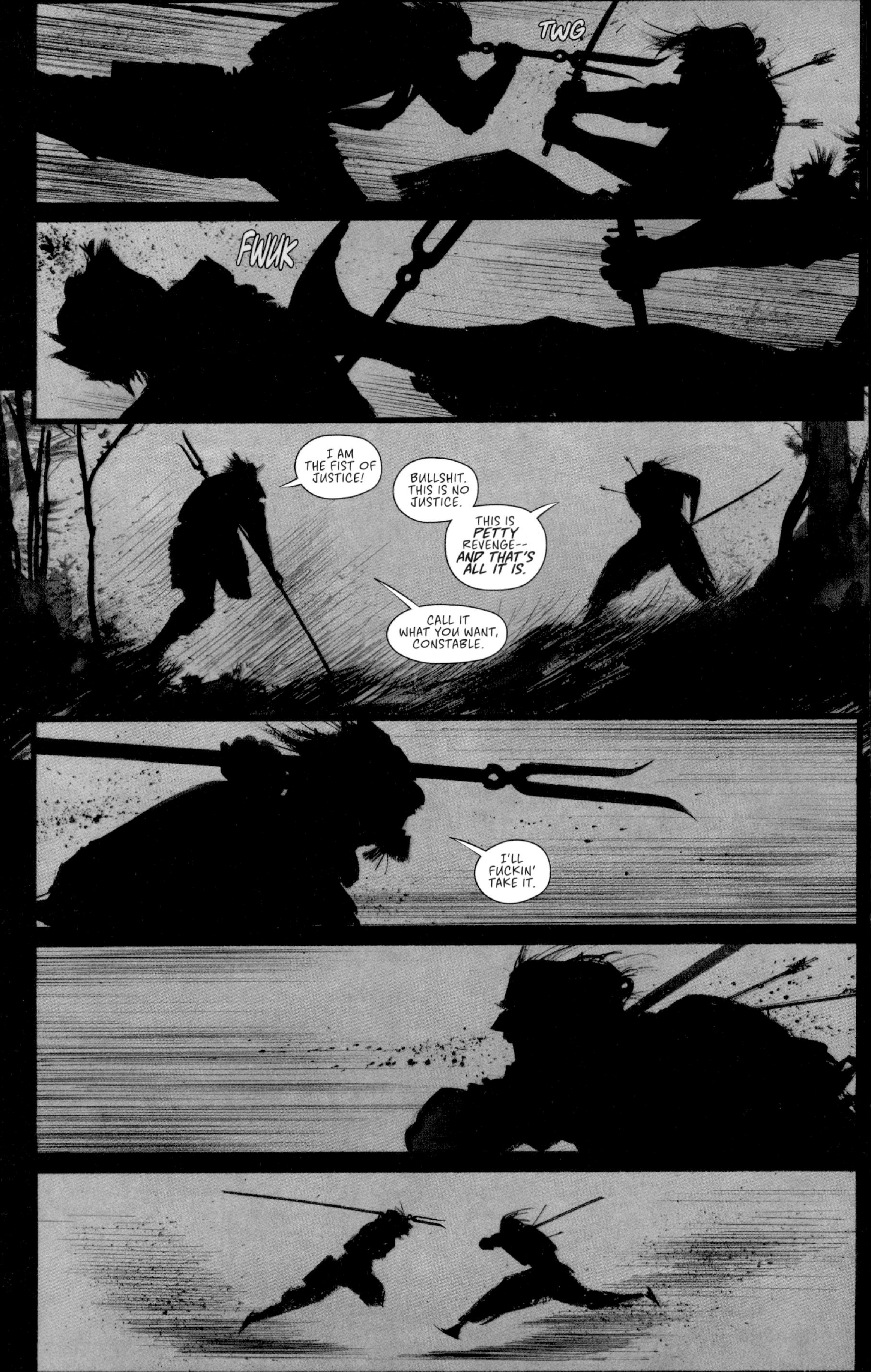
TWG
FWUK
I AM THE FIST OF JUSTICE!
BULLSHIT. THIS IS NO JUSTICE.
THIS IS PETTY REVENGE-- AND THAT'S ALL IT IS.
CALL IT WHAT YOU WANT, CONSTABLE.
I'LL FUCKIN' TAKE IT.

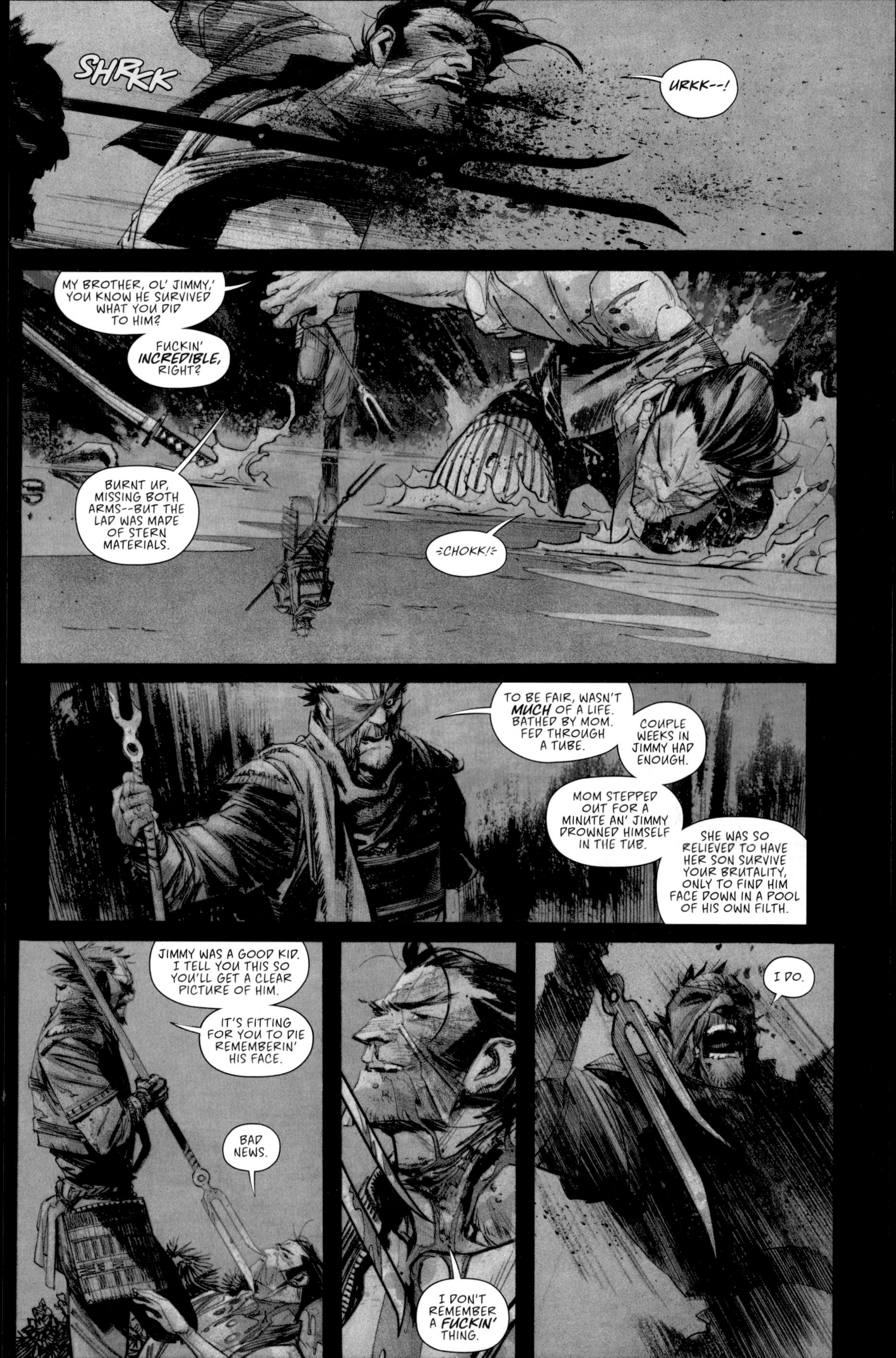
SHRKK
URKK--!
MY BROTHER, OL' JIMMY, YOU KNOW HE SURVIVED WHAT YOU DID TO HIM?
FUCKIN' INCREDIBLE, RIGHT?
BURNT UP, MISSING BOTH ARMS--BUT THE LAD WAS MADE OF STERN MATERIALS.
CHOKK!
TO BE FAIR, WASN'T MUCH OF A LIFE. BATHED BY MOM. FED THROUGH A TUBE.
COUPLE WEEKS IN JIMMY HAD ENOUGH.
MOM STEPPED OUT FOR A MINUTE AN' JIMMY DROWNED HIMSELF IN THE TUB.
SHE WAS SO RELIEVED TO HAVE HER SON SURVIVE YOUR BRUTALITY, ONLY TO FIND HIM FACE DOWN IN A POOL OF HIS OWN FILTH.
JIMMY WAS A GOOD KID. I TELL YOU THIS SO YOU'LL GET A CLEAR PICTURE OF HIM.
IT'S FITTING FOR YOU TO DIE REMEMBERIN' HIS FACE.
BAD NEWS.
I DON'T REMEMBER A FUCKIN' THING.
I DO.

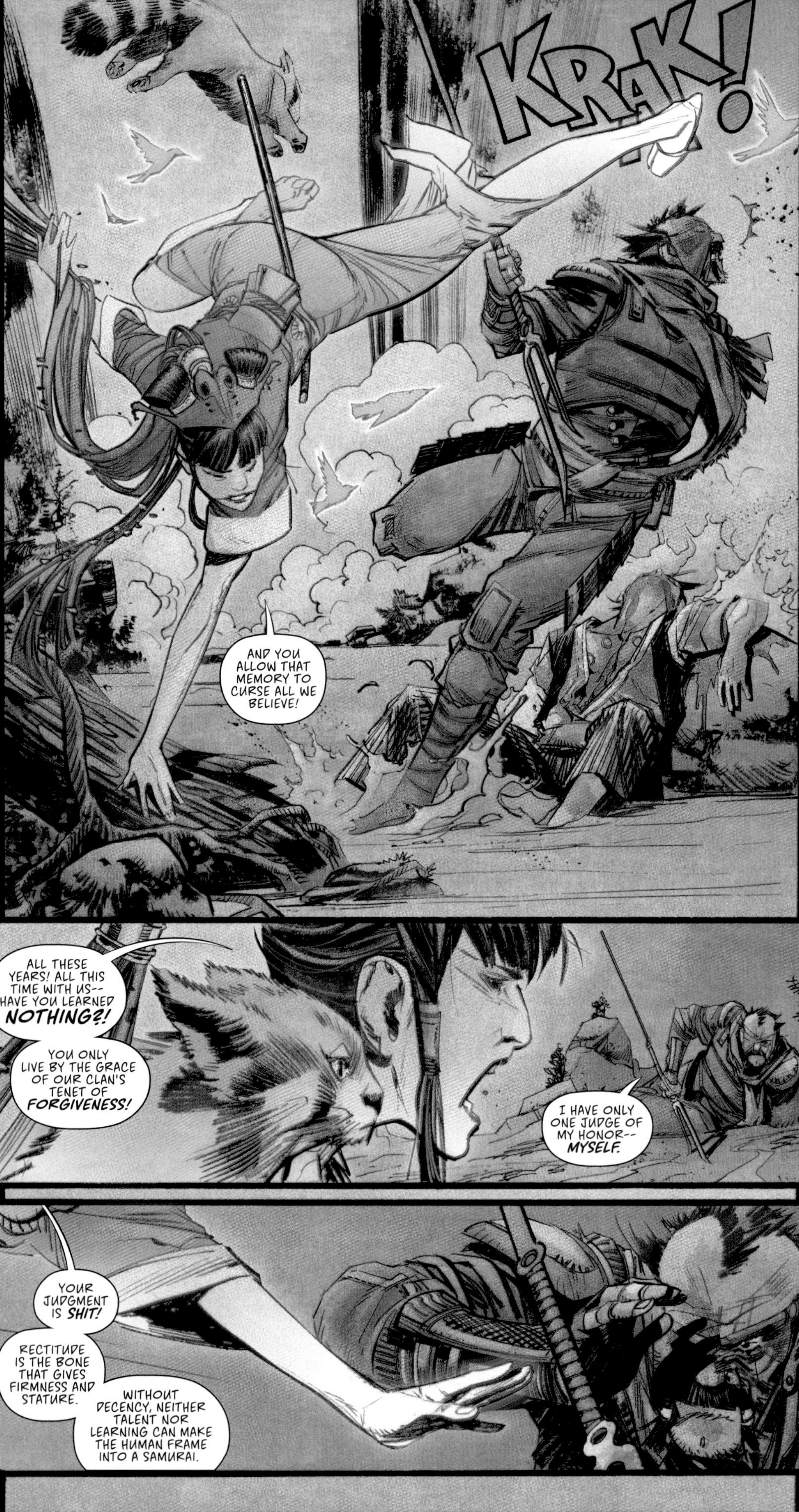
KRAK!
AND YOU ALLOW THAT MEMORY TO CURSE ALL WE BELIEVE!
ALL THESE YEARS! ALL THIS TIME WITH US-- HAVE YOU LEARNED NOTHING?!
YOU ONLY LIVE BY THE GRACE OF OUR CLAN'S TENET OF FORGIVENESS!
I HAVE ONLY ONE JUDGE OF MY HONOR-- MYSELF.
YOUR JUDGMENT IS SHIT!
RECTITUDE IS THE BONE THAT GIVES FIRMNESS AND STATURE.
WITHOUT DECENCY, NEITHER TALENT NOR LEARNING CAN MAKE THE HUMAN FRAME INTO A SAMURAI.

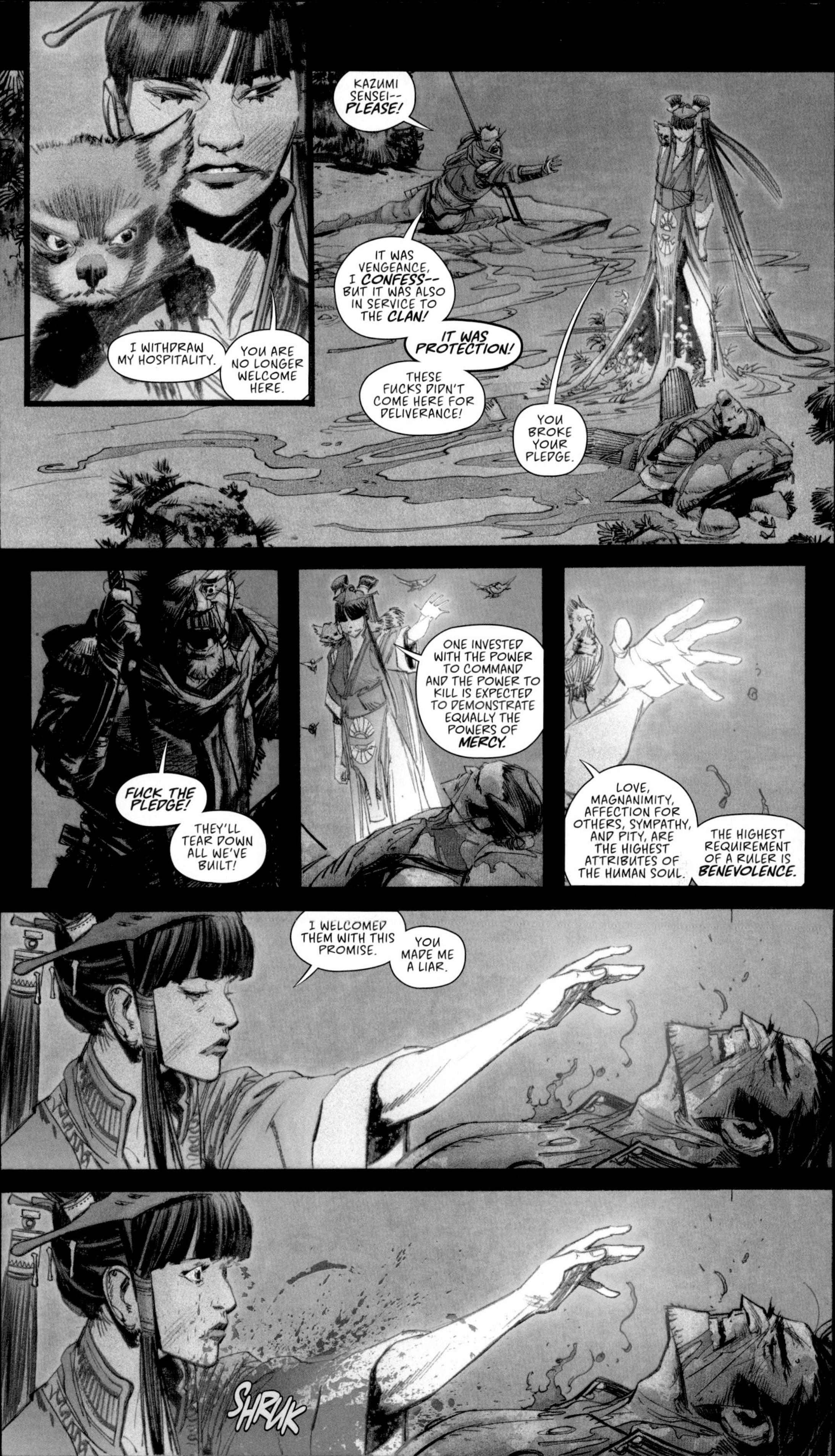
I WITHDRAW MY HOSPITALITY.
YOU ARE NO LONGER WELCOME HERE.
KAZUMI SENSEI-- PLEASE!
IT WAS VENGEANCE, I CONFESS-- BUT IT WAS ALSO IN SERVICE TO THE CLAN!
IT WAS PROTECTION!
THESE FUCKS DIDN'T COME HERE FOR DELIVERANCE!
YOU BROKE YOUR PLEDGE.
FUCK THE PLEDGE!
THEY'LL TEAR DOWN ALL WE'VE BUILT!
ONE INVESTED WITH THE POWER TO COMMAND AND THE POWER TO KILL IS EXPECTED TO DEMONSTRATE EQUALLY THE POWERS OF MERCY.
LOVE, MAGNANIMITY, AFFECTION FOR OTHERS, SYMPATHY, AND PITY, ARE THE HIGHEST ATTRIBUTES OF THE HUMAN SOUL.
THE HIGHEST REQUIREMENT OF A RULER IS BENEVOLENCE.
I WELCOMED THEM WITH THIS PROMISE.
YOU MADE ME A LIAR.
SHRUK

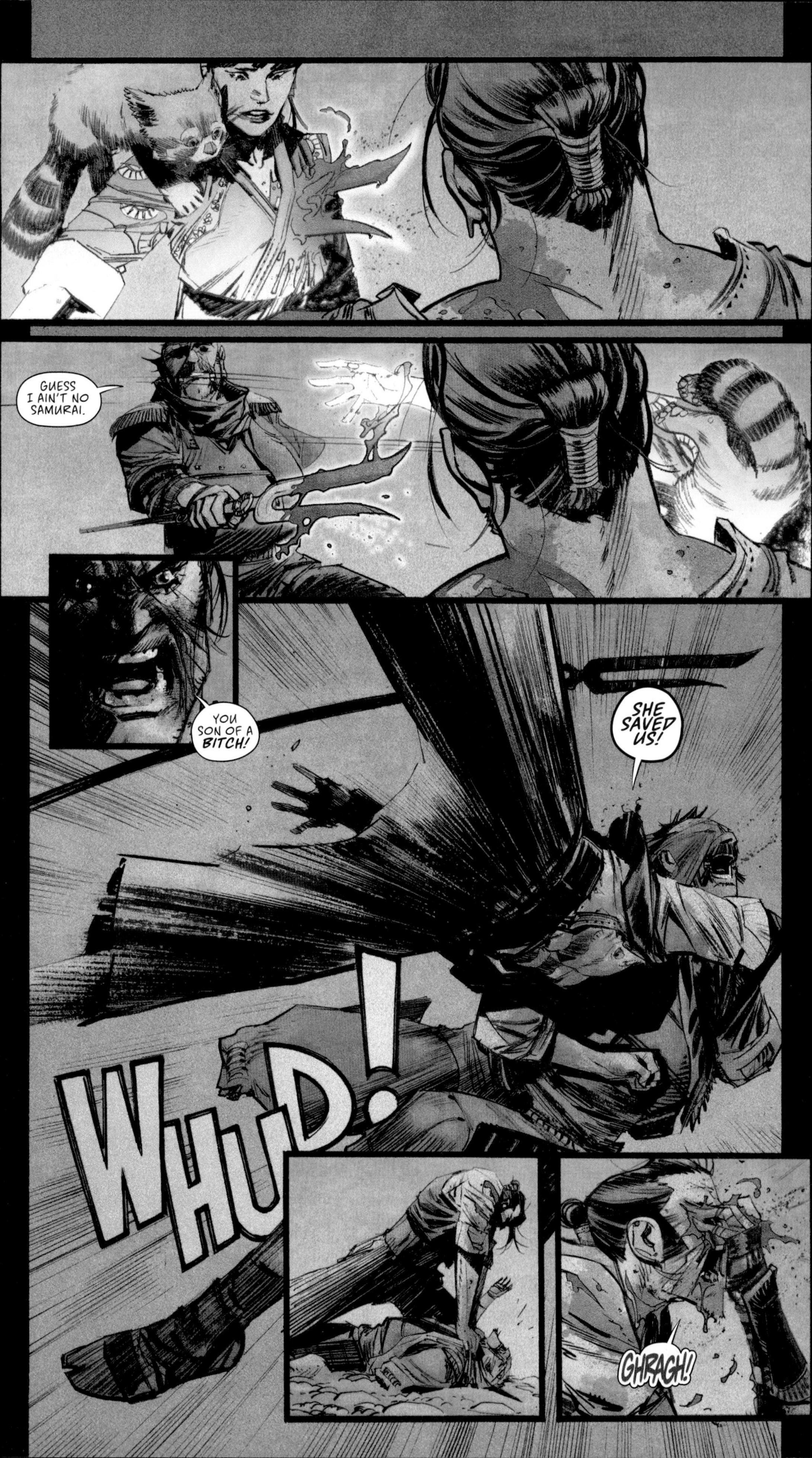
GUESS I AIN'T NO SAMURAI.
YOU SON OF A BITCH!
SHE SAVED US!
WHUD!
GHRAGH!

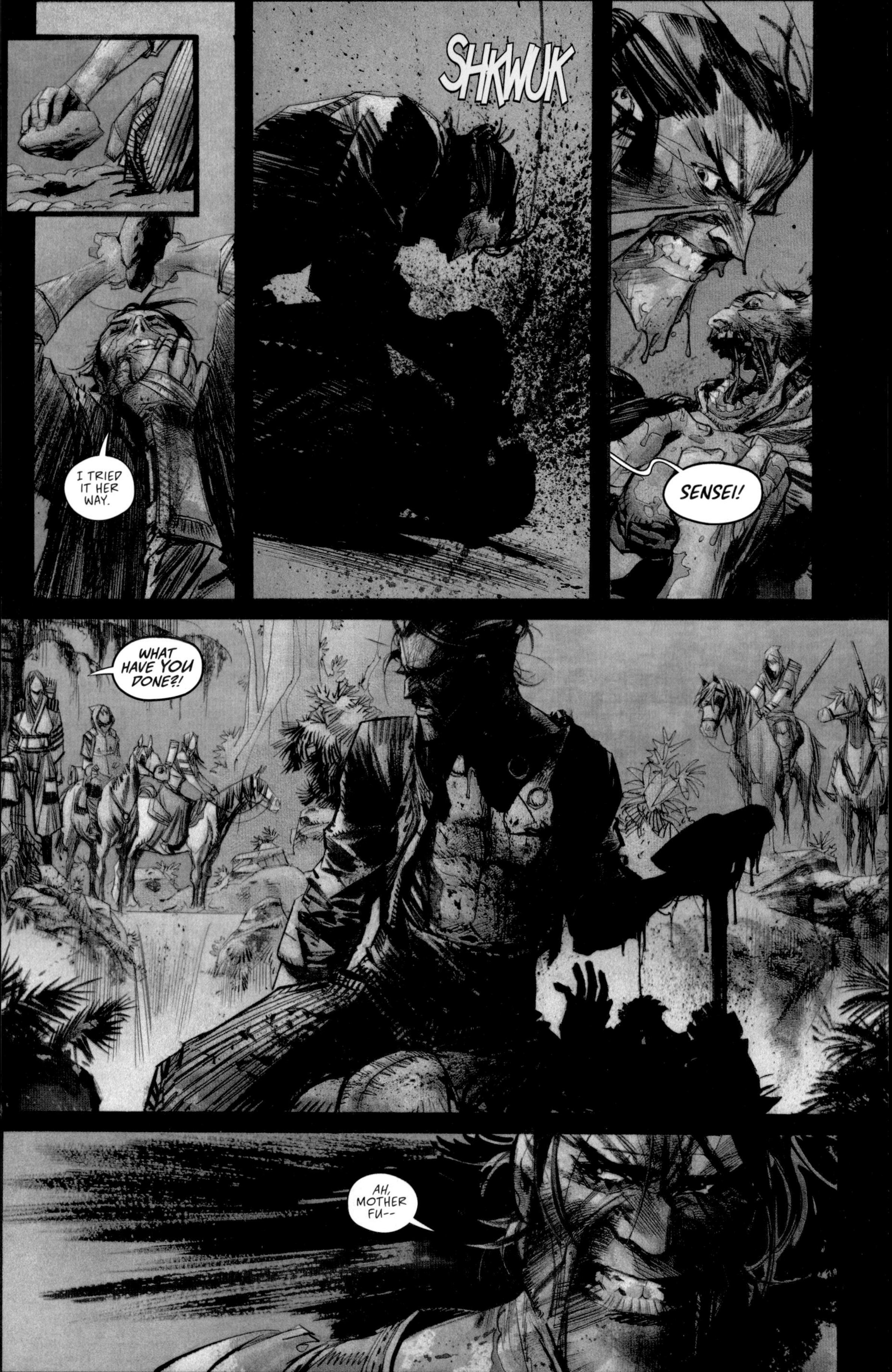

I TRIED IT HER WAY.
SHKWUK
SENSEI!
WHAT HAVE YOU DONE?!
AH, MOTHER FU--

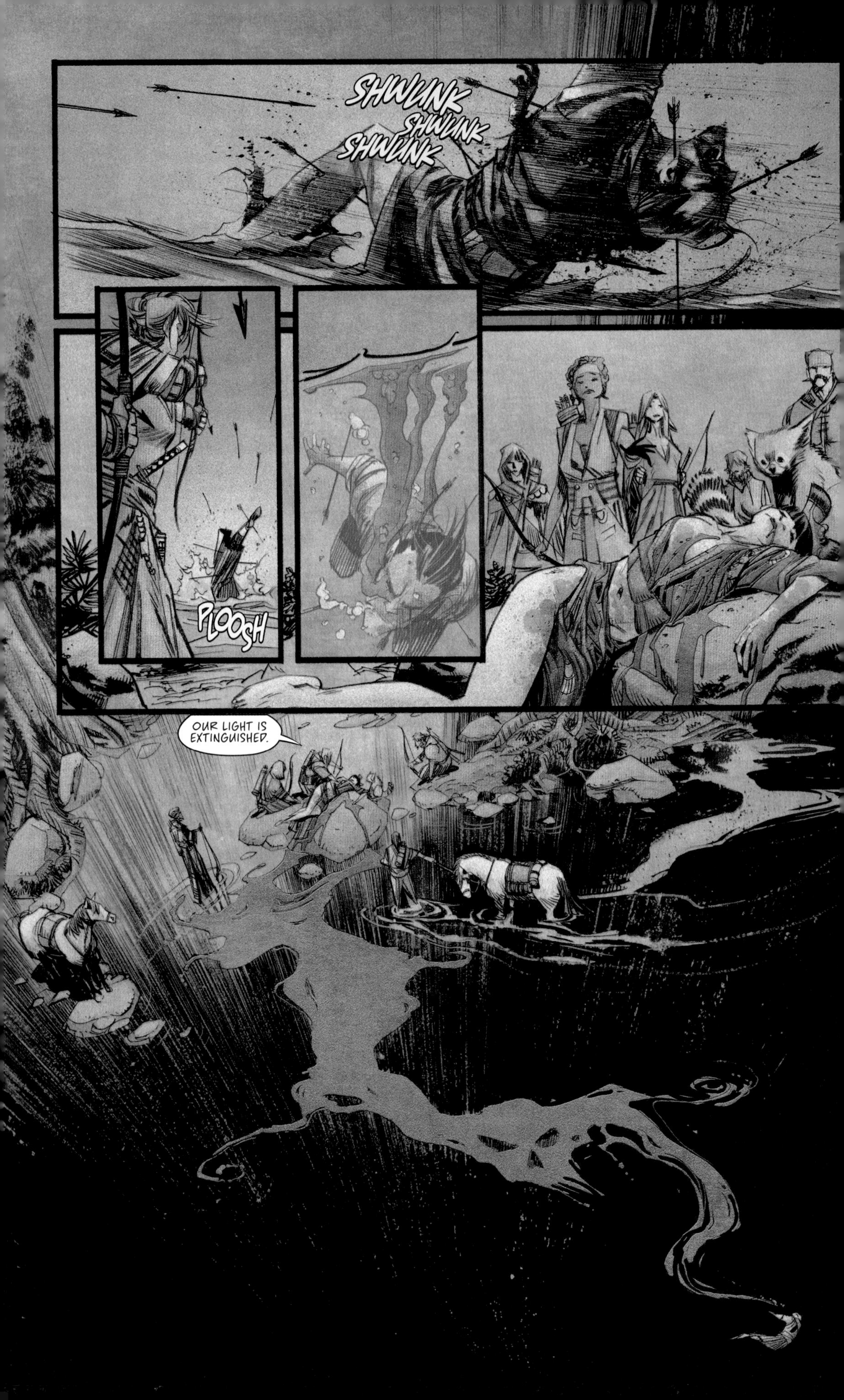
SHWUNK
SHWUNK
SHWUNK
PLOOSH
OUR LIGHT IS EXTINGUISHED.

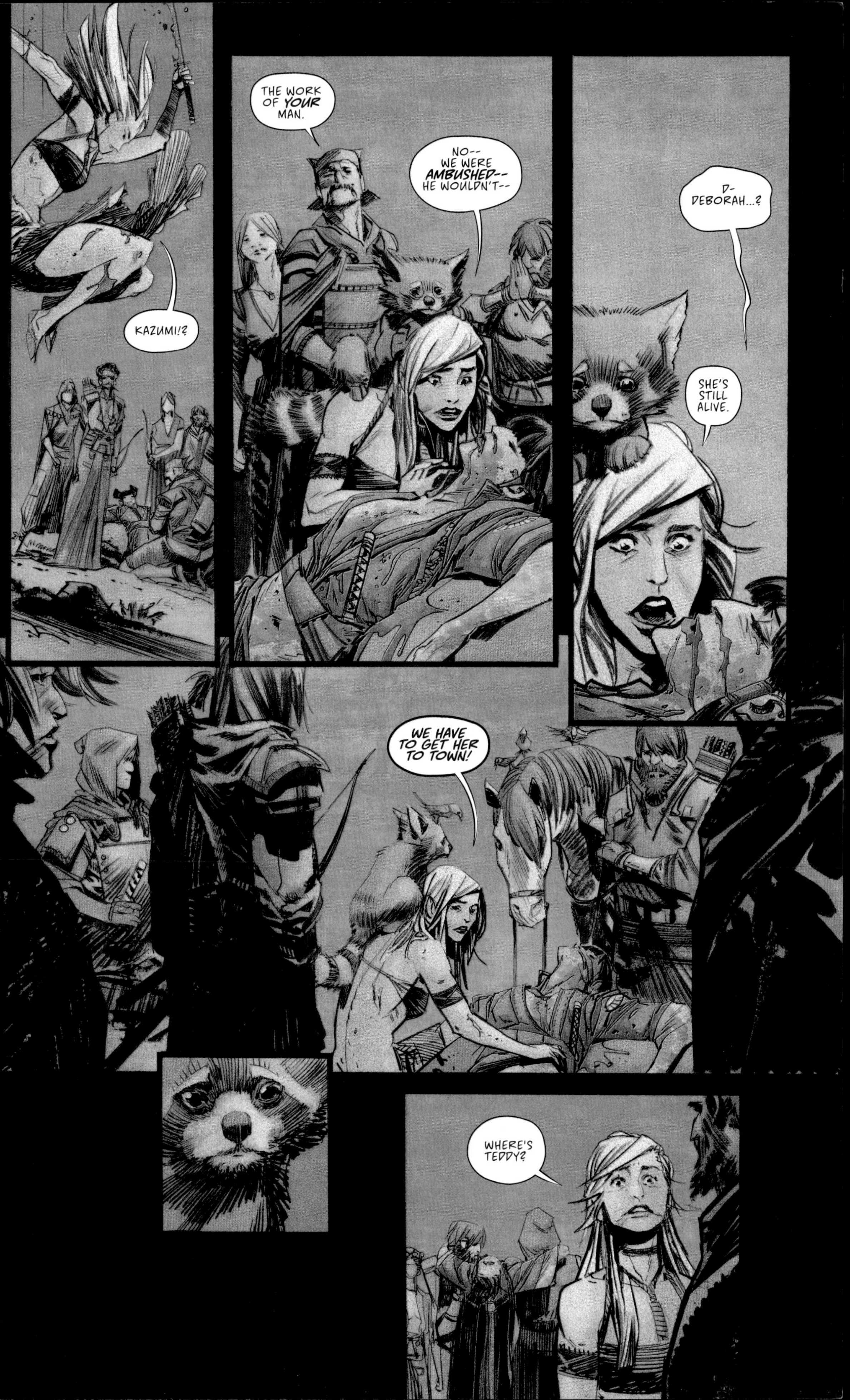
KAZUMI!?
THE WORK OF YOUR MAN.
NO-- WE WERE AMBUSHED-- HE WOULDN'T--
D- DEBORAH...?
SHE'S STILL ALIVE.
WE HAVE TO GET HER TO TOWN!
WHERE'S TEDDY?

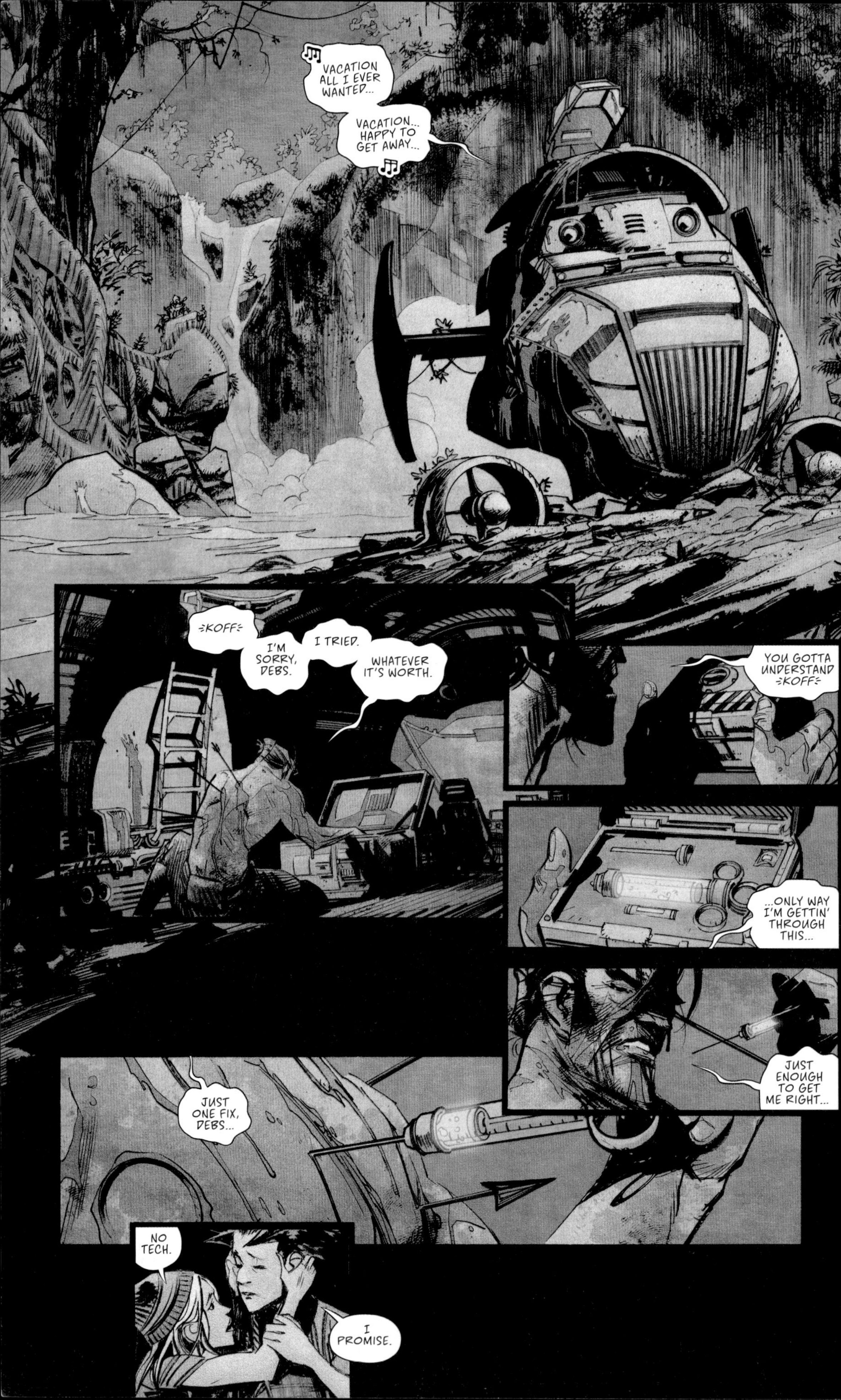

VACATION ALL I EVER WANTED...
VACATION... HAPPY TO GET AWAY...
KOFF
I'M SORRY, DEBS.
I TRIED.
WHATEVER IT'S WORTH.
YOU GOTTA UNDERSTAND KOFF
...ONLY WAY I'M GETTIN' THROUGH THIS...
JUST ENOUGH TO GET ME RIGHT...
JUST ONE FIX, DEBS...
NO TECH.
I PROMISE.

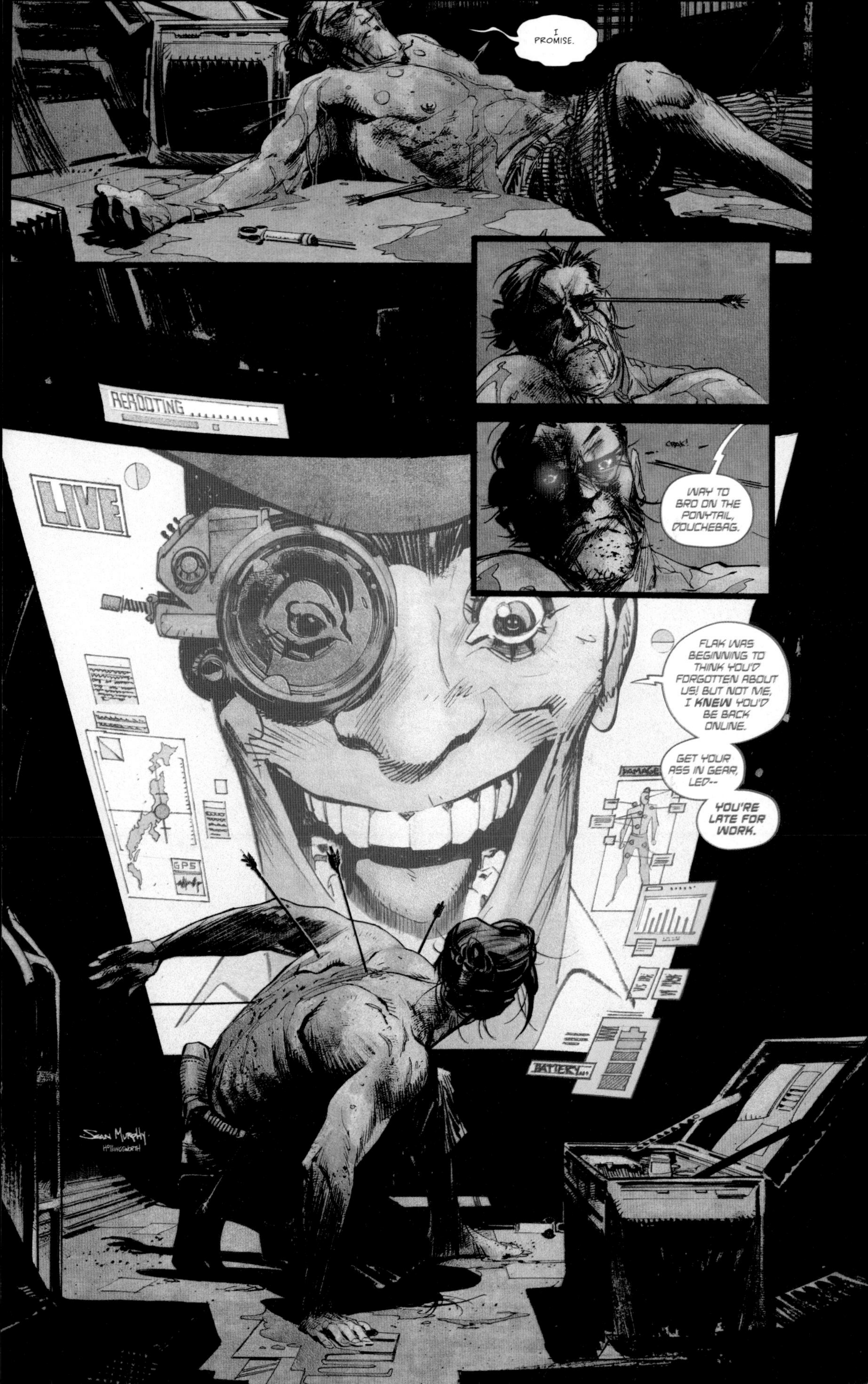
I PROMISE.
REBOOTING
LIVE
CRAK!
WAY TO BRO ON THE PONYTAIL, DOUCHEBAG.
FLAK WAS BEGINNING TO THINK YOU'D FORGOTTEN ABOUT US! BUT NOT ME, I KNEW YOU'D BE BACK ONLINE.
GET YOUR ASS IN GEAR, LEO--
YOU'RE LATE FOR WORK.
GPS
DAMAGE
BATTERY...
SEAN MURPHY
HOLLINGSWORTH

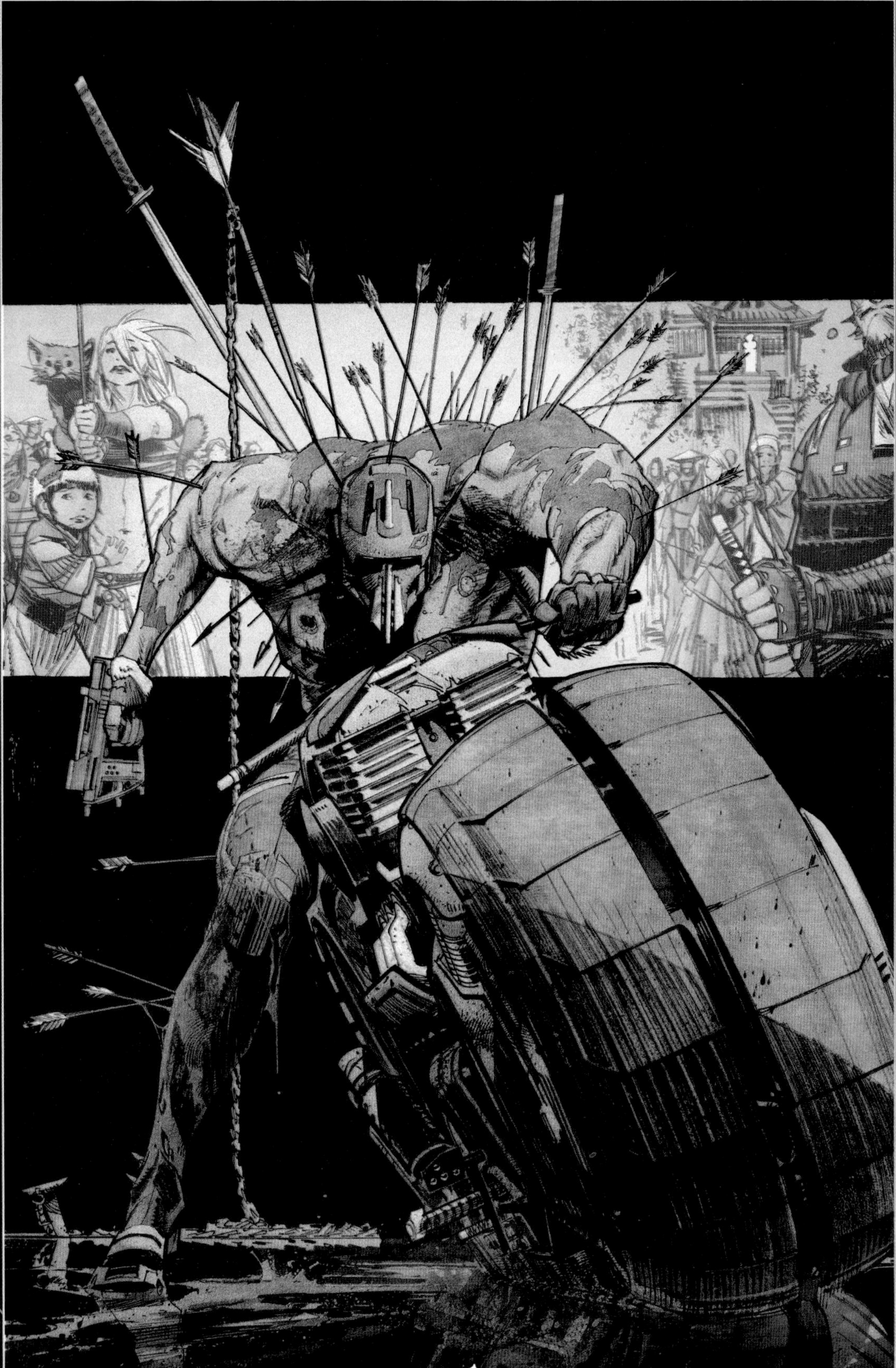

5

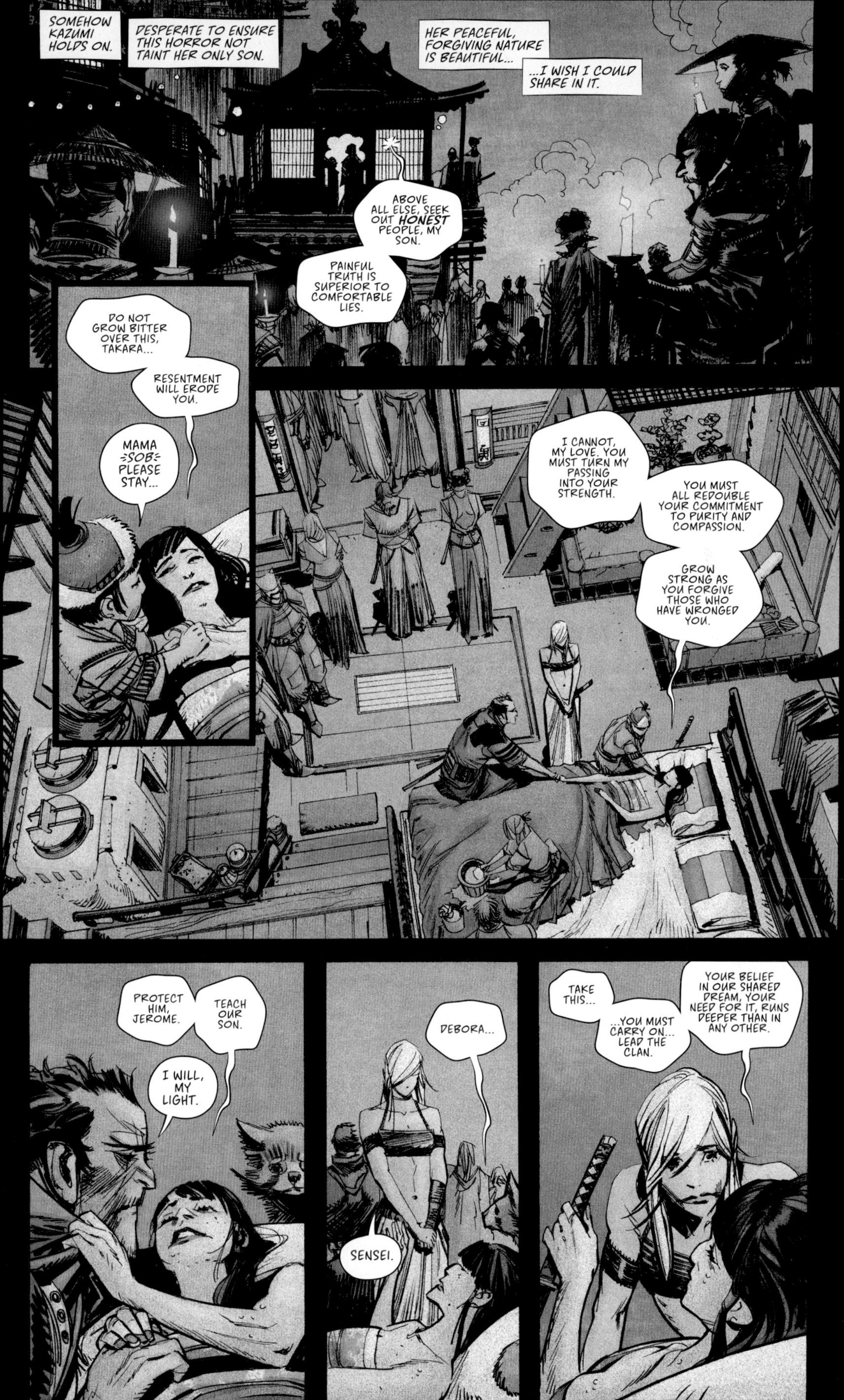
SOMEHOW KAZUMI HOLDS ON.
DESPERATE TO ENSURE THIS HORROR NOT TAINT HER ONLY SON.
HER PEACEFUL, FORGIVING NATURE IS BEAUTIFUL...
...I WISH I COULD SHARE IN IT.
ABOVE ALL ELSE, SEEK OUT HONEST PEOPLE, MY SON.
PAINFUL TRUTH IS SUPERIOR TO COMFORTABLE LIES.
DO NOT GROW BITTER OVER THIS, TAKARA...
RESENTMENT WILL ERODE YOU.
MAMA =SOB= PLEASE STAY...
I CANNOT, MY LOVE. YOU MUST TURN MY PASSING INTO YOUR STRENGTH.
YOU MUST ALL REDOUBLE YOUR COMMITMENT TO PURITY AND COMPASSION.
GROW STRONG AS YOU FORGIVE THOSE WHO HAVE WRONGED YOU.
PROTECT HIM, JEROME.
TEACH OUR SON.
I WILL, MY LIGHT.
DEBORA...
SENSEI.
TAKE THIS...
...YOU MUST CARRY ON... LEAD THE CLAN.
YOUR BELIEF IN OUR SHARED DREAM, YOUR NEED FOR IT, RUNS DEEPER THAN IN ANY OTHER.

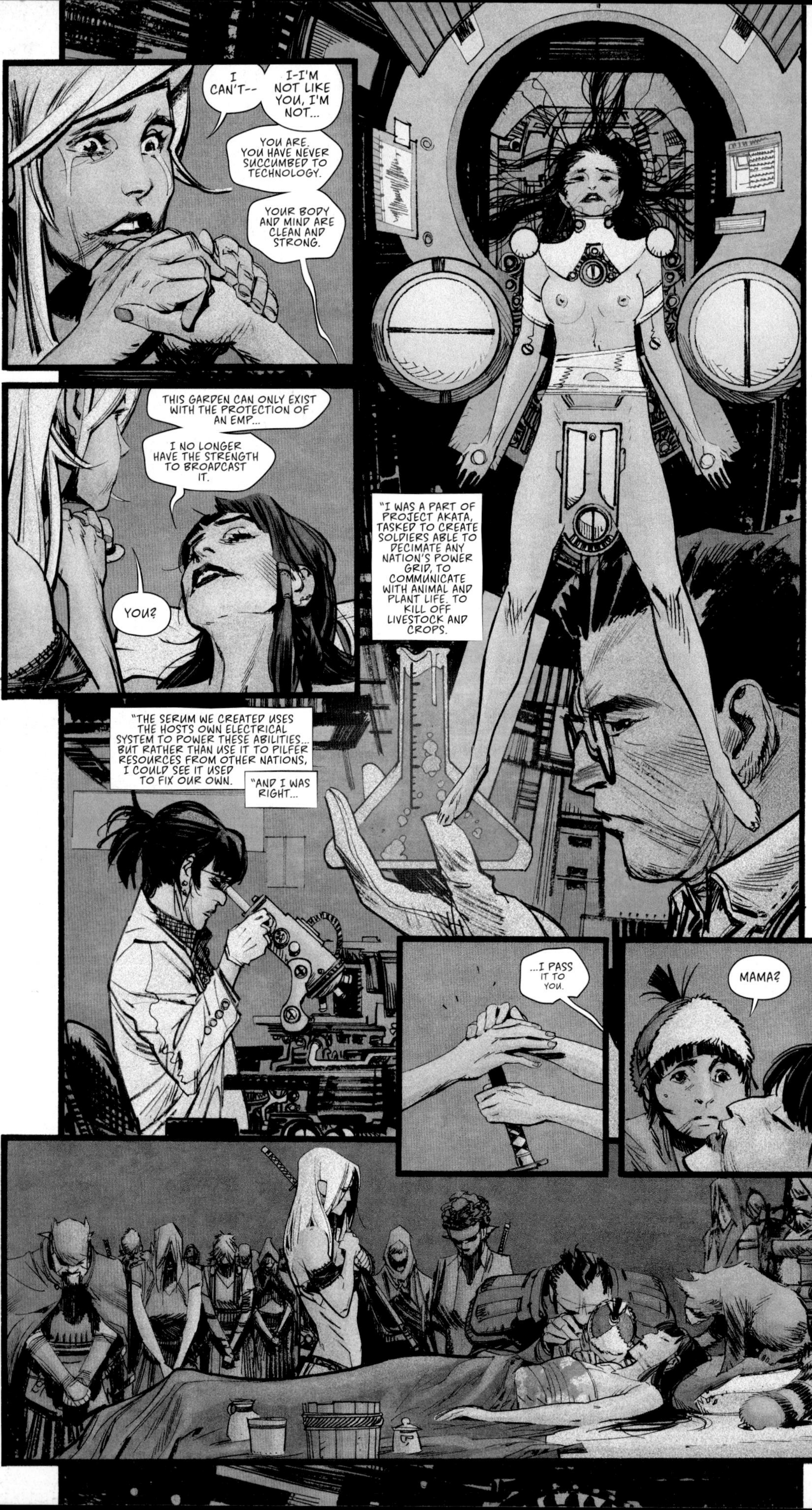

I CAN'T--
I-I'M NOT LIKE YOU, I'M NOT...
YOU ARE. YOU HAVE NEVER SUCCUMBED TO TECHNOLOGY.
YOUR BODY AND MIND ARE CLEAN AND STRONG.
THIS GARDEN CAN ONLY EXIST WITH THE PROTECTION OF AN EMP...
I NO LONGER HAVE THE STRENGTH TO BROADCAST IT.
YOU?
"I WAS A PART OF PROJECT AKATA, TASKED TO CREATE SOLDIERS ABLE TO DECIMATE ANY NATION'S POWER GRID, TO COMMUNICATE WITH ANIMAL AND PLANT LIFE. TO KILL OFF LIVESTOCK AND CROPS.
"THE SERUM WE CREATED USES THE HOSTS OWN ELECTRICAL SYSTEM TO POWER THESE ABILITIES... BUT RATHER THAN USE IT TO PILFER RESOURCES FROM OTHER NATIONS, I COULD SEE IT USED TO FIX OUR OWN.
"AND I WAS RIGHT...
...I PASS IT TO YOU.
MAMA?

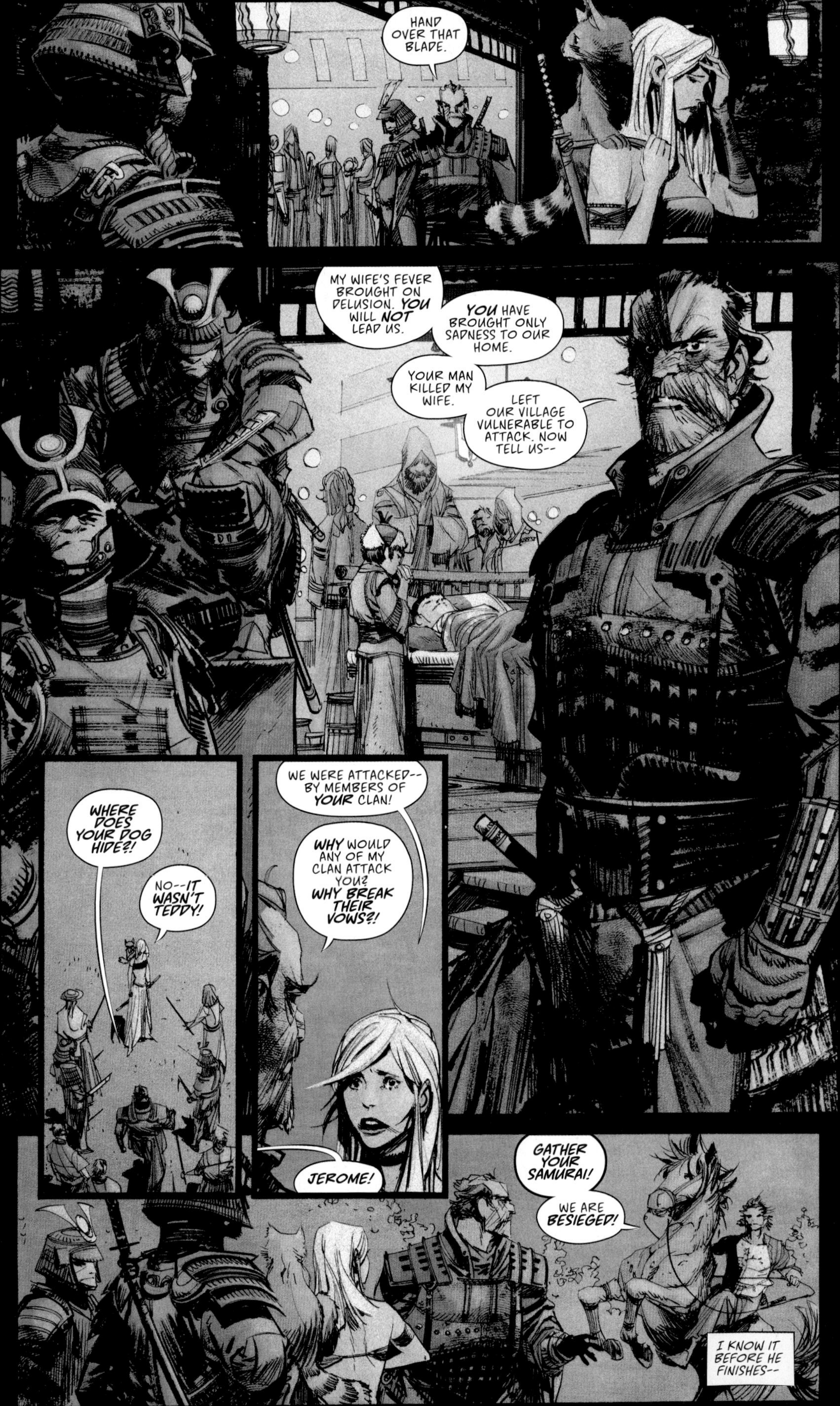

HAND OVER THAT BLADE.
MY WIFE'S FEVER BROUGHT ON DELUSION. YOU WILL NOT LEAD US.
YOU HAVE BROUGHT ONLY SADNESS TO OUR HOME.
YOUR MAN KILLED MY WIFE.
LEFT OUR VILLAGE VULNERABLE TO ATTACK. NOW TELL US--
WHERE DOES YOUR DOG HIDE?!
NO--IT WASN'T TEDDY!
WE WERE ATTACKED--BY MEMBERS OF YOUR CLAN!
WHY WOULD ANY OF MY CLAN ATTACK YOU? WHY BREAK THEIR VOWS?!
JEROME!
GATHER YOUR SAMURAI!
WE ARE BESIEGED!
I KNOW IT BEFORE HE FINISHES--

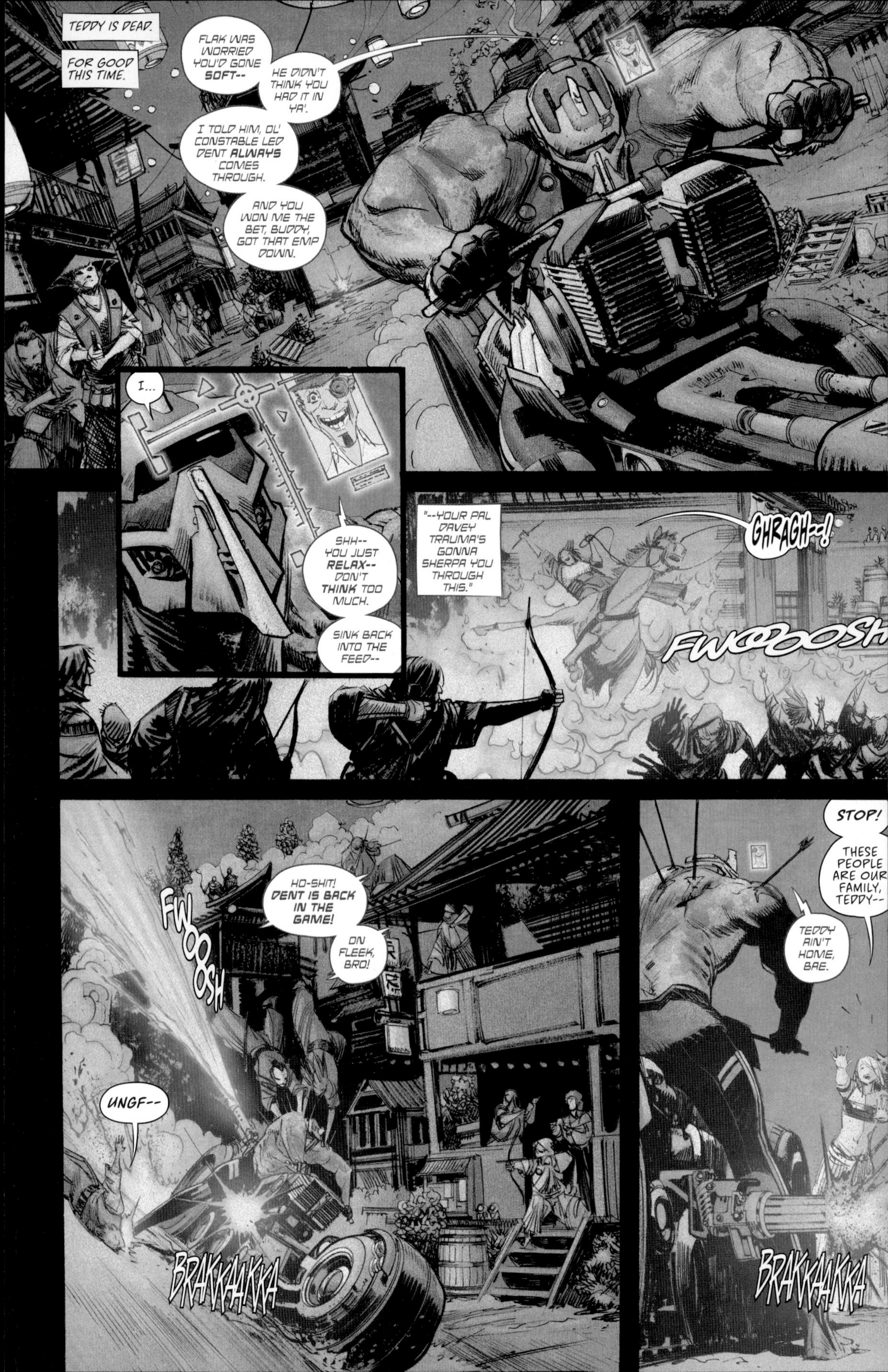

TEDDY IS DEAD.
FOR GOOD THIS TIME.
FLAK WAS WORRIED YOU'D GONE SOFT--
HE DIDN'T THINK YOU HAD IT IN YA'.
I TOLD HIM, OL' CONSTABLE LED DENT ALWAYS COMES THROUGH.
AND YOU WON ME THE BET, BUDDY, GOT THAT EMP DOWN.
I...
SHH-- YOU JUST RELAX-- DON'T THINK TOO MUCH.
SINK BACK INTO THE FEED--
"--YOUR PAL DAVEY TRAUMA'S GONNA SHERPA YOU THROUGH THIS."
GHRAGH--!
FWOOOOSH
FWOOOSH
HO-SHIT! DENT IS BACK IN THE GAME!
ON FLEEK, BRO!
UNGF--
BRAKKAAKKA
STOP!
THESE PEOPLE ARE OUR FAMILY, TEDDY--
TEDDY AIN'T HOME, BAE.
BRAKKAAKKA

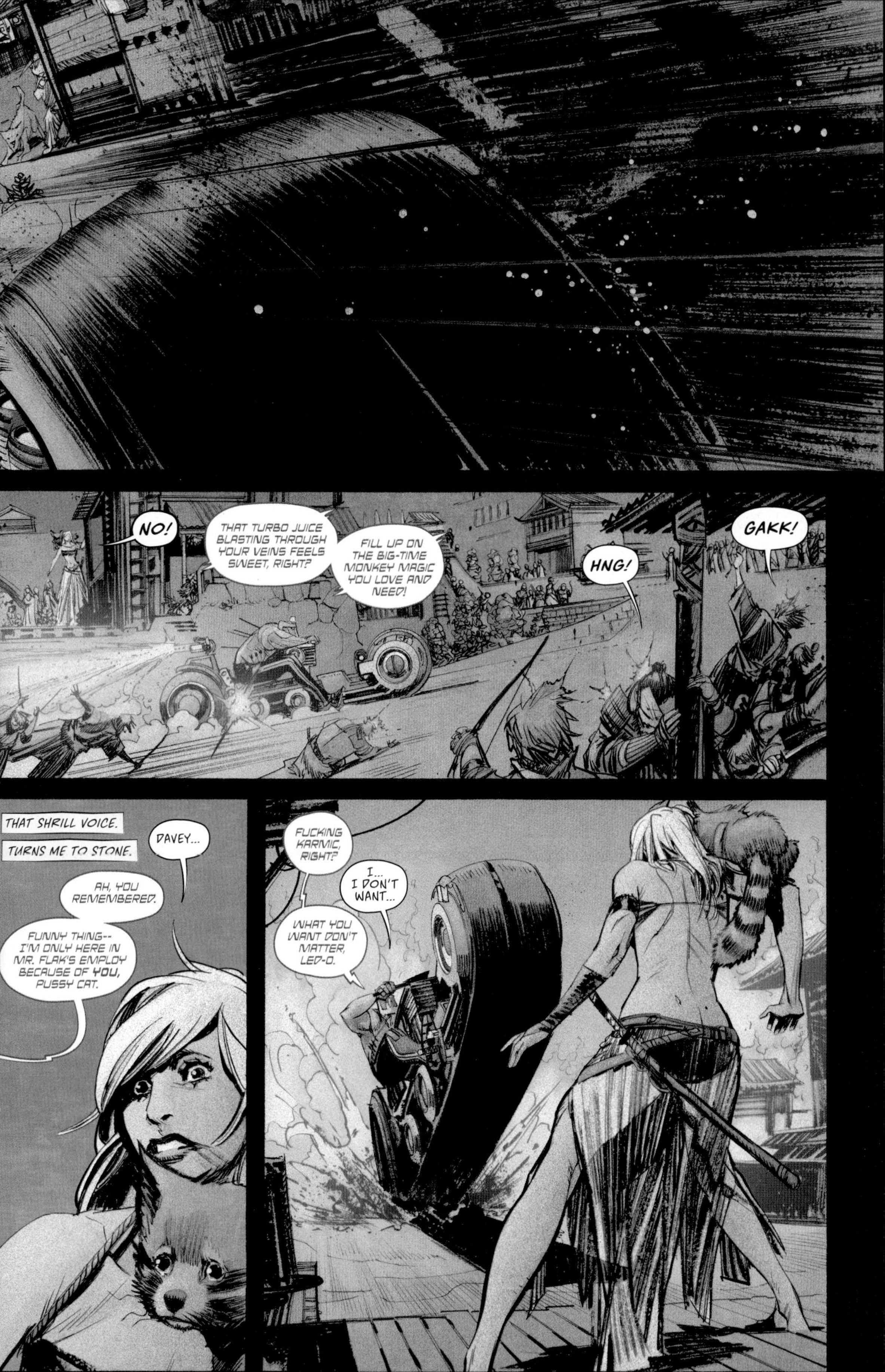
NO!
THAT TURBO JUICE BLASTING THROUGH YOUR VEINS FEELS SWEET, RIGHT?
FILL UP ON THE BIG-TIME MONKEY MAGIC YOU LOVE AND NEED!
HNG!
GAKK!
THAT SHRILL VOICE.
TURNS ME TO STONE.
DAVEY...
AH, YOU REMEMBERED.
FUNNY THING-- I'M ONLY HERE IN MR. FLAK'S EMPLOY BECAUSE OF YOU, PUSSY CAT.
FUCKING KARMIC, RIGHT?
I... I DON'T WANT...
WHAT YOU WANT DON'T MATTER, LED-O.

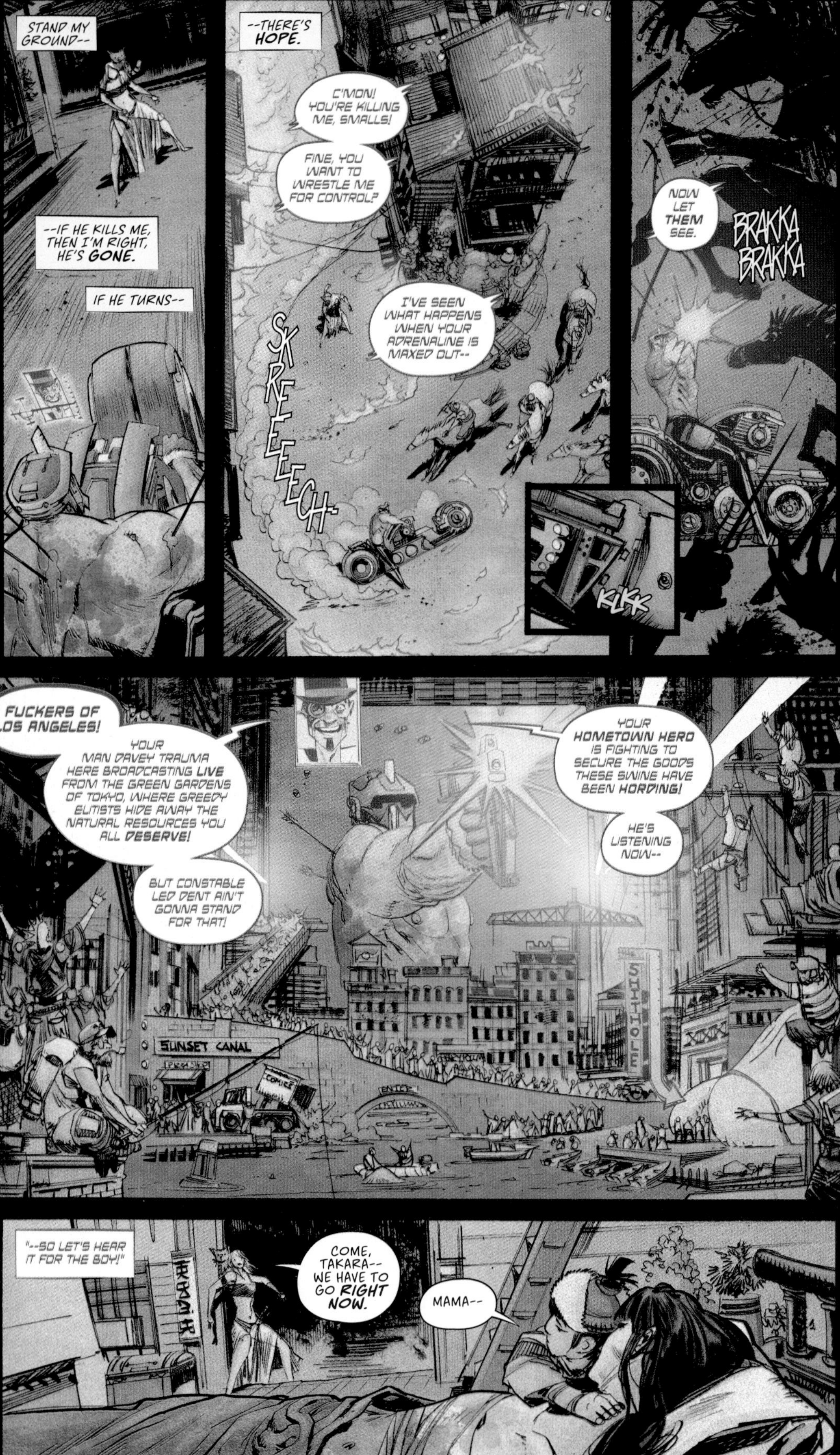
STAND MY GROUND--
--IF HE KILLS ME, THEN I'M RIGHT, HE'S GONE.
IF HE TURNS--
--THERE'S HOPE.
C'MON! YOU'RE KILLING ME, SMALLS!
FINE, YOU WANT TO WRESTLE ME FOR CONTROL?
I'VE SEEN WHAT HAPPENS WHEN YOUR ADRENALINE IS MAXED OUT--
SKREEEEECH--
KLIKK
NOW LET THEM SEE.
BRAKKA BRAKKA
FUCKERS OF LOS ANGELES!
YOUR MAN DAVEY TRAUMA HERE BROADCASTING LIVE FROM THE GREEN GARDENS OF TOKYO, WHERE GREEDY ELITISTS HIDE AWAY THE NATURAL RESOURCES YOU ALL DESERVE!
BUT CONSTABLE LED DENT AIN'T GONNA STAND FOR THAT!
YOUR HOMETOWN HERO IS FIGHTING TO SECURE THE GOODS THESE SWINE HAVE BEEN HORDING!
HE'S LISTENING NOW--
SUNSET CANAL
COMICS
SHITHOLE
"--SO LET'S HEAR IT FOR THE BOY!"
COME, TAKARA-- WE HAVE TO GO RIGHT NOW.
MAMA--

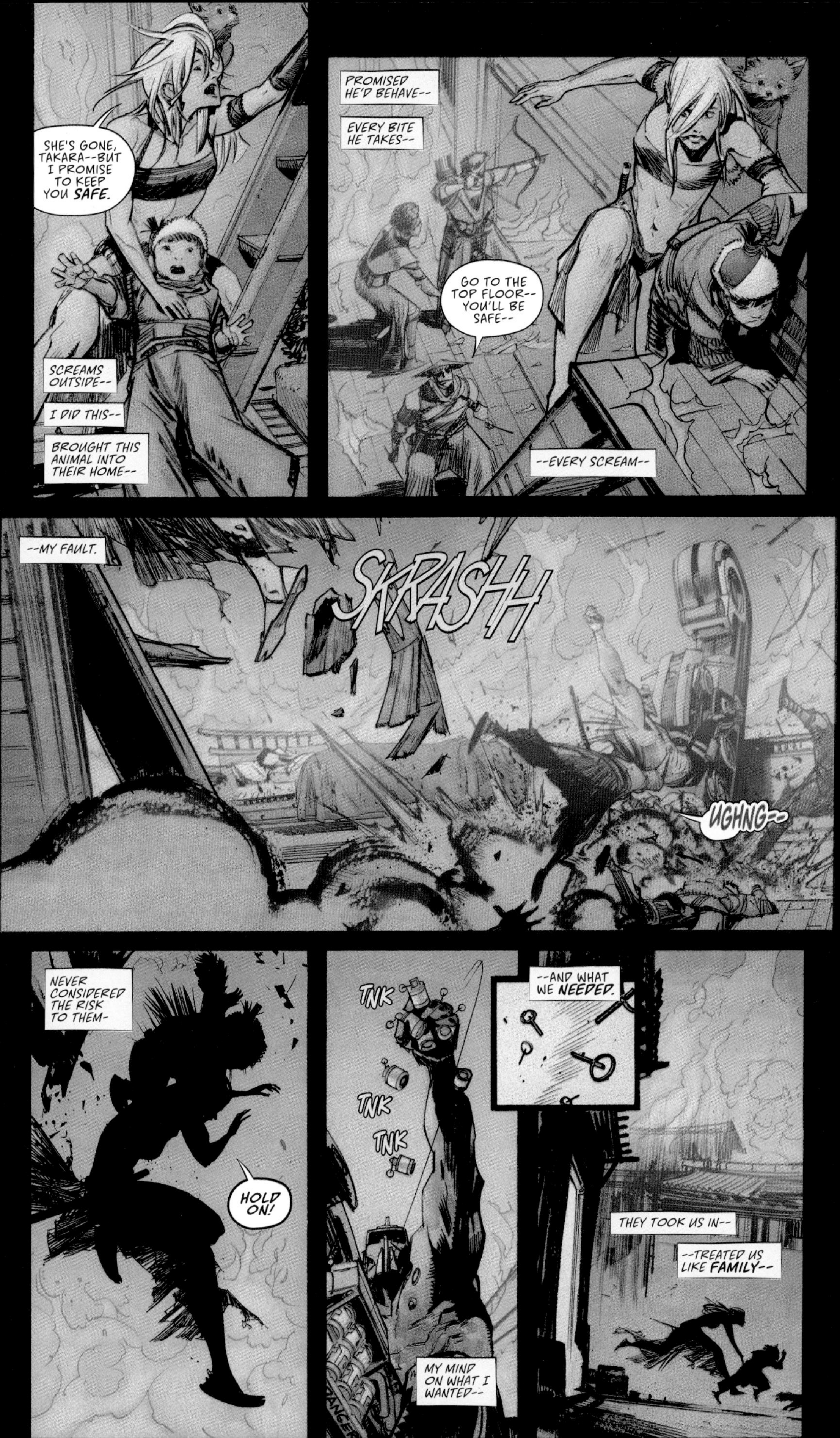
SHE'S GONE, TAKARA--BUT I PROMISE TO KEEP YOU SAFE.
SCREAMS OUTSIDE--
I DID THIS--
BROUGHT THIS ANIMAL INTO THEIR HOME--
PROMISED HE'D BEHAVE--
EVERY BITE HE TAKES--
GO TO THE TOP FLOOR--YOU'LL BE SAFE--
--EVERY SCREAM--
--MY FAULT.
SKRASHH
UGHNG--
NEVER CONSIDERED THE RISK TO THEM-
HOLD ON!
TNK
TNK
TNK
MY MIND ON WHAT I WANTED--
--AND WHAT WE NEEDED.
THEY TOOK US IN--
--TREATED US LIKE FAMILY--

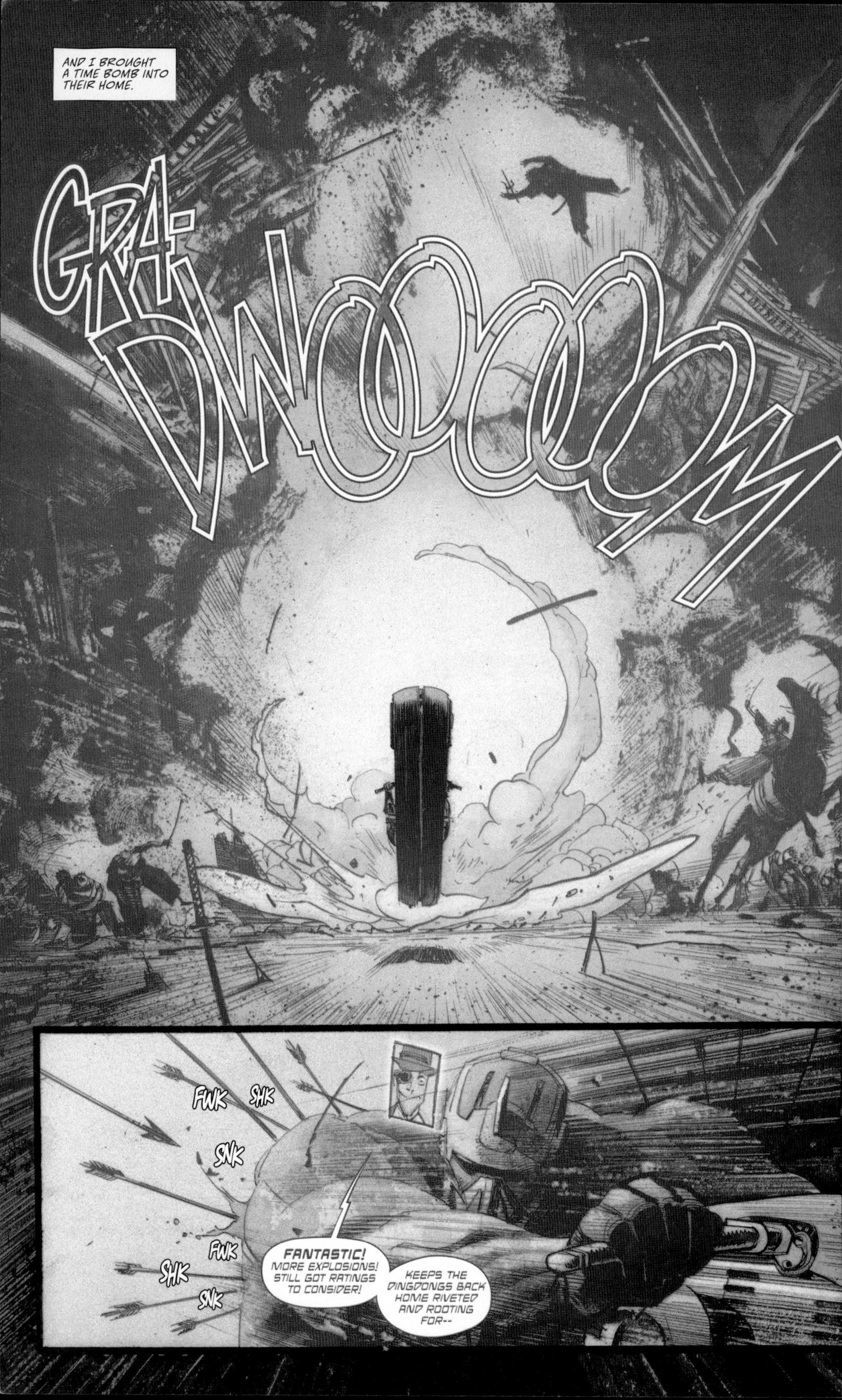
AND I BROUGHT A TIME BOMB INTO THEIR HOME.
GRA-DWOOOOM
FWK
SHK
SNK
FWK
SHK
SNK
FANTASTIC! MORE EXPLOSIONS! STILL GOT RATINGS TO CONSIDER!
KEEPS THE DINGDONGS BACK HOME RIVETED AND ROOTING FOR--

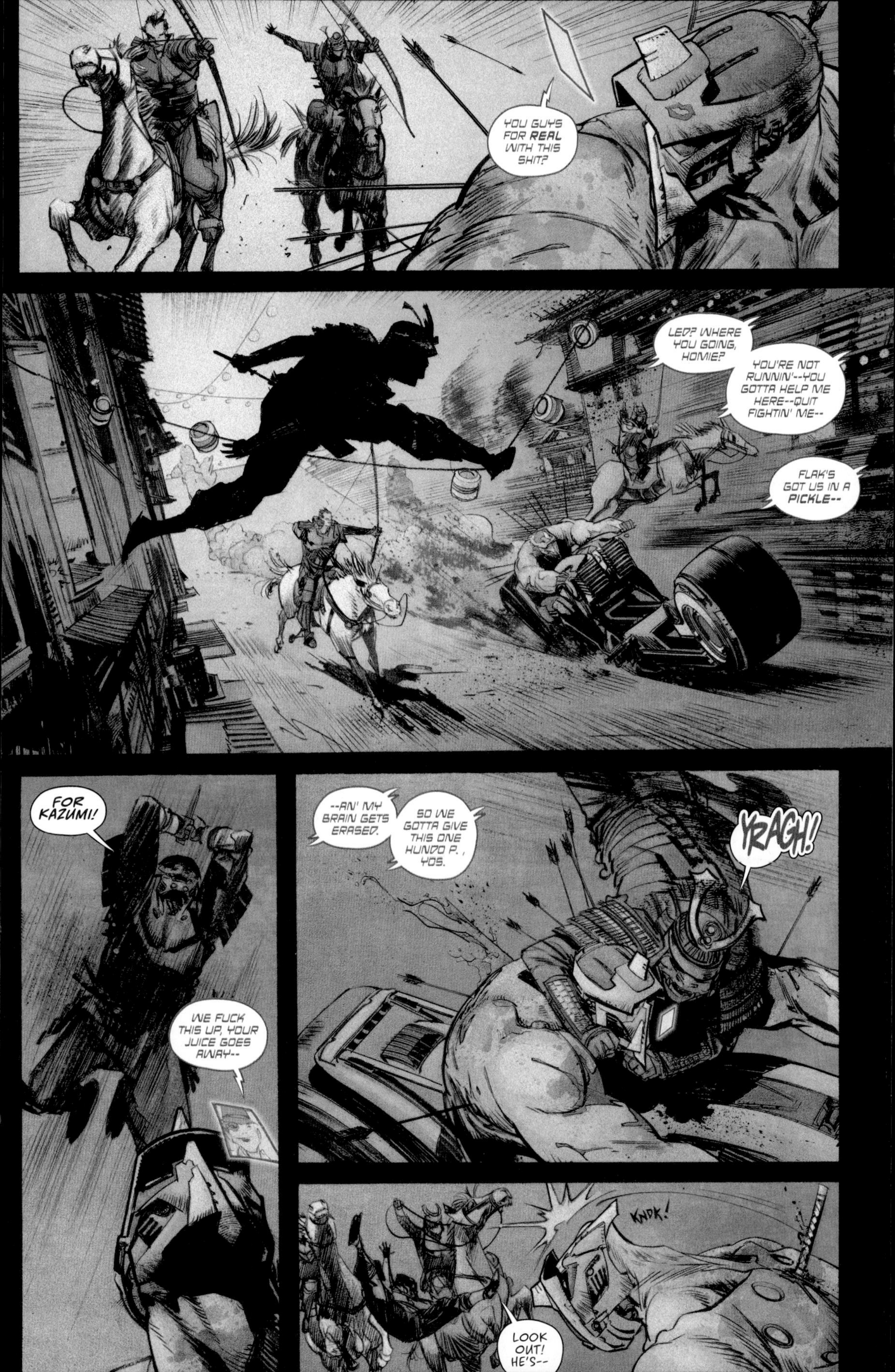
YOU GUYS FOR REAL WITH THIS SHIT?
LEO? WHERE YOU GOING, HOMIE?
YOU'RE NOT RUNNIN'--YOU GOTTA HELP ME HERE--QUIT FIGHTIN' ME--
FLAK'S GOT US IN A PICKLE--
FOR KAZUMI!
WE FUCK THIS UP, YOUR JUICE GOES AWAY--
--AN' MY BRAIN GETS ERASED.
SO WE GOTTA GIVE THIS ONE HUNDO P., YOS.
YRAGH!
KNOK!
LOOK OUT! HE'S--

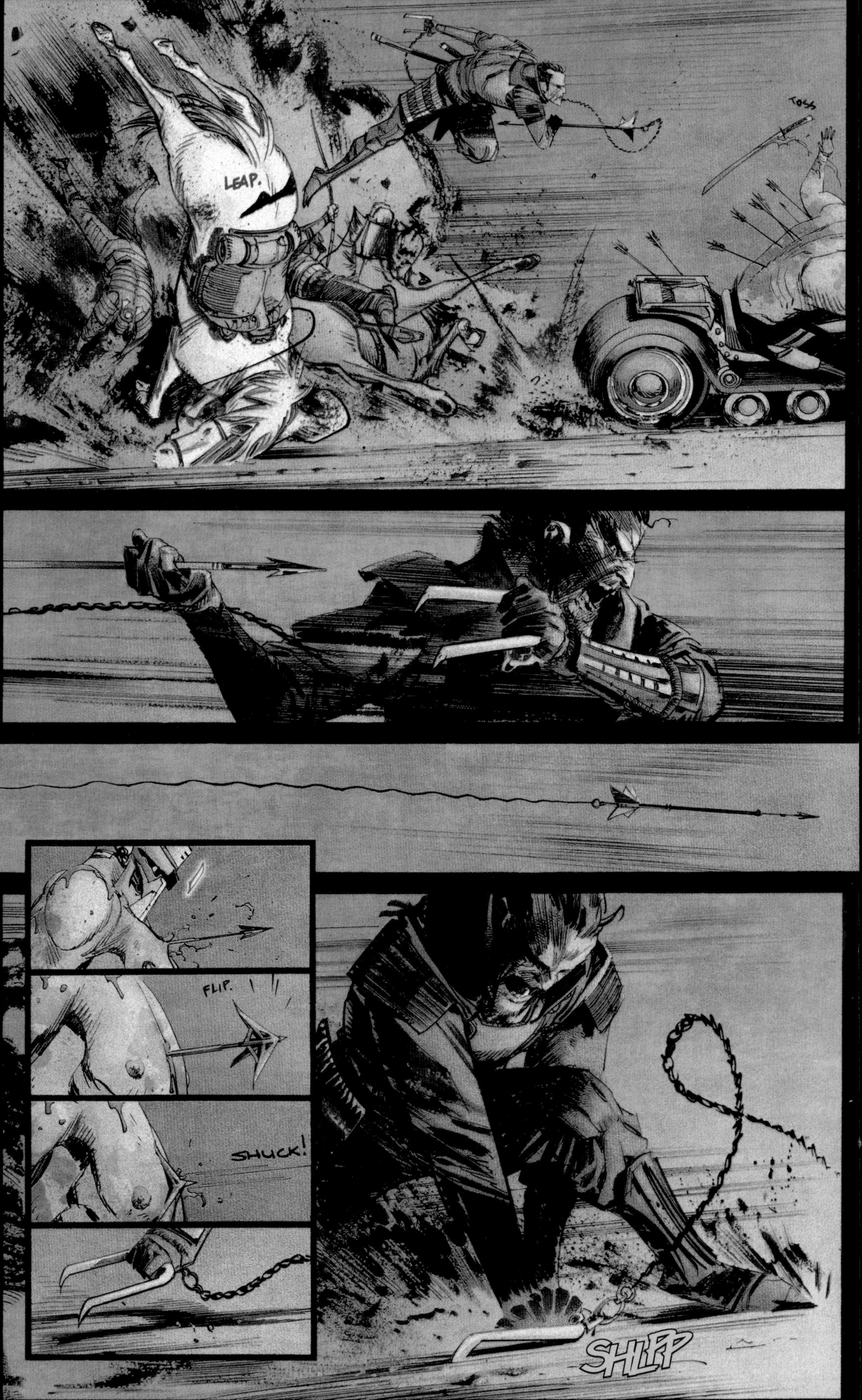

TOSS
LEAP.
FLIP.
SHUCK!
SHLRP

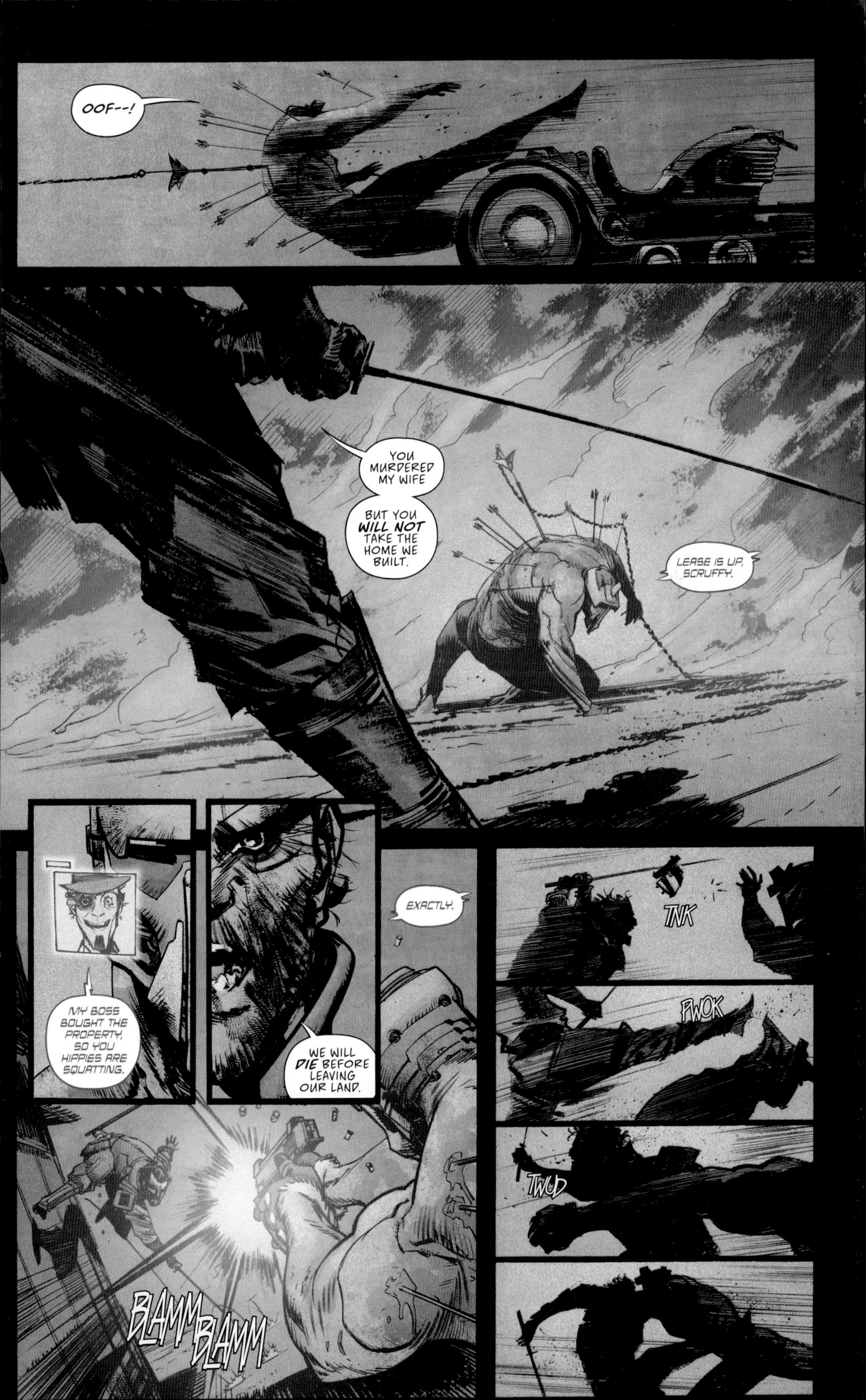
OOF--!
YOU MURDERED MY WIFE
BUT YOU WILL NOT TAKE THE HOME WE BUILT.
LEASE IS UP, SCRUFFY.
MY BOSS BOUGHT THE PROPERTY, SO YOU HIPPIES ARE SQUATTING.
WE WILL DIE BEFORE LEAVING OUR LAND.
EXACTLY.
BLAMM BLAMM
TNK
PWOK
TWUD

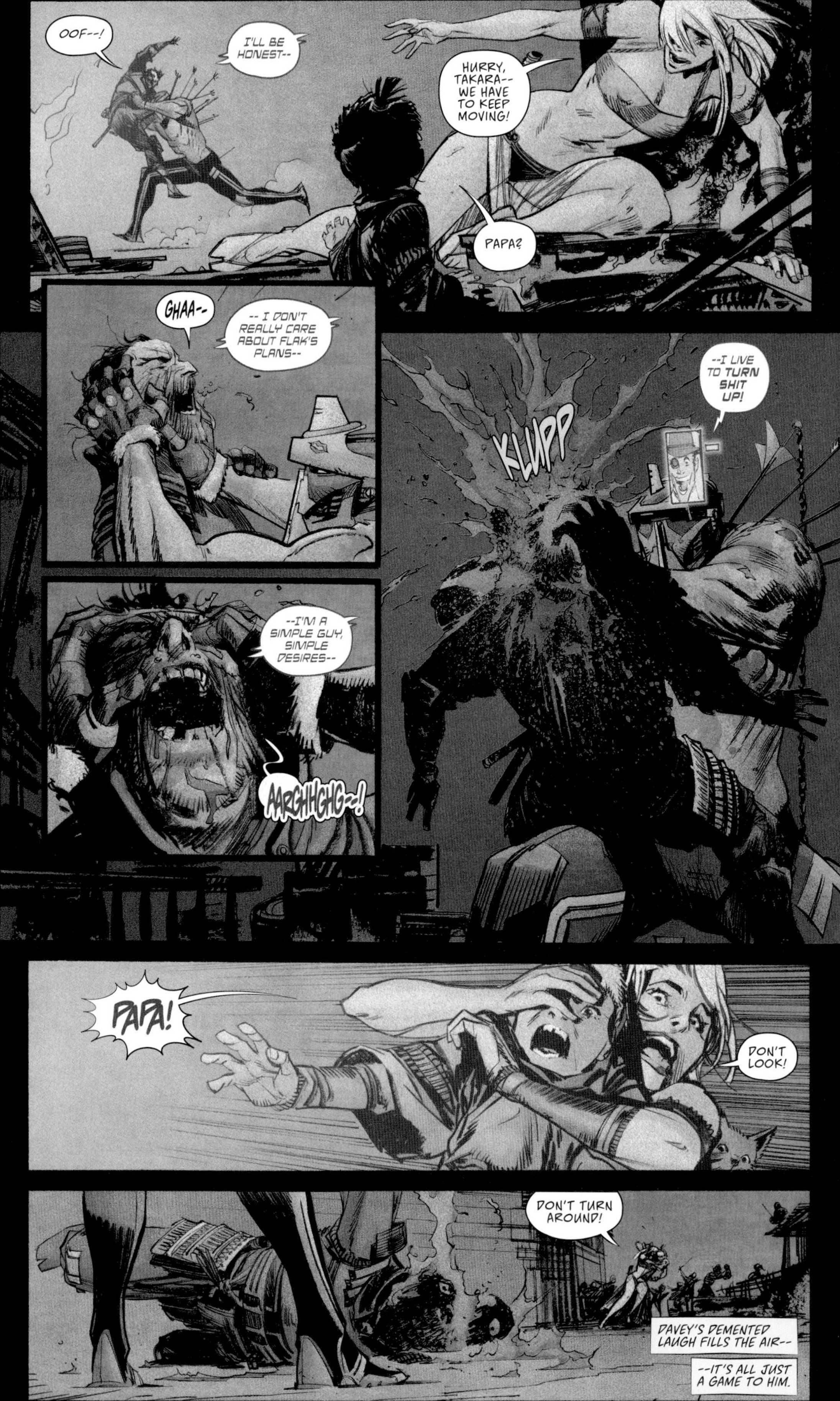

OOF--!
I'LL BE HONEST--
HURRY, TAKARA-- WE HAVE TO KEEP MOVING!
PAPA?
GHAA--
-- I DON'T REALLY CARE ABOUT FLAK'S PLANS--
--I'M A SIMPLE GUY, SIMPLE DESIRES--
AARGHHGHG--!
KLUPP
--I LIVE TO TURN SHIT UP!
PAPA!
DON'T LOOK!
DON'T TURN AROUND!
DAVEY'S DEMENTED LAUGH FILLS THE AIR--
--IT'S ALL JUST A GAME TO HIM.

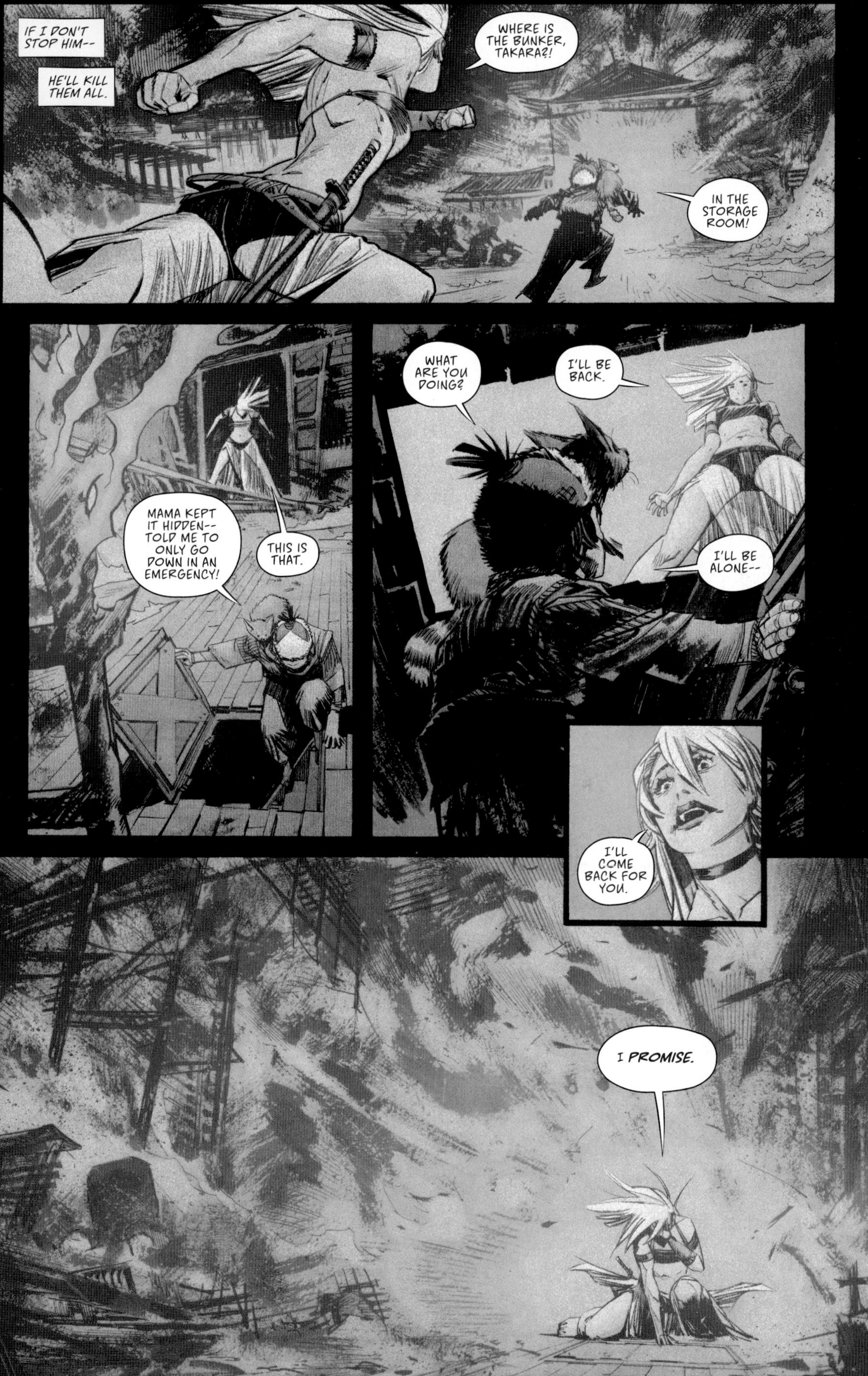
IF I DON'T STOP HIM--
HE'LL KILL THEM ALL.
WHERE IS THE BUNKER, TAKARA?!
IN THE STORAGE ROOM!
MAMA KEPT IT HIDDEN--TOLD ME TO ONLY GO DOWN IN AN EMERGENCY!
THIS IS THAT.
WHAT ARE YOU DOING?
I'LL BE BACK.
I'LL BE ALONE--
I'LL COME BACK FOR YOU.
I PROMISE.

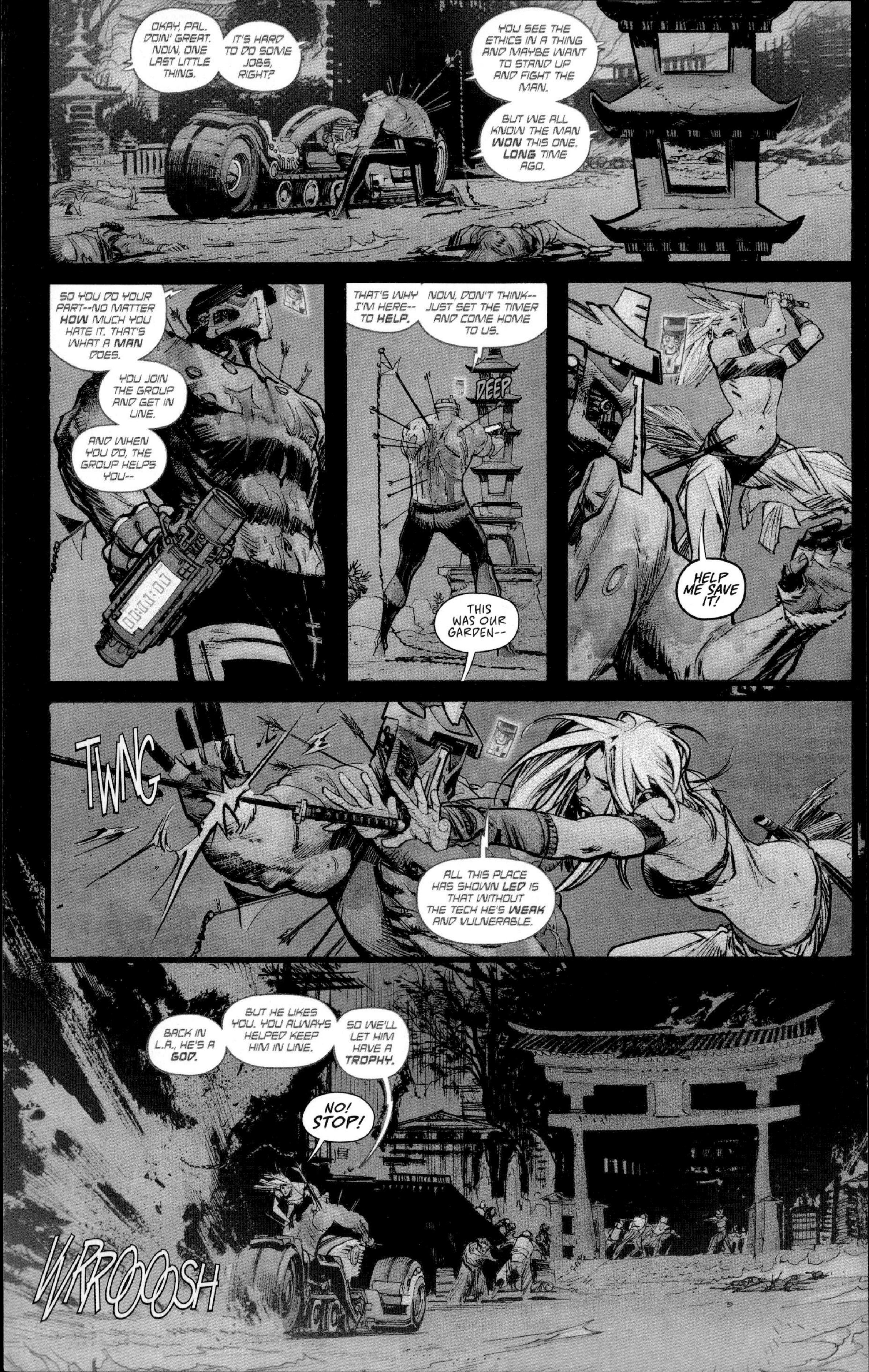

OKAY, PAL. DOIN' GREAT. NOW, ONE LAST LITTLE THING.
IT'S HARD TO DO SOME JOBS, RIGHT?
YOU SEE THE ETHICS IN A THING AND MAYBE WANT TO STAND UP AND FIGHT THE MAN.
BUT WE ALL KNOW THE MAN WON THIS ONE. LONG TIME AGO.
SO YOU DO YOUR PART--NO MATTER HOW MUCH YOU HATE IT. THAT'S WHAT A MAN DOES.
YOU JOIN THE GROUP AND GET IN LINE.
AND WHEN YOU DO, THE GROUP HELPS YOU--
THAT'S WHY I'M HERE--TO HELP.
NOW, DON'T THINK--JUST SET THE TIMER AND COME HOME TO US.
DEEP
THIS WAS OUR GARDEN--
HELP ME SAVE IT!
TWNG
ALL THIS PLACE HAS SHOWN LED IS THAT WITHOUT THE TECH HE'S WEAK AND VULNERABLE.
BACK IN L.A., HE'S A GOD.
BUT HE LIKES YOU. YOU ALWAYS HELPED KEEP HIM IN LINE.
SO WE'LL LET HIM HAVE A TROPHY.
NO! STOP!
WRROOOSH

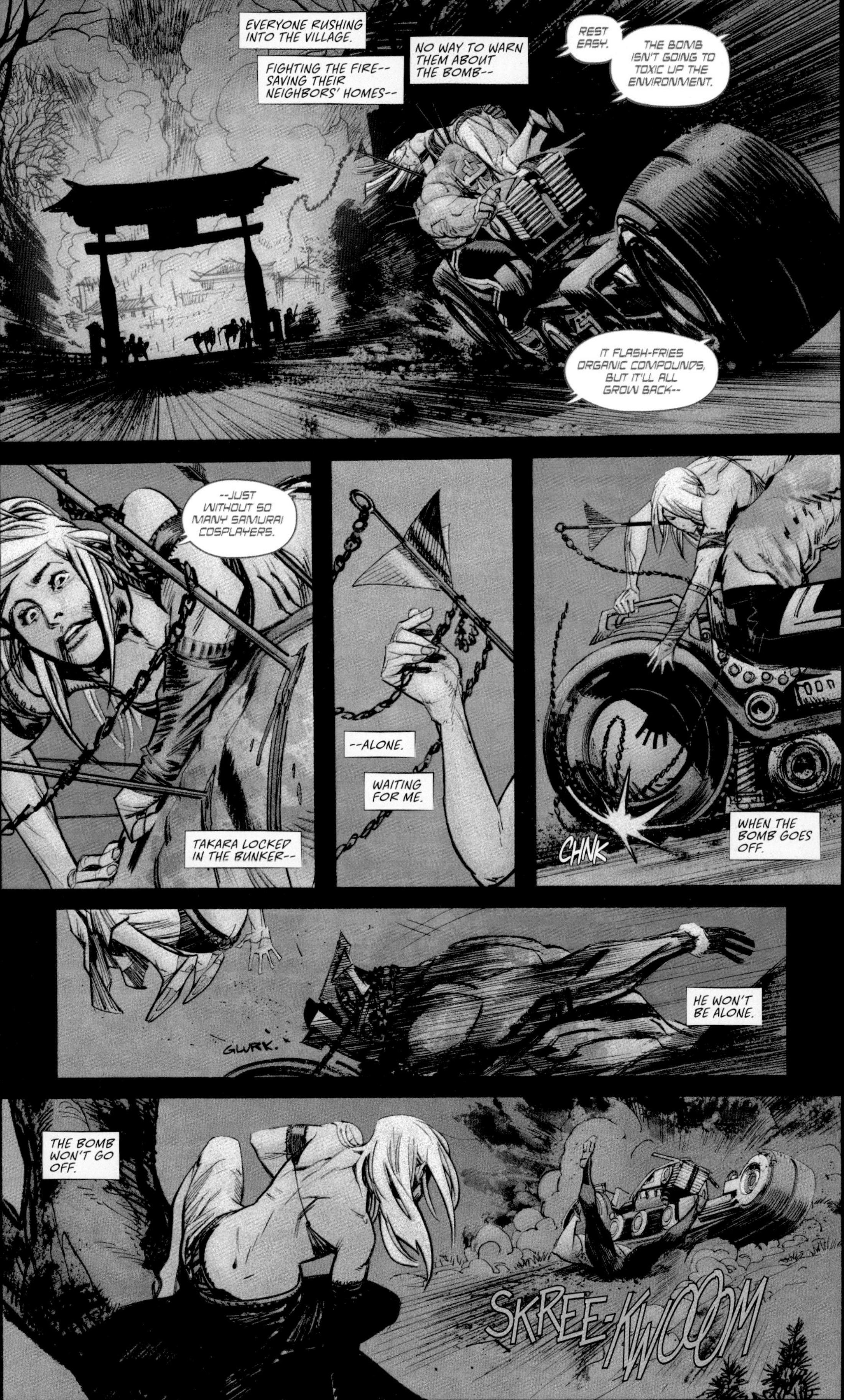
EVERYONE RUSHING INTO THE VILLAGE.
FIGHTING THE FIRE--SAVING THEIR NEIGHBORS' HOMES--
NO WAY TO WARN THEM ABOUT THE BOMB--
REST EASY.
THE BOMB ISN'T GOING TO TOXIC UP THE ENVIRONMENT.
IT FLASH-FRIES ORGANIC COMPOUNDS, BUT IT'LL ALL GROW BACK--
--JUST WITHOUT SO MANY SAMURAI COSPLAYERS.
TAKARA LOCKED IN THE BUNKER--
--ALONE.
WAITING FOR ME.
CHNK
WHEN THE BOMB GOES OFF.
GLURK.
HE WON'T BE ALONE.
THE BOMB WON'T GO OFF.
SKREE-KWOOOM

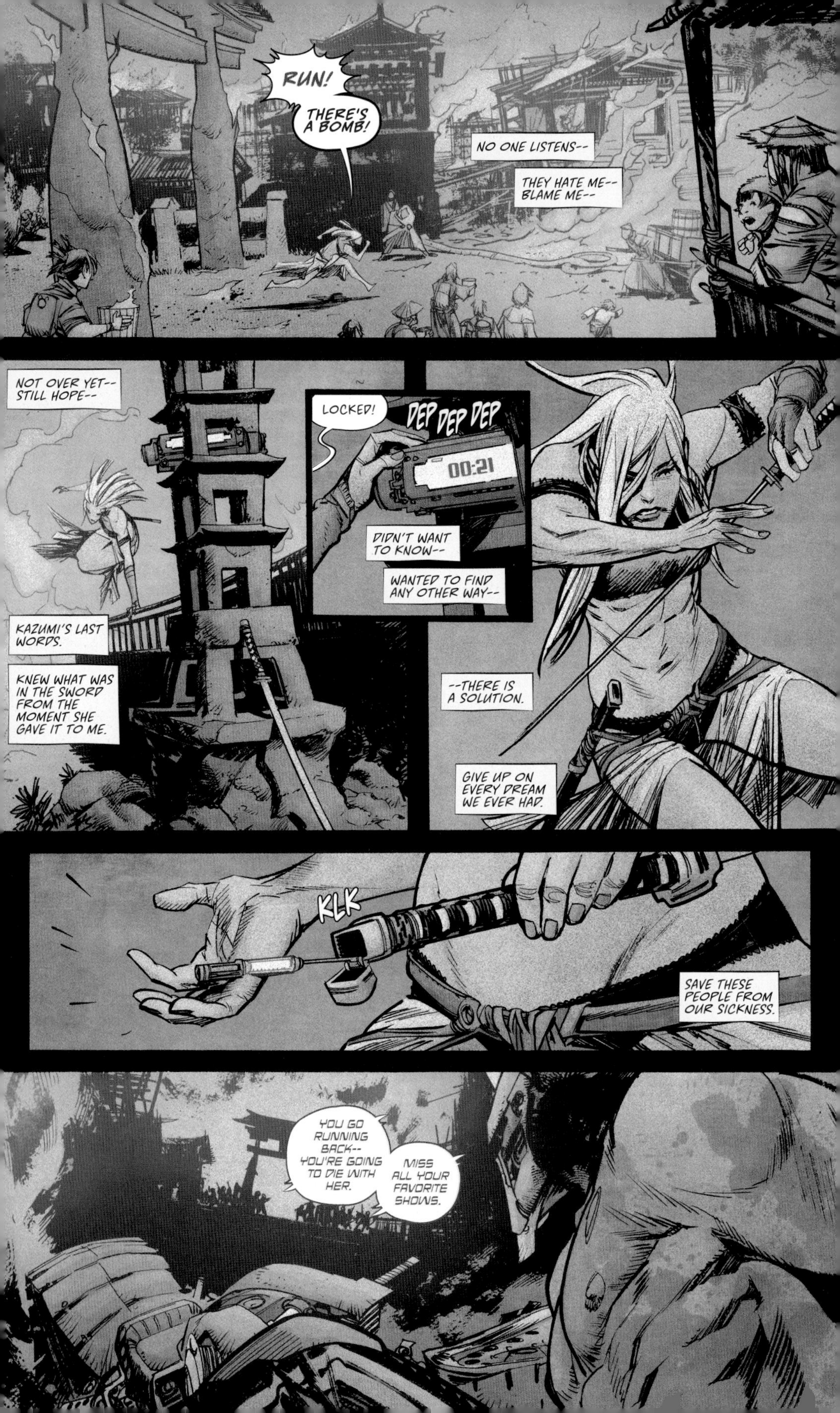
RUN!
THERE'S A BOMB!
NO ONE LISTENS--
THEY HATE ME-- BLAME ME--
NOT OVER YET-- STILL HOPE--
KAZUMI'S LAST WORDS.
KNEW WHAT WAS IN THE SWORD FROM THE MOMENT SHE GAVE IT TO ME.
LOCKED!
DEP DEP DEP
00:21
DIDN'T WANT TO KNOW--
WANTED TO FIND ANY OTHER WAY--
--THERE IS A SOLUTION.
GIVE UP ON EVERY DREAM WE EVER HAD.
KLK
SAVE THESE PEOPLE FROM OUR SICKNESS.
YOU GO RUNNING BACK-- YOU'RE GOING TO DIE WITH HER.
MISS ALL YOUR FAVORITE SHOWS.

I DO THIS--

--I BECOME AN
EMP BATTERY--

--SHORT
THE BOMB--

00:07

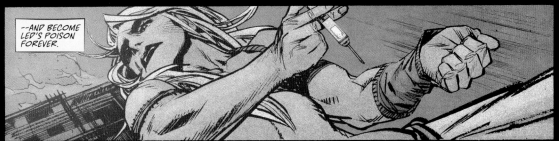

--AND BECOME
LEO'S POISON
FOREVER.

DUDE!
RETHINK
RUNNING AT
THE BOMB!

HE'S BEEN
MINE LONG
ENOUGH.

FOR FUCK'S
SAKE-- THERE
ARE MORE
FISH IN THE
SEA--

D-
D-D-
DEBB--

DEBBIE!

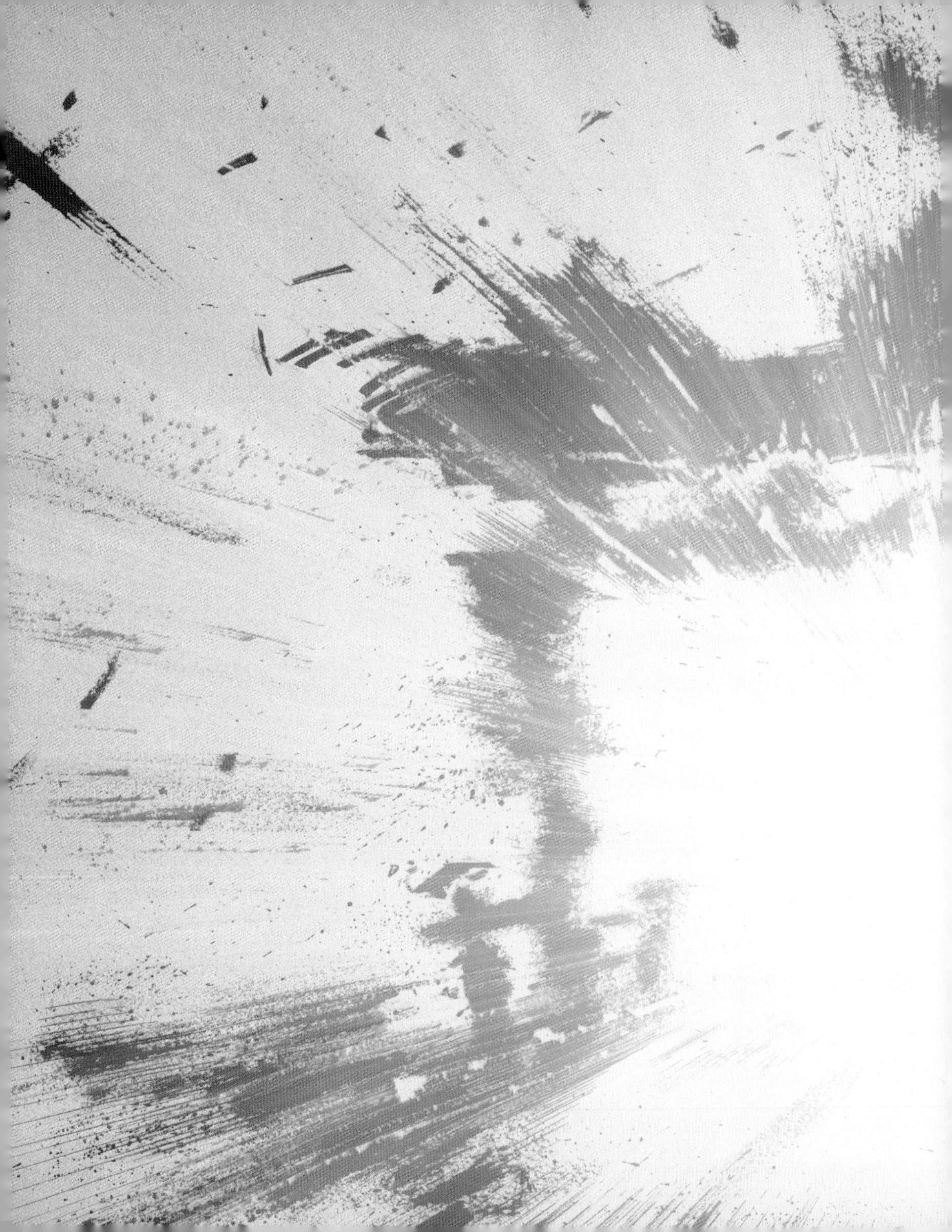

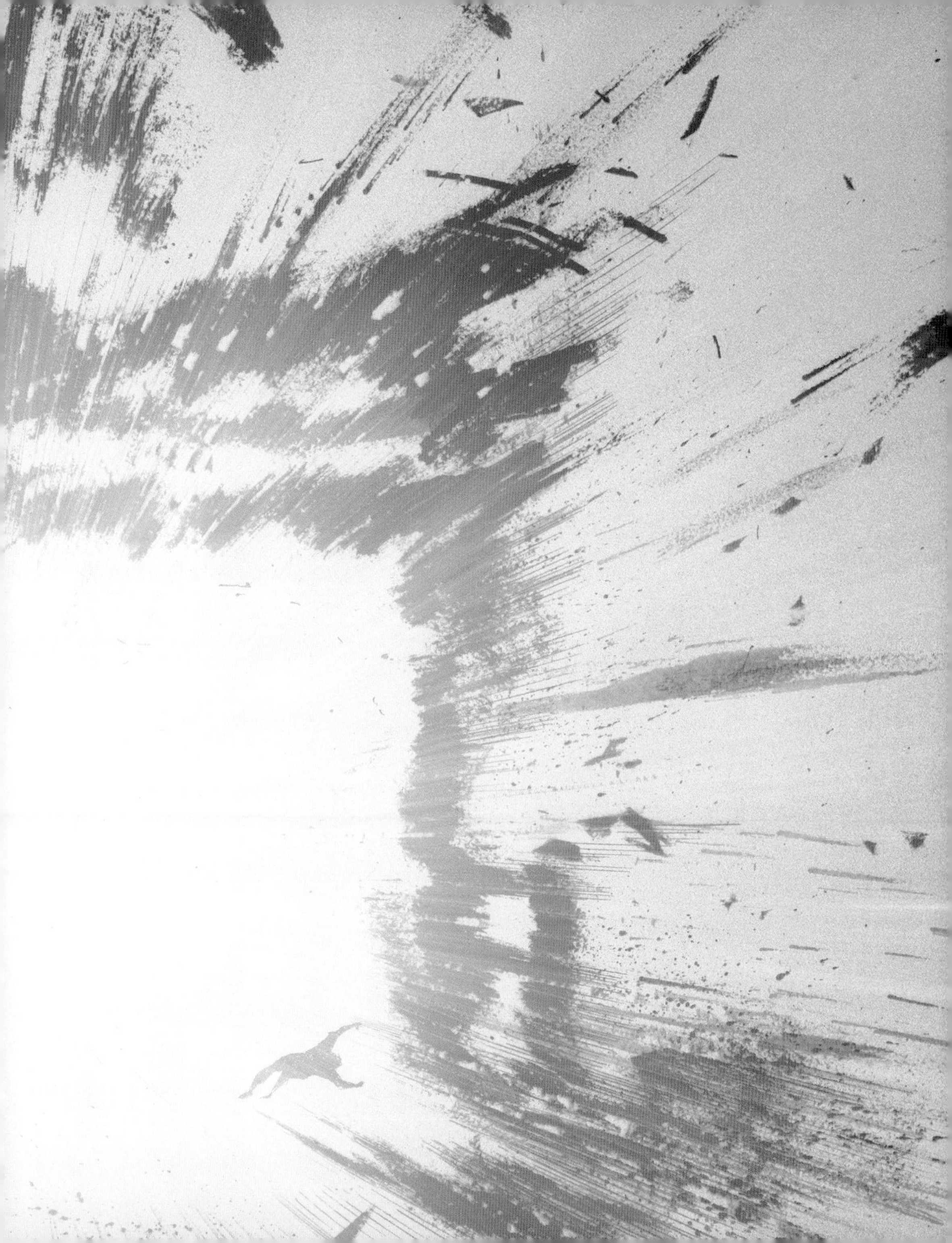

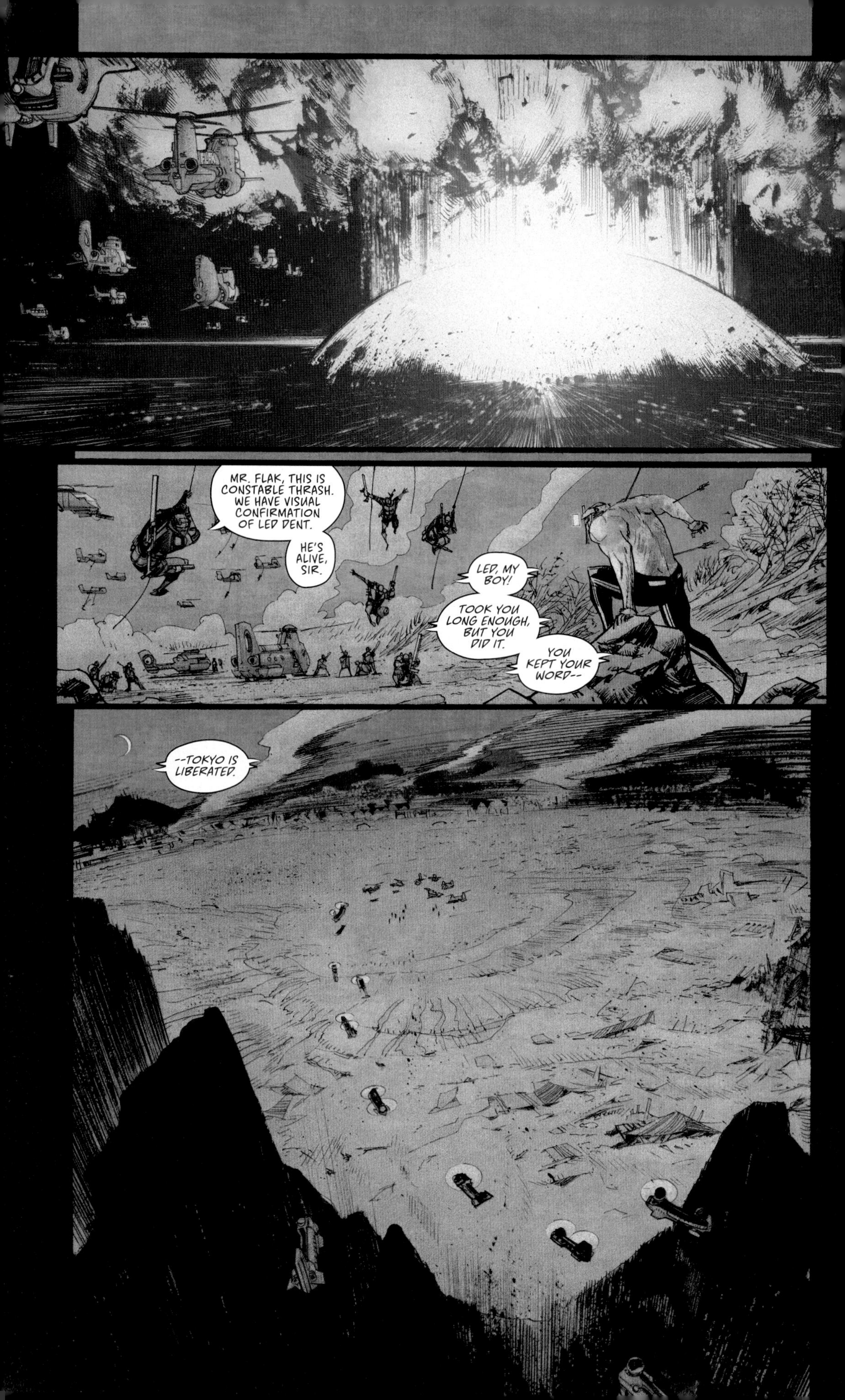
MR. FLAK, THIS IS CONSTABLE THRASH. WE HAVE VISUAL CONFIRMATION OF LED DENT.
HE'S ALIVE, SIR.
LED, MY BOY!
TOOK YOU LONG ENOUGH, BUT YOU DID IT.
YOU KEPT YOUR WORD--
--TOKYO IS LIBERATED.

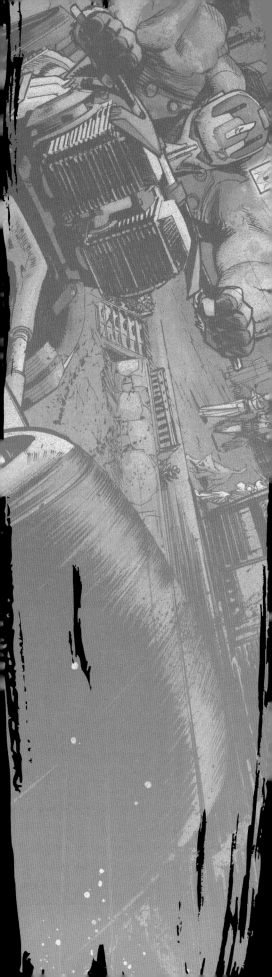

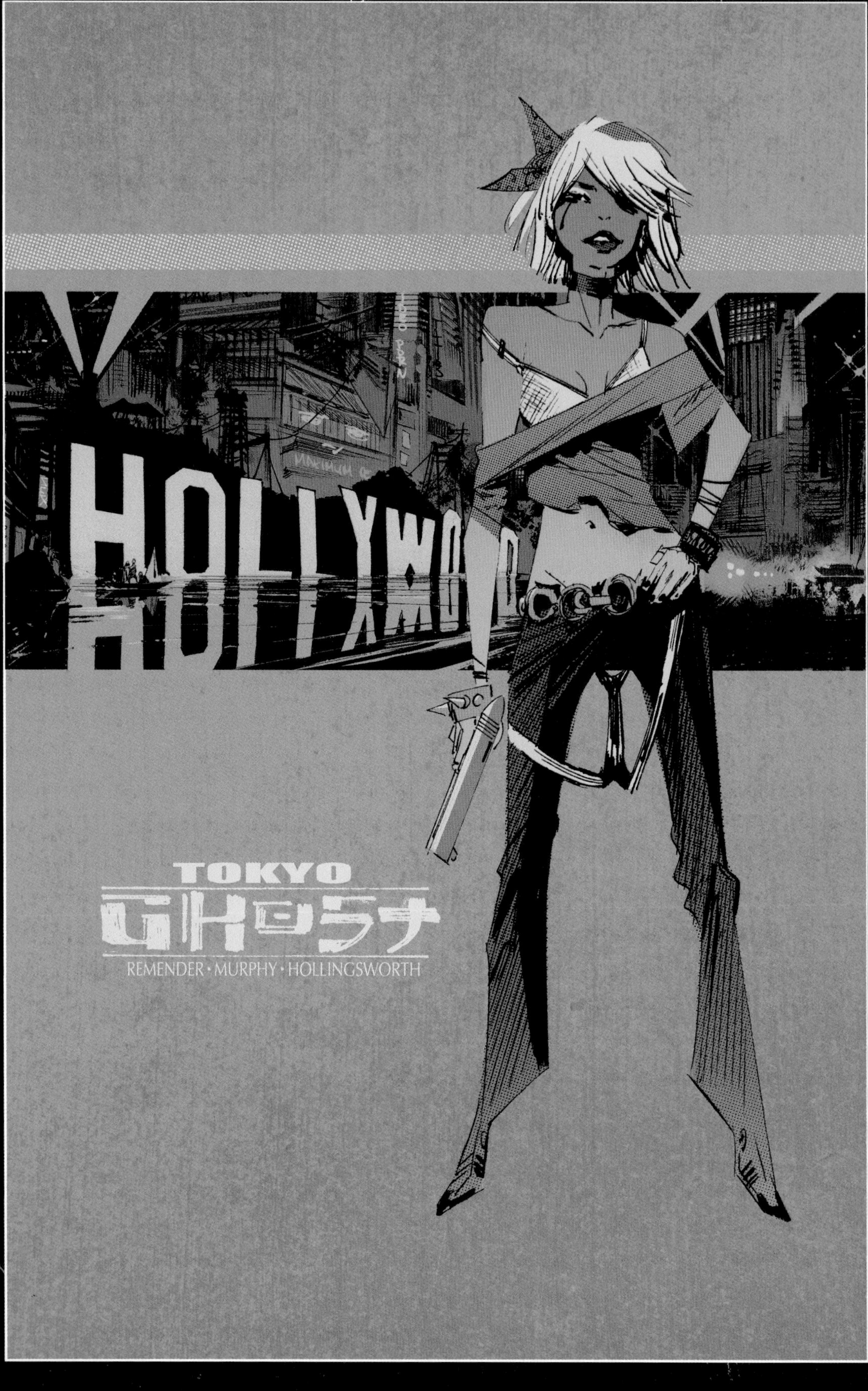
HOLLYWOOD
TOKYO
GHOST
REMENDER · MURPHY · HOLLINGSWORTH

#1 VARIANT BY SEAN MURPHY & DAVE McCAIG

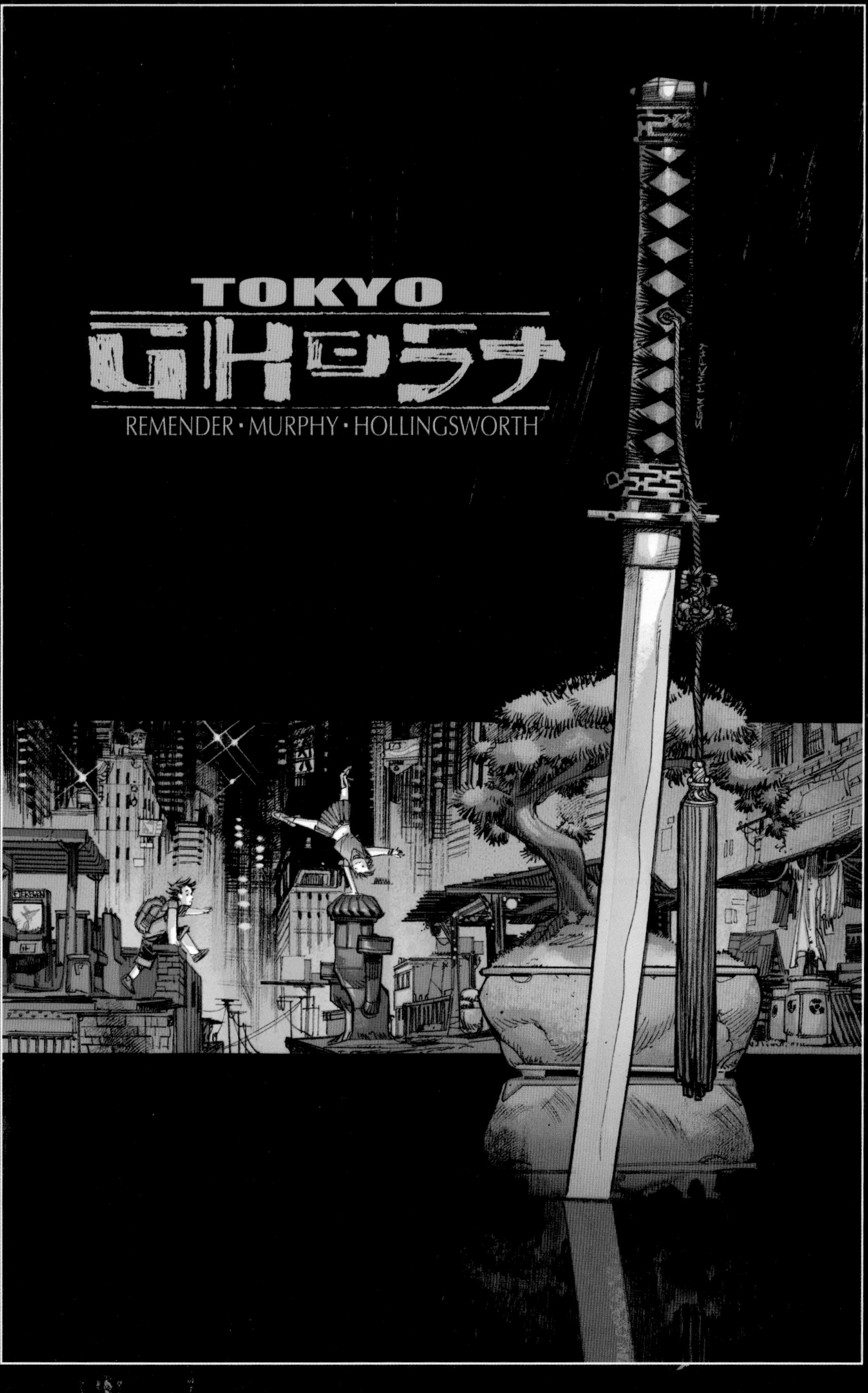
TOKYO
GHOST
REMENDER • MURPHY • HOLLINGSWORTH

#2 VARIANT BY SEAN MURPHY & DAVE McCAIG

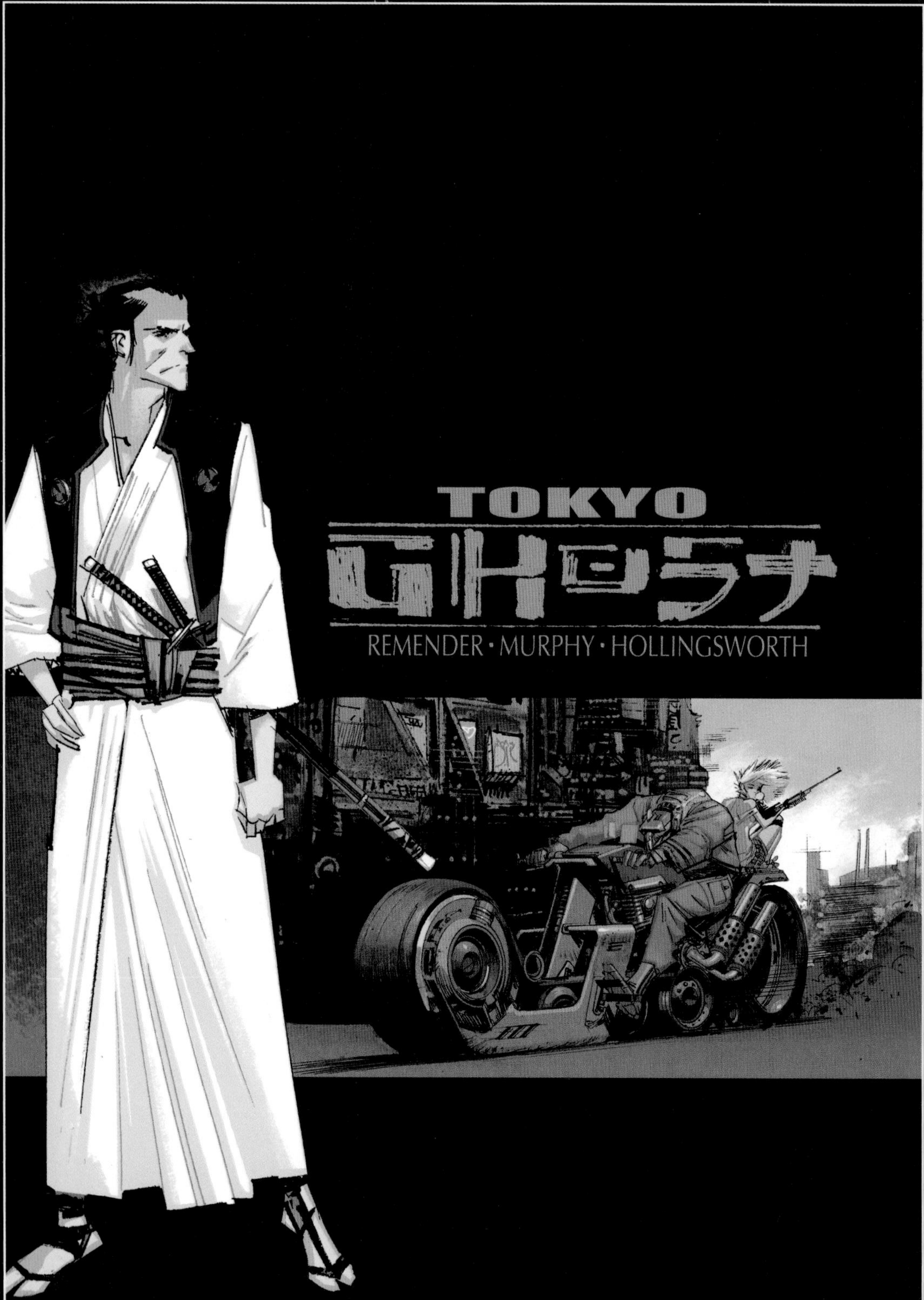
TOKYO
GHOST
REMENDER • MURPHY • HOLLINGSWORTH

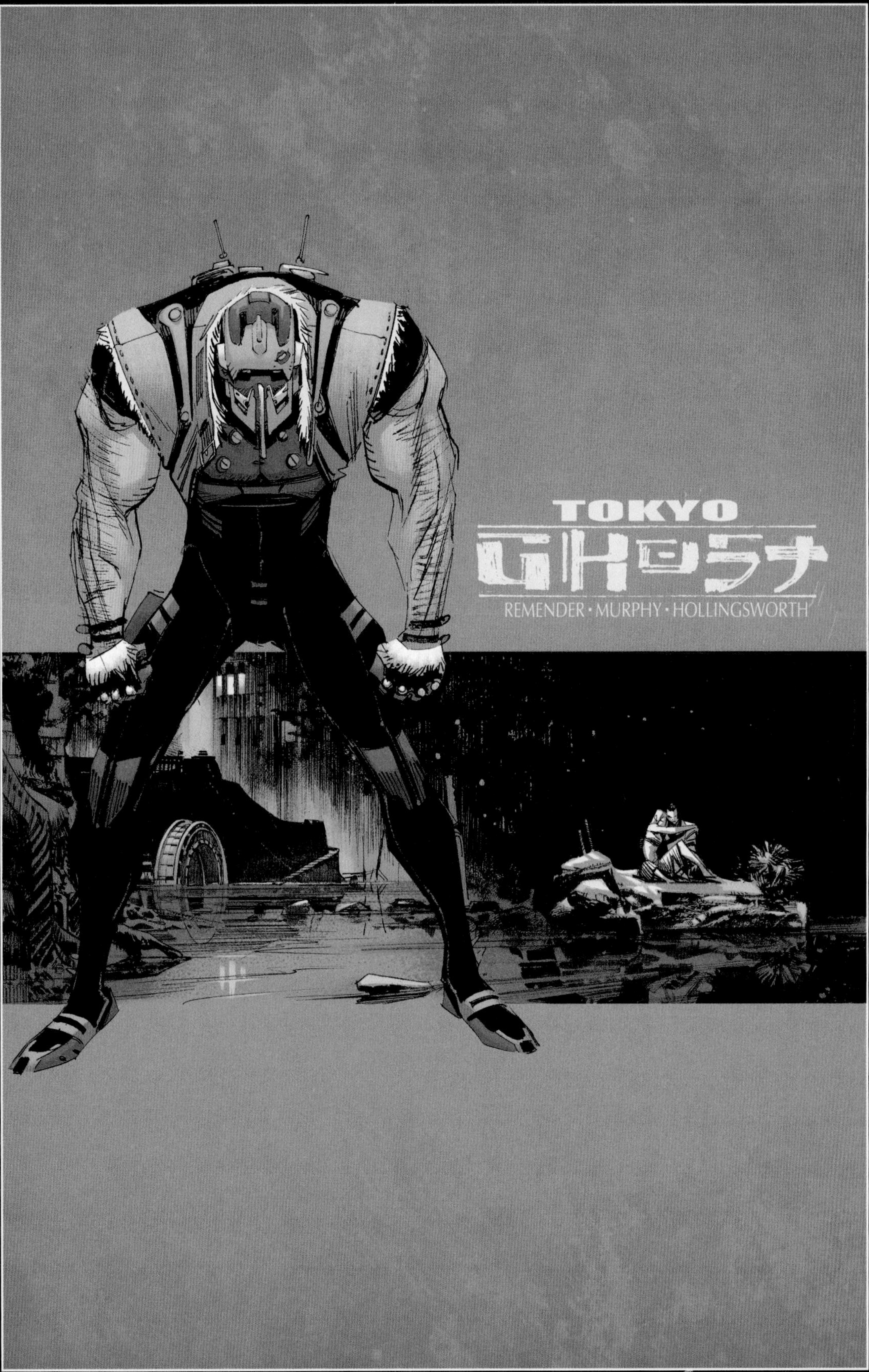
TOKYO
GHOST
REMENDER · MURPHY · HOLLINGSWORTH

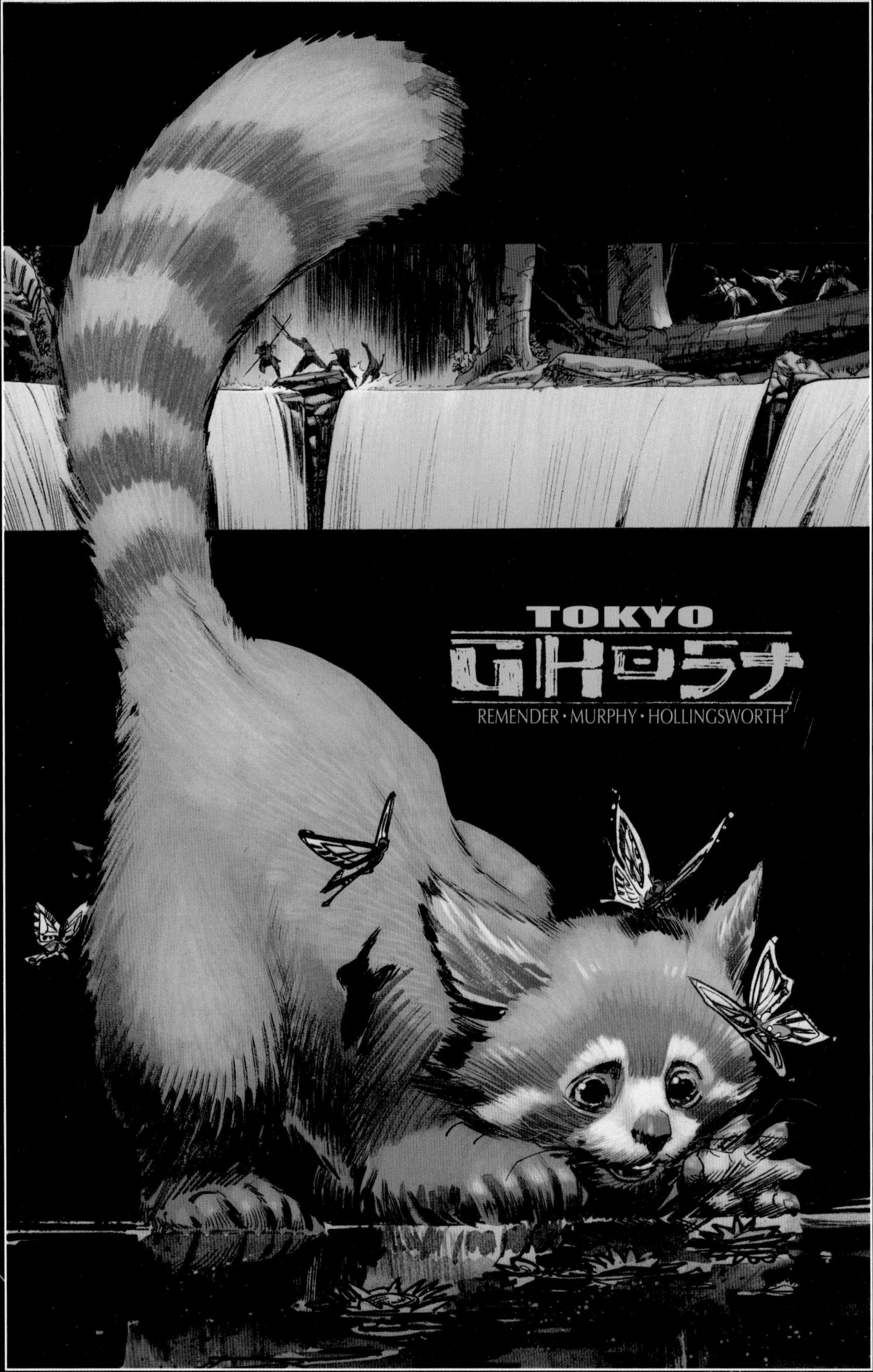
TOKYO
GHOST
REMENDER • MURPHY • HOLLINGSWORTH

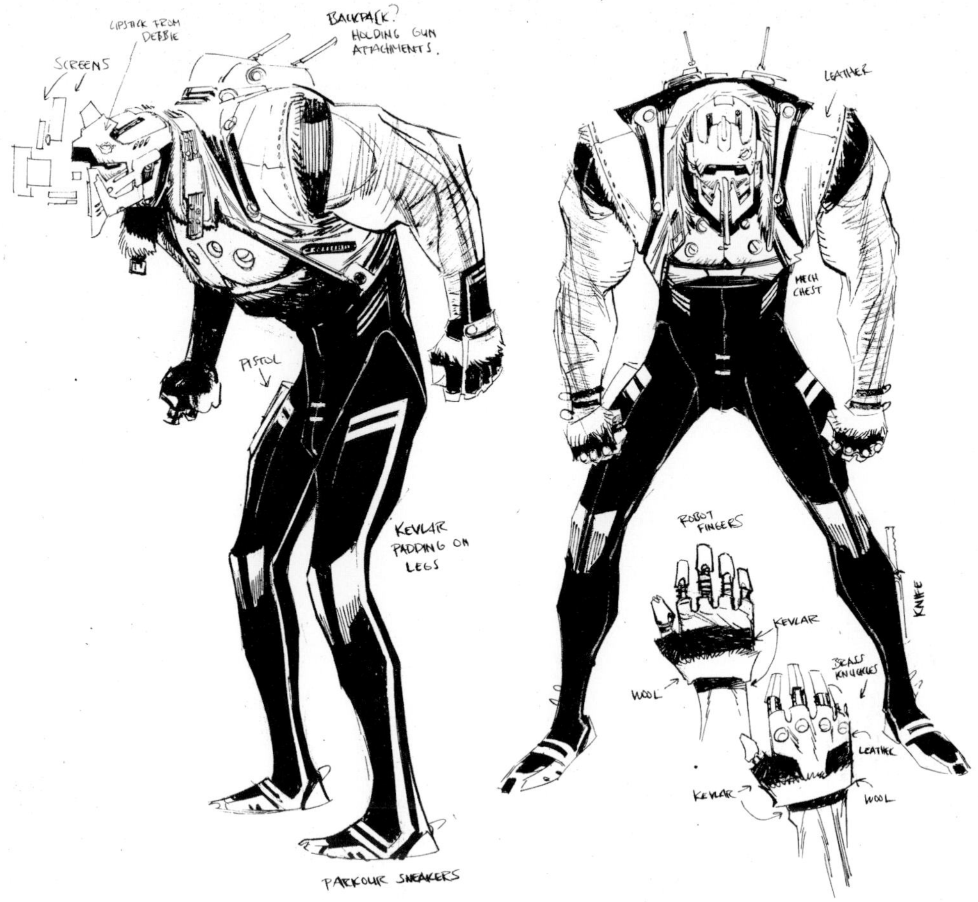
LIPSTICK FROM DEBBIE
SCREENS
BACKPACK? HOLDING GUN ATTACHMENTS.
LEATHER
MECH CHEST
PISTOL
KEVLAR PADDING ON LEGS
ROBOT FINGERS
KNIFE
KEVLAR
BRASS KNUCKLES
WOOL
LEATHER
KEVLAR
WOOL
PARKOUR SNEAKERS

TOKYO GHOST SKETCHBOOK

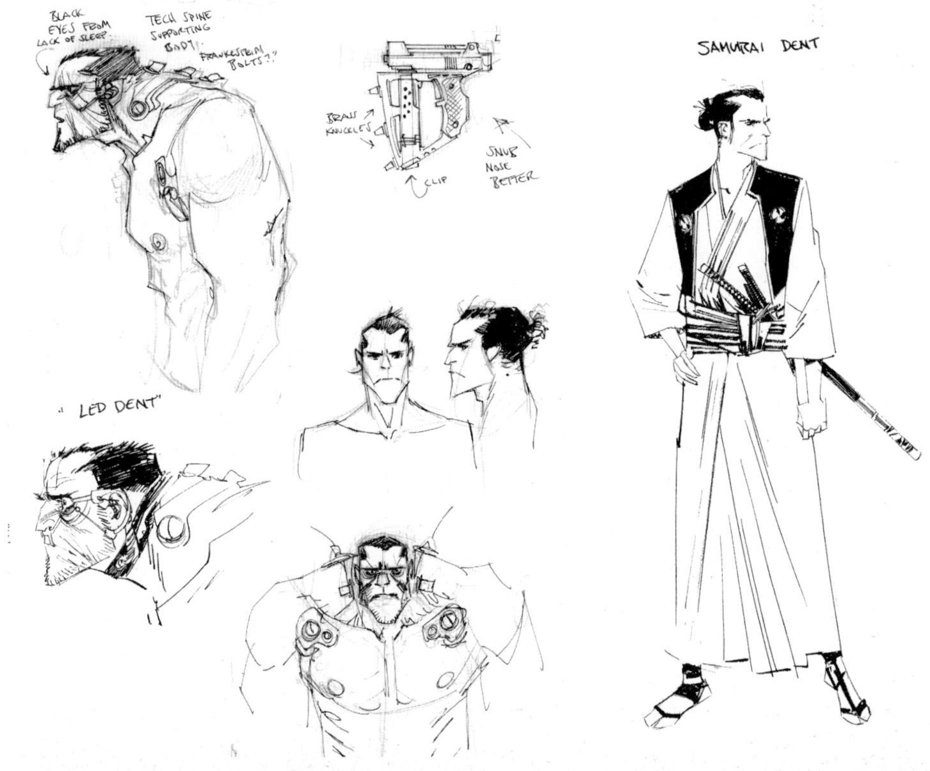
BLACK EYES FROM LACK OF SLEEP
TECH SPINE SUPPORTING BODY
"FRANKENSTEIN BOLTS?"
BRASS KNUCKLES
SNUB NOSE BETTER
CLIP
SAMURAI DENT
"LED DENT"

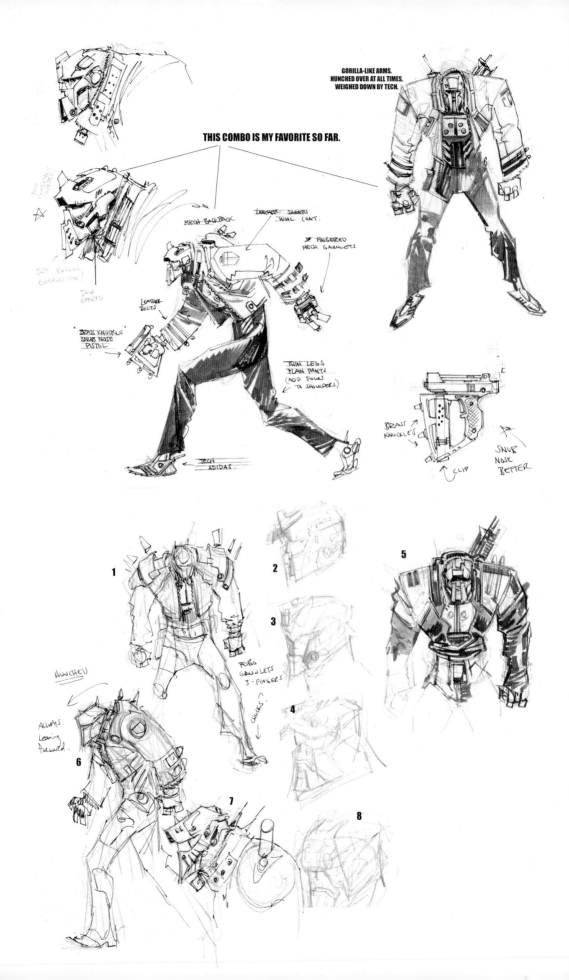

GORILLA-LIKE ARMS.
HUNCHED OVER AT ALL TIMES,
WEIGHED DOWN BY TECH.

THIS COMBO IS MY FAVORITE SO FAR.

MECH BACKPACK

LEATHER SHEERS
WOOL COAT.

3 FINGERED
MECH GAUNLETS

JUST ENOUGH
EVANGELION

JAW
EXPOSED

LEATHER
BELTS

BRASS KNUCKLE
SNUB NOSE
PISTOL

THIN LEGS
PLAIN PANTS
(ADD FOCUS
TO SHOULDERS)

TECH
ADIDAS.

BRASS
KNUCKLES

CLIP

SNUB
NOSE
BETTER

1

2

3

ROBO
GAUNLETS
3-FINGERS

CHUCKS?

4

5

HUNCHED

ALWAYS
LEANING
FORWARD.

6

7

8

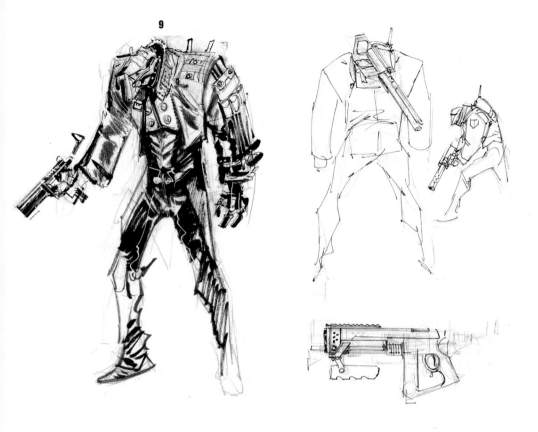

DAVEY

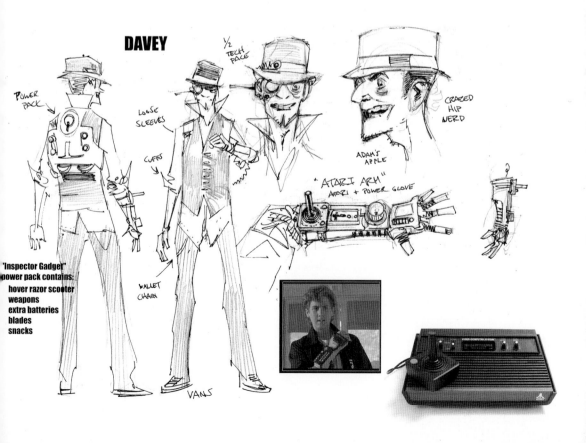

POWER PACK

LOOSE SLEEVES

CUFFS

½ TECH FACE

CRAZED HIP NERD

ADAM'S APPLE

"ATARI ARM"
ATARI + POWER GLOVE

"Inspector Gadget"
power pack contains:
    hover razor scooter
    weapons
    extra batteries
    blades
    snacks

WALLET CHAIN

VANS

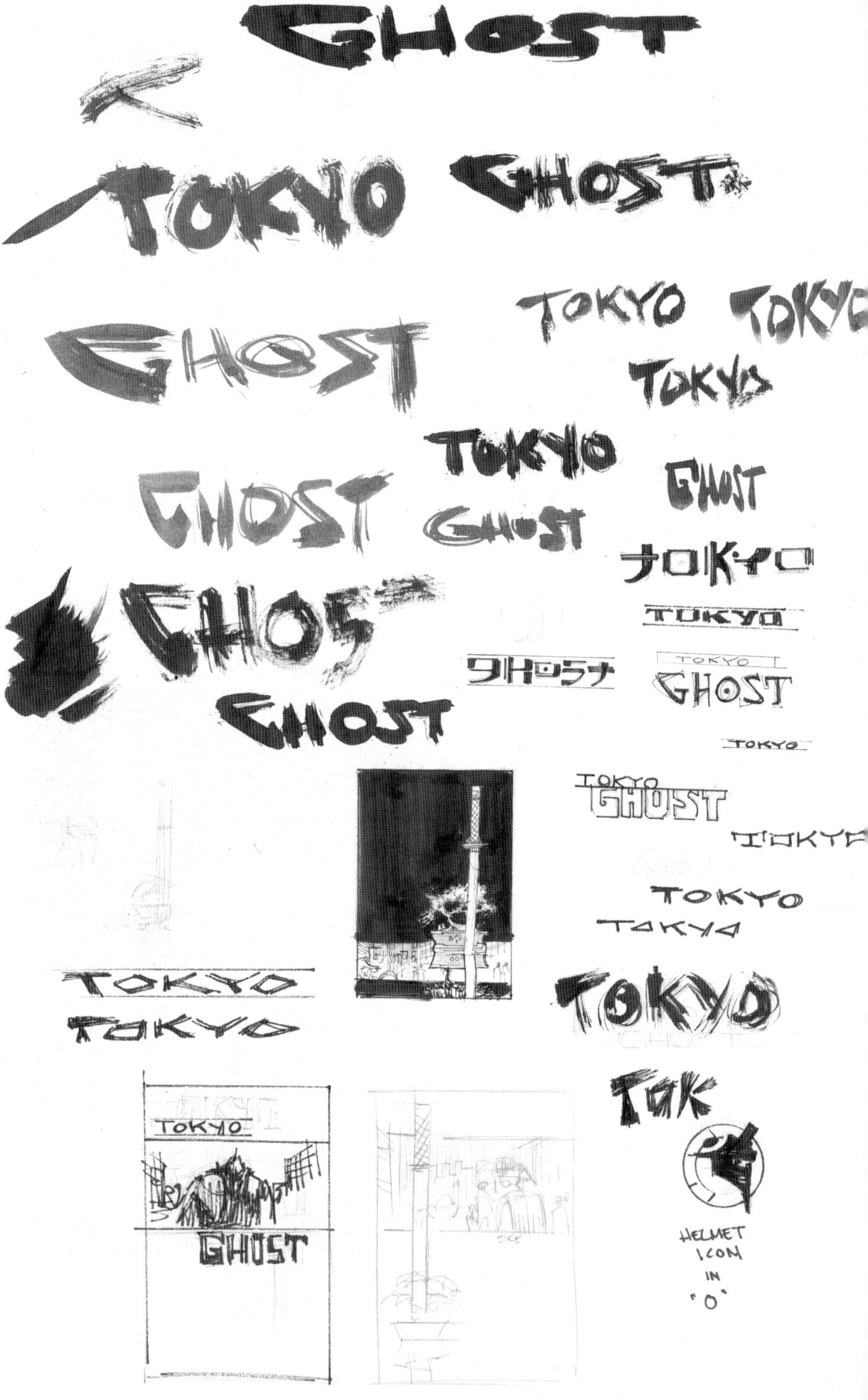
GHOST
TOKYO
GHOST
TOKYO
TOKYO
GHOST
TOKYO
TOKYO
GHOST
GHOST
GHOST
TOKYO
GHOST
TOKYO
GHOST
TOKYO
GHOST
GHOST
TOKYO
TOKYO
GHOST
TOKYO
TOKYO
TOKYO
TOKYO
TOKYO
TOKYO
TOKYO
GHOST
BIKE
TOK
HELMET
ICON
IN
"O"

1. TOKYO GHOST

5. TOKYO GHOST

2. TOKYO GHOST

6. TOKYO GHOST

3. TOKYO GHOST

7. TOKYO GHOST

4. TOKYO GHOST

8. TOKYO GHOST

DIGGING THIS ONE:

Cover theme:
Each will be mostly black with a panoramic panel in the background that's reverse of foreground. If SCI FI world in BG, then Japan world in FG.

Panorama in background of New Los Angeles. Dent on bike?

Future covers could play with Debbie, Dent's helmet, the bike, Japanese maple leaves, curves bridges, etc.

TOKYO GHOST
REMENDER MURPHY HOLLINGSWORTH

Katana, bonzai and reflection

Other covers I'm less into.

TOKYO
GHOST

GHOST

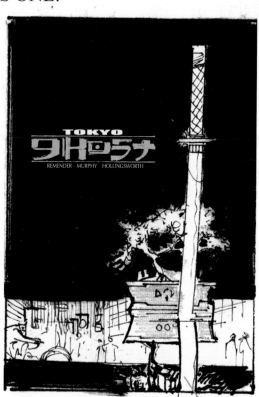

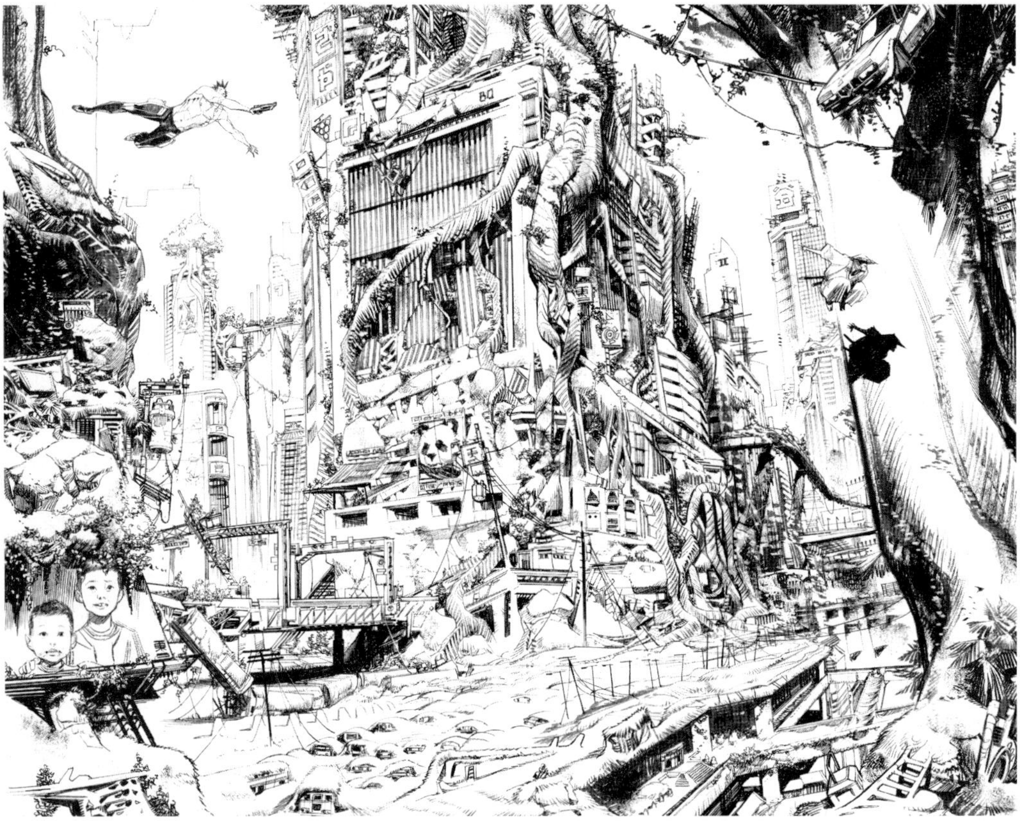

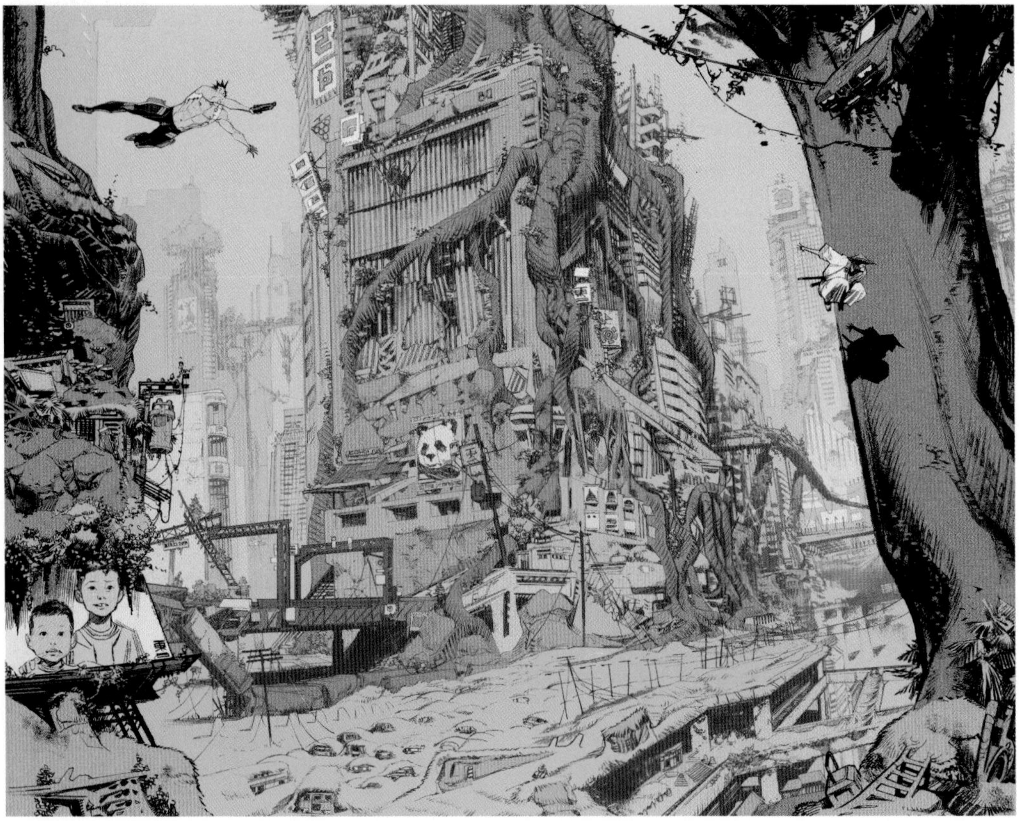

COLOR PROCESS BY MATT HOLLINGSWORTH

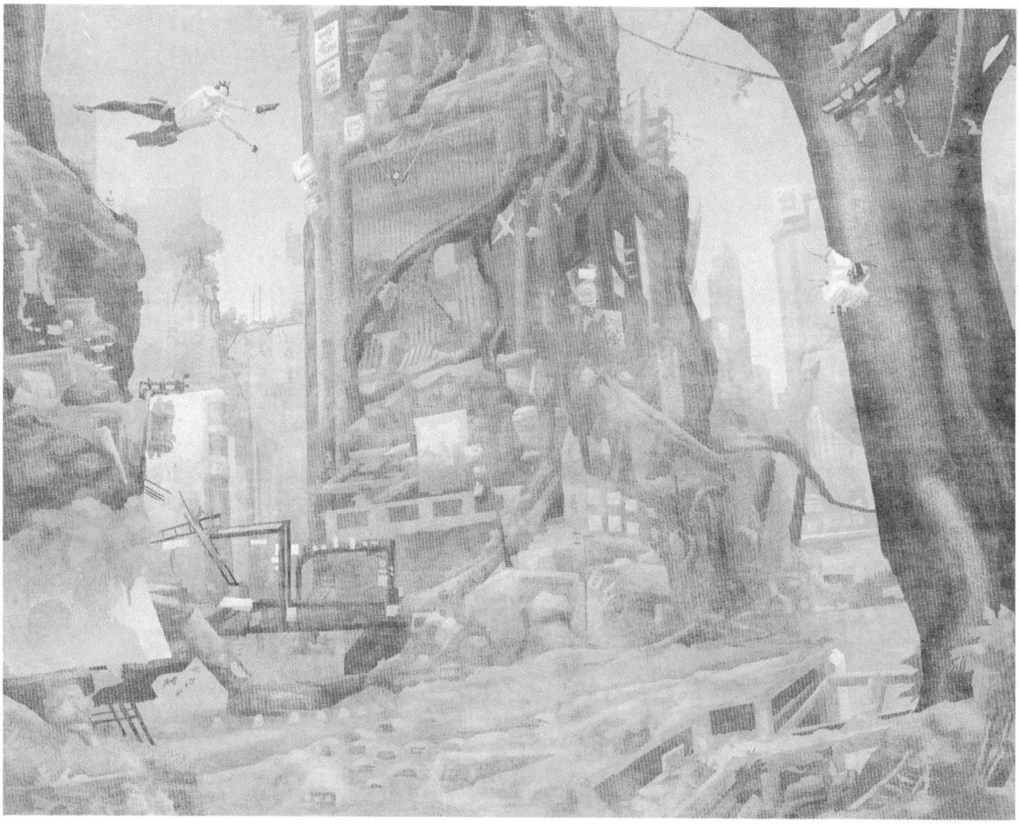

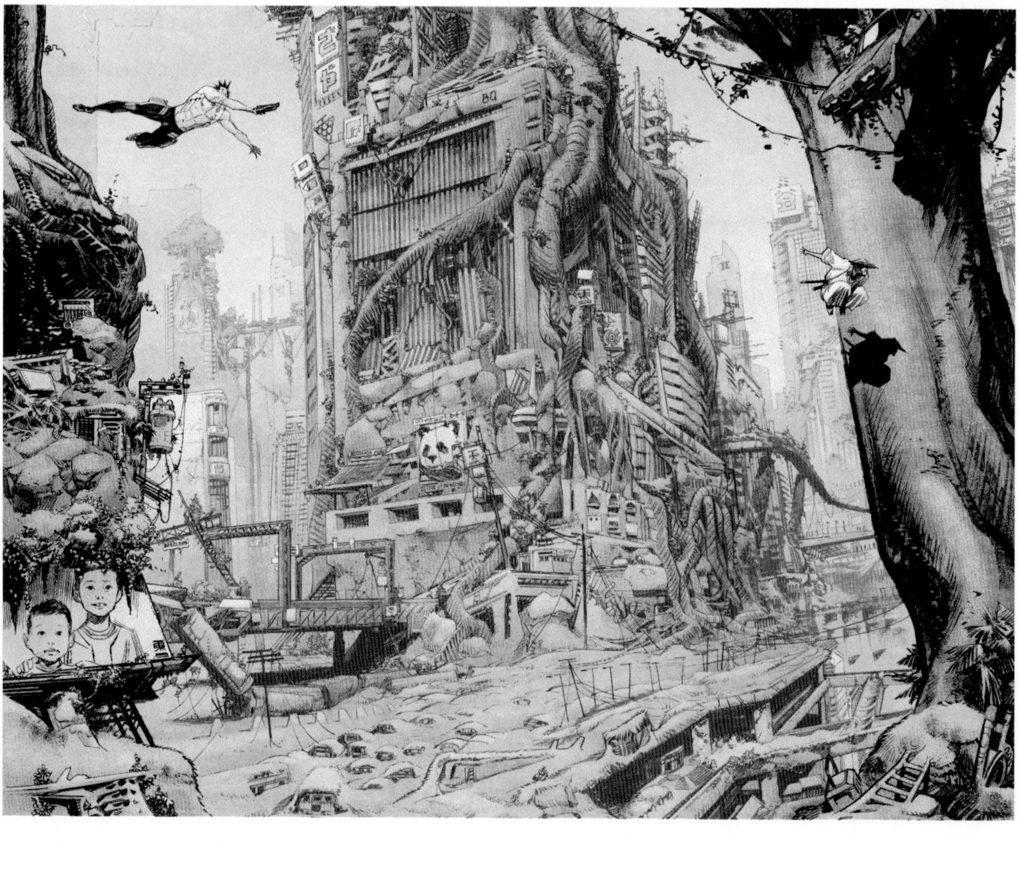

RICK REMENDER has fought the urge to do something clever and aloof to illustrate how above it all he is and simply list out his jive ass bio. Firstly, he's the writer/co-creator of comics such as *LOW*, *Fear Agent*, *Deadly Class*, *Strange Girl*, and *Black Science*. For Marvel he has written titles such as *Uncanny Avengers*, *Captain America*, *Uncanny X-Force*, and *Venom*.

Outside of comics he's written video games such as EPIC's *Bulletstorm* and Electronic Arts' *Dead Space*. Prior to that, served as an animator on films such as *The Iron Giant*, *Anastasia*, *Titan A.E.*, and *Rocky and Bullwinkle*. He also penciled comics such as *The Last Christmas*, *Bruce Campbell's Man with the Screaming Brain*, and *Teenage Mutant Ninja Turtles* and provided album art for bands such as NOFX, 3 Inches of Blood, and Lagwagon. He taught storyboarding, animation and comic art at San Francisco's Academy of Art University for many years. Now you know.

He and his tea-sipping wife, Danni, currently reside in Los Angeles raising two beautiful mischief monkeys.

SEAN MURPHY is the *New York Times* bestselling writer/artist of *Punk Rock Jesus*. He's also worked on such titles as *Batman*, *Hellblazer*, *The Wake*, and *American Vampire* with DC Comics. He lives with his wife and two dogs in Brooklyn, NY spending way too much money on rent.

MATT HOLLINGSWORTH has been an avid homebrewer of beer since 1997 and a beer judge since 1999. He's won a total of 18 medals, 13 of them gold medals, in competitions in New Jersey, Texas, Washington, Oregon and London. He's judged competitions in Oregon, Croatia, Slovenia, Slovakia, and Bulgaria.

In between beers, he's been coloring comics since 1991, including *Preacher*, *Daredevil*, *Hawkeye*, *The Wake*, *Hellboy*, *Chrononauts*, *Wytches* and, *We Stand on Guard*. Born in California, he lives in Croatia with his lovely wife Branka and his awesome son Liam.